a Whisper *in the* Shadows

DARCY BURKE

USA TODAY BESTSELLING AUTHOR

OLIVERHEBERBOOKS

Cover Design by Wicked Smart Designs

Published by Oliver-Heber Books

0 9 8 7 6 5 4 3 2 1

For our good friend Paul
Thanks for always putting up with Depeche Mode.
We will make sure your beloved Mickey is loved forever. He is a
wonderful cat—I'm so glad you had each other.

CHAPTER 1

London, May 1868

"Did you say you wanted me to be your wife?" Matilda Wren asked Inspector William Maxwell, a man she'd just met a few minutes ago. She wanted to make sure she'd heard him correctly.

"Yes," the inspector replied. He appeared to be in his late twenties and had light-brown curly hair and sharp, hazel eyes. "Not in actuality, of course. I'd like you to pose as my wife to assist me with an investigation."

Tilda slid a glance toward her friend and investigative partner, Hadrian Becket, Lord Ravenhurst. His features were inscrutable, but his gaze was fixed on the City of London inspector.

"Let us sit," Tilda said, gesturing toward the seating area in the parlor of her grandmother's house in Marylebone. She took one of the chairs while Hadrian claimed the other, and Inspector

Maxwell occupied the settee. "I confess I'm surprised by your request, Inspector. Or are you Detective Inspector?"

"Inspector," Maxwell replied. "Though I am hoping to be Detective Inspector at the conclusion of this investigation."

"I see." Tilda was more than surprised by the man's request—she was thrilled. While she'd worked in tandem with Scotland Yard on several cases now, they would never officially request her assistance. "Do your superiors know you are asking me to help?"

"They do. I'm conducting a secret investigation in which I will change my identity. The scheme requires me to have a wife, and, well, your recent success with helping to catch the Levitation Killer recommends you."

"Miss Wren did not just *help* to snare the murderers. She solved the case," Hadrian said with a bit of ice to his tone.

Tilda couldn't help feeling pleased that he would ensure she received credit. But she wanted him to have the same. "Lord Ravenhurst is being modest. He was instrumental throughout the investigation of the Levitation Killer. Rather, killers," Tilda corrected as there was more than one person responsible.

The inspector looked toward Hadrian. "I didn't realize you were so involved, my lord. There was no mention of you in any of the stories published about the case."

That was because Hadrian had asked that his name be left out of the reporting. While some of his peers and colleagues were aware he assisted with investigations, the majority would likely not approve of his involvement, particularly if it distracted from his duties. Though Hadrian had never indicated that was the case, Tilda sometimes wondered if their investigations took him away from his responsibilities in the Lords.

"I prefer my involvement to remain anonymous," Hadrian said blandly.

"I do understand," the inspector replied. "Well, I don't think this is a case where your assistance will be required," he added with a brief smile.

Tilda slid another glance at Hadrian. She didn't think he would like being excluded, but then again, perhaps it was time for him to pay more attention to his duties as earl.

"Tell me about this investigation," Tilda said to the inspector.

"Yes, of course." Maxwell positioned himself toward Tilda. "I'm investigating a friendly society. Are you familiar with them?"

"Somewhat," Tilda said. "They are organizations formed to provide for the welfare of their members. They are rather like a brotherhood, are they not?"

"In many cases," Maxwell said with a nod. "They are often organized with a specific goal or like-minded pursuit, perhaps centered on a trade or a religious belief. This society was started just over six months ago, and membership is confined to a specific ward in the City."

"Where is that?" Hadrian asked.

The inspector glanced in his direction but looked at Tilda as he responded. "It's called the Coleman Street Ward Amicable Society. Their headquarters are at the Swan and Hoop in Moorgate." This was all very close to the City of London Police headquarters in Old Jewry. "There is suspicion that this society is committing fraud. The Amicable Society provides the same sort of benefits as a burial club."

"I'm familiar with those," Tilda said, her curiosity piqued. "People pay a few shillings or pence a week in order to collect money to pay for a funeral in the event someone in the family dies."

"Precisely," the inspector said. "Friendly societies operate in much the same way but also offer benefits for illness and sometimes on the birth of a child. However, friendly societies are required to be registered. And yes, the Amicable Society *is* registered."

"How did the police become aware of this potential fraud?" Tilda asked.

"A widow of a member of the Amicable Society is the cousin of a sergeant's wife," Maxwell explained. "The member recently died, and when the widow tried to collect the benefit for her deceased husband, she was denied because it's the society's policy that benefits are not paid for one year."

Tilda cocked her head, uncertain of what the fraud could be. "Since the society has only existed for six months, why would the widow think she was eligible to collect?"

"Because when her husband joined and paid the entrance fee, he was told he would be eligible to receive benefits after six months." Maxwell frowned briefly. "The widow insists this is true but, unfortunately, does not have documentation to prove her claim."

"Does the society have record of him?" Tilda asked.

Maxwell nodded. "He is listed in their membership rolls. However, they refused to pay the benefit, citing that he wasn't yet eligible."

"That doesn't sound like fraud to me," Hadrian observed.

"It sounds like a dispute over what really happened," Tilda said.

The inspector pressed his lips together. "In addition to the potential discrepancy in the eligibility of benefits, the woman's husband was ill when he joined the society. I find it suspect that he was admitted since he was showing symptoms of consumption."

Tilda's curiosity was pricked, as was her sense that something wasn't right. "It's suspicious that a man who was ill was admitted to the society *and* that he was told he would be eligible for benefits in six months if the society's policy is actually one year."

"Precisely," the inspector said with a nod. "Sergeant Kilgore—his wife is the cousin of the widow—assigned an inspector to investigate. Inspector Dolen found that the deceased member of the society, Gilbert Cardy, had been recruited by a canvasser soliciting members when the society first began. However, Dolen wasn't able to locate the canvasser, Timothy Eaton, and the society's chair, Walter Phelps, said he left his post last week."

"Was Eaton committing fraud?" Hadrian asked. "What would be his motive for doing so?"

"That is what we must determine," Maxwell replied. "What fraud, if any, was perpetrated, why, and by whom?"

"Have you been assigned to this case along with Inspector Dolen?" Tilda asked.

"Sergeant Kilgore decided someone should investigate from within the society. The administrators of the society said they'd shared all they knew and did not appreciate Inspector Dolen causing a scandal over what amounted to a clerical error by an employee who no longer worked for the society."

"That doesn't sound evasive," Tilda quipped with a half-smile.

"Precisely." Maxwell nodded. "Inspector Dolen did not believe the society administrators were entirely cooperative. Sergeant Kilgore wants a thorough investigation of the society and thinks it can best be done under disguise. Since the society already knows Dolen, Kilgore assigned me to the case."

It all sounded rather suspect to Tilda. "I'm trying to determine why the society would accept members who are ill. In the case of this man who died of consumption, they don't have to pay the benefit because it has not been a year." Tilda met Hadrian's gaze and then the inspector's. "Is that the scheme? The society accepted members who they gambled would die in the first year and thus they wouldn't have to pay out?"

Maxwell smiled. "You are quite clever, Miss Wren. That is indeed my suspicion. My plan is to join the society in disguise to ferret out this information. I am hoping you will pretend to be my wife. Your presence will make me appear stable, and you will be able to assist with the investigation."

Tilda was already invested in uncovering the truth of whatever this society was doing. "Our job is to find proof of their fraud. Or at the very least, reveal the reasoning behind admitting members who are ill and may not live long enough to collect their benefits."

"Exactly so." Maxwell regarded her with admiration. "I'm already glad I've sought your assistance, Miss Wren."

"I'm intrigued by this case," Tilda said. "How will our disguises work?"

"I'm delighted to hear it," the inspector replied with a grin. "I've taken a position as a clerk at a mercantile house on Broad Street, where several society members are employed. I have taken lodgings for us to reside in, just off Coleman Street, in White Alley. First, however—"

"Wait just a moment," Hadrian interrupted, his dark brows drawn together over his brilliant blue eyes. "You can't expect Miss Wren to live with you. That would ruin her reputation."

Maxwell shifted on the settee as he regarded Hadrian. "We would sleep in separate rooms, of course. It is my hope that no one will ever know Miss Wren was a part of the investigation. We will be disguised and using different names."

Hadrian's features did not relax. Oddly, Tilda noted she still found him exceptionally handsome with his square jaw and aristocratic cheekbones, despite his vexation. Or perhaps even because of it—the fire in his gaze was most arresting. Even the slight bump in his nose added to his appeal.

"That is all well and good, however, it is still highly improper," Hadrian said. "Miss Wren is an unmarried woman, and to reside with a gentleman who is not her relative would be an irreparable blemish on her reputation. I am confident she would not wish to risk her future professional prospects by agreeing to such a scheme."

While Tilda didn't particularly care about her reputation when it came to marriageability, she absolutely needed to ensure that her professional reputation remained above reproach. It was difficult enough to be a woman investigator.

Still, Tilda could see where it would be most beneficial if she could reside in the City with her pretend husband. It would not only lend credibility to their ruse, but it would also aid her investigation to be in the thick of things.

She looked to Hadrian. "Is there any way I could protect my reputation and still reside in White Alley?"

Hadrian's lip curled with disdain. His disapproval of her even considering the arrangement was obvious. Tilda had never felt the difference in their positions so keenly. Someone of his rank had the expectation—and the privilege—of propriety. This was a job that would ensure Tilda's livelihood as well as that of her grandmother and the members of her household, which had grown of late as a result of the first two investigations she'd conducted with Hadrian. Indeed, it could have swelled even further with the last one, but Tilda had put her foot down. They were stretched as thinly as possible. Which was why she could not afford to decline this job, even if she wanted to. And she most certainly did *not* want to.

"You would require a chaperone," Hadrian replied. "She would need to be someone above reproach, but I still think it's a risk you oughtn't take."

"Duly noted." Whilst she desperately wanted to disagree with him, she understood the risk to her professional aspirations. If taking this job meant she may never have another, there would be no point in it.

"We can work around it." Maxwell gave Tilda a reassuring smile. "You'll simply pretend to live there, and we will ensure you are home safe and sound in Marylebone every evening."

"I suppose that must suffice," Tilda said, though she was disappointed. "You were going to say something before his lordship interrupted you."

"I was going to say that I need to be accepted for membership in the Amicable Society. An existing member will need to vouch for me."

"How shall we ensure that happens?" Tilda asked.

"You said 'we'. Does that mean you agree to assist me?" Maxwell appeared hopeful.

"What compensation are you offering?" Hadrian asked before Tilda could do so, though she had already decided to accept the inspector's offer.

Tilda gently pursed her lips toward Hadrian. Why was he cross? She wasn't going to reside in White Alley with Inspector Maxwell, though, in truth, she was still privately trying to work out a way in which she could.

Maxwell again looked toward Tilda when giving his response. "Twelve shillings per week." His gaze swept over Tilda. "I'm afraid I can't provide reimbursement for your wardrobe. You must dress as the wife of a clerk earning about thirty shillings a week. I am hopeful you can find something suitable."

"That is not a problem." Indeed, most of Tilda's outmoded wardrobe would suffice. She'd only recently been able to afford a few new ensembles from her investigative wages—largely due to what Hadrian had paid her to investigate the first two cases they'd worked on together.

The first had been to solve his attempted murder, and the second was to find the culprit of a murder for which Hadrian had been a suspect. In truth, Tilda didn't particularly care to waste money on her wardrobe, but her grandmother had convinced her that dressing well would convey her success as an investigator. Tilda had been hard-pressed to argue with that.

"I should be glad to assist you," Tilda added, anticipation bubbling inside her.

"Splendid," Maxwell said, with a smile that made him rather handsome. His beard and mustache directed more focus to his eyes, and they glimmered with good humor. "To answer your question about how we will find an existing member to vouch for me, I expect one of my coworkers at the mercantile house will agree. You and I will play the roles of a couple who wed a year ago and have just moved to the City for my new employment. I thought we could say that you make matchbooks at home. That would allow you to perchance conduct investigations in the neighborhood whilst I am working."

"I confess I'm impressed you've gone to so much trouble for this investigation," Tilda said.

"This case is very important to Sergeant Kilgore," Maxwell noted solemnly. "I do find preparation and planning to be tantamount to success."

Tilda was even more excited to accept this assignment. To work alongside a thoughtful inspector in this manner would be a brilliant experience. She could only hope it would lead to more work with the City of London Police.

"We are of a similar mind, Inspector." Tilda smiled. "How long do you expect this investigation to take?"

"Sergeant Kilgore has asked that we endeavor to complete our investigation within a fortnight." Maxwell grimaced faintly. "Indeed, he is insistent that we work as quickly as possible. This scheme is a considerable expense."

"Is he undertaking it because his wife's cousin is a potential victim of this fraud?" Hadrian asked.

Maxwell lifted a shoulder. "I can't say, but I imagine that is a strong reason for his interest in this case."

"When shall we begin?" Tilda asked.

"I am moving into the house in White Alley tomorrow, but you needn't come until Monday as there is a meeting of the Amicable Society at the Swan and Hoop in the evening that we will attend, assuming I have sponsorship to join the society, which I anticipate I will."

Tilda inclined her head. "Certainly. I will arrive early Monday morning before you leave for work."

"That would be most agreeable." Maxwell stood. "I'm delighted to be working with you, Miss Wren."

"Shouldn't you call me by my alias?"

"Mrs. Harwood," he said with a smile. "I accepted the clerk position and obtained lodgings as Mr. Albert Harwood. Your given name is up to you, though I doubt we'll use it much."

Tilda had risen and so did Hadrian. "I'll be Ivy." When she was a child, Tilda's only female friend had been named Ivy. She'd moved to Bristol when Tilda was eight. "I'm pleased you came to see me. You were prompted by seeing my name in the newspaper?"

"Yes, but I did speak with Inspector Teague about you as well," Maxwell replied. "He recommended you most highly."

Teague was the detective inspector Tilda and Hadrian had worked with several times at Scotland Yard. Tilda was delighted that he would recommend her.

"I look forward to working with you." Tilda offered Maxwell her hand.

Maxwell shook it, then Hadrian thrust his hand toward him as well. "Inspector."

"My lord." Maxwell removed his glove to shake Hadrian's bare hand.

Tilda watched as they shook and wondered if Hadrian was seeing any of the man's memories. After suffering a concussion during an attack on his person several months ago, Hadrian had been gifted—or cursed, depending on one's perception—with the ability to see others' memories, either by touching that person or an object they had handled. It had been an incredibly useful skill during their investigations, but the power did not come without turmoil. The visions caused him headaches that increased in intensity when he experienced several in a short time frame.

It was also confounding, as this ability had appeared seemingly out of nowhere. Shockingly, they had recently met a father and a son who possessed the same ability. Their experiences had been most helpful to Hadrian as he learned to navigate the new way in which he perceived the world.

After Inspector Maxwell took his leave, Hadrian turned a rather disgruntled expression on Tilda.

"Why are you looking at me like that?" Tilda asked.

"I suppose I wish you'd discussed this scheme with me before accepting Maxwell's offer."

"Why would I do so?" Tilda did not appreciate his paternalistic attitude. "I don't need your permission, Hadrian."

"Of course not," he said quickly. He exhaled. "My apologies. Of course, you must accept whatever professional assignment you wish. I do think you are worth far more than twelve shillings per week, however."

Indeed, Hadrian had paid her quite a bit more than that when he'd hired her on two separate occasions, as had his mother when she'd employed Tilda most recently. "I am accepting this assignment for the experience and the potential opportunity for future work with the City of London Police."

"But you need the income." He knew how tight their household finances were. That fact had been an intrinsic part of their first case together. "What good is working with the police if they can't pay you what you need? Or what you *deserve*."

Tilda appreciated his concern—and his unwavering confidence in her abilities. "I am hopeful the pay will increase once I demonstrate my capability."

He appeared placated by her argument. "I confess I'm greatly disappointed that I will not be part of this investigation."

"It will be strange conducting it without you." Tilda realized she was disappointed too. She now understood his irritation during her interview with Maxwell. "I would feel the same if you had been hired and I had not."

He let out a low, rather humorless laugh. "That is unlikely to happen since my participation in our investigations shall remain anonymous."

"Will they, though?" Tilda asked. "You worry about my reputation if I took up residence with Maxwell, but what of the inordinate amount of time we spend together during our investigations? Surely people recognize that you call here regularly, and we move about town together quite frequently."

Mostly, they visited places where no one would account for their presence. However, they'd once attended a reception at Northumberland House, which had required Tilda to dress as a high-society lady. They'd also traveled out of London by train on two occasions. "Don't you think there are people who have correctly assumed that you have something to do with my investigations?"

"Perhaps, and I would hope that is all they think," Hadrian replied with a touch of concern in his gaze. "I have made it clear to those in my inner circle that I assist you with investigations and that our association is purely professional. I admit there could be those who wonder if there is something else between us. Beyond professional association, I mean."

Tilda's breath snagged in her lungs. Just before Maxwell had arrived, there had been a charged moment between her and Hadrian. Their hands had almost touched. She'd been sorry they were interrupted but now reminded herself it was for the best.

They'd shared a kiss several weeks ago, and it caused an awkwardness between them. However, over the span of their last investigation, they'd returned to their easy, warm friendship, and, of course, their mutually satisfying professional partnership.

Still, the specter of something beyond those things hung about, as evidenced by the moment they'd shared before Inspector Maxwell had arrived and now again with Hadrian's comment regarding how they may be perceived.

Blast. Hadrian was a good friend and a trustworthy, valuable assistant. She hoped their relationship would continue in that manner. Anything else would potentially ruin what they had. Furthermore, Tilda wasn't interested in romance, and she was completely against marriage. That wasn't just because of her business aspirations—her parents' marriage had been unhappy, and Tilda did not wish to risk the life she currently enjoyed. She was independent and ran her grandmother's household. It was more than a woman could dare hope to attain, and Tilda was quite content. A husband would ruin everything she'd accomplished and what she hoped to achieve.

"Perhaps you've had similar concerns regarding our association," Hadrian said. "I noted you referred to me as 'his lordship' or 'Ravenhurst' in front of Maxwell rather than Hadrian."

"It seemed appropriate." Tilda hadn't given it much thought, but Hadrian was likely right. She hadn't wanted the inspector to think she and Hadrian were that familiar. But, of course, they were. A delicate heat fluttered through her, and she decided it was best to move on to a new topic. "Did you see anything when you shook the inspector's hand?"

Hadrian shrugged. "Nothing of import."

"But you saw *something*?" she prodded.

"I saw what seemed to be the interior of a police station. As I said, there was nothing remarkable."

"Well, we aren't investigating Inspector Maxwell," Tilda said with a sigh.

"*I* am not investigating anything." He did still sound a trifle cross or at least disappointed.

Tilda did not like leaving him out, but this wasn't her investigation to manage. "I will miss working with you," she said quietly. "I do have other inquiries from potential clients. Perhaps I'll have need of your assistance when this investigation is concluded." She gave him a hopeful look.

Hadrian's expression was enigmatic. "You know where to find me."

He turned and took his leave. Tilda frowned. She understood that he felt excluded and would hate to be in his position.

However, she was a private investigator, and he was an earl.

They'd been fortunate to work on several cases together, with excellent results. That didn't mean they would always be a partnership.

Tilda hoped this wasn't the beginning of the end of their association.

CHAPTER 2

*E*arly Monday morning, Tilda surveyed herself in the mirror in her bedchamber. The brown powder her maid, Clara, had used to darken her hair was effective in transforming Tilda from a blonde with hues of red to a brunette. Clara, whom Tilda still wasn't used to, stood just behind her.

Clara had worked for one of Tilda's past clients. When the client had been forced to return to her parents in the country, Clara, who had no family, had been without employment or even lodging. Tilda had invited her to join her grandmother's household temporarily while she sought a new position.

However, Tilda's grandmother liked having a maid in addition to their extremely capable housekeeper, Mrs. Acorn. Clara's presence had eased the housekeeper's workload and provided more direct assistance to Tilda and her grandmother, such as laundering their clothing and styling their hair. To please her grandmother, Tilda worked to make sure they could afford to keep Clara, though Tilda was certain the maid could earn better wages elsewhere. She was skilled enough to work in Mayfair or even Belgravia.

"Are you certain I can't do something more with your hair?" Clara asked hopefully.

"You are a marvel with styling hair, Clara," Tilda said. "However, this investigative assignment requires that I present myself as a working-class wife, which is why I'm wearing one of my older gowns that is no longer in fashion and have asked you to do something simple with my hair."

"I understand." Clara sounded a trifle disappointed.

Tilda had to admit she was beginning to dislike having to don her older gowns since purchasing a few new costumes in the last several months. Her new garments were simpler and less voluminous, which made them easier to wear. They also looked smarter and were generally more appealing to Tilda as a woman of business. Today, however, she would assume the role of a wife and matchbook maker.

"I think I look the part I need to play," Tilda said with a smile. "Thank you, Clara."

Grabbing her reticule, Tilda left the bedchamber and went downstairs.

Mrs. Acorn met Tilda at the bottom of the stairs. "Your grandmother would like to see you in the sitting room before you go."

"She's up this early?" Tilda asked.

In her early sixties, with kind brown eyes and dove-gray hair beneath a pristine white cap, Mrs. Acorn inclined her head. "She wanted to be sure to see you this morning. I believe she's concerned."

Tilda already knew that, for her grandmother had done nothing but express her worry about this new assignment over the past several days.

"I don't have much time," Tilda said. "I will speak with her briefly. Thank you, Mrs. Acorn."

Mrs. Acorn smiled. "You are a good granddaughter to alleviate her concerns."

Tilda made her way to the sitting room, where her grandmother was ensconced in her favorite chair near the hearth, sipping tea.

"Grandmama, why are you up so early?" Tilda asked. "You should be sleeping."

Her grandmother set her cup down and waved her hand. She lifted her bright blue gaze to Tilda. "Bah, I couldn't sleep much, thinking about you being gone all day and well into the evening."

Tilda had explained that this assignment would require her to be gone every day for a long period of time, as she was to pretend to be the wife of Inspector Maxwell. She needed to give the impression that she was living in White Alley without *actually* living there.

"What is it you're worried about, Grandmama?" Tilda asked. "This is not a dangerous case."

"It could be to your reputation," her grandmother said. "And you can't be sure there won't be danger. You'll be in the City, after all. I was thinking you should perhaps take your father's pistol."

Tilda had considered the same, but the weapon was large and heavy, and while it fit in her reticule, she didn't want to carry it, nor did she want anyone to guess she was carrying a pistol. She'd also considered buying a smaller pistol that she could carry with her, at least most of the time. However, it was not required for this case.

That her grandmother was suggesting Tilda carry her father's pistol was notable. In general, she did not like that Tilda had learned to shoot or saw the need to even own a weapon. Now, she was advocating it.

"I wish there was something I could say to assure you that this assignment is safe and that I will be fine," Tilda said. "Don't forget that I'll be working with a police inspector."

"You also said he would be away from the house all day, and you'll be there alone." Her mouth turned into a gentle frown.

Tilda gave her a reassuring smile. "All will be well. Now, I must be off." She bent and kissed her grandmother's cheek. "I'm not sure what time I'll be home this evening. If you are tired from rising so early this morning, you mustn't wait up for me, all right?" Tilda looked at her expectantly.

Her grandmother pursed her lips briefly. "We'll see. Do be careful, dear."

"I always am."

"I do prefer your natural hair color," Grandmama added.

"I do too," Tilda replied with a chuckle. "But this will help in preserving my reputation."

"Then we shall suffer it." Her grandmother sighed, and Tilda quashed a smile as she hastened from the sitting room. She strode to the entrance hall, where their butler, another retainer she'd acquired from an investigation, stood from his chair.

Vaughn was quite tall but stooped. He'd been Tilda's grandfather's cousin's butler, and upon his employer's death—a murder that Tilda and Hadrian had solved together—Vaughn had come to stay with Tilda and her grandmother. He'd needed to recover from a concussion sustained from the man who'd killed his employer. But by the time he had fully healed, he'd already made himself indispensable. It turned out Vaughn was uninterested in retirement, which was just as well since his employer hadn't provided a settlement for him.

As a result, Tilda felt it necessary to keep him in their household. Plus, she quite liked him. His presence also pleased her grandmother, though they had as much need of a butler as they did of a maid.

"Good morning, Miss Wren," Vaughn said with a smile. "You're fetching the omnibus to the City?"

Tilda plucked up a basket from the corner, which she'd set there last night. "I am. I'll tell you what I said to Grandmama: I don't know what time I'll return this evening, but if you're tired, you mustn't stay up to welcome me, just as you needn't have been at your post this early."

"It is no trouble to remain at my post later than usual," Vaughn said. "Just as it was not a problem to rise early. Anyway, I doubt I will be able to rest until you're home safely."

He gave her a warm smile, then opened the door for her. Tilda decided it was rather nice to be cared for, but she would draw the line at being fussed over.

"Have a good day, Vaughn."

Tilda stepped outside and hurried to catch the omnibus to the City. She departed at Poultry and found a market where she bought several items for the kitchen in Maxwell's house and tucked them into the basket. Then she walked to White Alley with her items, so that she would appear to everyone as a house-wife who had gone out to shop.

The house Maxwell had let was small and quite old. Tilda wondered if it was built just after the Great Fire. There were only two storeys, plus a garret, and it was so narrow as to only allow for the width of one small room.

Tilda let herself into the house and closed the door. "Good morning," she called.

Inspector Maxwell stepped into the narrow hall. He looked quite different, for he'd shaved his facial hair entirely. Without the beard, his cheeks appeared fuller and he looked younger. He was rather handsome, and she noted that attribute may be helpful in their investigation. "Good morning, Miss—" He stopped himself and shook his head with a faint smile. "Mrs. Harwood. Your hair is different."

"I wanted to disguise the true color. Your face is also changed."

"Since the police station isn't far and I've worked there several years, I wanted to make sure no one would recognize me." He wiped his hand over his chin. "It's been a shocking adjustment as I've worn the beard and mustache for nigh on a decade."

"Well, the loss has perhaps taken a decade from your age," she said with a smile.

Maxwell laughed. "I hope not, for then I would be a mere seventeen. I don't know that anyone would take me seriously."

"I spoke in jest," Tilda assured him, though he did not seem upset. "You're only a year or so older than me. I'll be twenty-six in November."

"My mother's birthday was Guy Fawkes Day," he said.

Tilda blinked in surprise. "Really? That is my birthday."

He smiled. "What a coincidence."

A moment stretched between them before Tilda wondered if it was becoming awkward. She held up the basket. "Where is the kitchen?"

"This way," Maxwell replied. "Such as it is." His gaze swept over her. "You've done very well with your costume."

"Thank you." Tilda didn't plan on telling him that until somewhat recently, her entire wardrobe looked similar to this. She also surrendered, finally, to the realization that she ought to stop wearing her older gowns, at least when she left the house.

"Allow me to give you a tour of our new lodgings, not that it's very large." He showed her the front sitting room, which was as small as Tilda expected. The furniture was minimal and the decoration nonexistent.

"I hope I won't be required to entertain," Tilda said as she glanced about. "The guests would find my housewifery skills lacking." She gave him a sardonic smile.

"No one will think that. We are fortunate to afford a house like this." Was there a note of affront in his response?

Tilda realized he, as an unmarried man, likely lived at the police station. Perhaps *he* would like to have a house like this, even with its spartan furnishings and dingy walls and floor. Whilst she couldn't fix the furniture, she could ensure the house was tidy. "I will spend the day cleaning and sprucing it up. By the time you return, you won't recognize it."

He smiled. "Your housewifery skills sound exceptional. And I am glad to have them, especially after several days alone. Come, this way is the dining room."

He led her through a doorway to the rear room on the ground floor, which was even smaller than the front sitting room. Then he escorted her downstairs to the compact kitchen with its low ceilings. The air smelled of coal, and the walls were gray. Tilda had a new appreciation for how hard Mrs. Acorn worked to keep their kitchen looking clean and relatively bright.

This made Tilda think of how her mother might have felt when she'd married a young constable and set up their household. They'd been fortunate to have a little money that Tilda's father had inherited from his grandfather, so they'd had a maid of all work. Even so, Tilda's mother had overseen the household and handled a great many tasks. Though she'd never cooked. Tilda had learned what little she knew about kitchen work from that maid. She was not looking forward to preparing meals here and was rather hoping she wouldn't have to.

Tilda set the basket of food on the scarred worktable in the center of the main room. She dipped her head into a doorway and saw the tiny scullery.

"The front is where the coal is stored, along with a cupboard with a cot," Maxwell said, gesturing toward the opposite end of the kitchen. "In addition to the scullery, there is a narrow pantry and a small room for bathing."

They went back up to the ground floor, then Maxwell led her up to the first. As they reached the landing, Maxwell turned his head. "I'm pleased to report that one of my coworkers at the mercantile house has agreed to propose me for membership to the Amicable Society this evening."

"That is excellent news. How is the job going?" she asked.

"Honestly? It's drudgery." Maxwell showed her into the front room, a small bedchamber. "I confess I would not want to do it permanently. Thankfully, I will only have to endure it a fortnight or less. I wouldn't have bothered at all, but I thought it prudent to immerse myself in the ward. And since several society members work at the mercantile house, I've an opportunity to befriend them and hopefully gather information about how the society operates."

Tilda was glad she didn't have to go to a job as part of her disguise.

The bedchamber contained a somewhat narrow unmade bed, a dresser, and a chair. The curtains on the grimy window were old and in need of replacement. It did not look as though Maxwell was sleeping here. "There's another bedchamber?" Tilda asked.

"Just one, at the back of the house. It's smaller, and that's where I've been sleeping. That could change, however. I've had an idea that could allow you to live here. If you wanted to."

Tilda turned to face him. "I do, actually. What is your idea?"

"I confess I was concerned that someone may suspect you aren't actually living here, so I've been trying to come up with a solution that would protect your reputation. You need a chaperone, and I know just the person. You recall that Sergeant Kilgore is overseeing this investigation. His wife works for the police as a searcher. She could live here as your 'older sister' and be your chaperone. She would also prepare meals and clean. I think her presence would provide you with the necessary propriety to preserve your reputation."

Indeed, a married woman in residence *would* keep Tilda's reputation safe. And if Tilda didn't have to cook or clean, she was definitely in favor. "That's a brilliant idea. Is Mrs. Kilgore amenable?"

Maxwell inclined his head. "She is, in fact, and her husband is in agreement."

Tilda wondered at the resources the City of London police were putting into this investigation. It was no small amount with

Maxwell and his lodgings, hiring Tilda, and now reassigning another employee.

"Inspector Maxwell, I find it curious that so much is being invested in this investigation. Is the suspected fraud so great as to warrant this large amount of time and money?"

"It isn't just the fraud, though that is bad enough," Maxwell replied. "The friendly society is an extraordinary benefit to the Coleman Street Ward, and its success may spawn others in neighboring wards, which would be a good thing. A society like this binds people together and offers stability, as well as security. It's really in everyone's interest that we determine what went wrong here, if anything, and ensure it doesn't happen again."

That made Tilda even more glad she was working with Maxwell on this investigation. "It may be helpful to our investigation to have Mrs. Kilgore here, since it was her cousin's husband who was a member of the Amicable Society and died."

Maxwell nodded. "I had the same thought. And I'm sure it's why she's keen to help. My thought is that you and Mrs. Kilgore would each take a bedchamber, whilst I will sleep upstairs in the garret."

"I don't wish to displace you," Tilda said. "I don't mind sleeping upstairs."

"I wouldn't hear of it." Maxwell smiled. "It's no trouble at all. I'll arrange for Mrs. Kilgore to join the household tomorrow."

"Then I shall also move in tomorrow." Tilda was not looking forward to having that conversation with her grandmother.

Maxwell started toward the door. "I should be on my way to work now. I'll hurry back after to fetch you for the Amicable Society meeting this evening."

"I'll be waiting." Tilda followed her "husband" downstairs to the front door, then waved at him as he departed. She made eye contact with a woman sweeping the stoop next door and smiled. The woman paused in her sweeping and seemed uncertain for a moment, then smiled in return.

Tilda went back into the house and looked about at all that could occupy her time today. She could spend the entire day in the kitchen and likely not complete all that needed to be done. There was also much to do and plan if she was going to take up residence tomorrow.

Unfortunately, she didn't want to do any of that. Tilda realized her investigation had revealed one thing so far: she still wasn't interested in actually being a wife.

~

Tilda and Maxwell walked along White Alley to Moorgate and found the Swan and Hoop. It was quite ordinary for societies such as the one they were investigating to meet in public houses.

They entered the pub and looked about the common room. Tilda noted that several people were gathered near a doorway to another chamber.

"There is Mr. Draper, my colleague." Maxwell inclined his head toward a stocky man with light brown hair and a rounded chin. He stood with a woman who was only slightly shorter than him but several years younger. Tilda estimated him to be around thirty, whilst she appeared to be about Tilda's age.

The man's expression brightened with recognition as he saw them approach. "Evening, Harwood." Draper held out his hand, and Maxwell shook it.

"Good evening to you, Draper. May I present Mrs. Harwood?" Maxwell gestured to Tilda.

"I'm pleased to make your acquaintance," Tilda said.

Draper indicated the dark-blonde woman beside him. "This is Mrs. Draper."

She met Tilda's gaze with a slight nod. Tilda perceived an edge of nervousness in her.

"Are we to be allowed into the meeting?" Tilda asked her.

Mrs. Draper's pretty cornflower-blue eyes rounded briefly. "Goodness, no. They would never include us. They'll close the doors to the private dining room, and we'll sit out here and wait. There will be at least a half dozen of us, I should think." She held up a basket. "I brought some mending to do. Did you bring anything?"

"I did not. We are just settling into our new house, and I'm afraid I'm not entirely sure where I put my mending," Tilda lied with a laugh.

Mrs. Draper nodded in commiseration.

"The meeting won't start for a little while yet," Mr. Draper said. "Why don't you come meet the society's leadership council."

"I should like that," Maxwell said.

The four of them walked into the adjoining private dining room. It was set with rows of chairs and a table at one end with three chairs behind it. A dark purple cloth covered the table, and two branches of candles sat on either end. There was a gavel upon which was carved a cock and a snake, as well as a large leather-bound book which also bore a cock and snake. A pen and inkpot were situated beside the book. Finally, there was a Bible.

Tilda understood that these sorts of societies often had some kind of ceremonial aspect, but it seemed she would not be allowed to witness it. She would have to settle for hearing Inspector Maxwell's description.

Several gentlemen mingled about the room, but Mr. Draper led them to the table where three men stood in front of it.

"Evening, Draper," one of the men said. He had dark hair and long side whiskers. His small brown eyes regarded Mrs. Draper and then Tilda. She didn't particularly care for the way his gaze lingered on her. He had a somewhat heavy paunch, and his nose bore the reddish hue of someone who enjoyed more than the occasional glass of wine.

"Good evening, Mr. Phelps," Draper replied. "This is my colleague, Mr. Harwood."

"Ah, yes," Mr. Phelps replied with a placid smile. "Welcome." He glanced toward Draper. "We're delighted you brought someone to join our membership."

"Not just yet," the man next to Phelps said with a hearty laugh. He appeared a few years older and had a thick head of gray hair and round brown eyes. His nose was rather bulbous, and he had a cheerful smile. Tilda noted that of all the men in the room, he dressed the smartest. He wore an exceptionally well-tailored coat made of fine claret wool. She wondered at his occupation.

"I'm Harvey Nevill," he said. "Pleased to meet you." His gaze flicked to Tilda. "Have you brought Mrs. Harwood with you?"

"I have," Maxwell replied. "This is my lovely wife."

"She is lovely indeed," Mr. Nevill said affably. He looked to Maxwell with a more serious expression. "I meant no offense when I said that you were not a member yet, but the truth is you are not until you've taken your oath."

"An oath isn't absolutely required, but you're getting ahead of things, Nevill," the third man said, sounding almost cross. He had sable hair and an equally dark mustache. His coffee-brown eyes were sharp and perhaps a trifle cold, or perhaps they only seemed that way after Nevill's open charm. He snapped his gaze to Draper. "Shouldn't you set up the collection table?"

"Of course." Draper looked toward Maxwell. "If you recall, I assist with collecting the weekly dues." He took himself off, and Mrs. Draper followed behind him as if she too had been dismissed.

The terse gentleman cleared his throat. "As I was saying, Harwood must meet the requirements of membership first."

"Yes, yes, of course," Nevill said with a wave of his hand. He looked back to Tilda and Maxwell. "This is Ernest Furnier. He is the bursar, and what he means by meeting the standards of membership is that he wants to know you can afford it."

"I would not have come if I could not," Maxwell assured them. "Draper said it was six farthings a week."

"The cost depends on your age," Furnier said with a frown. "How old are you?"

"Twenty-seven," the inspector replied.

"Then yes, six farthings a week. Plus the entrance fee, which is two shillings, six pence—*if* you are accepted," Furnier said sharply. "Are you prepared to pay that?"

"I am. When will I—or my wife—be eligible to collect benefits?"

"In one year. What is your occupation?" Furnier demanded.

Nevill gave the treasurer an exasperated look. "He's a clerk like Draper, isn't that right?"

"Yes," Maxwell said. "I heard we may be eligible for benefits in six months."

Furnier exhaled, then cast an angry look toward his colleagues. "I wish I knew where that rumor started. I would make sure to bury it once and for all."

Tilda took note of Furnier's irritation, as well as him saying the six-month eligibility was a rumor.

"Who told you it was six months?" Nevill asked, his wide brow furrowed.

"I can't recall," the inspector said with a light shrug. "Perhaps I was mistaken."

"You were indeed." Furnier turned his expectant gaze on Tilda, his thin brows drawn together. "And do you have employment, Mrs. Harwood?"

"Yes, I make matchbooks."

Furnier looked immediately satisfied. He returned his attention to the inspector. "And where do you reside?"

"In White Alley," Maxwell replied. "Number Five."

"I know it," Nevill said with a wag of his finger. "It's been empty for a bit. I'm sure it will keep you busy to clean it properly." He chuckled as he looked at Tilda. Of course that would be entirely her duty.

Tilda merely smiled and nodded. She was making a great

effort to remain quiet. In this situation, she thought it best to let her "husband" do the talking.

"Is my membership application accepted then?" Maxwell asked.

Mr. Phelps scrutinized him a moment. "The three of us must decide together, but you've met the financial requirements. Let us discuss your character. How long have you and Mrs. Harwood been married?"

Maxwell smiled at Tilda. "Just over a year."

"And you're new to the City?" Phelps asked.

"Yes, we've just moved from Essex," Maxwell replied. "I was fortunate enough to be hired by the mercantile house. I thought it would be beneficial for me to join a society such as this, so I was quite pleased when Draper mentioned it to me."

"How long has the society been in operation?" Tilda asked. Though Maxwell had told her it was six months or so, she wanted to hear it from the society administrators.

"About six months," Phelps replied. "Our membership already boasts nearly two hundred and fifty members."

"Indeed?" Maxwell's brows climbed. "That is impressive."

Phelps puffed up a bit, his shoulders arching back as his chin notched up. "For the final stage of admission, we must ask about your health. If you'll excuse us, Mrs. Harwood, we will take your husband to meet our society physician, Dr. Giles."

He indicated a gentleman with dark blond hair who stood talking to another gentleman near the first row of chairs. He was younger than the three administrators, who all looked as if they were in their forties. The doctor appeared to be in his late twenties. He smiled broadly—and rather charmingly—at something the other man said.

"Of course," Tilda murmured as Mr. Phelps took Maxwell to meet the doctor.

"It's a shame women can't join your society," Tilda said to Nevill and Furnier.

Nevill chuckled. "I'm afraid that's not possible, however, you ladies are welcome to sit in the common room of the pub and have your own little club of sorts." There was an air of condescension in his tone.

Furnier narrowed his eyes at Tilda. "You will be taken care of should your husband die tragically. This society ensures your well-being. Is that not pleasing?"

Tilda summoned a mild smile. "Indeed it is. I am very grateful my husband has the opportunity to be considered for membership in this wonderful congregation."

Furnier gave her a slight nod of approval, but it didn't matter. Tilda had already decided she didn't care for the man.

"Pardon me," Furnier murmured before moving to the doorway where Draper had relocated a small table and a pair of chairs.

Tilda cast a glance toward where Maxwell was speaking with the doctor and Mr. Phelps. The other gentleman had moved away. Another man walked into the room and recognition sparked in Tilda before she even saw his face. She knew that form, never mind that he was dressed in a simple dark blue suit. Taking in his blond hair and long side whiskers, she suffered a moment's doubt. But his familiar features banished that immediately.

Sucking in a breath, she narrowed her eyes at Hadrian. What in the devil was he doing here?

CHAPTER 3

*T*he moment Hadrian's gaze met Tilda's, he could see her surprise. He probably should have warned her that he'd decided to attend the meeting. However, the truth was that he hadn't wanted to tell her, in the very likely case she would ask him not to come. As he made his way to her, he hoped she would grasp his plan and accept it.

"Good evening, Sister," he said, noting her darkened hair. It was a bit jarring to see her without her reddish-blonde locks.

"I wasn't sure you would be able to come," she said smoothly, but with a gentle flare of her nostrils that no one but Hadrian likely noticed.

He was relieved—and pleased—that she didn't call him out. "I was able to arrange my shift at the club so I could attend this meeting tonight. I hope it's all right." He glanced about and saw that Inspector Maxwell stood with another pair of gentlemen.

Tilda narrowed her eyes at him slightly before turning her attention to the man beside her. "Allow me to present my brother, Mr. Beck. Nigel, this is Mr. Nevill, a member of the society's leadership council."

Nigel? Hadrian had known a Nigel at Oxford. He was a sneaky fellow, always getting into trouble. Perhaps it was a good name for this scheme.

"I hope it's all right that I invited my brother," she said to Nevill. "He's interested in joining the society as well."

"Does he have someone to propose his membership?" Nevill asked.

"I'd hoped my brother-in-law could," Hadrian replied easily. "His interest in joining sparked mine."

"Well, technically, Mr. Harwood isn't yet a member." Nevill narrowed his eyes toward Furnier. "But he will be shortly, so I say it's fine that he proposes you. The society is always looking to expand its membership." He grinned at Hadrian. "Let me smooth the way with my colleagues. It may be best if Mr. Beck waits in the common room for a few minutes."

"Certainly," Hadrian replied eagerly. "Would you care to accompany me, Sister?"

"I will, yes." Tilda smiled prettily at Nevill, then glanced toward Inspector Maxwell, who was watching them with a somewhat hooded gaze.

When they were in the common room, Tilda led Hadrian to a corner. "What on earth are you doing here?" she asked quietly but urgently, her dark-blonde brows pitched together.

"Participating in the investigation," he replied in an equally low tone. "I decided I could join the society as well."

"As my brother." She blinked. "It doesn't work like that, as you've just learned. You can't just show up and seek membership. You must be proposed by an existing member."

"I understand that now, but it doesn't seem to be a problem according to Nevill, since Maxwell is apparently becoming a member tonight."

"I hope he is. He's currently undergoing a medical evaluation with the society's doctor. If he passes, I believe he will be welcomed or initiated, or whatever it is they do."

"There's an initiation?" Hadrian asked.

"Some sort of ceremony," Tilda said. "Did you see the table at the front of the room with the candles and other items?"

"I did, but I wasn't sure what that was for. Sounds intriguing. Knowing your curiosity, you must be looking forward to seeing that." He half-smiled.

"I'm not allowed," she said with disgust. "Women are not permitted to attend the meetings, but neither will you be if you aren't accepted for membership. What is it you hoped to accomplish in coming here?"

"I told you—to join the investigation. I thought I could be helpful. Particularly with my special ability."

She exhaled, her expression still perturbed. "You are always helpful—with and without your ability. Alas, you were not invited. I can't think Inspector Maxwell will be in favor of this."

Hadrian knew he'd made a gamble coming here, but he'd hoped Tilda would be pleased. "Do you want me to go?"

A long moment stretched as she studied him, then looked toward the meeting room. "No." She turned her gaze to him. "I must say, you've done an excellent job with your disguise. The blond hair threw me."

"Your darker hair also gave me pause," Hadrian said.

She swept her gaze over him, and he felt a jolt of awareness. "Your costume is very plain—and doesn't appear costly. It doesn't reveal you to be an earl. I'm impressed."

"Thank you, though I can't take the credit. I called on Mrs. Longbotham at the Hen and Chicken." They'd met Mrs. Longbotham, who was actually a man who preferred to dress as a woman and be addressed as such, during one of their investigations. Mrs. Longbotham had aided them in disguising Tilda as a man so that she could visit a gentlemen's club with Hadrian.

Tilda's eyes rounded. "Did you? Well done. Your simple costume doesn't advertise your nobility."

"It was Mrs. Longbotham's idea that I take on the role of a footman at a gentlemen's club. Such a position allows for my speech. I didn't think I'd be able to speak differently, not like you can." Tilda had employed an excellent Cockney accent on several occasions during their investigations.

"I'm not speaking too differently," Tilda said. "We are saying we came from Essex, so I suppose you should be from there too."

Hadrian saw the inspector leave the meeting room and move toward them. "Here comes Maxwell."

Inspector Maxwell, who was now clean-shaven, kept his features placid, but his jaw was tight. "What is going on?" he asked softly. The question held an edge of irritation.

"His lordship wanted to offer his help as an investigator," Tilda replied. "He has fabricated a disguise as Nigel Beck, a footman at a gentlemen's club."

"Has he now?" Maxwell asked, giving Hadrian a frosty look. "You are muddling our investigation. You should have discussed this with me first, particularly since I said your assistance would not be required."

"I do apologize," Hadrian said.

"It will be fine," Tilda interjected. "Lord Ravenhurst is an excellent investigator. I am confident his presence will provide valuable assistance. He would join the Amicable Society, but he does not have anyone to propose his membership. You can after you become a member. How did it go with the doctor?"

Hadrian noted Tilda did not wait for Maxwell to agree. He had to stifle a smile.

"Fine," Maxwell replied. "He asked me about my general health and whether anyone in my family had suffered from certain illnesses, such as consumption. He also asked if we had any children, or if you had ever been with child. I said you have not, but that we hoped to be blessed."

Though Hadrian knew this was all make-believe, the thought of Tilda having a child with Inspector Maxwell was shockingly distressing. Perhaps it was because Tilda had never expressed a desire to become a mother—or a wife.

Tilda nodded. "Does that mean you will be inducted, or whatever they call it, this evening?"

"I will."

Maxwell narrowed his eyes at Hadrian in what appeared to be irritation. "Your intrusion in this investigation is highly irregular. If you were not an earl, I would ask you to leave forthwith."

Hadrian tamped down his annoyance. He *had* intruded on the inspector's investigation uninvited. And Maxwell couldn't know what...*unique* perspective Hadrian would offer by way of his special ability to experience others' memories.

"Consider what he may contribute," Tilda argued. "You work all day, whereas Lord Ravenhurst's pretend employment is in the evenings. Perhaps there is investigative work he can do during the day."

The inspector fell silent a moment, his brow creased with contemplation. "I suppose that would be helpful." He continued speaking to Tilda as if Hadrian weren't there. "They're going to ask where he lives." Now, he looked to Hadrian. "What will you say?"

Hadrian lifted his shoulder. "I thought I would say I live with you."

Maxwell's expression flashed with discomfort as he looked toward Tilda. There was something Hadrian didn't know.

"Is there something wrong with your lodgings?" Hadrian asked.

"No," Maxwell replied. He fixed his gaze on Hadrian. "Would you actually want to stay there or just pretend to?"

"I can pretend as Miss Wren is doing."

Tilda exhaled. "I will not be pretending. As of tomorrow, we have arranged for a chaperone to stay at the house. She is Mrs. Kilgore, the wife of a sergeant at the City of London Police, and she will be residing with us as my sister." She met Hadrian's gaze with a wry look. "*Our* sister."

Now it was Hadrian's turn to be surprised—and irritated. He

did not like that Tilda had arranged to reside with the inspector. Though he supposed he had to give them credit for providing a chaperone.

"I believe we're getting ahead of ourselves," Maxwell said. "Let us even determine if the society is willing to consider his lordship's membership."

Tilda's brows arched briefly. "Here comes Mr. Nevill. He seemed to think it would be possible."

Nevill flashed a smile at them. "Mr. Beck, I just need to ask a few questions to assess your eligibility for membership. Where are you employed?"

Hadrian looked down at the man, for he was several inches shorter than Hadrian's six foot two inches. "I work at a club in the West End. I prefer not to name it for discretion's sake." And so that no one would go asking about him and learn he was not actually an employee.

"I understand," Nevill said with a vague nod. His brown eyes lit with interest. "Do you rub elbows with the elite?"

"I *serve* them," Hadrian said rather flatly.

"Of course," Nevill replied with a laugh. "Well, in my opinion, you will make an excellent addition to the Amicable Society. We've just a few formalities. Would you like to come with me and meet the other administrators?"

Hadrian smiled eagerly. "I should be delighted."

Nevill turned and started toward the private dining room. Hadrian followed the man, and Tilda and Maxwell trailed behind. However, when they reached the doorway, Nevill turned and gave Tilda an apologetic smile.

"I'm sorry, Mrs. Harwood, but we will be starting shortly. You'll need to remain here in the common room."

"I see," she murmured.

Hadrian could see the curiosity brimming in her gaze and also the disappointment and annoyance that she was to be excluded.

She forced a smile. "I understand."

Mrs. Draper came from the meeting room and joined her. "Mrs. Harwood, allow me to introduce you to the other wives." She guided Tilda to a table where several other ladies were seated.

Hadrian was now doubly glad he'd come, for he could report every detail of the meeting to Tilda. He supposed the inspector would have done the same, but Maxwell didn't know Tilda as Hadrian did. He would not be aware of the information she would hope to learn. Hadrian, however, knew her quite well and would do his best to satisfy her boundless curiosity.

Someone closed the doors behind them, and Mr. Nevill took Hadrian toward the purple-covered table where three other men stood. Maxwell joined them, though he loitered a bit behind.

"We have another potential member," Nevill told them. "This is Mr. Harwood's brother-in-law, Mr. Nigel Beck. He works at a gentlemen's club in the West End. Mr. Harwood, allow me to present Mr. Phelps, the society's chair, Mr. Furnier, our bursar, and Dr. Giles, our physician."

Furnier, a small, thin man with a pinched expression did not appear pleased. "We mustn't rush anything." He sent Hadrian a look that was even colder than the one Maxwell had delivered earlier. "You should come back next week."

"I can try." Hadrian scrubbed his cheek. "However, I'm typically working at this hour."

"I'm afraid that will not do," Furnier said. "We expect members will attend meetings as much as possible, and at least once each quarter."

Hadrian wondered if they actually required that. If they did, it would seem someone would have noticed the member who had died was ill. "Is it a problem if members don't attend?"

"It is the easiest way to collect the weekly membership fees, as we meet every Monday evening." Nevill glanced toward a table near the doorway, where a man sat taking payments from members as they entered. He placed the funds in a money box on the table and recorded the deposit in a ledger. "If someone is not able to attend, they typically send their payment along with someone else, so it's not really *required* that they attend." He sent a suffering glance toward Furnier.

"What happens if someone doesn't make their weekly payment?" Hadrian asked.

Furnier pursed his lips tightly. "We call on them to ensure all is well. However, if two consecutive payments are missed, we issue a written warning of dismissal from the society. After the third missed payment, we remove them from our membership roll."

"If I can't attend, perhaps I can send my fee with my brother-in-law." Hadrian inclined his head toward Maxwell, who'd moved to the rows of chairs that were aligned for the meeting.

"Certainly," Nevill said.

"What is your income?" Furnier asked, looking harassed and prompting Hadrian to wonder if he ever smiled or appeared pleasant.

"Twenty-five shillings per week."

Nevill smiled. "That is sufficient. Are you in good health?" He glanced toward the doctor.

"He certainly looks it," Dr. Giles commented after sweeping his gaze over Hadrian's person. "What is your age?"

"Thirty," Hadrian replied.

"Have any of your family died of consumption?" the doctor asked.

"No."

"Do any of them suffer with gout?" When Hadrian replied in the negative, Dr. Giles rattled off several more diseases, to which Hadrian also said no.

"Are all members subject to this interview?" Hadrian asked.

The chair, Mr. Phelps, fixed his dark-brown eyes on Hadrian.

"Of course. Are you prepared to pay the entrance fee this evening?"

"I believe so," Hadrian replied. "Two pence?"

"Three shillings to join," Mr. Furnier said crisply. "Two pence per week after that. The amount varies based on age, and you are not young."

Hadrian nearly scoffed at that assessment. He certainly didn't feel *old*. Withdrawing the necessary funds from his coat, he held the coins out to the bursar.

Furnier frowned and did not take the money. "You haven't been approved yet."

Hadrian didn't withdraw his hand. He was very close to being admitted—it was clear Nevill wanted him. "My apologies. I thought I had."

"Of course, you are," Nevill said jovially before casting an exasperated glance toward Furnier. "We would be glad to accept your application. Don't you agree, Walter?" He looked expectantly at the apparent man in charge.

Mr. Phelps hesitated, then stretched his lips into a thin smile. "Yes, of course. We'll take down your information after the meeting, as we must begin. You may give your entrance fee to Mr. Draper over there." He gestured toward the man sitting at a table near the door. "Then please take your seat."

Hadrian grinned with what he hoped was the proper amount of enthusiasm. "Thank you very much." He'd learned a great deal about playing a role from watching Tilda. He went to the man Phelps had indicated—Draper—just as he was closing a wooden box.

Hadrian glimpsed a cock and snake carved into the top before as he handed over his entrance fee. Draper opened the lid and dropped the coins inside the box. "Your name?"

"Nigel Beck."

Draper recorded Hadrian's payment in a ledger, then dropped

the coins into the box. He looked up and smiled warmly. "Welcome. I'm Draper. Who sponsored your membership?"

"My brother-in-law, Albert Harwood."

"I work with Harwood," Draper said amiably. "He didn't mention you."

Hadrian wasn't sure if Draper meant anything by that. The man didn't appear suspicious, so Hadrian decided it was an innocuous statement.

"Please take your seats," Phelps announced.

Draper closed the box and turned the key in the lock before taking it to Furnier whilst Hadrian sat down with Maxwell in the middle of the rows. The room was not quite full, but it was close.

"They admitted you?" Maxwell whispered.

Hadrian nodded. "Nevill was quite zealous in his desire to welcome me. Furnier was…less so."

"He seems prickly."

"So I gathered." Hadrian was quite pleased with how that had gone. He only wished he'd had time to shake at least one of their hands.

The three administrators moved behind the table whilst the doctor sat in a chair on the right side near the wall. The man at the table near the door closed it and went to sit in one of the rows. Phelps stood in the middle and reached beneath the table. He pulled out something feathered and set it atop his head.

Hadrian realized it was a hat adorned with the plumage of a cock. He bit the inside of his cheek to keep from smiling or, worse, laughing.

Phelps picked up the gavel and tapped it on the table three times, then once, then three more times. The sound was muffled by the tablecloth.

"I hereby call the meeting of the Amicable Society of the Coleman Street Ward to order," Phelps called out, then turned his head toward Nevill. "Let us introduce our new members since our last meeting, not all of whom are present this evening."

How was it that they admitted members who weren't present? Furnier had made a fuss about Hadrian attending meetings. Furthermore, how were those members approved for membership if they weren't subjected to the same interview process? These questions were pertinent to the investigation.

Nevill sat down and opened the ledger, then announced several names. Taking a pen from his coat, he wrote several more as he spoke them, including Albert Harwood and Nigel Beck. Presumably, he was adding those who had been offered membership this evening.

The secretary set the pen aside and rose once more. "Let us recite our oath. Will the new members come forward?"

Hadrian and Maxwell exchanged a glance as they stood and moved to the front of the room along with four other men.

Nevill set a piece of parchment on the front of the table toward them. "This is our oath. We will ask you all to put your hand on the Bible and repeat the oath in turn."

Hadrian patiently waited while the other gentlemen completed their recitations. He'd practically memorized the oath by the time it was his turn to put his hand on the Bible.

"I, Nigel Beck, swear to uphold the benevolent purposes of the Amicable Society of the Coleman Street Ward. I will strive for hard work, good health, and a happy home. I will support my brethren and encourage our expansion, and if God should take me from this earth, I shall be glad to know that I was an amicable brother and served the society well."

Then it was Maxwell's turn. Finally, they were finished, but Nevill bade them remain in place.

Phelps let out a crowing sound that Hadrian supposed was meant to mimic a cock's call at dawn. Again, he had to keep himself from revealing his amusement.

"The cock is the emblem of the Coleman Street Ward," Phelps announced. "So, of course, it is ours too. We also revere the snake, which signifies health and wellness. As members of the

Amicable Society, you will rise each morning with the joy and fervor of the cock and proceed through your day with the ease and confidence of the snake. Do you agree?"

"I do," they all replied, mostly in unison.

"Let me now teach you the handshake," Phelps said.

Hadrian slid a glance toward Maxwell, whose face was blank. Hadrian could hardly wait to tell Tilda about everything.

"The handshake and the oath are secret," Phelps said sternly. "You must not share them with anyone outside of the society. It is how we identify one another. Those who are not amicable members must not be brought into our sacred knowledge."

Starting with the first gentleman standing before the table, Phelps taught him the handshake. Hadrian was assured of shaking at least Phelps's hand. He hoped he would learn something about the man and perhaps the society.

But how would he convey what he learned to the inspector without revealing the manner in which he'd obtained that knowledge? He couldn't very well explain his ability to see others' memories, nor did he want to. That was his own secret, and there were only three people in the world who knew it: Tilda and two gentlemen—a father and son—who shared the same power.

The handshake was rather simple. The two men clasped hands, then Phelps showed them how to fan the fingers and hold them away from the other's hand. Phelps then moved his fingers. "Like they're feathers fluttering, you see?" he asked. The man copied Phelps.

"Very good," Phelps said. "Shake once, then glide back and forth and side to side a bit, as if our hands and forearms are a snake slithering." He demonstrated the movement, and the man smiled. "Now you try."

The man repeated the handshake. Satisfied, Phelps congratulated him and moved to the next gentleman. As he proceeded down the line, he no longer needed to demonstrate first. The new members had watched and performed the shake without prompting.

When it was Hadrian's turn, he clasped Phelps's hand. The edges of his vision blurred as one of the man's memories came into focus. Hadrian did not close his eyes, for when he did, that ended the vision.

He saw Phelps transfer coins from a purse to a metal box that already contained money. Before Hadrian could try to determine where this was taking place or how Phelps might have been feeling, the handshake was over, and the memory disappeared. Pain shot through Hadrian's head, which he expected. Hopefully, the headache would be short-lived.

After Maxwell shook Phelps's hand, the new members returned to their seats. The rest of the meeting was rather boring, as they discussed plans for a parade in July. Someone suggested the ladies could organize a picnic. Maxwell endorsed this idea, and Hadrian knew why. It would involve Tilda in the matters of the society, assuming the planning happened soon, and that would be helpful.

Indeed, knowing that Tilda could not join the society, Hadrian wondered what her role in the investigation would be. He supposed she could learn things from the wives. He wondered if any of them in the common room were married to the administrators. They seemed to be the men on which to focus their investigation. If the society was, in fact, corrupt, they would be the likely culprits, along with the canvasser, Eaton.

Just before the meeting concluded, a man raised his hand. Phelps called his name, and the man stood to ask what was happening with the possible corruption committed by the former canvasser. This was met with murmurs and Phelps holding up his hands. He said they were still looking into the matter and asked everyone to be patient. Then he adjourned the meeting.

As the gentlemen began to make their way from the room, Maxwell turned to Hadrian. "That was interesting. And helpful—

it gives us the perfect opportunity to ask about Eaton and potential corruption."

"Agreed," Hadrian said eagerly. "I'd also like to ask a few questions about membership admissions."

Nodding, Maxwell accompanied Hadrian to the front of the room, where the administrators were placing the items on the table into a crate. "We wanted to thank you for welcoming us into the Amicable Society," Maxwell said with a smile.

"We're delighted to have you," Nevill replied with enthusiasm.

Hadrian stepped up to the table as Furnier pulled the purple cloth away and began to fold it. "You mentioned there are new members who aren't here this evening. I'm curious how they're assessed and admitted to the society? I had the impression it was important to be present." He glanced at Furnier, who narrowed his eyes briefly.

"It is, but we understand it isn't always possible with work and family," Phelps said, sounding rather smooth.

"Is there another day and time when people may apply for membership?" Hadrian pressed.

"Not specifically," Phelps replied. "If a member wants to recommend someone and that person can't attend the meeting, they arrange to meet with one of us, and we conduct the membership interview and collect the entrance fee." He cocked his head and studied Hadrian a moment. "Why are you so interested?"

Hadrian summoned a brief smile. "Merely curious."

"I'd heard there was a canvasser until recently," Maxwell said. "What happened with him?"

Phelps's jaw tightened. "His practices have come into question, and he is no longer with the society."

"How unfortunate." Maxwell's brow creased. "Were some of those questionable practices to do with not having members sponsor the men he recruited and not conducting medical assessments?"

"In fact, we endeavored to have Mr. Eaton call on men whom members endorsed," Nevill explained. "He would conduct the interview and collect the entrance fee."

"What about having Dr. Giles assess their health?" Maxwell asked.

Phelps flashed a smile, but it did not reach his dark eyes. Indeed, his gaze held a glint of annoyance. "You must excuse us, Mr. Harwood. We need to clean up and be on our way."

"Of course." Maxwell inclined his head and turned from the table.

Hadrian bade the administrators good evening and accompanied Maxwell from the room. They found Tilda, who'd already excused herself from the other ladies, then left the pub together. They did not speak until they'd reached White Alley.

"How was the initiation?" Tilda asked.

"Ridiculous," Hadrian replied. "Phelps wore a hat to make him look like a cock and then made the sound of one."

"We heard that," Tilda said with a chuckle. "The other ladies almost universally rolled their eyes."

"Would you like to learn the handshake?" Hadrian asked.

She met his gaze with avid interest, and it was clear to Hadrian that she wanted to know if he'd seen anything. However, he couldn't reveal that in front of Maxwell. "There was a handshake?" she asked.

"We're not supposed to share any of that," Maxwell said with faint disapproval. "It's a secret for members only."

Hadrian scoffed. "You're not really buying into all that, are you?"

Maxwell allowed a smile, and it occurred to Hadrian that, without his facial hair, the man was rather attractive. He also looked young, which made Hadrian think of Furnier's comment that, at thirty, Hadrian wasn't young. He felt an irrational prick of irritation. Was that provoked by the inspector's youth?

"I found the ceremony ridiculous as well," Maxwell said. "And it doesn't seem as though it's necessary. What I mean is, I don't think every member is formally initiated."

"I agree." Hadrian nodded as he looked to Tilda. "There were a few members who were recruited since the last meeting but who weren't present tonight. I found that odd after Furnier made a point of telling me I should attend a certain number of meetings. But then Nevill seemed to disagree, so perhaps that isn't a policy."

"Though I've just met Furnier, I had the impression he's a stickler," Maxwell said.

"Definitely," Hadrian agreed. "I also found it odd that they required Maxwell and me to be proposed by existing members and yet employed a canvasser to recruit people who may not have been proposed."

"That was why I asked the question," Maxwell said. "Though they did say they tried to have the canvasser call on houses recommended by other members. Still, I don't know how they ensured that was the case. Did you note how they didn't respond to my query about the doctor's approval of those members?"

"I did."

"It seems as though it may have been easy for a member to hide an illness," Tilda said.

"Such as Mr. Cardy?" Hadrian wasn't sure what Tilda was implying, if anything. "You think the Cardys perpetrated the fraud instead of the society?"

Tilda shrugged. "I think it's possible Cardy lied about his illness in order to obtain benefits, and Mrs. Cardy could have lied to the society about being told there was a six-month eligibility policy in an effort to collect the money early. I'm not saying I believe that's what happened, just that we must think of this from all perspectives."

"You are correct," Maxwell said with a hint of admiration. His gaze met Tilda's, and she smiled at him.

Hadrian noted the connection between them and had to ignore another pang of frustration. He forced himself to think of the investigation. "I could easily have lied to Dr. Giles about my health. He did not conduct a physical examination. Is that odd for a friendly society?"

"I'm not certain." Maxwell frowned. "I believe it varies. I wanted to ask more questions, specifically how they collect the weekly dues from people who aren't in attendance."

"I have the answer to that." Hadrian shared what Furnier and Nevill had told him. "When I mentioned I may not be able to attend every week, they said I would need to find a way to make my payments, as that is when they collect. I'm allowed to send it with someone, such as my brother-in-law here." He inclined his head toward Maxwell. "That means I must trust him not to steal it." He added the last with a smile, but he realized he harbored an irritation toward the inspector. Not dislike, exactly, but something about the man grated on Hadrian's nerves.

"And I have an answer about whether it's odd not to conduct a physical examination," Tilda said. "There was some discussion about Gilbert Cardy's death and the fact that he was ill when he was admitted. Everyone finds that strange—according to Mrs. Burley. She is clearly the society's gossipmonger."

"What else did Mrs. Burley say?" Maxwell asked with interest.

"That last week's meeting was lively, as several people voiced concerns about ill members being admitted. There is also a question as to why the Cardys may have misunderstood the eligibility period." Tilda looked from Maxwell to Hadrian. "Apparently, Mr. Phelps assured everyone that the administrators would deal with the issues. Did they address anything during your meeting?"

"No, they did not." They reached Number Five, and Maxwell unlocked the door. He held it open for Tilda and Hadrian to precede him inside.

After closing the door, the inspector moved to light a lantern that sat on a small table against the wall, where the stairway rose. "If you give me your hand, Miss Wren, I will demonstrate the handshake."

Tilda extended her hand, and Maxwell clasped it, fluttering his fingers. "Those are supposed to be feathers, and this is a snake." He moved their hands and forearms, pumping forward and pulling back with a gentle glide.

Hadrian watched with a surprising sensation of disappointment. *He'd* wanted to show her. He realized he would take any opportunity to touch Tilda. They'd come so close last week before the inspector had arrived at her house. Their hands had almost touched, and it was the most intimate moment they'd shared since they'd kissed several weeks ago. Hadrian had been unaccountably disappointed that they'd been interrupted.

Now, as he watched her shake the inspector's hand, along with the knowledge that they would be residing together under the same roof, Hadrian realized a horrible and undeniable fact, and perhaps the reason for why Maxwell troubled him.

Hadrian was jealous.

CHAPTER 4

*P*erplexed, Tilda released Maxwell's hand. "I'm afraid I
don't understand the application of this handshake.
Are you to offer this randomly to other gentlemen you
encounter?"

"Apparently so?" Maxwell shook his head. "I confess, I'm not
entirely clear on the matter." He looked to Hadrian.

"I wouldn't think we would do so randomly. I suspect we
ought to use the handshake when greeting known members of
the society." Hadrian shrugged. "Whatever its purpose, it seems a
bit silly."

"Your gentlemen's clubs don't have such handshakes?"
Maxwell asked with perhaps the barest hint of derision. It was
the way he'd said "your gentlemen's clubs."

"No." Hadrian narrowed his eyes briefly. "Are you predisposed
to dislike these sorts of clubs and societies?"

Tilda had wondered if he'd caught Maxwell's scorn—if it was
that—and now she knew.

"They seem exclusive for the sheer purpose of exclusion,"
Maxwell replied.

Tilda could not find fault with the inspector's assessment.

Indeed, she didn't understand the need to join such a club, though she did see the financial benefits of the Amicable Society. She smiled at the inspector, appreciating their shared belief. "What an invigorating perspective."

Hadrian's brow furrowed slightly, and his eyes darkened. Had he not cared for her response on the matter? Or was his head paining him? She was eager to learn what he'd seen when he'd shaken hands during the meeting.

She was also worried as to how many hands he'd shaken. When he had multiple visions in a short period of time, the accompanying headache could be quite horrid. But she hadn't seen him touching his head or massaging his temple. Alas, she'd have to wait to ask him about it, as they could not discuss his ability in front of Maxwell. It wasn't just that the inspector might not understand, or even believe them, but that it was up to Hadrian with whom he shared his ability. Tilda would never reveal his secret.

"Should we adjourn to the sitting room to discuss what we learned this evening?" Maxwell suggested.

"Yes, I'd like to share what else I discovered from the wives." Tilda picked up the lantern and led them into the sitting room.

The seating included a wooden settle and a pair of worn cushioned chairs that were probably red at some time but had faded to a dingy pink. Tilda had spent a great deal of time working to rid them of dust that afternoon.

Hadrian glanced about. Tilda had to think this was perhaps the meanest room he'd encountered. Actually, it wasn't—they'd seen worse a time or two during their investigations.

Tilda set the lantern on a small table and perched on the settle. The two men each took a chair.

"Before I tell you about the wives, is there anything else from the meeting that I should know, aside from the ceremonial claptrap?" Tilda asked.

"It was somewhat dull," Maxwell said.

Hadrian inclined his weirdly blond head—Tilda much preferred his dark-brown hair. "In that assessment, we are agreed."

Maxwell looked to Tilda. "What did you learn, Miss Wren?"

"With regard to the administrators, only Mr. Furnier has a wife," Tilda said. "She is rather quiet. She was darning a pair of socks and kept her focus on them almost entirely. Mr. Phelps is a widower, and Mr. Nevill has never been married. Dr. Giles is betrothed. He's to wed next month. Apparently, he was engaged to be married a few years ago, but his fiancée died. He and Mr. Phelps are quite dedicated to the benefits of the society because they both understand how difficult it is to lose a loved one. It's especially awful if one cannot afford a proper funeral."

"Is that why they accept ill members?" Hadrian mused. "It's not a sound business practice, as they may need to pay out if the member survives the first year." He shook his head. "I can't see Furnier allowing that."

"I agree," Maxwell said. "He was meticulous in making sure I met the qualifications of membership."

"That was also my experience," Hadrian noted. They all fell silent a moment.

Tilda continued with what she'd learned from the wives. "I asked where the society keeps its records, since all meetings are conducted at the Swan and Hoop. Mrs. Draper said there's a financial ledger where her husband records the weekly dues as people enter the meeting and pay. Then Mrs. Burley told me there's a membership roll that sits on the ceremonial table. I asked if the canvasser kept a record of his recruitment."

Maxwell smiled. "Brilliant."

"That was when Mrs. Burley took the opportunity to discuss last week's meeting. Phelps announced that the canvasser had been sacked, and they were looking into possible corruption."

"He mentioned that during our meeting," Hadrian said. "But only because someone asked—probably because Phelps hadn't provided an update. Seems as though it should have been the first thing discussed in the meeting."

"Did Mrs. Burley have anything to say about the canvasser's record?" Maxwell asked.

"Only that she wasn't aware of one. She did say it would be helpful if it existed, for then they could hopefully determine whether Eaton had committed any wrongdoing. That was when Mrs. Furnier finally spoke up and said Mrs. Burley didn't know *everything*. She said there was a record of Mr. Eaton's recruitment and that they must trust the administrators to solve that issue." Tilda recalled Mrs. Burley's affronted reaction. "Mrs. Burley didn't appreciate being scolded."

"I can imagine," Maxwell murmured.

Tilda frowned slightly. "I will say Mrs. Furnier seemed almost suspicious about my questions regarding the records. It was one of the few times she looked up from darning her socks. I explained that I was interested in recordkeeping because my husband is a clerk." She looked to Maxwell. "Mrs. Draper endorsed my curiosity as another clerk's wife."

"We also learned at the meeting that there's to be a picnic and the wives are to plan it," Hadrian said.

Tilda blinked. "Nobody mentioned that."

"I think it was just decided at tonight's meeting." Hadrian inclined his head toward Maxwell. "Your husband was keen to endorse the idea."

"I most certainly was," the inspector said. "It will give Miss Wren an excellent opportunity to meet with the other ladies."

"It does indeed." Tilda tapped her fingertips briefly against the wood seat. "Perhaps I can persuade Mrs. Furnier to host a meeting, which would give me an opportunity to search for the society's financial records. Although, I don't know if she would agree. She seems unlikely to."

"I want to find Timothy Eaton, the canvasser who disappeared, since Inspector Dolen was not able to speak with him," Maxwell said. "I'd like to see his recruitment records."

"What information do you have about him?" Tilda asked.

"He was living at a boarding house in Ironmonger Lane. Dolen interviewed the landlady, but she didn't have much to say. She described Eaton as charming and attractive, as well as extremely friendly—just the sort of person one might hire to recruit members."

Tilda would hope she could persuade the woman to say more. "I should like to talk to her, if you don't mind."

"Not at all, but will you do so as Miss Wren, investigator, or Mrs. Harwood, curious matchbook maker?" Maxwell smiled briefly.

"I can't think of a reason Mrs. Harwood would be asking about Eaton," Tilda replied. "And I should like to protect my disguise. I shall have to speak with this woman as myself—an investigator."

Maxwell's brow furrowed. "You must be very careful not to be detected by anyone who knows you as Mrs. Harwood."

"We should determine who hired Eaton and for what purpose," Tilda said. "Did they direct him to recruit people who were ill and to offer a shorter eligibility for benefits in order to persuade them to join? Was the intent to simply fill the society's coffers, or was it something more nefarious?"

"Such as what?" Hadrian asked. "Do we know if all the money that was collected actually made it into the society's locked box?"

"That is also a good question," Tilda said, with anticipation for the coming investigation.

The inspector shifted his attention to Hadrian, a slight frown marring his expression. "I am still slightly peeved that you inserted yourself into my investigation without speaking with me first. Henceforth, I require that every method and scheme must be approved by me. This is *my* investigation. Do you both agree?" He looked to Tilda then back to Hadrian.

"I understand," Hadrian replied.

"Of course," Tilda said softly.

Maxwell exhaled. "Very good. Ravenhurst, you aren't going to be compensated as Miss Wren is—not that you need it."

"I'm perfectly content to not receive compensation," Hadrian said. "Particularly since I involved myself in your investigation without your consent. I am grateful you are allowing me to continue."

"Thank you for saying so, my lord," Maxwell said.

Hadrian gave his head a shake. "Ravenhurst is fine, or Raven, if you'd like. That is how my colleagues address me."

"I think I'd best get in the habit of calling you Beck." Maxwell turned his head toward Tilda. "How did you know his name was Nigel Beck when you introduced us at the pub? Did you know that he was going to come?"

"I did not. I gave him that name. His lordship's surname is Becket. I borrowed part of it."

"And why Nigel?" Hadrian asked with a half-smile.

Tilda's gaze found his. "When I was a child, the neighbors had a cat named Nigel."

Hadrian smirked. "You named me after a cat."

Maxwell laughed.

"It was the first name that came to me," Tilda said. "I liked Nigel. He was a good cat."

Hadrian chuckled, then sobered as he focused on the inspector. "What of the living arrangements?"

Maxwell pivoted toward him. "I imagine you'll be sleeping at your home, since your position at the club would likely require you to work well into the night or even until morning."

"I suppose that makes sense," Hadrian said, flicking a glance toward Tilda. She didn't think he liked that, because that left her here alone with Maxwell and the chaperone, but would Hadrian's presence make it any better? He wasn't a chaperone.

"When you are here, you will share the garret on the top floor with me," Maxwell said. "Miss Wren and Mrs. Kilgore will take the bedchambers on the first floor."

"I will be sure to arrive here around sunrise after my work at the club is completed." Hadrian glanced toward Tilda. "We should probably be going."

"Will you ride back to the West End together?" Maxwell asked. "I was going to offer to escort Miss Wren, since it's getting late."

"That is most kind of you," Tilda said. "However, since Lord Ravenhurst is here and going in that direction, I'll accompany him. I'll return in the morning before you leave for work."

"As will I," Hadrian said. "We can come together."

Tilda nodded. She rose and bid Maxwell good evening. Hadrian did the same, and they started toward the entrance hall.

"You should leave through the scullery," Maxwell said. "You can make your way to Coleman Street and avoid detection, in case any of the neighbors happen to be looking out."

"Smart," Tilda said, before leading Hadrian down to the kitchen.

"This place is rather dirty," Hadrian noted.

"And that's after I spent the day cleaning it—or starting to, anyway." Tilda couldn't keep the bitterness from her tone. "I did not realize this assignment would require me to clean."

"Perhaps the chaperone will help?" Hadrian suggested.

"That is my hope." Tilda led him through the scullery to the rear door. They ascended a short flight of stairs to a small rear yard where there was a privy.

"How clean is that?" Hadrian asked.

"Cleaner than when I arrived this morning," Tilda replied.

"You must be exhausted." Faint lines creased his forehead.

Was he concerned?

Tilda wasn't sure what Hadrian might think of her cleaning. While it wasn't a typical chore for her, she knew she had more experience with it than he did. She wondered if he'd ever actually cleaned something. She returned her thoughts to his query. "Somewhat, but I'm invigorated by the investigation."

They found their way through a narrow alley. It wasn't much more than a path to Coleman Street.

Tilda glanced at him as they emerged onto the thoroughfare. "I hope we can find a hack."

"No need," Hadrian said. "We only need to walk down to Gresham Street. Leach is waiting there."

"Is he?" Tilda asked. "He dropped you off there, I presume?"

Hadrian nodded. "I was careful not to be seen."

They started toward Gresham Street.

She cast him a sideways glance. "How did you know I was going to caution you about that?"

Hadrian chuckled. "I know you. That's how."

Tilda smiled. "I am glad you're involved in the investigation. I am eager to hear what you saw during the meeting. I know you shook someone's hand to learn that handshake." She looked over at him as they walked. "You *did* see something?"

He cast a glance toward her and nodded. "I only shook Phelps's hand because he demonstrated the handshake. It was a quick vision. I only saw Phelps take money from a purse and place it into a metal box. I also felt that Phelps was anxious. I can tell you the box he deposited the money into was not the same as the box at the society meeting. That one was made of wood, and the lid was carved with a cock and a snake."

"That is an excellent observation," Tilda said. "Do you think Phelps was putting some of the society's money into his own personal box?"

"I can't say, but it wasn't the same box I saw at the meeting, so I have questions."

"As do I." Tilda was once again very grateful for his strange ability.

They'd arrived at Gresham Street. "This way," Hadrian said, guiding her to the right.

There was a pair of rather fierce-looking men up ahead on the pavement. Tilda slipped her arm through Hadrian's.

He looked over at her and put his hand over her arm with a faint smile and the barest nod. "The coach is just there." He gestured across the street with his head.

The traffic was light at this hour, and Hadrian guided her across the street. They arrived at the coach as Leach jumped down to greet them.

The coachman grinned broadly at Tilda. "Good evening, Miss Wren. Always a pleasure to see you."

"And you, Leach," Tilda replied with a smile. "Particularly this evening, as I was not looking forward to taking the omnibus."

"Glad I can be of service." Leach moved to open the door of the coach.

Tilda climbed inside and immediately felt a sense of comfort. She'd spent more time in this coach than any other in her life. Her family had never owned a vehicle.

Hesitating the barest moment, she took the forward-facing seat and left plenty of room for Hadrian to sit beside her. They didn't always share the same seat, and she couldn't help thinking of the one time they had when it had resulted in a kiss.

Best not to think of that now. Or ever, really.

Hadrian sat beside her, and she had to admit it was nice to have his warmth nearby. The night was cool.

"What does your grandmother think of you residing with Inspector Maxwell?" Hadrian asked.

"She doesn't know yet. We only came up with the plan today." Tilda exhaled. "She won't like it, but the presence of a married chaperone will make her feel better." She slid a glance at him. "I sense you don't care for the arrangement either."

"Not particularly, but the chaperone is good. And I will be there much of the time."

"Your presence is somehow beneficial to my reputation?" Tilda laughed. "The situation would not be improved if you were in Maxwell's place." Her gaze met his, and for the barest moment, she felt a flash of heat. More alarming, she had the sense he felt it too. She quickly looked away.

"I only meant that we already spend a great deal of time together and with good, practical reason," Hadrian clarified.

Tilda could not argue with that, and yet she began to wonder if they, in fact, spent *too* much time together. Preferring not to think about that, she turned her thoughts to the investigation. "When we visit the boarding house tomorrow, we should try to see Eaton's room."

"So I can touch some things in the hope I'll see one of his memories?" Hadrian asked.

"If you are amenable."

"Of course," he said without hesitation. "I inserted myself into this investigation so I could do exactly that."

"Must I remind you that you provide value beyond your visions?" Tilda had assured him of this before. "Indeed, your investigative skills have grown immensely. You were most helpful this evening. It's too bad you're an earl. We might have formed a true professional partnership."

Hadrian angled himself toward her, his features faintly lined with consternation. "We can't because I'm an earl?"

Tilda lifted a shoulder. "I wouldn't think so. You've loftier responsibilities, and you certainly don't need the income."

"I can think of little more important than what you do, Tilda," he said softly. "You help people, and you are keeping London safer."

His words were earnest, and she felt them most keenly. "Thank you. And you are a part of what I do."

"I consider it an honor to be aligned with you." Their eyes met, and the connection between them seemed to strengthen. "Professionally, I mean."

Yes, professionally. And as friends.

Nothing more.

CHAPTER 5

*T*he following morning, Hadrian arrived at Tilda's just as the sun was rising over London. He wasn't surprised when Vaughn answered the door. The butler was incredibly dedicated, and he would not allow Tilda to leave without being present in the entrance hall.

They exchanged brief pleasantries as Hadrian picked up Tilda's somewhat small valise. "Is this everything?" he asked.

"I am playing the role of a working-class wife in the City," Tilda said wryly. "That is all I will need."

Vaughn held the door as Tilda preceded Hadrian from the house. She wore one of her older gowns, and Hadrian realized he'd become used to her newer wardrobe that was far more fashionable. He also realized it didn't really matter what she wore because she was lovely at all times.

"You are not only playing a working-class wife, however," Hadrian noted as they walked toward the coach. "When we visit the boarding house, you said you would go as an investigator."

"That is true. I did bring one of my newer costumes for just such occasions."

Leach was waiting for them at the coach and took the bag

from Hadrian whilst Tilda climbed inside. "Shall I carry this with me on the box?" the coachman asked.

"We can put it in here," Tilda said.

Hadrian sat down beside her and grasped the valise. "Thank you, Leach." He placed the bag on the opposite seat.

Leach closed the door, and they were shortly on their way.

Hadrian pivoted slightly toward her. "We were discussing your disguise. What about your hair when you transform from Mrs. Harwood to Miss Wren? I can simply remove my hairpieces before we call on the boarding house."

"Since the darker color is powdered onto my hair, I shall need to hide it under my hat as much as possible." Tilda had brought a hat with a brim for this purpose. It was out of fashion and would likely clash with her more current gown, but the discrepancy could not be helped. "It would be better if I had a wig, but I did not wish to incur the expense."

"Mrs. Longbotham might have lent you one," Hadrian suggested.

Tilda blew out a breath. "I should have thought of that, although I'm not sure when I would have had time to fetch it. The hat will have to do. We'll need to change our appearance at the house in White Alley, then steal from the back into that small corridor to Coleman Street as we did last night."

"That was the plan I also devised," Hadrian said, settling back against the squab.

"There isn't any other way. We'll simply need to be careful." Tilda stifled a yawn.

"Is this early for you?" Hadrian asked.

"Yes." She gave him a sheepish look. "I confess, it's rather difficult to rise before the sun this time of year."

"I agree. I generally only wake at this hour if I'm taking an early morning ride," he said. "But this is even early for that. Do you ride at all?"

Tilda shook her head. "I have not had occasion to."

"Would you like to?" he asked. "I could teach you."

"No, thank you," she replied firmly.

"I'm surprised you aren't interested." And perhaps a trifle disappointed. He would have enjoyed teaching her to ride. "You're so curious about everything. But not about riding horses?"

"No, I don't have any curiosity about that. I don't see a need for it. If I did, I would learn."

"I suppose that makes sense. You are efficient in all things." He smiled at her.

She lifted a shoulder. "I try to be."

"How did your grandmother take the news that you would be staying in the City?"

"As I expected, she was not enthusiastic. However, she was pleased there will be a chaperone." Tilda met Hadrian's gaze. "She was also happy to hear that you are now involved in the investigation."

"Was she?" Hadrian asked.

"She likes you very much," Tilda said. "And she knows that you and I have been in dangerous situations together before—not that this case is dangerous. Still, it makes her feel better knowing you're there."

Hadrian couldn't help feeling flattered. He liked her grandmother too. "She didn't think Inspector Maxwell would keep you safe?"

Tilda narrowed her eyes slightly. "I can keep *myself* safe. I think it's more that she knows you, whereas she is not acquainted with Maxwell."

"I've asked Leach to drop us off in a different location today," Hadrian said. "I thought it would be better if we didn't arrive in the same place we left from last night."

"That makes sense," Tilda said with a nod.

"He's taking us to Fore Street," Hadrian said. "Do you plan to return to your grandmother's house at all, or will you remain in the City for the duration of the investigation?"

"I will stay in the City. The investigation is supposed to take no more than a fortnight, and I do hope it may be less than that, as I've other investigative inquiries I must attend to."

A short time later, they arrived at the intersection of Basinghall and Fore Streets. Leach opened the door for them.

"Let me carry your bag," Hadrian said as he plucked up her valise. "It's what brothers do." He flashed her a smile before turning his attention to Leach. "Pick me up down at Moorgate later this afternoon."

The coachman inclined his head, then climbed back into his seat.

Hadrian and Tilda started walking toward Coleman Street. Despite the early hour, people were moving about. They came abreast of an alley that cut down to London Wall, and Tilda paused.

She touched his arm. "There's a police constable in front of that house."

"I see them," Hadrian said. "Shall we walk by? It will not take us out of our way."

"Let's. I can't imagine it's anything to do with our investigation, but I'm curious, which will be of no surprise to you."

Hadrian chuckled. "Absolutely not. I would wonder what was amiss if you did not want to walk that way."

As they neared the house, a woman came out the front door. She passed the constable on her way to the pavement.

"That's Mrs. Burley," Tilda whispered. "I met her at the meeting last night."

"You mentioned her," Hadrian said. "She was the one who talked a great deal."

Mrs. Burley's gaze fell on Tilda and Hadrian, and she made her way toward them. She appeared to be in her early forties with blonde hair pinned atop her head and a turned-up nose that gave her a rather inquisitive look. "Good morning, Mrs. Harwood." Her gaze flicked over Hadrian.

"This is my brother, Nigel Beck," Tilda said. "Nigel, this is Mrs. Burley. We met at the society meeting last night. Well, outside the meeting, since we are not permitted inside. Perhaps you met Mr. Burley?"

"I did not," Hadrian said. "I'm sure I will next week. Pleased to meet you, Mrs. Burley." He tried not to sound too much like a peer from the West End.

"You won't believe what's happened!" Mrs. Burley's brown eyes were bright with excitement. She glanced back at the house and lowered her voice. "Mr. Phelps has been murdered."

Hadrian swept his gaze toward Tilda at the same moment she looked at him. She appeared just as shocked as he was by this development. Was she also thinking the same thing? Namely, why were people always murdered during their investigations?

Mrs. Burley clucked her tongue. "The society will be thrown into turmoil."

"How awful," Tilda said. "About Mr. Phelps. I'm sure the society will survive."

"I hope so." Mrs. Burley pursed her lips. "There have been rumors of disagreements between Phelps, Nevill, and Furnier, and I saw Phelps and Nevill argue last week after the meeting."

"Indeed?" Tilda rounded her eyes in mock surprise. "I didn't hear anything about that last night."

Mrs. Burley gave her head a shake. "Oh no, we wouldn't speak of that there, not in front of Gladys Furnier."

"What were you doing in the house?" Hadrian asked, taking the question right out of Tilda's mouth, which was fine by her.

"His cleaning woman—Mrs. Rudge—comes twice a week and found him this morning. She came right over to tell me. I live across the street." She gestured to the small, narrow terrace opposite Phelps's house. "She didn't know what else to do."

Tilda's brow creased, and Hadrian imagined she was trying to determine a way to ask why the woman would go to her. Hadrian certainly wanted to ask that.

"You know her well then?" Tilda asked.

"I know everyone on the street, even those who don't live here," Mrs. Burley replied. "I do aim to be helpful. I went and found a constable, who sent for the inspector at the station in Old Jewry."

"There's an inspector?" Tilda asked.

Mrs. Burley nodded. "He's interviewing one of the neighbors. I was in the house consoling poor Mrs. Rudge and confirming that the dead body was indeed Mr. Phelps." She shuddered, but Hadrian had the sense it was for show and not a genuine reaction. "It was quite horrible. His head was bashed in. There was blood and other...matter. Utterly gruesome."

"Do you know when he was killed?" Tilda asked. "It's so shocking that we just saw him last evening."

"Sometime overnight." Mrs. Burley edged closer to them and slid a hooded glance toward Phelps's house. "He walked home last night with Nevill. They do that fairly often."

"Nevill may have been the last one to see him alive then," Hadrian said.

Mrs. Burley nodded. "He left just before eleven, but who knows if Phelps was alive then or not?" She arched her brows and widened her eyes briefly.

Hadrian could see that Mrs. Burley was well-versed on what happened along this street. He wondered what her neighbors thought of her.

Tilda gasped softly, but Hadrian believed she was playing a role. She was quite good at that when they were making inquiries. "Do you think Nevill had a reason to kill Phelps? You said they—and Furnier—were rumored to have had a disagreement."

"There's that business with Mr. Cardy dying and his widow trying to collect his death benefit, though it's only been six months since he joined." Mrs. Burley waved her hand. "I told you all that last night, didn't I?"

"Do you think the administrators argued about what happened with Cardy being admitted against the society's policy?" Tilda asked.

"I don't know for sure, but that's my guess. I had the impression from Mrs. Furnier that her husband was quite angry when he learned that Cardy had been ill."

"Wouldn't everyone have noticed his illness?" Hadrian asked.

"Mr. Cardy didn't attend meetings." Mrs. Burley cocked her head. "In fact, I'm not sure how his weekly dues were collected."

"It's my understanding that a member can send their dues with someone else," Hadrian said, citing what he'd learned last night. "Perhaps someone was doing that for Mr. Cardy."

"That makes sense," Mrs. Burley said. "I wonder who…" she added in a murmur, and Hadrian surmised that she wanted to gather this information. It seemed as though they'd met someone whose curiosity would rival Tilda's. Though their curiosity did not appear to be borne of the same purpose. Tilda liked to learn things and uncover the truth. Perhaps Mrs. Burley enjoyed collecting information and details that would make her feel important.

Mrs. Burley sniffed. "I must be on my way. I need to inform the other neighbors what's happened. They'll want to hear of this tragedy." She frowned sadly.

"How lucky they are to have you to inform them," Tilda said, with a gentle smile and just the barest hint of sarcasm, which Hadrian caught.

"Indeed." Mrs. Burley nodded sagely, appearing oblivious to the irony. She walked across the street and went to the house next to hers, where she knocked on the door.

Tilda blinked as she watched Mrs. Burley. "She was serious about telling everyone."

"I didn't doubt it," Hadrian said.

Pivoting toward Phelps's house, Tilda's brow creased.

Hadrian narrowed his gaze at her. "I recognize that pensive expression. You're trying to think of a way we can gain access to Mr. Phelps's house."

"Of course." She glanced at him. "Don't you want to view the scene of the murder?" She didn't wait for him to answer, because the answer was yes, and she likely knew that. "I can't think of a reason that an employee at a gentlemen's club and a matchbook maker would need to stick their noses in this situation." She pouted faintly. "Unfortunately."

"Perhaps we could be helpful to the police," Hadrian suggested. "We did see Phelps last night. Furthermore, don't the police know Maxwell has infiltrated the society?"

Tilda's eyes lit. "That's true. We should definitely speak with them."

They walked up to Phelps's house, and the constable at the door turned to greet them. His expression was wary but curious.

"Move along now. There's nothing to see here," the constable said.

"We heard Mr. Phelps has been murdered," Tilda said. "We are working with Inspector Maxwell on the investigation into the Coleman Street Ward Amicable Society. Perhaps you're familiar with that?"

The constable nodded. "A little. I know we're supposed to act as though we don't know him if we encounter him in the ward."

"We were at the society meeting with him last night," Tilda explained. "We saw Phelps. Might we go inside? We'd like to see if there's anything pertinent to our investigation. Inspector Maxwell would appreciate that."

"I don't see why not," the constable said. "There's another constable inside speaking with the housekeeper. Tell him who you are but be quick about your business."

Tilda smiled at him. "Thank you. We will."

The constable opened the door to let them inside. Tilda

preceded Hadrian into the entrance hall. To the right was a parlor, and right away, Hadrian saw Phelps. He lay face-down on the floor, his head turned toward the hearth and split open. The wood floor beneath him was stained dark brown-red.

Hadrian escorted Tilda into the parlor. To the left, a doorway opened into a dining room. Another constable sat at the table, his back to them, with a woman who blew her nose into a handkerchief.

"Phelps is wearing the same clothing as last night," Tilda noted softly, her gaze darting toward the dining room, as if she were trying not to draw the constable's attention. "That would seem to indicate he was killed before he retired for the evening. His body does appear as though he's been dead several hours."

"How can you tell?" Hadrian asked as they moved closer to Phelps.

"He looks very stiff," Tilda whispered. "Rigor mortis has set in." She bent to look more closely at his head. "I wonder if they've found the murder weapon."

Hadrian glanced about. "I don't see anything that looks like the weapon—no blunt objects covered in blood. Perhaps the police moved it."

"Or the killer may have taken it." Tilda met his gaze. "Should you touch something? The question is what." Her brow creased. "I don't want to provoke several visions when they are so very taxing for you."

There was no use in trying to touch Phelps, for Hadrian almost never saw the memories of the dead. Instead, he would hope to see the memory of the murderer, if he could. He'd done that on several occasions, though he often didn't realize that was whose memory he was seeing until later. It was one clue amongst many that he and Tilda collected to solve the crime.

Hadrian surveyed the room. "There's a desk in the corner. Shall I touch that?"

"Why not? Perhaps you'll find something to do with the society."

As Hadrian moved toward the desk, he transferred the valise to his left hand. The constable came from the dining room and asked Tilda what she was doing. Hadrian took advantage of her explanation to press his bare right palm against the desk.

The parlor fell away, and he saw Phelps. His expression was deeply furrowed with concern or perhaps irritation. Whoever's memory Hadrian was seeing was agitated in this moment. The man—not Phelps—reached for an open diary atop the desk. Focusing on the writing in the diary, Hadrian saw names and payments. The man's flesh was pale, his fingers thick. The sleeve of his coat was the color of claret. Hadrian had seen that color just last night.

"Hadrian." Tilda's voice broke into his vision.

He blinked, which ended what he was seeing. A dull ache spread through his temples.

She touched his sleeve. "We have to go."

Hadrian noticed the constable was still in the parlor and was frowning at them. "I take it he doesn't think we should be here, despite our involvement in the fraud investigation?" he whispered.

"Apparently not. He said Inspector *Chisholm* wouldn't care for our presence."

Tilda had stressed the inspector's name to convey something, but Hadrian would have realized it without the clue: they'd met Chisholm during the first case he'd worked on with Tilda. Chisholm had become involved when the man who'd attacked Hadrian had been found murdered in the City. Inspector Chisholm had likely acted improperly, ensuring another man was initially arrested for the murder. However, Chisholm hadn't been prosecuted, nor had he even lost his position with the police, apparently.

"Let us depart," Hadrian said, thinking it was best if they

didn't encounter Chisholm like this and perceiving Tilda felt the same.

"Quickly." Tilda was already moving toward the entrance hall.

However, it was too late, as Chisholm was just closing the front door. His small, dark eyes rounded before narrowing slightly as he regarded Tilda and Hadrian.

"Lord Ravenhurst, isn't it?" Chisholm asked, his square jaw clenching the barest amount. He was tall but did not reach Hadrian's height.

"Yes, though I am in disguise under the name Nigel Beck as a new member of the Coleman Street Ward Amicable Society. This is my 'sister,' Mrs. Harwood."

Chisholm scrutinized Tilda. "I thought she might be the female private investigator you were with at Fitch's inquest, but she's not blonde."

"I am her," Tilda said tersely. "I'm also in disguise and working with Inspector Maxwell on the fraud investigation of the Amicable Society. Ravenhurst is not my sibling."

"I see. Well, you shouldn't be here." He glowered at them.

"We were looking for clues that may relate to our investigation," Tilda said. "Maxwell would have done so if he were with us."

Chisholm peered past them toward the parlor. "And why isn't he?"

"We were just returning to the ward this morning when we happened by," Tilda replied. "Maxwell is at our house in White Alley, preparing to go to his fake job with other members of the society."

"That's right." Chisholm gave them a condescending nod. "I would tell Maxwell the same I'll tell you—if we find anything pertinent to your investigation, we'll let you know."

Hadrian cast Tilda a sideways glance and could tell she was gritting her teeth as she forced a smile. "Thank you, Inspector. Did you find a murder weapon?"

"I think it's best if that information remains with the police for now," Chisholm replied with an irritating smile of his own. "If I have time, I'll seek Maxwell out. Or he can come to me at the police station. If he can take time away from his *fake job*."

"I'll tell him that," Tilda said icily. She started toward the door, and Hadrian hastened to open it for her.

They walked past the constable outside and made their way toward the London Wall.

Hadrian glanced back at Phelps's house. "What a patronizing clod. He clearly remembered us and, given his demeanor, I wonder if he knows I asked the superintendent about his behavior during that investigation. I still believe he was behind the dodgy evidence that saw John Prince wrongly arrested."

"I agree, but we didn't have proof. I'm just glad Prince went free." She looked over at Hadrian. "I didn't realize you'd spoken to the superintendent."

"I wrote a letter," Hadrian said. "I indicated my strong recommendation that Chisholm ought to be investigated, though I don't know if he was."

"Regardless, he's still an inspector," Tilda said with disdain. "And we must work with him."

"Should we tell Maxwell about our past interaction with Chisholm?" Hadrian thought they should. He worried about whether they could trust the man.

Tilda nodded. "I think we must, particularly since it seems he may be disinclined to share information with us. I hope he will not allow his opinion of us to affect his communication with Maxwell. That would be most unprofessional."

They turned from London Wall to Coleman Street. "What did you see when you touched the desk?" Tilda asked.

Hadrian detailed the vision. "You saw who was wearing a claret-colored coat last night?"

Her gaze met his briefly. "Mr. Nevill. You think it was his

memory? Because you wouldn't have seen Phelps's since he is dead."

"Correct. I do believe it was Nevill's." Hadrian thought through his vision once more. "I didn't see anyone else, though I suppose there could have been another person—or people— present."

Tilda glanced at him as they turned down Coleman Street. "I wonder why Nevill was upset."

Hadrian often gleaned a sense of what the memory-holder was feeling, but it wasn't always clear. In this case, he had at least an inkling. "I think it may have been an argument, particularly with Phelps's expression."

"I would very much like to question Nevill about what happened last night after the meeting," Tilda said. "But we are not assigned to solve Phelps's murder."

"Has that ever deterred us?" Hadrian asked wryly.

Tilda smiled, then shook her head. "Why is it our investigations always somehow lead to murder?"

They turned into White Alley. "I was wondering the same thing, and I've no answer." Hadrian looked over at her, and her eyes shone with anticipation.

"It's fortunate we've a knack for solving such crimes."

CHAPTER 6

*T*ilda and Hadrian arrived at Number Five White Alley just as Maxwell was preparing to leave. He set his hat on his head as they entered. Tilda was anxious to tell him about Phelps's murder. She was also sorry he would have to rush off.

"I was beginning to wonder if something had happened," Maxwell said.

"In fact, something has." Tilda glanced toward Hadrian as he set her valise down near the stairs. "Lord Ravenhurst's coachman dropped us in Fore Street, and as we walked past Second Postern, we noticed a constable. We decided to walk that way instead."

Maxwell's gaze turned wary. "Why was there a constable?"

"He was at Mr. Phelps's house," Tilda replied. "Phelps was murdered sometime in the night."

Eyes rounding, Maxwell sucked in a breath. "What were you able to discover?"

Tilda shared the information they'd learned from Mrs. Burley and detailed their encounter with the constable.

"He allowed you to go inside the house?" Maxwell sounded quite surprised.

"He did." Tilda then revealed what they'd seen, though she did not tell him about Hadrian's vision, of course.

Maxwell frowned. "Wasn't there an inspector present?"

Tilda exchanged a look with Hadrian. "There was, in fact. We encountered Inspector Chisholm as we were leaving. How well do you know him?"

"Well enough, though we haven't ever worked directly together," Maxwell replied.

"We crossed paths with him during an investigation somewhat recently." Tilda tried to think of how to gently say that Chisholm was likely corrupt. "An innocent man was arrested for murder, and we believe Inspector Chisholm was bribed to ensure that happened—in order to protect the real killer."

Maxwell's brows shot up. "You have evidence of this?"

Tilda shook her head. "We'd hoped there would be an investigation, but it seems there wasn't."

"I wrote a letter to the superintendent," Hadrian said. "The murderer had bribed other officers within the Met, and we know he bribed someone with the City Police. Unfortunately, we could not discover whom before he died."

"Then how can you be sure Chisholm is corrupt?" Maxwell did not appear convinced.

"We just are," Hadrian said firmly.

Tilda knew Hadrian was certain, but then he, unlike her, sometimes allowed his emotions to influence his conclusions. "We don't have proof, but he has earned our suspicion. He did not seem very pleased to see us today. He did not like that the constable had let us enter Phelps's house, and he would not share any information with us, even when I said it would be for your benefit. He said he would find you or you could call on him at the station."

"Whilst it's frustrating that he wouldn't just give you the information so you could share it with me, I do understand his hesitance." Maxwell rubbed his hand over his mouth and chin, then shook his head. "I can't believe Phelps was murdered. How I wish I didn't have to go to this mundane job at the mercantile house."

"It's not as if we're assigned to investigate the murder," Tilda said with a sympathetic smile. "We aren't even investigators right now—at least not publicly." Though she was going to become one when they visited the boarding house later.

Maxwell blew out a breath. "No, we're not." Tilda sensed his frustration, and she shared it.

"What do you think will happen with the Amicable Society?" Hadrian asked. "Phelps was the leader."

"I suppose we'll have to wait and find out," Maxwell said. "I wonder if Chisholm has any idea who the killer might be."

Tilda had been thinking of that. "It seems to me that the person with the obvious motive would be Mrs. Cardy, the wife of the member who died."

Maxwell glanced behind him toward the back of the house. "Mrs. Cardy's cousin is downstairs."

Tilda's thoughts were so preoccupied that she'd forgotten Mrs. Kilgore would be there.

"We should tell her about the murder," Maxwell said, his lips pressing together grimly.

"Can you spare the time?" Tilda asked. "If not, I can tell her."

"I will be a few minutes late to the mercantile house. I should like to tell Mrs. Kilgore about Phelps's death."

They hastened to the stairs leading down to the kitchen.

Mrs. Kilgore was at the worktable chopping potatoes. She was in her middle thirties with pale blonde hair and rosy cheeks, heated perhaps from the hearth. Thick blonde brows crested her round brown eyes. She paused in her work.

Inspector Maxwell moved toward the table. "Mrs. Kilgore, allow me to introduce Miss Wren and Lord Ravenhurst." Maxwell gestured toward Tilda and Hadrian. "Otherwise known as Mrs. Harwood and Mr. Beck."

"I'm pleased to meet you." Mrs. Kilgore set the knife down.

"Thank you for being here," Tilda said. "I appreciate you taking on the role of chaperone."

"I'm always eager to help the police."

Maxwell glanced at Tilda. "Miss Wren has news to share." His tone was slightly ominous.

Tilda didn't smile, but she did maintain a pleasant expression. "On our way here this morning, Lord Ravenhurst and I walked by the house of the leader of the Amicable Society—Mr. Phelps. He was murdered last night."

Mrs. Kilgore blinked rapidly. "What happened?"

"We don't know yet." Tilda didn't see the need to detail what they *did* know.

"Well, I'm sorry to hear he's dead," Mrs. Kilgore said. "I have my reservations about the society and what they did to my cousin's family—taking their money and then not paying Gil's benefit—but I wouldn't wish ill of the man."

Maxwell nodded at her. "Inspector Chisholm is assigned to the murder investigation. I expect he will speak with your cousin today."

Mrs. Kilgore's lips pursed in a stubborn expression. "Hester won't have anything to say. She didn't even know Mr. Phelps. She only dealt with the man who recruited her husband."

"Timothy Eaton," Maxwell said.

"Aye." Mrs. Kilgore picked up the knife, her lip curling with disdain. "Terrible that he took their money, knowing her husband was poorly and likely wouldn't live long enough to receive his death benefit. She has five children and must now support them on her wages as a seamstress. I hope they don't think she killed him. How on earth would she find the time?"

"Chisholm will discover the truth," Maxwell said. "I'll speak with him later, before I return for dinner. Now, I need to be on my way." He inclined his head at Tilda before dashing off.

Mrs. Kilgore looked toward Tilda. "I left you the larger bedchamber."

"You didn't have to. Thank you." Tilda smiled at the woman. "After we settle in for a bit, Lord Ravenhurst and I will be going on a few errands. We will be changing our appearances, so don't be alarmed when we look different."

"Is this to do with the investigation?" Mrs. Kilgore asked.

"Yes." Tilda didn't want to explain, since they were inquiring after Timothy Eaton, and the man had a connection to Mrs. Kilgore's family—an unpleasant one.

Mrs. Kilgore looked at Hadrian hesitantly. "Will you be here much, my lord?"

"During the day, mostly," he replied with a charming smile.

"Will you be taking dinner here?" Mrs. Kilgore asked with a touch of uneasiness. Tilda thought she must be nervous, perhaps because Hadrian was an earl.

"Not generally, no. I will be sure to let you know when I plan to be here for dinner." He spoke with a warm kindness that seemed to put Mrs. Kilgore at ease. "I would hate to cause you any trouble by showing up unplanned."

Mrs. Kilgore's apprehension seemed to return as lines gathered between her brows. "Are you sure you want to do that, my lord? I'm not used to cooking for one such as yourself."

"I am delighted to partake of whatever you make, Mrs. Kilgore. I am sure it will be delicious." And he gave her another smile that bordered on dazzling. "In fact, perhaps you'd like to prepare tea before we depart on our errands."

Tilda wondered if Hadrian smiled like that when he was out in Society. She imagined him when he'd been looking for a wife a few years ago, attending balls and soirées, outfitted in his pristine evening wear. She'd seen him that way once—the night he'd escorted her to Northumberland House. However, that was not the Hadrian she knew.

"You are too kind, my lord," Mrs. Kilgore said. "I will make the tea straightaway. I did stock the pantry with some items when I arrived."

"We'll leave you to it," Tilda said. She turned and left the kitchen, leading Hadrian upstairs.

On the ground floor, they made their way to the stairs that would take them to the first floor.

"I assumed there was tea and perhaps I should not have." Hadrian picked up Tilda's valise before climbing the stairs with her. "I was trying to put her at ease. It didn't occur to me that there may not be supplies."

"It's all right. Though, I am glad Mrs. Kilgore brought tea, for I did not." Yesterday, Tilda had purchased the bare minimum of food supplies at the grocer.

When they reached the first floor, Tilda took the valise from Hadrian.

"I suppose I'll go up and investigate the garret," he said.

"And remove your hair pieces," Tilda said. "Do you have glue to reattach the side whiskers?"

"I do not. I shall have to remain myself until I return to Mayfair." He frowned. "I should have thought to bring that and a change of clothing, since we'd planned to call at the boarding house as investigators."

"I should have prepared you," Tilda said. "You can fetch the necessary implements and clothing this evening when you return home."

"Indeed, I shall." He pivoted. "I'll see you downstairs for tea in a bit?"

"Yes." Tilda recalled that the larger bedchamber faced the street. The bed was dressed, which was not how it had appeared yesterday. Tilda had been busy with other chores and hadn't seen to it. Mrs. Kilgore must have done.

There was a small dresser, which Tilda used for her belongings. She set her hairbrush and other personal items on top.

Moving to the window, she pushed the thin curtain aside and

looked down at the narrow alley. She'd seen worse places in London, but this was a far cry from Marylebone and her grandmother's house, let alone the terrace she'd shared with her parents on Charlotte Street.

Tilda turned away and began to change her clothing. Her mind pivoted to the coming interview with the boarding house owner. She was eager to become her true self once more—Matilda Wren, private investigator—even if her hair wasn't the right color.

A short while later, Tilda and Hadrian took tea in the small dining room. There was only a crude table with four chairs and a wobbly sideboard table, plus the hearth. Two windows, which Tilda cleaned yesterday, provided meager light. They were on either side of the hearth and hung with faded blue curtains that barely covered the length of each window.

Mrs. Kilgore served the tea, along with a few biscuits she'd brought with her that morning. "I'll make a fresh batch this afternoon," she said, again appearing a bit nervous.

"Don't go to too much trouble," Tilda said. "We didn't employ you to be a housekeeper or a cook."

"Well, neither were you employed to do those things," Mrs. Kilgore said. "I'm happy to contribute as I can. You are busy investigating." She eyed Tilda with something akin to admiration. "It's remarkable to see a woman investigator. I confess I was surprised when I heard the police had hired you. Inspector Maxwell was adamant he needed someone to pretend to be his wife and that she must possess investigative skills."

"I'm thrilled he asked me," Tilda said. "And I appreciate your presence, which facilitates this ruse. Thank you, Mrs. Kilgore."

"It's my privilege to help as I may. I'll be in the kitchen if you need me." Mrs. Kilgore turned and departed.

"It's remarkable," Hadrian said before sipping his tea. There wasn't any sugar or milk.

Tilda couldn't tell what he thought of the beverage. She

considered asking him to bring sugar and milk tomorrow. He probably wouldn't mind, but he wasn't even supposed to be here. And now she was looking to him for help—and not just with the investigation.

"I suppose it is," Tilda murmured in reply to his comment. "I'm glad to participate in the investigation, and it's my intent to obtain helpful information today. I'm anxious to be on our way, though I suppose it's a trifle early yet."

Hadrian chuckled. "I'm not surprised by your enthusiasm—and I share it. We'll go as soon as we finish our tea."

They departed via the back of the house. Tilda wore her out-of-fashion bonnet, and Hadrian had pulled his hat low on his head to hopefully mask his hair. The lack of side whiskers could not be helped.

They emerged onto Coleman Street and quickly crossed it before heading toward Gresham Street. Hadrian glanced over at Tilda, his expression uncertain.

"Is there something you want to say?" she asked.

"Do you think Mrs. Kilgore would be affronted if I brought tea for the household tomorrow?"

"I don't think so. In fact, I considered asking if you might want to bring sugar and milk. Our supplies are a bit meager." Tilda grimaced faintly. "I imagine for you, they're appalling."

"There's not that great a distance between you and me," Hadrian said. "You noticed the lack of milk and sugar. And do we not drink similar tea?"

"I don't know." Tilda assumed he drank something more expensive. "I would think you drink a special blend. We buy ours already made."

"We do, in fact." He looked a bit sheepish.

Tilda smiled. "The Ravenhurst blend?"

"It's not called that. You had it at my mother's."

"That was delicious." She'd taken tea at his mother's house when the dowager countess had hired her to investigate a medium with whom she'd wanted to consult. That had been Tilda's most recent case, and—like this one—it had become a murder investigation.

"I have always enjoyed tea at your grandmother's house," Hadrian said earnestly.

"I've never had occasion to think otherwise." Tilda sensed a slight awkwardness to this conversation, and she did not want there to be. The truth was that their social and economic positions were different. "I hope you will bring whatever tea you like tomorrow. It will be a welcome addition to our pretend household. Indeed, it's most thoughtful of you to contribute."

They fell silent a moment, until they turned onto Gresham Street toward Ironmonger Lane.

Tilda sent him a sideways glance. "I've been thinking about the vision you saw this morning. I think it's likely that Phelps and Nevill were having an argument of some kind, particularly given the rumor Mrs. Burley shared about them and Furnier disagreeing over something. I should like to know what they quarreled about. Alas, we will only hear Nevill's perspective now that Phelps is dead."

"I'm curious how the three men came together to form the society," Hadrian said. "They seem to possess rather different temperaments, at least in the case of Furnier. My impression is that he's far more rigid than the other two. I realize we've only just made their acquaintance."

"That was also my impression," Tilda replied. "I too would like to know how the society started."

They turned onto Ironmonger Lane, and Tilda gestured to the left. "There's the boarding house." She paused and looked at him. "I wonder if you should just be Hadrian Becket for this interview. Your title is often useful, but in this case, I worry it might be something that someone would want to share. We mustn't draw attention to ourselves."

"You make a good point." Hadrian smiled. "I've no problem being Mr. Becket."

Tilda nodded before going to the door and knocking upon the wood. There was no immediate answer, and they waited a few moments.

"Should we knock again?" Hadrian asked.

"Perhaps."

Hadrian lifted his hand to do so just as the door opened. A woman with blazing red curls topped with a white cap stood just over the threshold. She swept her blue gaze over them and narrowed her eyes.

"Good morning," Tilda said pleasantly. "We've come to speak with you about one of your prior tenants, Timothy Eaton."

"Who are you?" the woman asked, her red brows pitched together.

"I beg your pardon, I am Miss Wren, an investigator hired to find Mr. Eaton. This is Mr. Becket. Please forgive us, for we do not know your name."

"Mrs. Vickers. Come in." She opened the door wider for them to enter. "We can come into the parlor 'ere." She waved her hand as she led them to the room just off the small, dim entrance hall. The parlor was cozy, with mismatched furnishings and a single window that looked out onto the street. "Would you like to sit?"

"For a few minutes, thank you." Tilda perched on a worn settee covered in purple damask, and Hadrian sat down beside her.

Mrs. Vickers sat opposite them. "You're looking for Tim?"

Tilda nodded. "Do you know where we can find him?"

"I don't, and I'm worried about 'im." Mrs. Vickers frowned. "'E left so quickly."

"Did he?" Tilda asked. "When was that?"

"Over a week ago now. When I went to bed one night, 'e was 'ere, then 'e was gone in the morning. Didn't give me any notice, and that wasn't like 'im." Mrs. Vickers smiled faintly. "Tim was a good lodger. Always paid on time, except when 'e lost 'is job."

"When was that?" Tilda suspected she knew but wanted to hear what Mrs. Vickers would say.

"Last autumn. 'E worked for the Prudential Assurance Company, but they sacked 'im."

That was not what Tilda had expected. "I thought you were referring to his employment with the Coleman Street Ward Amicable Society. He worked for the Prudential Assurance Company before that?" At Mrs. Vickers's nod, Tilda asked if the woman knew why Eaton had been dismissed.

Mrs. Vickers shook her head. "'E didn't say, but I know 'e was unhappy about it. I was worried for 'im at first because 'e worked very 'ard, and I couldn't understand why the company would do that, but 'e quickly found work with the Amicable Society doing the same work—'e recruited members. 'E liked the society, said it was a good community and service they provide, though not for women." She sent Tilda a slightly disgruntled look.

Tilda responded with an understanding nod.

"Tim agreed with that sentiment," Mrs. Vickers added. "'E said more than once that 'e wished 'e could offer me membership."

"Did he recruit members on his own?" Hadrian asked. "Specifically, we'd like to know if anyone from the society approved the men he recruited."

Mrs. Vickers's brow puckered. "It was my impression 'e offered memberships when 'e called on people, but I don't really know." Her features smoothed, and she smiled. "I do know 'e was very good at it. Tim was right friendly, and 'e 'ad a bit of charm about 'im. Everyone liked 'im. I'm sure part of 'is success was due to 'is amiability and 'is ability to talk."

Tilda found it interesting that Eaton may have had the authority to extend offers of membership without input from the doctor, at least. But perhaps the problem was that he *hadn't* possessed the authority. "Do you know who hired Mr. Eaton for his position with the Amicable Society?"

"I don't, but Tim sometimes mentioned there was one person 'e didn't care for as much as the others."

"And who was that?" Tilda asked.

"I don't recall 'is name, but I think 'e was the man in charge of the money." Mrs. Vickers seemed to think a moment. "Farrier, perhaps?" She shrugged.

Tilda exchanged a look with Hadrian. Mrs. Vickers had to mean Furnier. Tilda had no trouble believing someone wouldn't care for him.

Hadrian moved his gaze to Mrs. Vickers. "Do you have any idea why Mr. Eaton left in a hurry?"

Mrs. Vickers shook her head.

"Do you know of any family or friends he may have gone to stay with?" Tilda hoped Mrs. Vickers could give them something that would help them find Eaton.

"Never mentioned any family," Mrs. Vickers replied. "I asked 'im once, and 'e said he didn't 'ave any. I don't know 'bout friends, but 'e spent a fair amount of time at the Wolf and Dove up on Gresham Street."

The pub would be a helpful avenue to investigate. "I don't suppose you'd allow us to look in Mr. Eaton's former bedchamber?" Tilda asked.

Mrs. Vickers gave them a brief, apologetic smile. "I have another lodger in there now."

"The person who hired us to find Mr. Eaton hasn't seen him in some time," Tilda said. "I wonder if you could describe what he looks like now? For instance, does he still have a mustache?" Tilda made that up to give the impression that they at least had some idea of his appearance—and it didn't matter that it wasn't true because Eaton could have shaved.

Mrs. Vickers surprised Tilda by blushing. "Tim's a handsome one. Bright blond curls and shining blue eyes. And a smile that turns 'eads. 'E still has the mustache, and I've never seen a finer one, truth be told. But it's the dimple in 'is chin that drew my eye. Not as tall as you, Mr. Becket, but not short."

Tilda looked over at Hadrian and gave him a subtle nod to convey she was finished with the interview. She rose. "Thank you for speaking with us, Mrs. Vickers. We appreciate your time."

Hadrian also stood as Mrs. Vickers jumped to her feet.

She escorted them to the entrance hall. "I do 'ope you find 'im. Why are you looking for 'im anyway?"

"We aren't able to say," Tilda replied with bland smile.

"In fact, it might be best if you didn't mention that we came here today asking after him." Hadrian gave Mrs. Vickers one of his thoroughly charming smiles. "Would that be all right?"

Mrs. Vickers blushed again. "Certainly, whatever you say."

"Thank you, Mrs. Vickers," Hadrian said warmly. "You've been most helpful."

As they started back toward Gresham Street, Tilda chuckled softly. "Were you trying to charm Mrs. Vickers into keeping our visit secret?"

Hadrian shrugged. "It seemed like a good idea."

"It was indeed. You quite dazzled her, I think. It seems she has a penchant for handsome men. She was clearly drawn in by Timothy Eaton."

"I'm glad you asked what he looks like. If I see him in a vision, I'll be better able to recognize him." Hadrian looked over at her as they walked. "We should visit that pub. To see if anyone there knows Eaton and might have an idea where he went."

"I was thinking the same thing," Tilda said. "I'd also like to visit the Prudential Assurance Company to find out why they sacked him." She frowned slightly. "Though I'm concerned about doing too much work as investigators. I don't want to expose our identities. Word could spread that someone is conducting an investigation."

"We could visit the Wolf and Dove in our disguises, and I

could pretend to be a friend of Eaton's who's just moved to the neighborhood." Hadrian frowned. "Except I don't have any glue to reapply my hair pieces."

"Perhaps if you keep your hat pulled down, it won't matter. It's not ideal, but at least your clothing is appropriate to your disguise." She glanced down at the newer garment she was wearing, a dark gray gown. "Unlike mine."

"I agree that it should be fine this once for the pub, especially at this hour of the day," Hadrian said. "I don't expect it will be busy. However, I don't think I should visit the Prudential Assurance Company without my full disguise."

"I agree. In fact, it's probably best if you and I don't go there at all." An idea struck her. "I know the perfect person we could ask to make an inquiry."

Hadrian's brows elevated briefly. "Who?"

"Ezra Clement." He was a journalist they'd run into several times during their last investigation. Ultimately, he and Tilda had ended up helping one another and agreeing to perhaps assist each other in the future, should it benefit them. "He might like a story about a corrupt society, if indeed it is corrupt."

Hadrian's brows pitched low over his eyes. "Clement would certainly like to write a story about a murder." He sounded perturbed.

"You don't like him," Tilda said.

"I didn't like that he was going to pester my mother."

They'd encountered Clement as he'd been about to call on Hadrian's mother to inquire about her connection to the society of mediums that Tilda and Hadrian were investigating.

"He was only trying to do his job," Tilda said. "But I agree that he was aggressive. However, I think we've come to an understanding about how we may aid one another, and this would be an excellent opportunity to test that."

"I suppose it could work," Hadrian allowed. "Before we do

anything, you should speak to Maxwell. He's been clear that this is *his* investigation."

"True. I suppose we should also speak with him before visiting the pub, but I don't want to wait. Let's return to White Alley and become Beck and Harwood once more."

"I much prefer us as Ravenhurst and Wren." Hadrian smirked. "Or Raven and Wren, since my colleagues generally call me Raven. I rather like the pair of birds solving crimes together."

Tilda blinked at him. "I didn't realize you had a whimsical nature."

"I don't usually. But I've changed a great deal since I hit my head on the pavement and acquired an inexplicable power to see things."

"*Blast*," Tilda said softly. "I should have asked you to touch something at the boarding house, since we weren't able to gain access to Eaton's room."

He smiled. "What makes you think I didn't? Alas, I didn't see anything."

"That is unfortunate. But thank you for trying."

"I'll try again at the pub," Hadrian said. "I'm keen to find Eaton. I do feel he'll be helpful."

"Particularly now that Phelps has been killed," Tilda pointed out.

"We aren't investigating his murder, however."

Tilda smiled. "As you pointed out earlier, when has that stopped us before?"

7

CHAPTER 7

*A*fter returning to White Alley so Tilda could change her clothing back to that of Mrs. Harwood, Tilda and Hadrian made their way to the Wolf and Dove public house on Gresham Street.

They passed St. Stephen's Church on Coleman Street. A gate stood partially open to the small graveyard. Hadrian admired the building. "Is it strange to think your ancestor designed that?" Hadrian referred to Tilda's many times great-grandfather, Christopher Wren, the famous architect.

"Not strange exactly. I do enjoy stepping into his buildings. He rebuilt all the churches that were destroyed by the fire. Is it odd that while I don't consider myself an overly religious person, I appreciate the architectural beauty of the structures?"

"Not at all," Hadrian replied. "One might say it's in your blood."

Tilda laughed softly. "I suppose that's true."

They continued toward Gresham Street. "I presume we'll be speaking with either the owner of the pub or an employee," Hadrian said. "Since I'm pretending to be Eaton's friend, shall I begin the conversation?"

"Yes. As we are in our disguises now, I should probably defer to my brother." Tilda rolled her eyes with a faint smirk.

Hadrian chuckled softly. "I know it bothers you not to take the lead. Have you struggled with that while working with Maxwell, since it's his investigation?"

"It's only been a day, so I can't say. I was rather disappointed to be left out of the Amicable Society meeting last night."

"I hope it was satisfying to be an investigator, at least for a short while, earlier today."

She nodded. "It was, thank you."

They turned onto Gresham Street, and Tilda pointed out that the pub was just ahead. "We ought to have a reason for asking questions about Eaton. Since he's moved out of the lodging house, you—as his friend—can simply be trying to find where he's gone."

"That seems reasonable." Hadrian opened the door to the pub for Tilda, and she preceded him inside.

"You must also do whatever you can to make your speech sound less cultured," Tilda advised.

Hadrian grimaced briefly. "I've been working at that. I've been trying to think of words I oughtn't say."

"Such as 'oughtn't'?" Tilda flashed a smile.

Hadrian swallowed a laugh.

The common room was spacious but not well lit. As it was early afternoon, there weren't many patrons. A man in his forties worked behind a bar in the back left corner. He was barrel-chested with dark hair that came to a widow's peak at the top of his forehead.

Hadrian escorted Tilda to the bar and inclined his head at the man. "Afternoon," he said genially. "I'm looking for a friend of mine, Timothy Eaton. He's moved out of his lodgings, and I don't know where he's gone."

"I know Eaton," the barman replied in a deep voice, then narrowed his eyes. "'Ow do you know 'im?"

"We met a couple months ago," Hadrian replied. "He convinced me to join the Coleman Street Ward Amicable Society. I wanted to thank him, as well as collect a wager. He bet me that I wouldn't actually do it." Hadrian glanced at Tilda to see her reaction to the lie he'd just concocted. Her gaze held a sheen of approval. "Did he try to recruit you too?" Hadrian asked the man.

The barman let out a short laugh. "My pub is just outside Coleman Street Ward, so Eaton doesn't solicit members for that friendly society 'ere. It was different when 'e worked for that assurance company. Eaton is one of the friendliest blokes I know. 'As a smile fer everyone. 'E'll talk yer ear off if you give 'im 'alf a chance."

"Have you seen him recently?" Hadrian asked.

The man braced his hands on the bar, his features pensive for a moment. "Not for a few days. Saturday, I think." He nodded as if he were agreeing with himself. "'E was in 'ere Saturday night."

Tilda and Hadrian exchanged a glance. That was fairly recently. Perhaps he was still in the area.

"That's good to hear," Hadrian said, trying to sound relieved. "Do you know where he's lodging now?"

The barman shook his head.

"Any idea when he might be in again?" Hadrian asked.

"'Ard to say." The man frowned. "Now that I think about it, it's strange 'e 'asn't been in since Saturday. 'E's usually in 'ere every couple days, sometimes every day."

"Is there anyone who spent time with him here and may know his whereabouts?" Hadrian glanced about, though there were only a handful of people present.

"There's a fellow from the assurance company. They meet 'ere most Saturday nights."

"Is that who he saw last Saturday?" Hadrian asked.

The barman's brow furrowed. "Come to think of it, no. It was another man, older."

"Did you know him?"

The man shook his head again. "Might 'ave had dark 'air. Can't recall." He narrowed his eyes at Hadrian. "Why are you asking all these questions 'bout Eaton and 'is friends? 'E must owe you a decent sum."

Hadrian shrugged. "Aside from the wager, I'm only concerned about him is all. His former landlady said he moved out in a hurry. If I can talk to one of his friends, mayhap I can find out where he is."

The barman nodded. "The man from the assurance company is called Rippon, I think. 'E wears glasses."

"That's helpful to know. Thank you," Hadrian said.

"Pardon me," Tilda said in a somewhat small voice that didn't sound at all like her. "Can you think of anything else about the man Mr. Eaton saw on Saturday? Do you recall where they sat?"

The man narrowed his eyes again, this time at Tilda.

"This is my sister," Hadrian hastened to say.

His features smooth, the barman nodded vaguely. "Eaton always sits in the same place—that table in the corner over by the window." The man pointed to the opposite corner of the common room before locking his gaze on Hadrian. "You drinking anything?"

"I'll have a pint," Hadrian replied with a faint smile. "Nothing for my sister." He put a coin on the bar—more than the pint would cost—as the man pulled a pint of ale.

Dark beer dribbled down the side of the glass as the man set it atop the bar. He plucked up the coin. "Eaton'll turn up, or mayhap 'e's moved on. Wouldn't be the first bloke who 'ad to strike a new path for 'imself."

Hadrian inclined his head in agreement as he picked up the ale. He turned from the bar, and Tilda accompanied him toward the center of the common room.

"I wasn't sure if we should go straight to Eaton's table," Hadrian said softly.

Tilda sent him a faint nod. "You have good instincts. We've

already drawn enough attention with our questioning. We'll still make our way in that direction. I know you want to touch the table."

"I do." Hadrian sipped the ale. It wasn't bad.

A pair of men came in and went toward the bar. Their arrival was just the distraction Hadrian and Tilda needed to investigate Eaton's table.

Tilda turned her head toward the bar. "He's busy now. Let's go."

They moved quickly to the corner with the table. "Shall we sit?" Hadrian asked.

"I think for a few minutes, yes." Tilda slid into a chair while Hadrian sat opposite her.

He set his ale on the table, then pressed his bare palms against the scarred wood. Dressed as Nigel Beck, he wasn't wearing gloves.

Immediately, he saw a series of images. But they weren't very clear—just flashes of faces and an overall sensation of conviviality.

Frustrated, Hadrian sought to focus on Eaton, in the hope he would see something related to the man. During their last investigation, Hadrian had met another gentleman who possessed the same ability to see others' memories. Captain Vale had been helpful in explaining how the gift—or affliction, depending on one's perspective—was passed within families and could affect people differently. It seemed everyone with the ability suffered headaches of varying degrees, and they may diminish over time. Others struggled a great deal with being overwhelmed by the power.

Hadrian didn't always have a vision when he touched something or someone, and there was no way to know if and when it would happen. He had absolutely no control over the ability. The visions could also be different for each person with the power. Hadrian did not ever hear anything, but some others did.

He'd begun to smell things from time to time, which wasn't universal.

Vale had also told Hadrian how he might begin to try to steer his visions. If Hadrian focused on someone, he may be able to see their memory—if it was possible. Hadrian did not see the memories of those closest to him, such as his mother, his valet, or Tilda.

Resisting the urge to close his eyes in order to focus on Eaton —because the visions always stopped when he closed his eyes— Hadrian tried to conjure what the man looked like based on Mrs. Vickers's description. He pressed his hands into the wood and repeated Eaton's name in his mind.

Eaton had sat here with the man from the assurance company. What was his name? Rippon.

Hadrian began to see a face. The man sat across the table from him. He had blond hair and a blond mustache and a rather deep cleft in his chin. He talked animatedly, and Hadrian wished he could hear what was being said. The man laughed. He seemed to match what Hadrian had learned about Eaton from Mrs. Vickers.

From past experience, Hadrian knew it was best if he could detect every possible detail about the vision. He looked at the man's hands—he was missing almost half of the little finger of his left hand. Hadrian was certain he was seeing Timothy Eaton. But whose memory was he seeing?

The vision faded, and Hadrian was once again in the pub on a Tuesday afternoon, sitting across from Tilda. She watched him anxiously.

"I think I just saw Eaton," he said, wincing faintly as pain shot through his temple. "He was sitting where you are."

"What made you think it was him?"

"Blond hair and mustache, cleft chin. And he seemed…cheerful, which is, I think, how Mrs. Vickers and the barman described him. He also has an abnormality that could verify his identity. He's missing nearly half the little finger on his left hand."

Her gaze shone with admiration. "Excellent detail."

"What I don't know is whose memory I was seeing. I wonder if it might have been Rippon, since we know he met Eaton here on Saturdays. Also, the image came when I thought of his name."

Tilda drew in a breath. "That is *fascinating*. Perhaps you're learning how to control what you see."

"It does seem so, as I was able to guide things just now. We'll see if that continues." Hadrian was not yet ready to declare his efforts a success. He took another sip of ale.

"I shall remain cautiously optimistic." Tilda smiled. "Did you glean anything else from what you saw?"

"No. It appeared to just be a conversation. Eaton spoke animatedly and appeared in high spirits. I would say whoever he was speaking to is a friend."

"This was a successful inquiry." Tilda glanced back toward the bar. "We have a name for someone to speak with at the assurance company—Rippon. I'd like to take an omnibus to Fleet Street to speak with Mr. Clement, but I should speak with Inspector Maxwell first to ensure he supports asking for Clement's assistance." She let out a soft exhale of disappointment.

"I'll escort you back to White Alley, then I should probably return home, since it will be time for me to go to work at the gentlemen's club." Hadrian scowled briefly with disappointment. "I would much rather remain with you to continue the investigation, particularly given Phelps's murder."

Her gaze was sympathetic. "I understand. I wouldn't want to leave either."

"Perhaps I should lose my job and try to obtain employment as a canvasser at the Amicable Society," Hadrian suggested. "With Eaton gone and now Phelps murdered, it would seem they are in need of help."

"That is an intriguing thought." Tilda fell silent for a moment, her expression pensive. "We shall have to propose it to Maxwell."

"I would hope he'd support it. Working for the society would give us a great deal of access to its function."

Tilda's eyes gleamed with anticipation. "It would indeed. I shall speak to Maxwell about this scheme this evening."

How Hadrian disliked having to gain Maxwell's approval during this investigation. He was used to making the decisions with Tilda and them guiding their own inquiries. "I'm sure you'll convince him of the benefits. After all, he was clever enough to hire you."

"I should like to persuade him to allow me to make inquiries without discussing them with him first. I will try. Shall we go?" She started to rise.

Hadrian took a long drink of his ale as he stood. "Ready."

He hoped Tilda would find success with Maxwell. They had established an excellent and effective investigative process. It wasn't helpful for them to have to seek the inspector's approval at every turn.

Hadrian missed when it was just the two of them.

CHAPTER 8

*I*nspector Maxwell returned from his workday, eager to hear what Tilda might have learned. Mrs. Kilgore served them a robust stew for dinner.

Before they sat down at the table, Maxwell informed her that he'd gone to the police station to speak with Inspector Chisholm. Unfortunately, he hadn't been there. Tilda didn't mask her disappointment. There was no reason to, for Maxwell shared it.

During the meal, Tilda revealed what she and Hadrian had learned from Mrs. Vickers and the barkeep about Timothy Eaton. She did not, of course, disclose anything to do with Hadrian's visions, but they hadn't yielded anything terribly helpful as of yet. Furthermore, she'd have to come up with a way to share that information without explaining how they'd actually learned it. Meaning, she and Hadrian had to first confirm it in another way.

As they finished eating, Tilda told Maxwell about Rippon, Eaton's colleague at the Prudential Assurance Company and frequent companion at the Wolf and Dove. "I should like to speak with him, but I worry we—that includes you and Ravenhurst—

ought not to conduct too many inquiries, lest we stir up suspicion."

Maxwell's brows drew together as he set his spoon down and leaned back against his chair. "That is a concern."

"I've a suggestion that I hope you might find agreeable," Tilda said. "I've worked with a journalist in the past, Mr. Ezra Clement at the *Daily News*. We've shared information, and he was very helpful in solving the last case I worked on. We could have him make inquiries at the assurance company."

"I'm not sure I want to work with a reporter." Maxwell frowned briefly. His hesitation reminded Tilda of Hadrian's disdain for Clement in particular, though he was coming around. "You trust him?"

"I do," Tilda said with confidence. "I think he would be interested in the story of the murder of Mr. Phelps, particularly given the alleged fraud."

Maxwell sat forward, his eyes sparking with alarm. "It would be best if he didn't publish anything whilst we are in the midst of our investigation."

"Of course, and that would be a requirement," Tilda said firmly, seeking to ease Maxwell's concern. "We'll share the details with him for his story, so that he may publish the exclusive account. In exchange, he'll interview Mr. Rippon at the Prudential Assurance Company about Mr. Eaton. We'd like to know why his employment was terminated and his reaction to that, as well as anything Rippon can tell us about Eaton joining the Amicable Society. Ideally, Rippon will also be able to tell us where we can find Eaton now."

After thinking a long moment, Maxwell brushed his hand over his jaw. "I suppose that seems reasonable. I trust your judgment, so if you think this scheme will work, I am in favor of it. Will you speak with Mr. Clement?"

"Yes, I can call on him in Fleet Street tomorrow morning with Lord Ravenhurst."

Mrs. Kilgore walked into the dining room and surveyed their empty bowls. "All finished, then?"

"Indeed, and it was delicious. It's one of my favorite dishes that you bring to the station," Maxwell said with a smile.

Mrs. Kilgore only nodded as she expertly cleared the table.

Tilda noted she did not smile often. "Thank you, Mrs. Kilgore. We are lucky to have you here," Tilda said. She was most grateful for Mrs. Kilgore's cooking, as it was not her forte.

"I am glad to help." Mrs. Kilgore carried the dishes from the dining room.

Alone with Maxwell once more, Tilda met his gaze. "There is one more thing I'd like to share. Or discuss, I suppose."

Maxwell settled back in his chair and crossed his arms over his chest. "What's that?"

Tilda hoped the inspector would support Hadrian's idea as he'd done with asking Clement to assist them. "Lord Ravenhurst came up with a scheme that will be most helpful. It seems the Amicable Society is without a canvasser, and now they are without their chief administrator. His lordship thinks he ought to seek the vacant canvasser position. He would likely learn a great many things if he were an employee of the society—even more than you can learn as a member."

Blinking in what appeared to be surprise, Maxwell uncrossed his arms. He shifted his attention away from Tilda as he seemed to ponder the suggestion. "That is a good idea." He returned his gaze to Tilda. "I suppose that would mean he would be living here all the time then?"

"Yes," Tilda replied. "He would quit his pretend job at the gentlemen's club in order to work for the society. If Furnier and Nevill agreed to hire him."

Maxwell didn't react immediately. His gaze was once again trained on nothing as his brow creased.

"You seem hesitant," Tilda observed.

"I'm not." Maxwell exhaled, and a lopsided smile flashed over his features. "I suppose I wish I'd thought of it."

"Why would you have? We didn't realize the canvassing position was potentially vacant."

"That's true." The inspector inclined his head. "Yes, let's see if they'll hire Lord Ravenhurst." He regarded Tilda a moment. "You and he seem to work well together."

"We've conducted several investigations, and I would say we've formed an excellent working relationship," Tilda replied.

"It's entirely professional then?" Maxwell asked. He quickly added, "I don't mean to pry."

"Not at all. Lord Ravenhurst and I are business associates as well as friends, but it's not as if we attend social engagements together." Tilda chuckled. "We hardly move in the same circles."

"No, I can't imagine you do," Maxwell said with a smile. "I'm curious why you wanted to be an investigator. Some would say it's an odd occupation for a woman."

"I find *most* men think *most* occupations are odd for women." Tilda didn't mask the edge of disdain in her tone.

"I don't," Maxwell assured her. "I think it's wonderful that you're an investigator."

Tilda felt a surge of pride—and pleasure. So few people endorsed what she did. Even her own grandmother wasn't entirely supportive. She would greatly prefer Tilda marry instead. "Thank you for saying so. I did not believe you found my occupation strange," Tilda clarified. "How could I, when you hired me whilst the Metropolitan Police would not?"

Maxwell met her gaze with a pointed look. "That is their loss. Still, I imagine it stings, since your father worked for the Met."

"It does," Tilda admitted. "However, I'm glad to have a good relationship with Inspector Teague there. I believe he would hire me if he could."

"Well, it's not as if women don't already work for the police,"

Maxwell said. "Mrs. Kilgore works as a searcher for the City, and I believe she's helped her husband with a few cases in the past—posing in a role as you are doing, though not necessarily conducting inquiries on her own as you are. I'm sure Scotland Yard has women searchers and likely utilizes police wives in a similar fashion."

"They do," Tilda said. "I could angle for one of those positions, but I don't really want to search females who are arrested. I want to be an investigator."

Maxwell cocked his head. "And why is that?"

Tilda lifted her shoulder. "I suppose I inherited my curiosity and interest in investigation from my father. He was a sergeant but was going to move to the detective branch when he was killed."

"I'm sorry to hear that." Maxwell gave her a sympathetic look that made Tilda shift in her chair. She didn't like pity any more than she cared to speak of losing her father.

"Why did you want to work for the police?" Tilda asked, eagerly changing the subject.

"My father was a dock worker," Maxwell replied. "I saw how hard he labored. He was exhausted and in pain from the back-breaking work. He died when I was fifteen."

"That's the same age I was when my father died," Tilda said quietly. Hadn't she wanted to avoid talking about her father? And yet here she was offering information. She sought to redirect the conversation back to the inspector. "You didn't wish to be a dock worker?"

Maxwell gave his head an infinitesimal shake. "I wanted to help people. I was actually interested in becoming a doctor—my mother works for an apothecary and enjoys it. But I wasn't able to go to school for that."

Tilda found it sad that Maxwell couldn't pursue his dreams. "Do you have siblings?"

"An older sister. She's been married a few years now. There

were younger siblings—a brother and a sister—but we lost them rather young."

Tilda's chest constricted. "That must have been difficult."

"It was very sad, especially for my mother." Maxwell's voice had softened along with his features. His hazel eyes took on a deep melancholy. "I remember how expensive it was to have funerals for them. That's why this case matters a great deal to me. People struggle enough to provide a good life for themselves and their families without others trying to take advantage of them."

"I agree." Tilda was glad to learn more about the inspector. They had similar beliefs and losing their fathers at the same age made her feel a surprising connection to him. "Though you are not a doctor, I hope you're glad to be working to help people, because you are."

He smiled faintly. "I hope so."

A knock on the door prompted them to turn their heads toward the entrance hall.

Maxwell braced his hands on the edge of the table. "I wonder who that could be." He stood and moved toward the door.

Tilda rose and followed Maxwell but remained in the parlor. Maxwell opened the door. Surprisingly, it was Inspector Chisholm.

"Good evening, Inspector Chisholm. I'm glad you came by. Are you aware I stopped at the police station to speak with you?" Maxwell opened the door wide and invited the older man inside.

Chisholm looked to be in his middle-thirties. His dark gaze swept the entrance hall and moved into the parlor, where it collided with Tilda's. "Yes, I'd heard. Sergeant Kilgore asked me to come and share information with you."

For the sake of discretion, Tilda thought it may have been better for the inspector to call at the back door. Though, if anyone noted Chisholm's identity and wondered why he was there, she and Maxwell could just say he was interviewing them about the meeting last night.

Tilda moved to stand near one of the chairs in the parlor. "Good evening, Inspector Chisholm."

"Miss Wren." Chisholm removed his hat to reveal his mostly bald head. A band of dark hair stretched from ear to ear.

Tilda gestured to the seating area in the parlor. "Would you care to sit?"

Chisholm entered the parlor and sat on the wooden settle. He set his hat beside him.

Maxwell took the other chair as Tilda sat in hers. "I'm eager to hear what you learned today regarding Phelps's murder."

"I'll share what may be helpful to you. It would probably be best if you attend the inquest tomorrow afternoon at the Swan and Hoop." He fixed a dubious stare on Maxwell. "Will your fake job allow you to attend? I imagine that's a bloody nuisance."

"It is, and I'll be there," Maxwell replied. "There was much conversation at the mercantile house today regarding Phelps's death. One of the other Amicable Society members who works there indicated he wanted to attend the inquest whenever it would be, so I imagine all the members—and there are about five or six of us—will attend."

"Then it won't be odd for you to attend." Tilda thought that was good.

Maxwell briefly met her gaze. "Exactly."

"Good," Chisholm said. "That way you can hear everything firsthand, and I won't need to repeat it."

Tilda found Chisholm's demeanor dismissive. She wondered if he was always like that or if he was behaving that way because of her involvement. And if it was the latter, did Chisholm object to her because of their past association, however fleeting it was, or because of her sex?

Maxwell smiled benignly. "You will need to repeat what you learned today. I'd ask that you share everything, so that I may determine if it's useful to our investigation or not."

Pressing her lips together to quash a smile, Tilda greatly approved of Maxwell's response.

"We questioned most of the neighbors around Phelps's house," Chisholm said. "One or two were not at home, so I've assigned a constable to hopefully catch them this evening.

"We learned from one neighbor that Mr. Nevill, one of the society administrators, walked home with Phelps to his house last night, following the meeting." Chisholm didn't know that Tilda had heard that from Mrs. Burley or that she'd already shared that information with Maxwell. "I questioned Nevill today at his tailoring shop in Moorgate. He said he left before eleven and Phelps was fine at that time."

"How did Nevill seem when you spoke with him?" Tilda asked.

Chisholm turned his attention to her, and his brows arched briefly before he replied. "He was upset to learn of his friend's death. He did seem surprised, but he could simply be a good actor."

Tilda noted Chisholm's description of Nevill as a friend. "Were Nevill and Phelps actually friends and not just colleagues?"

"Nevill referred to Phelps as such," Chisholm said. "He said they met about seven months ago, not long after Maxwell moved into the neighborhood. They were acquainted through a friend of Nevill's, a man called Isaiah Jarret."

Maxwell looked to Tilda. "I haven't heard that name before. Have you?"

Tilda shook her head.

Chisholm went on. "Apparently, he was the person with whom Phelps was originally going to start the society, but they had a disagreement of some kind, and Phelps ended up working with Nevill and then Furnier."

"I wonder what that disagreement was about," Tilda mused. "I don't suppose you were able to speak with Mr. Jarret today?"

"No, but I have his direction and will do so tomorrow morning," Chisholm said. "He lives off Old Jewry and works as a senior clerk for the Imperial Bank on Lothbury."

Tilda was surprised but pleased that Chisholm was sharing so much. She'd been prepared to have to pry information from him.

"So, Phelps originally planned to work with Jarret, the two had a disagreement, and Phelps moved on to Nevill. They joined with Furnier after that?" Maxwell summarized.

Chisholm nodded. "I confirmed this with Furnier, as I interviewed him and his wife after I spoke with Nevill."

"How did they take the news of Phelps's death?" Tilda was curious if they'd been upset, or if they were even capable of expressing such emotion.

"They were more reserved in their reaction than Nevill, though they did seem troubled." Chisholm made a sound in his throat that was almost a scoff. "Furnier seems a cold bloke."

"That was our impression as well," Maxwell said. "What did they know of Jarret?"

"Nothing. Furnier only vaguely knows the man. Neither the Furniers nor Nevill had any idea who might have wanted to kill Phelps—outside of the Cardy family."

Tilda noted Chisholm's use of the word *family*, and not just Mrs. Cardy, the widow. The family would include Mrs. Cardy's cousin, Mrs. Kilgore, as well as Mrs. Kilgore's husband, Sergeant Kilgore. Were the Kilgores suspects? Tilda would find that surprising, given the effort the sergeant was devoting to this investigation. "Did the Furniers or Mr. Nevill have any information that would support Mrs. Cardy or another member of her family committing the murder?"

"No, they didn't provide any evidence," Chisholm replied gruffly. "Mrs. Cardy was just the only person they could think of when I posed the question." Since he now said *person*, perhaps he'd only meant the Widow Cardy.

Chisholm straightened in his chair, appearing to stretch his spine. "Mrs. Cardy was my final interview today. I can't imagine she has the strength to kill Phelps. He was bludgeoned in the head with something quite heavy, given the damage it made, but she is petite and slight. I would describe her as overworked and undernourished. She has five children, one of whom is not even a year of age." He gave his head a sad shake.

The inspector's wordless reaction to what he said improved Tilda's impression of him. She thought of the poor woman with five mouths to feed and no husband to provide for them. Nor would she receive a death benefit after paying into the Amicable Society. Tilda shared Maxwell's thoughts about people who took advantage of others who were already at such an extreme disadvantage.

Chisholm continued. "Mrs. Cardy also had an alibi provided by her oldest child, a nine-year-old daughter. Mrs. Cardy takes in sewing, and the daughter helps her now. They were working late to complete their work for the day, so they were together at home. I can't completely discount her as a suspect, but I prefer Nevill at the moment."

In the interest of establishing a mutually beneficial working relationship with Inspector Chisholm, Tilda wanted to share what she and Hadrian had learned. "I was able to gather some information today about Timothy Eaton, the canvasser who solicited Mr. Cardy's membership."

"What's that?" Chisholm turned his attention toward Tilda.

She repeated everything she'd already told Maxwell, leaving out Hadrian's visions, of course. When she mentioned Rippon from the Prudential Assurance Company, she did not share their plans to have Clement interview him. Nor did she reveal Hadrian's scheme to potentially infiltrate the Amicable Society as their new canvasser. She would leave it to Maxwell to disclose that information to his colleague. Or not.

It happened that Maxwell did not inform Chisholm of those plans.

Chisholm rose. "I appreciate you sharing what you've

learned. I would advise you to steer clear of conducting any inquiries that will intrude on my investigation." He gave them each a pointed look, his gaze lingering on Tilda, as if he expected her to disobey his edict. Or perhaps he was simply trying to assert his authority. Whatever the reason, Tilda maintained a serene expression.

After Chisholm departed, Tilda turned to Maxwell. "You didn't tell him about using Clement to interview Rippon or about Lord Ravenhurst angling for the canvasser position at the Amicable Society."

"Chisholm made it clear that our investigations are separate. I saw no need to inform him of our plans. If we find Eaton, I'll inform Chisholm, as interviewing him could help the murder investigation."

"He seemed a bit disagreeable," Tilda said cautiously, hoping Maxwell wouldn't think she was overstepping. "Is he always like that?"

"He's sometimes abrupt in his manner," Maxwell said. "He did seem curt this evening, but he's likely had a long day."

Tilda supposed that was true. Perhaps she was anticipating conflict when there really wasn't any.

Maxwell narrowed his eyes slightly. "I do wonder if he objects to your position in the investigation. He may have thought you would serve to play a role and not actively participate in making inquiries, as most women would do."

It made Tilda feel a bit better to hear Maxwell voicing her thoughts—that Chisholm might take issue with working with a female in this manner. "Should I endeavor to remain silent, if possible?"

"Not at all," Maxwell said quickly. He smiled at her. "Chisholm seemed to become accustomed to you, at least a little. I want him to see that you're a capable and clever investigator."

Tilda warmed at his compliments and his open support. "Thank you, Inspector. That is kind of you to say." She decided this was as good a time as any to seek his approval regarding how she conducted her investigations.

"Would you mind if Lord Ravenhurst and I make inquiries or enact schemes without your directive or permission? I ask because we could have sought out Clement today about interviewing Rippon. We may already have the results of that interview this evening if we'd done so."

A faint grimace passed over Maxwell's features. "I do understand your perspective, and you make a good argument. Since I hired you because of your competence and skill, you should be able to conduct this investigation in the best, most efficient way possible. Please proceed at your discretion."

"Thank you. I will be thoughtful and careful."

Maxwell smiled. "I've no doubt." He sobered. "However, I don't want Lord Ravenhurst conducting any investigative business without your—or my—approval and consent. You must supervise his activities."

Tilda would not share the word "supervise" with Hadrian, though she wasn't sure if he'd take offense—at least from her. They'd worked together long enough now, with her mostly taking the lead, that she didn't think he would mind. But if Maxwell said that to Hadrian, she wondered if he would be affronted.

"Will Ravenhurst mind having to report to you?" Maxwell asked, his tone carrying the barest sardonic lilt.

"Not at all. As I've said, we've worked together before, but *I* am the investigator and he assists as needed. Sometimes, it's quite useful to have an earl with me when I make inquiries."

Often, in fact. And it wasn't just his title. Hadrian had proved himself to be a capable investigator. There were also his visions, which had sometimes driven them to important revelations, not that she could share that with Maxwell.

"How fortunate for you," Maxwell said. "He is not an earl in this case, however. I do hope he remembers that."

"Certainly." Tilda felt as though she had to defend Hadrian somewhat. "He did an admirable job of appearing as Nigel Beck during our inquiries today. Lord Ravenhurst has always followed my direction, and he will do so now. I appreciate you trusting me to make decisions about the investigation."

"I do trust you, Miss Wren." He smiled at her, his eyes gleaming with appreciation. "Indeed, I admire you greatly."

Tilda noted a surprising jolt of awareness under his warm regard. She'd only ever felt something similar with Hadrian. On many occasions, in fact. Notably, when he'd kissed her.

No, this wasn't as strong as that. But it was…something.

Shoving the sensation away, Tilda shook out her shoulders and announced that she would be retiring. She suddenly felt too close in this house and desperately wanted to be alone.

CHAPTER 9

The following morning, Hadrian hesitated outside the door of Number Five White Alley. He carried a basket of items his cook had sent for the pantry, as well as a valise full of his personal items. He'd brought different clothing, along with the glue for his hair pieces. It was early, but the sun was up, not that its light penetrated the narrow alley.

He felt strange just walking into the house without knocking, but since he was supposed to be a resident, it made sense he would do so. He hoped the door wasn't locked, as he'd failed to obtain a key from Maxwell.

Briefly setting the valise down, he tried the door. Thankfully, it pushed open. Hadrian plucked up the valise and stepped into the entrance hall, then closed the door with his elbow. He had a sudden and very deep appreciation for butlers.

Leaving his valise in the hall, he carried the basket downstairs to the kitchen where, judging from the smell, Mrs. Kilgore was making breakfast.

He greeted her with a smile and set the basket on the end of the worktable. "Good morning. I brought some things for the pantry, including tea."

She looked over the large basket of goods that included the aforementioned tea, bread, jam, butter, and eggs, among other things, her eyes rounding. "This is most generous of you, my lord." She sniffed the tea and blinked. "I've never smelt tea like that before. Should I make some now?"

"Unless you already have some brewed." He didn't want her to do additional work.

"It's no trouble," she said. "I'm making eggs and toast for Inspector Maxwell and Miss Wren. Would you like some too?"

"Thank you, but I've eaten already. There are kippers in the basket if you'd like to make those as well."

"You brought food that isn't for you?" She appeared perplexed.

"It's for everyone, including you," Hadrian said with a smile.

"Thank you, my lord," she said, still seeming slightly baffled. "I did think that was a great deal of food. It's unexpected, but very kind. Now, off with you. I'll bring breakfast to the dining room shortly. Inspector Maxwell and Miss Wren will be there soon, I expect."

"Thank *you*, Mrs. Kilgore."

Hadrian went back upstairs and found that Maxwell was already in the dining room.

"I assumed that was your valise in the entrance hall," Maxwell said in lieu of a greeting.

"Good morning," Hadrian said. "Yes, it's mine. I appreciate you leaving the door unlocked for me, but perhaps it's best if I can let myself in."

"I was thinking the same thing." Maxwell fished a key from his pocket and handed it to Hadrian.

"Thank you." Hadrian pocketed the key.

"Inspector Chisholm called last night." Maxwell gestured toward one of the four chairs at the square table. "Sit and I'll tell you about it."

Hadrian eagerly sat and listened to Maxwell recount the

meeting. After hearing everything, Hadrian could well imagine all the new lines of inquiry Tilda would wish to follow. He looked forward to discussing it with her.

She came into the dining room then, her gaze falling on Hadrian with a gleam of warmth. "Good morning, my lord."

Hadrian didn't like her calling him that—it felt stiff and unfriendly. He considered asking both her and Maxwell to call him by his given name, just so he and Tilda could return to addressing themselves as they'd become accustomed to. But he wasn't sure Maxwell would feel comfortable with the familiarity, at least not yet. Perhaps if Hadrian were to live here full time, that might change. He hoped Tilda had been able to persuade Maxwell to allow Hadrian to try to obtain the canvasser position.

Mrs. Kilgore brought the breakfast and served it on the table. "I'll fetch the tea in a moment," she said. "His lordship brought a fancy tea. It's steeping."

Maxwell's brow arched. "Did you?"

"I brought several things for the pantry," Hadrian said. "I wanted to contribute to the household."

"There are even kippers," Mrs. Kilgore said. "But I'll make those tomorrow." She looked to Maxwell. "Unless you'd like them now?"

"Tomorrow will be fine," Maxwell replied. "Thank you, Mrs. Kilgore."

"I'll just fetch the tea." She took herself off.

Hadrian waited while Tilda and Maxwell ate for a few minutes.

After swallowing a bite of toast, Tilda turned her attention to Hadrian. "Inspector Maxwell liked your idea of trying to become the new canvasser for the Amicable Society. The inquest is this afternoon, and I expect Mr. Nevill and Mr. Furnier will attend. Perhaps you can speak with them about the position."

"I'll do that," Hadrian said, delighted Maxwell had agreed to their plan. He looked toward the inspector. "Thank you for endorsing this idea. I think it will be helpful."

"Miss Wren has assured me that you possess the necessary skill to conduct this aspect of the investigation. You must keep Miss Wren and me apprised of what you learn as soon as possible."

"Of course." Hadrian worked to keep himself from feeling defensive. Maxwell's tone seemed to carry a hint of skepticism as to Hadrian's abilities.

Tilda sent a smile toward her fake husband. "Inspector Maxwell has also agreed to allow us to ask Mr. Clement to interview Mr. Rippon at the Prudential Assurance Company."

Hadrian was pleased to hear that Tilda had been successful in her endeavors with Maxwell. Hadrian had never doubted her persuasive ability, but he didn't know the inspector well enough to assume he would agree.

"I don't typically like to work with reporters," Maxwell said with a hint of disdain. "I find some of them to be unscrupulous."

"I agree." At least here was something Hadrian and Maxwell could agree upon. Not that they disagreed, but Hadrian sensed a…divide between them. "Clement rather put me off at first, but he redeemed himself by assisting us on our last investigation. I'm optimistic he'll also be helpful with this investigation, particularly since we are trying to be careful about how and with whom we make inquiries."

"It's a clever plan." Maxwell looked at Tilda with a warm smile. "But then, I expect nothing less from Miss Wren. She has proven herself to be a most competent investigative partner."

Hadrian bristled at Maxwell's use of the word *partner*—Tilda was *Hadrian's* partner, not Maxwell's.

"We should tell his lordship everything we learned from Inspector Chisholm last night," Tilda said.

"I've already done that," Maxwell replied.

Tilda's gaze flashed with surprise. "Well, that's…good." She turned her head toward Hadrian. "After we visit Clement, I would like to call on Mrs. Cardy. I'd thought to take her some food from the market. That gives us a reason for calling, and it will also help her and her children. I'm very sorry for their plight."

"That's a wonderful idea," Hadrian said. "Though I think my cook packed enough food for us to share with the Cardys. Let's ask Mrs. Kilgore to prepare a basket from what I brought."

As if summoned by his mention of her, Mrs. Kilgore entered with the tea. She poured out and set a cup down in front of each of them. "I suppose you want sugar?" She picked up the small tin of sugar cubes that Hadrian's cook had included in the basket.

"Yes, please," Hadrian said. She put the tin on the table.

Tilda looked to Mrs. Kilgore. "His lordship and I are going to call on Mrs. Cardy later this morning, and we'd like to share some of the food he brought with her and the children. Will you pack a basket?"

"I'd be happy to," Mrs. Kilgore replied earnestly. "I'm so pleased you want to help my dear cousin."

"My cook baked some biscuits that Mrs. Cardy's children might like," Hadrian said.

Mrs. Kilgore sniffed. "You are truly kindhearted, my lord. Thank you. It's so unfair what's happened to poor Hester. To lose her husband is bad enough, but to be without the funds he paid into the Amicable Society is salt in her wound. They should at least refund what he contributed."

"Why didn't they?" Hadrian asked.

"I don't know," Mrs. Kilgore replied with a deep frown. "I think they said there wasn't a record of what he paid, but I don't know if that's true."

"We'll do our best to recover the Cardys' money," Hadrian vowed. Indeed, he'd supply it to them himself if necessary.

"Thank you, my lord." Mrs. Kilgore left the dining room.

Tilda turned her gaze to Hadrian. "Is this the tea you brought?"

"I believe so. It certainly smells like it, and I did suggest she use it." Hadrian moved the sugar closer to Tilda so she could help herself first.

After she added a cube to her tea, she offered the small silver tongs, which Hadrian's cook had also sent, to Maxwell. But the inspector shook his head. "I've never put sugar in my tea. It's a luxury we could ill afford, and I've never wanted to take up the habit."

A faint bit of color stained Tilda's cheeks very briefly as she handed the tongs to Hadrian. His fingers brushed hers, and he made sure not to reveal his reaction to her. Every time they touched, he felt a rush of awareness and heat. Indeed, the sensation had only increased the longer he'd known her.

Hadrian stirred his sugar into his tea as Maxwell sipped his. The inspector took a second sip before returning his cup to the saucer. "That is excellent tea, Ravenhurst. Thank you for bringing it."

"It's my pleasure to contribute to the household, particularly since I will be living here all the time now."

Maxwell met his gaze across the table. "*If* you're hired to be the Amicable Society canvasser."

Hadrian didn't care for the man continuing to direct doubt at him. "Hopefully, that will happen this afternoon at the inquest. Either way, I do plan to stay, unless you take issue with that."

"I do not." Maxwell's reply sounded a bit strained.

"Miss Wren and I will be sure to apprise you of all that transpires at the inquest, since you will be working." A small—and perhaps petty—part of Hadrian was glad that he and Tilda would be together without the inspector.

"Oh, I will be at the inquest," Maxwell said rather fervently. "I must report to the mercantile house this morning, but those of us who are members of the Amicable Society will attend."

"Well, that's certainly helpful," Hadrian said, tamping down his disappointment. "I'm sure you would have been frustrated to miss it."

Maxwell's lips pressed into a grim line. "Most certainly. I should be off now. I look forward to hearing about your interview with Mrs. Cardy and what this journalist says."

"I'm sure Mr. Clement will want to attend the inquest," Tilda said. "You can at least observe him there, if not meet him."

The inspector stood. "I'll see you there." He inclined his head, then left the dining room.

Hadrian sipped his tea and did not speak until he heard the front door of the house close. "Perhaps I should have not brought the sugar."

Tilda grimaced. "I had not considered that Inspector Maxwell may not have had much opportunity to consume it. I hope he did not take offense."

"I don't think so. I confess I feel a trifle awkward bringing what is, I suppose, extravagance into the household. Mrs. Kilgore was somewhat flabbergasted by some of the items in the basket my cook sent."

"I think that was nice of your cook, and I'm sure Mrs. Kilgore is grateful."

"Assuredly, but, like you, I don't mean to cause any upset."

"I understand how they may feel," Tilda said. "I am sometimes too aware of our class and economic difference. I think of the evening you took me to Northumberland House, and it seems as though it was a dream."

"A nice one, I hope?" Hadrian had enjoyed that evening with her, and not just because it had provided a turning point in their case. Tilda had looked incomparably beautiful in her finery, and he'd been proud to have her on his arm.

"It was shockingly different from what I'm used to," she said with a light chuckle. "This household is probably closer to my reality."

Hadrian took that to mean that she would have more in common with Maxwell, or a man like him. That pricked at Hadrian quite sharply.

Tilda took another drink of tea. "That really is delicious. I would not be opposed to drinking that every day." She flashed him a smile as she stood.

It was silly, but Hadrian's chest puffed, and a sense of triumph stole through him. Because she liked his fancy tea.

"Let us prepare to visit Mrs. Cardy," she said. "It's early yet, so perhaps you'd like to settle in first."

Hadrian rose. "I'll take my things up to the garret." He hadn't spent much time considering that he would be sharing the small space with Maxwell. There were two beds and a dressing screen, so he could count on at least a small measure of privacy.

"Will you manage without a valet?" Tilda asked with a half-smile.

He couldn't tell if she was teasing or genuinely curious. "I do not require my valet's assistance. Not even for shaving," he added.

Though now, he wondered how he would accomplish that. He supposed he'd have to bring water up from the kitchen. Or would he just shave downstairs? He'd have to ask Maxwell. Better yet, he'd observe what Maxwell did and copy him.

"I'm impressed," Tilda said. "And pleased. This investigation will speed up a little, I believe, with you here full time."

Whilst Hadrian loved to see her enthusiasm, one thing he never wished was for his time with Tilda to be short.

~

*L*ater that morning, Tilda and Hadrian took an omnibus to Fleet Street, where they found Ezra Clement at his favorite coffee house. He'd been eager to help with their investigation, particularly when it meant he could report on a fraud and a murder. He'd understood they were working under different identities and that, if their paths should cross, he was to pretend he didn't know them. They would certainly encounter one another that afternoon, since he planned to attend the inquest at the Swan and Hoop.

After fetching the basket of food from White Alley, Tilda and Hadrian had made their way to Mrs. Cardy's house at the end of Nuns Court. The tenement was terribly shabby, and Tilda felt even worse about the fact that Mrs. Cardy's husband had given money to the Amicable Society and not received a benefit when he died.

As they approached the door, Hadrian briefly touched Tilda's arm, and they paused. She pivoted to face him.

"Inspector Chisholm said Mrs. Cardy is small and slight," Hadrian said. "He doesn't think she has the strength to have killed Phelps, given the blow to his head."

Tilda didn't like to make assumptions. "Perhaps, but one should never underestimate another's anger, particularly when that person's family's livelihood is at stake."

"You make a valid point." Hadrian inclined his head toward the tenement, and they continued to the door.

He carried the basket containing items his cook had sent. Tilda had been surprised to see it also included beeswax candles. Hadrian insisted on giving all of them to Mrs. Cardy, for which Mrs. Kilgore had thanked him profusely.

Tilda glanced at Hadrian. "You knock." She eyed his fake blond hair and long side whiskers. He just didn't look like the Hadrian she knew, and she didn't particularly care for it.

Hadrian knocked. After a few moments, there came the sound of running feet, and the door opened.

A young girl, whom Tilda took to be the nine-year-old Chisholm had mentioned, blinked at them. Her dark brown hair hung to her shoulders. The locks needed a good washing.

Tilda gave her a warm smile. "Good morning. You must be Miss Cardy. I am Mrs. Harwood, and this is my brother, Mr.

Beck. We wish to convey our condolences about your father, and we brought something for your family. May we come in and speak with your mother?"

Normally, Tilda would not call on a widow, but customs were different amongst the working classes. They could not afford to sequester themselves and adhere to strict mourning rituals. There was work to be done and mouths to feed.

The girl's round, dark eyes fixed on the basket in Hadrian's hand. She backed up slightly and pulled the door open wider.

Tilda stepped into the room, which seemed to be both a parlor and a bedroom. Two younger girls sat cross-legged on a pallet and played with what looked to be dolls made of clothes-pins. Tilda gave them a warm smile, and the smaller of the two smiled back.

"I'll fetch Mama," the girl who answered the door said. She moved through a doorway into another room.

Tilda glanced at Hadrian, but his features were nonreactive. He maintained a pleasant expression.

The girl returned with her mother, who was only a few inches taller. She had the same dark hair and round brown eyes as her daughter, but her face was thinner and her chin square. She wiped her hands on her apron. It was white, though somewhat dingy, but the rest of her clothing was black and ill-fitting. Tilda wondered if it had been borrowed.

"Good morning, Mrs. Cardy," Tilda said. "We were sorry to hear of your family's loss and have brought you some things to help in this sad time."

Mrs. Cardy regarded them with caution. "'Oo are ye?"

"I'm Mrs. Harwood," Tilda said. "And this is my brother, Mr. Beck. He and my husband are members of the Amicable Society."

Mrs. Cardy's eyes narrowed, and her nostrils flared. "We don't speak o' them in this 'ouse."

"I do understand," Tilda said quickly. "I don't mean to cause any upset. We do not support what happened to your husband

and your family. The society should not have taken his money if he wasn't eligible."

"That's right," Mrs. Cardy said sternly. "But Gil insisted they didn't care if 'e was ill. The man what recruited him said the purpose of the society was to 'elp people. 'E saw Gil was poorly and said the Society could 'elp 'im and us—'is family. We thought it was a boon."

Sadness lined Mrs. Cardy's thin features, and Tilda tamped down her anger at the injustice of this poor woman's situation. "The man who sold him the membership was Mr. Eaton?" Tilda asked.

Mrs. Cardy nodded. "Friendly fellow. Called 'ere one Sunday. We liked 'im very much, which makes what 'appened even worse. After Gil died, I asked the doctor what signed the death notice why they took my 'usband's money and told 'im I could 'ave the death benefit if Gil could just last six months. 'E wouldn't answer. Said it was Eaton's fault." Her dark gaze filled with anguish. "Do ye know 'ow 'ard Gil tried to stay alive? 'E died six months and one day after paying 'is entrance fee."

Tilda hadn't known that. Somehow, it made the situation even sadder. "I'm truly sorry."

Hadrian held the basket toward Mrs. Cardy. "We have some things for you."

Mrs. Cardy reached for the handle, and Hadrian deftly moved his hand so that he touched her. Then he acted as if he lost his grip and brought his other hand to clasp the handle so that it also touched her hand. This allowed him to prolong their connection. Tilda hoped he was seeing one—or more—of her memories and knew that was his intent.

"My apologies, the basket's a bit heavy," Hadrian said. "Shall I set it down for you?"

Taking her hand from the basket, she pivoted toward the doorway from which she'd come. "Yes, in 'ere."

She led them into the back room that appeared to be a

kitchen, dining room, and also a bedchamber. It contained a rickety table cluttered with garments in various states of assembly or repair, and there was a cradle near the hearth where a babe was sleeping. Mrs. Cardy's fifth child, a small boy who was barely more than a babe himself, sat at the table, gnawing on what looked to be a piece of cloth.

"I'll make some space." Mrs. Cardy moved a stack of garments and set them on another pile. Hadrian set the basket on the table and took a step back.

Mrs. Cardy looked through the contents of the basket and sucked in a breath. "This is all for us?" She eyed them with suspicion. "Ye didn't steal these, did ye?"

"No, a wealthy benefactor donated them," Tilda said. They'd decided that was what they would tell her. How else would they have candles, biscuits, jam, and smoked fish, among other things?

"Look at the candles here, Susan," Mrs. Cardy said, her eyes gleaming with joy.

The girl smiled at her mother. "Ye look 'appy, Mama."

"I am, my sweet. There are biscuits." Mrs. Cardy's tone held a poignant awe. She handed one to Susan and gave another to the boy at the table.

He took a bite, and a look of sheer rapture moved over his small face. Tilda's heart wrenched.

"Is it good?" Mrs. Cardy asked with a laugh.

The boy nodded vigorously, then tried to shove the rest of the biscuit in his mouth. Mrs. Cardy clasped his hand and kept him from devouring the remainder. "Slowly, Bertie, slowly."

Tilda looked to Susan. She was nibbling at the biscuit, taking very small bites. Her eyes glowed with wonder.

Mrs. Cardy looked back at Tilda and Hadrian. "This was very kind of ye. Please thank whoever gave ye these things. They can never know 'ow wonderful this is for my children." The woman sniffed.

"I'm so glad." Tilda had to work to keep her own emotions at bay.

"I'm going to speak to the society administrators," Hadrian said firmly. "They must return the funds that your husband paid into the Society. It's the right thing to do."

"That's what I said, but they say it wasn't their fault. Perhaps now Mr. Phelps is dead, things'll be different." Mrs. Cardy blinked at them. "Did ye know 'e was murdered?"

Tilda nodded. "Why do you think things will be better without him?"

Mrs. Cardy shrugged. "He was the one in charge. With 'im gone, perhaps the others'll 'ave more sympathy." She moved her attention to her daughter, who was eating her biscuit very slowly.

"How well did you know Mr. Phelps?" Hadrian asked. He regarded Mrs. Cardy with interest, and Tilda wondered if his question was prompted by the vision he'd seen when he'd touched the woman—assuming he'd seen one of her memories.

"Only met 'im once." Mrs. Cardy kept her focus on Susan.

Hadrian's interest in the woman seemed to intensify. "When and where was that?"

Tilda felt certain he'd seen something to do with Phelps and was eager to hear what it was.

"Can't recall exactly." She glanced at Hadrian, and her gaze seemed wary.

"I hope you'll tell us if you can remember the circumstances of your meeting with Mr. Phelps," Hadrian said.

Mrs. Cardy didn't respond.

Tilda took the woman's silence to mean she was unlikely to reveal anything. Rather than press her on the subject of Phelps, Tilda moved to a new line of inquiry. "Are you aware of any others in your position? As a widow of a member of the Amicable Society, I mean."

"Not widowed, but I know of a few others 'oo were sold memberships and are ill." Mrs. Cardy looked toward Tilda and now seemed more at ease. "They're trying to 'old on for the full year now they know there's no money after six months like they were promised."

"And none of you have any paperwork to confirm any of this?" Hadrian asked.

"Just a worthless certificate of membership," Mrs. Cardy said. "I burned Gil's."

Tilda looked at Mrs. Cardy with sympathy. "Why did you think it was worthless?"

"The doctor said it didn't matter that we 'ad it, that the rules were the rules. Blamed it on Eaton again."

Tilda looked forward to Dr. Giles's testimony at the inquest later and to potentially speaking with him herself. "Have any of the families you mentioned spoken to the police?"

Mrs. Cardy let out a sharp laugh. "Why would they bother? Police aren't much 'elp to folk like us. The only reason they're doing anything is because of my dear cousin."

"I'd like to speak with these families." Hadrian's eyes flashed with outrage. "I'm a member of the society, and I want to see justice done."

Mrs. Cardy sniffed. "Thank ye, Mr. Beck. Ye could try to speak with Joseph and Meg Lenton. They live down the court at Number Twelve."

Hadrian nodded. "I'll do that. You all deserve resti— To be put right."

Tilda was certain he'd been about to say "restitution" and was proud of him for taking care to sound like someone from a lower class with decidedly less education. She looked to Mrs. Cardy. "We'll take no more of your time." Then she smiled at Susan as the girl finished her biscuit. "I'm glad you enjoyed that."

"Thank ye, ma'am."

"Walk them to the door, Susan," Mrs. Cardy said. "Your baby brother is starting to fuss."

Tilda glanced toward the cradle and saw that the smallest

child was sucking on his hand. Tilda turned and walked back into the main room, to the front door.

Hadrian came around and opened it for her.

"Goodbye, Susan," Tilda said before departing. Hadrian closed the door and followed her into the court.

When they'd moved a short distance from the house, Tilda turned to Hadrian. "Did you see something when you touched Mrs. Cardy? I think you must have, given your questions regarding Phelps."

"I saw Phelps in his parlor. I had the sense Mrs. Cardy was angry. Phelps appeared perturbed and perhaps a bit…cold."

"You saw Phelps where he was killed? That's why you asked her when and where she'd seen him. You were trying to determine if she was there the night of the murder."

"Just so," Hadrian said. "I was not able to ascertain the time of day—not from a window or a clock."

"What about his clothing? Was Phelps dressed the same as the night he was killed?"

Hadrian frowned faintly, his brow creasing. "I'm not sure if the garments were the same, but they were at least similar. The image came quickly and was gone before I could see everything I wanted to."

"It's all right. It's still helpful to know she spoke to him," Tilda said with a reassuring nod. "And you did try to discover the truth. Well done."

"I had the sense she was unnerved by my questions," Hadrian noted.

"I did too." Tilda cocked her head. "Did you or Maxwell receive a membership certificate?"

"We did not," Hadrian replied. "When Mrs. Cardy mentioned her husband had one, I became curious. We must ask one of the administrators about that. Should we stop and see the Lentons?"

"We may as well," Tilda said.

They found the Lentons' house and spoke with Meg Lenton.

She did not invite them in, but she did show them the membership certificate her husband had received, though she now assumed it was worthless after what had transpired with the Cardys.

The certificate bore Joseph Lenton's name and his date of admission. It wasn't signed by anyone, nor did it contain any remarkable details.

"I rather expected the certificate to have the society's cock and snake," Hadrian said as they turned onto Coleman Street following their brief interview of Mrs. Lenton.

"It was utterly nondescript," Tilda said. "It's almost as if the certificate was an afterthought. Or not actually an official document issued by the society," she added cynically.

"I'll wager it's the latter," Hadrian said. "I don't know if anyone besides Eaton is responsible, but Cardy, Lenton, and likely many others were fraudulently admitted to the society. I'm going to make sure Mrs. Cardy receives what she's owed. I'll cover the expense myself, if necessary."

Tilda touched his arm and smiled up at him. "I'm not surprised you would do that, but thank you. I confess I'm quite moved by the Cardys' plight."

"As am I, and that was before I met them. Now, I am doubly so." His eye twitched, and he touched his temple.

"Does your head ache from touching Mrs. Cardy?"

He nodded gently. "The pain is already starting to fade. It wasn't a very long vision."

"I was impressed with how you juggled the basket and were able to touch her hand for more than a fleeting moment."

"I was doing my best," he said with the flicker of a smile. "I can't imagine Mrs. Cardy killed Phelps. Aside from not appearing strong enough, there is also the issue of her alibi. Susan told Inspector Chisholm that she and her mother were sewing together at home."

"Unfortunately, even children can lie," Tilda said, though she hoped that was not the case. She didn't want Mrs. Cardy to be a murderer. Her children needed her.

And yet, Tilda could easily see how the woman might have been moved by fear and suffering to avenge her husband's death. In the heat of an argument during which Mrs. Cardy sought to regain what her family had lost and so desperately needed, she could very well have simply lost control of her emotions.

"I'm not sure I can blame the Cardys whatsoever," Hadrian said with a flash of intensity.

She turned her head toward him. "Your anger at their plight is true, isn't it?"

"Absolutely." He met her gaze. "You doubted that?"

"Not at all," she said firmly. "It's admirable. I was also most impressed with your ability to sound like someone with less education."

"I nearly slipped up a few times." He chuckled. "I'm even more impressed with your ability to take on various roles during our investigations."

They arrived at White Alley and were surprised to find Inspector Chisholm waiting in the parlor. He held his hat and regarded them with a furrowed brow. His expression was rather grim.

Tilda did not think his visit was due to good news. "What brings you here before the inquest?"

"I'm hoping to see Maxwell. I don't suppose you're expecting him?" the inspector asked.

Tilda shook her head. "He's meeting us at the Swan and Hoop."

Chisholm nodded vaguely, and his brows drew together tightly. "I'm afraid we've another murder to contend with. A body was found on the banks of the Thames yesterday. We're fairly certain it's Timothy Eaton."

CHAPTER 10

*H*adrian saw Tilda's nostrils flare at the news of Eaton's body being discovered, just as he felt his own jolt of surprise.

"You're only 'fairly certain?'" Tilda asked.

"The body is not in the best condition," Chisholm said with a grimace. "The coroner estimates he's been dead a few days. He did not drown, however. He was stabbed several times."

Tilda's brows arched briefly. "Stabbing is convenient, otherwise the gases in his body may have built up too much and then, well, he might have been unidentifiable. Why do you think it's Eaton?"

"Blond hair and mustache, as well as a cleft chin, but his face is distorted and...damaged." Chisholm's features briefly flashed with disgust. "I won't go into details. He's missing the end of the little finger of his left hand, which apparently Eaton was as well."

Hadrian met Tilda's gaze. Silent communication passed between them: this was most certainly Eaton. "Since he was stabbed, this is another murder," Tilda said.

Chisholm nodded. "Still, there's to be an inquest. The coroner examined the remains earlier this morning, but he had to shift his attention to Phelps, since that inquest is this afternoon. In fact, I must be on my way. I came in through the back and will depart the same way. I didn't think it wise to call at the front door a second time." He left the parlor, heading toward the back of the house and the stairs to the kitchen.

"This is a shocking development," Hadrian said.

"Indeed," Tilda agreed. "We should leave for the inquest so we can hopefully catch Maxwell before it starts and inform him of Eaton's death. I think we both know the man they found near the river is Eaton."

Hadrian nodded as he went to the door and held it open for Tilda. "Do you think whoever killed Phelps also killed Eaton?"

"If they were working together to defraud the society, it's probable," Tilda said. "But we don't know Phelps's role, nor are we even entirely sure of Eaton's. I'm curious to see who attends the inquest today and what information we may learn."

"I do hope to speak with Nevill and Furnier about the canvasser position after the inquest. I will try to gather more information about how the society operated, particularly with regard to Eaton's recruitment process and those membership certificates that weren't given to me or Maxwell."

Tilda pursed her lips. "I would love to join you, but they may not wish to speak about society details with a non-member present. Perhaps Maxwell should accompany you when you approach them."

Hadrian bristled. "Why? Am I not capable of questioning them on my own?"

Tilda's eyes flashed with surprise. "Of course. I was just thinking that Maxwell's presence might be reason enough for me to come too."

"It would be preferable—or easier, at least—if you were pretending to be *my* wife," Hadrian said.

A pulse of excitement ran through him. The sensation was akin to joy or pleasure. The thought of Tilda as his wife, of spending every day with her, investigation or not, was shockingly appealing. Pretending, he supposed, would be the next best thing. He slid her a glance, wondering at her reaction to what he'd said. Her features didn't reveal anything beyond an expression of contemplation. And perhaps mild irritation.

Well, damn. He didn't care for that.

"I'm not sure it matters whose wife I'm pretending to be," she said. "I dislike not being an investigator—outwardly, I mean."

Perhaps that explained her annoyance, and it wasn't due to what he'd said. He would hope so.

They arrived at the Swan and Hoop a few minutes later and walked into the common room. Inspector Chisholm stood near the doors to the room where Hadrian had attended the Amicable Society meeting.

Before Hadrian and Tilda could make their way in that direction, Mrs. Burley blocked their path. "I'm so pleased to see another wife here today," she said to Tilda. "But where is Mr. Harwood?"

"He should be here shortly," Tilda replied.

"Mr. Burley was also given leave from his employer to attend." Mrs. Burley inclined her head to a man standing in the corner sipping an ale. He did not look in their direction. Indeed, he seemed quite intent on his beer.

"What do you think will happen with the Amicable Society?" Mrs. Burley asked, her gaze moving from Tilda to Hadrian.

"Why should something happen to it?" Tilda asked. "Mr. Nevill and Mr. Furnier are capable of managing it, aren't they?"

"I suppose, but Phelps's murder is a scandal." Mrs. Burley spoke rather breathlessly. "Between that and the admitting of members who are ill and perhaps misrepresenting when they are eligible for benefits, it may be best if the society folded. And refunded everyone's money, of course. They need to call a meeting as soon as possible. No one wants to wait until Monday to discuss these matters." She looked at Hadrian expectantly. "Don't you agree?"

"I do think a meeting should be called." Hadrian wasn't going to agree with anything else she said.

"We should go in and sit before there are no seats remaining," Tilda said to Hadrian. "We need to save one for Mr. Harwood."

"Certainly." Hadrian looked toward Mrs. Burley. "We'll see you later."

Mrs. Burley nodded. "I need to fetch Mr. Burley. We must obtain seats as well."

The room was crowded with chairs in addition to the table on which Phelps's body lay covered with a cloth. A man of small stature with gray hair stood at the head of the table speaking with a sergeant.

Hadrian leaned toward Tilda again. "That's the coroner from the inquest we attended here in the City a few months ago. Do you suppose that's Sergeant Kilgore with him?" he asked quietly.

"Perhaps," Tilda murmured.

A group of men who had to be the jury gathered on the other side of the table away from the door. There were chairs set out for them, and some sat, whilst others stood.

She led Hadrian to the end of the table opposite the coroner and sergeant. There were a few rows of chairs for spectators, and she moved to the end of the first one to sit. She left the chair on the end vacant, presumably for Maxwell. Hadrian sat on her left.

"There's Clement," Tilda said softly.

Ezra Clement, garbed in bright orange and purple trousers—Hadrian had concluded that loud pants were the reporter's signature—entered. He looked over the assembly, his gaze moving past Hadrian and Tilda without recognition. Rather than take a seat, he assumed a position in the corner. He pulled his notebook from his pocket.

Nevill entered next. Chisholm came in right behind him and motioned for him to sit in a row of chairs against the wall. Over the course of the next few minutes, several other people joined him in those chairs, including Mr. Furnier, Dr. Giles, a man Hadrian didn't recognize, and Mr. and Mrs. Burley.

A well-dressed woman swept in, a short, somewhat opaque veil partially covering her face. When she turned her head to survey the room, Hadrian could see enough of her features to assess her to be around sixty or so. She wore dove-gray, perhaps indicating she was a widow.

"I wonder who that is," he whispered to Tilda. "She doesn't look as though she belongs here." Her clothing and stature were not working class.

"I've no idea, and you're right."

Chisholm also guided the mystery woman to sit along the wall.

"I've been thinking those people are the witnesses who will be questioned today," Tilda said. "This inquest will be quite intriguing."

Another man entered and loitered in the doorway. He removed his hat to reveal brown wavy hair. And he wore glasses.

"I wonder if that's Rippon," Tilda whispered to Hadrian.

"Eaton's friend from the Prudential Assurance Company?" Hadrian glanced at her. "Seems a logical assumption."

Chisholm greeted the man—perhaps Rippon—and directed him to sit in the witness chairs. He then ushered a woman wearing black from head to toe, including a thick veil, to the same area. Despite her face being covered, Hadrian recognized her to be Mrs. Cardy.

The coroner inclined his head toward Chisholm, who moved toward the door. Just when Hadrian thought Maxwell would be shut out of the inquest, the inspector slipped into the room, along with Draper and a few other men, who were likely the society members from the mercantile house. The inspector glanced about, and as soon as his gaze settled on Hadrian and

Tilda, he made his way toward them. The other men sat elsewhere.

Chisholm closed the door, and the coroner addressed the room. They would have to inform Maxwell about Eaton later.

The coroner wore a sober expression, his gaze dark and assessing. "I am the coroner, Abraham Thetford." He glanced toward a clerk seated behind a small table in the corner at that end of the room. "We're here to conduct an inquest into the death of Mr. Walter Phelps, who died mysteriously. If you are not here for that purpose, you may wish to leave. If you are upset by discussions of death and do not care to see the body of a dead man, I invite you to depart."

Thetford paused as he scanned the room once more, but no one left. He took a deep breath, then looked to his left, where the jury was now seated in the row of chairs. "I thank you, gentlemen, for your service today."

The coroner then explained when and how Phelps had died. "The murder weapon has not been found, but Mr. Phelps was killed by a blow to his head from a heavy object that cracked his skull. In reviewing items present in the house, the police found a single brass candlestick, the size and shape of which indicate it could have been used to kill Phelps. However, if it was indeed used in the murder, it has been cleaned meticulously. We have a great many witnesses to speak with today. We will begin with Inspector Chisholm, who has been assigned the oversight of this case."

Inspector Chisholm and the other members of the police were sitting at the front of the room behind Thetford. The coroner pivoted so his back was to the witnesses and the jury would easily be able to see and hear him speak with Chisholm.

Thetford questioned Inspector Chisholm about the murder, then spoke to the constables who had been at Phelps's house when Hadrian and Tilda had happened by. Hadrian tensed, wondering if the constable stationed at Phelps's door would tell the coroner that he and Tilda had been there that morning. Thankfully, he did not. Had he been directed not to say anything?

Next, Thetford called upon Mrs. Burley. "You are a neighbor of Mr. Phelps?"

Mrs. Burley sat forward in her chair and nodded eagerly. "I am."

"Please tell the jury what you saw on Monday evening, the eleventh of May."

"Well, Mondays are when the Amicable Society meets here at the Swan and Hoop. My husband and I walked home from the meeting." She flicked a glance toward her husband, who sat to her right. "We saw Mr. Phelps walking to his house in the company of Mr. Nevill, but that wasn't unusual."

Hadrian looked at Nevill to see his reaction. He kept rubbing the palm of his hand against his knee. The repetitive action made him appear nervous. Beside him, Mr. Furnier looked annoyed, his face pinched. His lips pursed when Mrs. Burley said it was typical for Nevill and Phelps to return to his house after a meeting.

Was that because Furnier was perturbed to be left out of whatever Phelps and Nevill may have discussed on their walk? Or perhaps Furnier hadn't been aware that the two men often went to Phelps's house together after meetings.

"Did you notice when Mr. Nevill left?" Thetford asked.

"Just before eleven," she replied. "I know because I was pulling the draperies closed in the bedchamber as I was preparing to retire. I looked down and saw him leaving."

"And did you see anyone else enter or leave Mr. Phelps's house that evening?"

"I did not, but I also wasn't watching the entire time," she added with a light laugh. "Some will say I know everything that goes on in our street, but that isn't entirely true. I do have a household to run."

The coroner cocked his head. "Mrs. Burley, would you describe yourself as an observant person?"

"I would," she replied proudly.

"Had you noticed any of the society administrators or the physician arguing?"

"Mr. Burley said that Mr. Furnier seemed annoyed with Mr. Phelps and Mr. Nevill at last week's meeting. Then, afterward, I saw Mr. Phelps and Mr. Nevill arguing, though I don't know what they said."

"That was the meeting on the fourth of May?" Thetford clarified.

"Yes. I noted that Mr. Nevill did *not* accompany Mr. Phelps back to his house that night."

Thetford shifted his gaze to her husband. "Mr. Burley, did you note anyone else calling on Mr. Phelps?"

Mr. Burley, his face pink, shook his nearly bald head. "I went to sleep as soon as we arrived home."

"I see." Thetford clasped his hands behind his back. "You are a member of the Amicable Society?"

"Yes."

Mrs. Burley drew herself up and lifted her chin. "He was one of the first to be offered membership. We met Mr. Phelps not long after he took his lodgings across the street from us."

"When was that?" Thetford asked.

"Late September," she replied.

Again, Thetford looked to Burley. "You've been happy with your membership?"

Burley nodded. He appeared to be a man of few words, but perhaps that was because his wife used them all.

Thetford unlocked his hands and took a step toward Burley. "Who do you think killed Mr. Phelps?"

Burley shrugged. "How would I know?"

The coroner looked to Mrs. Burley, who was clearly having difficulty not speaking. She'd moved even more to the edge of her seat. Indeed, Hadrian feared she may slip to the floor in her eagerness.

"What is your opinion, Mrs. Burley?" Thetford asked.

"I don't know that I have an *opinion*. I just know that some people were unhappy with the Amicable Society because of certain memberships that were offered to people who weren't well."

"Which people?"

She shifted in her chair and glanced furtively toward Mrs. Cardy. "There was a member who was admitted despite being quite ill. It is my understanding that you must be in good health to join the society. Unfortunately, he died, and his family was not given the benefit because he hadn't been a member for a year. His wife insists he was told he could collect benefits after six months, so I believe there is some contention." She pressed her lips together and clasped her hands tightly in her lap.

"Who was the man who died?" the coroner asked. His gaze flicked toward Mrs. Cardy, indicating he knew, but wanted Mrs. Burley to state it for the record.

"Gilbert Cardy," Mrs. Burley said, her shoulder twitching.

"Thank you, Mrs. Burley. Next, I should like to speak with Mr. Nevill." The coroner pivoted to address the man.

Mr. Nevill looked somewhat pale. His hand stilled on his knee, wrapping around the front and clasping it.

"You are one of the administrators of the Amicable Society," the coroner said. "What is your occupation?"

"I own a tailoring shop," Nevill replied, straightening in his chair.

"And how did you come to meet Mr. Phelps?" Thetford asked.

"We were introduced by a friend of mine, Isaiah Jarret." Nevill glanced toward one of the men in the witness row. "He is a long-time patron of my shop."

Hadrian turned his head toward Tilda just as she glanced at

him. They exchanged a meaningful look. He knew she was keen to hear what Jarret would say.

Thetford studied Nevill. "Did you become acquainted with Phelps because of the prospect of the Amicable Society, or did you become friends first?"

"Jarret had told me that he and Phelps were considering starting a friendly society. They were looking for a third person to help with the administration, and Jarret thought of me. I was interested. Phelps and I became friends because of that."

The coroner nodded. "But Mr. Jarret did not become an administrator of the Amicable Society. Why not?"

Nevill rubbed his knee again and slid another glance toward Jarret. "He and Phelps had a disagreement as to the core beliefs of the society. Phelps wanted it to be focused on the ward and the people who live here. Jarret agreed with that but was also insistent that the society be teetotal. Phelps refused, and Jarret ultimately removed himself from the planning."

Thetford seemed to think a moment and glanced at Furnier before addressing Nevill once more. "After that, you approached Mr. Furnier to be the third administrator?"

Nevill nodded. "He was also a client, as well as a bank clerk—the same as Jarret. Jarret would have overseen the financial matters, so I suggested Furnier to take his place."

Thetford's brows gathered together. "How was your relationship with Mr. Phelps? You said you were friends. Did you ever disagree, particularly about matters pertaining to the Amicable Society?"

"We were good friends. I am greatly distressed by his death." Nevill's jaw tightened. "He was the primary driver behind the society."

Hadrian noted that Nevill did not answer Thetford's question. Since Hadrian had seen a vision in which Nevill and Phelps appeared to argue, Nevill's prevarication seemed suspect.

"What about the matter of the ill members who were

recruited and told they could collect benefits after six months?" Thetford asked. "How did that happen?"

"Walter—Phelps, that is—hired a canvasser. Timothy Eaton had worked for the Prudential Assurance Company, and we thought he would be an excellent person to help us grow the society quickly." Nevill grimaced, his features creasing into deep lines. "However, it seems Eaton was recruiting members who were ill and lying to them about when they would be eligible for benefits." He dashed a pained look toward Mrs. Cardy.

"That is unfortunate," Thetford stated. "Why has the money collected from those members, such as Gilbert Cardy, not been returned to them?"

Nevill paled. "I, ah, you must ask Mr. Furnier. I do not manage any of the financial matters."

Taking a deep breath, Thetford pivoted slightly. "Why did you accompany Phelps home the night of his death?"

"He invited me for a nightcap, which he often did after the meetings."

"Why was Furnier not included?" Thetford asked.

A pink flush crept up Nevill's neck and flooded his cheeks. "We knew Furnier would decline. He always preferred to return home with his wife following the meetings."

"What time did you leave Phelps's house that night?"

"Nearly eleven, as Mrs. Burley said."

Thetford narrowed his eyes at Nevill. "Did you see anyone on the street?"

Nevill shook his head. "I was in a hurry to return home. It was late."

"And Mr. Phelps was alive when you left him?"

"Of course!" Nevill sat stock straight, his eyes rounding. "I'm deeply saddened by what happened. It's unconscionable." He pulled a handkerchief from his pocket and dashed it over his eyes.

"Thank you, Mr. Nevill." Thetford turned to the jury. "We will adjourn for a short break. You may stretch your legs, but please don't speak with anyone and do not leave the room." The coroner regarded the witnesses next. "I give you the same instruction, including those of you who have already testified. You may be called upon again." Finally, he looked toward the spectators. "You may stand, but do not speak to the jury or the witnesses. If you choose to leave the room, you will not be readmitted."

Thetford turned and went to speak with the clerk.

Hadrian turned his body toward Tilda as Maxwell did the same.

Tilda looked to Maxwell. "Eaton has been murdered."

Maxwell's eyes rounded. "That changes everything."

CHAPTER 11

*T*ilda wasn't sure how it changed things, though it did complicate their investigation. "What do you mean? Other than that we can't interview him now." That was a major disappointment. Now the two men who would know the most about whatever the fraudulent membership scheme may be were dead.

"Yes, that is what I mean. Our investigation has become more difficult." Maxwell frowned. "How did you find out about Eaton?"

In a hushed tone, Tilda explained what Chisholm had told them earlier.

"Eaton's murder poses many questions and seems directly connected to our investigation." Maxwell looked at Hadrian. "It will be most helpful if Nevill and Furnier agree to hire you. Will you speak to them after the inquest?"

"That is my plan," Hadrian said.

Thetford addressed the room once more and announced the inquest would begin again. He turned toward the witnesses and addressed Furnier. "Mr. Nevill explained how you came to know Mr. Phelps. Was what he said accurate?"

Furnier's mouth was tightly set. "Yes."

"Would you say that you and Mr. Phelps developed a friendship like he and Mr. Nevill?" the coroner asked.

"We were not friends, no. We were colleagues."

Thetford cocked his head. "Why weren't you friends?"

"We didn't have a great deal in common. He and Nevill are not married and, apparently, shared an affinity for a *nightcap*." Furnier sniffed as if he smelled something unpleasant.

"Does it bother you that they didn't invite you to share their nightcap routine?"

"Not at all," Furnier replied sharply. "I do not imbibe."

"You are teetotal then?" Thetford clarified.

"Yes." Furnier lifted his chin. His expression was that of someone who believed themselves superior.

"Did you have a problem with the society not being teetotal?"

Furnier's brow creased as he looked up at the coroner with irritation. "Clearly, I do not, or I would not have worked so hard to found it with Nevill and Phelps. I shared their belief that the Amicable Society would be a benefit to the Coleman Street Ward."

"Thank you, Mr. Furnier. I appreciate your candor," Thetford said. "Can you tell us how Mr. Eaton was hired to be a canvasser?"

"That was Phelps's idea." Furnier's tone held a faint note of derision, and Tilda wondered if he'd been against hiring Eaton. "I would tell you to ask him, but obviously you cannot. Phelps thought a canvasser would grow our membership more quickly and suggested Eaton. Nevill and I asked to meet with him, which we did. I was impressed with his experience working for the Prudential Assurance Company. However, given what he did whilst recruiting members for the Amicable Society, I regret not speaking with someone there about his tenure. I took Phelps's assurances."

"Can you please state what Mr. Eaton did whilst recruiting

members for the Amicable Society?" Thetford asked. "Specifically, I would ask that you speak to your knowledge of the collection of fees."

Tilda leaned forward slightly. This was most important to their investigation.

Furnier's gaze was cool. "You've already heard that Eaton was recruiting members who were ill and telling them they could collect benefits after six months, which was against our established policy. We require a year of membership before one may collect benefits. Eaton added their names to the membership roll and gave me the entrance fees every Sunday, which I added to the lockbox on Mondays before our weekly meeting."

"Did you ever find a discrepancy in the amount Eaton gave you?"

"No," Furnier replied firmly. "All the required funds were accounted for."

Thetford's gaze was fixed intently on Furnier. "Did Mrs. Cardy ask for her husband's fees to be refunded?"

"I'm not aware of her doing so."

"Thank you, Mr. Furnier. One last question. Who, in your opinion, would want to kill Mr. Phelps?"

"Someone with no moral compass," Furnier said with disgust.

The coroner turned his attention to the next witness in the row of chairs. "Dr. Giles, you are the society's physician. What is your exact role?"

The doctor's gaze fixed on the coroner as he responded. "I assess the health of potential members in order to determine if they are eligible for benefits. I will also ensure members are deceased before benefits are distributed."

"What method do you use to establish someone's eligibility?"

Shifting in the chair, Dr. Giles looked away from Thetford. "I interview them regarding their age, state of health, and the existence of illness within their family."

Tilda sensed the doctor was uneasy with this question.

Thetford regarded him expectantly. "Do you conduct examinations to ensure they are providing accurate information about their health?"

The doctor still did not meet the coroner's gaze. "Not always."

His response seemed to carry an edge of regret, which Tilda could understand. The process Dr. Giles used to ascertain a member's eligibility seemed rather inadequate.

"How did you come to work for the society?" Thetford held up a hand. "Forgive me, I'm not sure if you are a paid employee. Are you?"

Dr. Giles flattened his spine to the back of the chair and pushed his shoulders back as he returned his focus to Thetford. "I will be paid when it comes time to review claims for benefits."

"You are not currently compensated for assessing potential members?" Thetford asked.

"No."

"Let us return to my question. How did you come to work for the society?"

The doctor smoothed his hands over his thighs. "Phelps had placed an advertisement in the newspaper. I called on him to discuss the position, and he hired me."

"Since you are not currently paid for your work with the society, are you employed elsewhere?"

A slight frown marred Dr. Giles's classically handsome features. "I work with another physician on Gresham Street."

Thetford cocked his head. "I'm curious why you would accept a position with the society in addition to your other employment. What was your reasoning?"

"I live in Coleman Street Ward, and I was eager to be involved in a friendly society dedicated to the ward's benefit." The doctor's voice sounded tight, and Tilda wasn't certain he was being entirely honest. Perhaps he was nervous.

"What was your relationship with Timothy Eaton?" Thetford asked, his eyes narrowing slightly. "Were you aware he was admitting members who did not meet the health requirements?"

"I barely knew him, and no, I was not aware."

Thetford blinked. "You said that you interview potential members about their age, health, and illness within their family. Did you not assess every member? Let me be specific. Did you assess Mr. Cardy's health prior to his membership?"

Dr. Giles's face flushed. "I did not."

"Then why was Mr. Cardy allowed to become a member?" The coroner watched Giles intently, but he also cast glances toward Mrs. Cardy, as well as Furnier and Nevill.

"You'll have to ask them." Dr. Giles flung his hand toward the two living administrators. "I did not approve Cardy or anyone else who may be ill. That is not what I agreed to do." His voice rose slightly.

Thetford's brows darted up. "What do you mean? What *did* you agree to do?"

Tilda was glad he asked the question, for she found Dr. Giles's choice of words notable. She was also watching—and noting—the others' reactions. Mrs. Cardy watched the interrogation with open hostility, whilst Nevill appeared pale, and Furnier looked peeved.

"Precisely what I already told you. I assess potential members."

"But you did not assess Mr. Cardy?" Thetford confirmed.

"No." The doctor gave his head several vigorous shakes for good measure.

"You seem angry about this," Thetford noted quietly. "Why?"

Dr. Giles took a breath and rolled his shoulders. "I do not like my reputation impugned. I would not misrepresent someone's medical state. I was not aware Eaton was admitting members. I am not an administrator. The three of them did not include me in all the society's business." He sent a perturbed glance toward Nevill and Furnier.

"I understand," the coroner said evenly. "Thank you, Dr. Giles."

Thetford turned his attention to Furnier. "You said Eaton recorded new members in the membership roll and that you accounted for the entrance fees. Did you not account for the health qualifications of these members?"

"That is not my responsibility," Furnier said coolly. "That is up to Dr. Giles and Nevill, since he is our membership director."

Nevill's face turned scarlet. "I— Walter said anyone Eaton admitted was fine! I didn't realize they hadn't been assessed by Giles!"

"It is a shame we can't ask Mr. Phelps if that's true," Thetford said with a humorless smile. "May I assume that your recollection would be at odds with his, and that you may have argued about such matters?"

"We did not argue," Nevill grumbled, his gaze shifting to the floor.

"Others have testified that you have," Thetford noted. He drew a deep breath and returned his attention to the doctor. "Thank you, Dr. Giles."

Thetford took a few steps as his gaze moved to the next person in the row of chairs and asked his name.

"Isaiah Jarret."

"You knew Mr. Phelps?" the coroner asked.

"I did." Jarret sent a dark look toward Phelps's body and gave his head the barest shake. The man was middle-aged, with thinning sable hair and long side whiskers that were sprinkled with gray. His eyes were hooded beneath brown, bushy brows.

"Mr. Nevill said you introduced him to Mr. Phelps. How did you come to be acquainted with the deceased?" Thetford asked.

"I met him at St. Stephen's one Sunday," Jarret replied. "We shared an affinity for Wren's architectural designs. We would visit his buildings and discuss them."

"It sounds as though you became friendly," Thetford observed. "But then you fell out over the teetotal business?"

A faint scowl marred Jarret's high forehead. "I took issue with Phelps about more than just his penchant for drink. He was not from this area, and I found it strange that he'd come to this ward to start a friendly society." Jarret crossed his arms over his chest. "He said his grandfather was born in the ward and that he wanted to reestablish roots here."

Thetford nodded. "Do you know where Phelps originated from?"

"Somewhere in Kent. He was always vague about it, just as he was concerning his wife. She died year before last, and that's what prompted him to come to London."

"Phelps does not seem to have been employed," Thetford said. "Do you know how he came to have money?"

"He said it was from his wife's family. Though he seemed to live modestly, he had a few nice things at his house—decent table linens and a fancy pair of brass candlesticks—and he dressed well enough." Jarret unfolded his arms. "He had plenty of liquor too." He made this comment with derision.

"You argued with Phelps about whether the society should be teetotal?" Thetford asked.

"We disagreed. I didn't really argue with him," Jarret said with a shrug. "There wouldn't have been any point. I withdrew my involvement."

The coroner shifted his attention to Mrs. Burley. "Ma'am, did you witness Mr. Jarret arguing with Mr. Phelps?"

"I did." Mrs. Burley pursed her lips briefly as she glanced toward Jarret.

"That was last autumn," Jarret interjected, his brows pitching into a V as he glared at Mrs. Burley. "And it was more of a disagreement."

The coroner leveled a cool stare on Jarret. "I'm speaking with

Mrs. Burley just now." He returned his gaze to her. "Have you seen Mr. Jarret at Mr. Phelps's house recently?"

Mrs. Burley nodded. "He called on Mr. Phelps on Sunday evening. He wasn't there long, and when he left, he stalked away from the house with an angry expression."

Thetford inclined his head. "Thank you, Mrs. Burley." He clasped his hands behind his back as he addressed Jarret. "Why did you call on Phelps on Sunday?"

Jarret crossed his arms again. "I'd heard about Gilbert Cardy being admitted to the society whilst ill and that he'd been told he'd be eligible for benefits after six months. I went to Phelps to ask him what happened and what could be done to help the Cardys."

"And what did Phelps say?"

"He said it was the canvasser's fault—Eaton. Phelps refused to take any responsibility, nor would he commit to providing any relief." Jarret scowled. "What sort of friendly society leaves a widow and her children unprotected? Especially if Phelps truly wished to improve the lives of the residents of Coleman Street Ward."

Thetford nodded vaguely. "You mentioned a pair of brass candlesticks, however the inventory of the house conducted by the police show a single brass candlestick. You are sure there were two?"

"Completely," Jarret replied with firm confidence.

The coroner exchanged a look with Chisholm, who then wrote on his notepad. Tilda felt certain they'd just identified the murder weapon. Thetford had said the candlestick could have caused Phelps's wound, but that it had been thoroughly cleaned. It made more sense that a second candlestick was used and then removed from the house.

"Thank you, Mr. Jarret." Thetford moved on to the man wearing glasses. "Mr. Amos Rippon?"

Tilda exchanged a glance with Hadrian. Their assumption had been correct.

Rippon was perhaps a few years older than Tilda. He seemed nervous—his jaw was clenched, and his eyes kept darting about. At last, he managed to fix his gaze on the coroner. "Yes."

"Thank you for coming today, Mr. Rippon. I hope it wasn't too much trouble. Please tell us what you do for employment."

"I'm—" His voice scratched, and he cleared his throat. "I'm a clerk at the Prudential Assurance Company."

"Are you acquainted with Mr. Eaton?" Thetford asked.

"Yes. We worked together for Prudential as canvassers."

"Were you also friends?"

Rippon hesitated and cast his gaze toward the floor. "Er, yes."

"Why did Mr. Eaton stop working at the Prudential Assurance Company?"

Again, Rippon didn't immediately answer. His neck reddened above the collar of his shirt. "He was sacked."

"You know I'm going to ask why, don't you?" Thetford regarded Rippon expectantly.

"They accused him of pocketing money he collected from people," Rippon replied. He looked up at the coroner. "But he didn't. Tim's a good sort."

"You speak of him in the present tense," Thetford noted. "Are you not aware that Mr. Eaton was found dead on the banks of the Thames yesterday?"

Gasps filled the room, followed by whispers. "Silence, please," the coroner called out sharply.

Rippon paled. "I didn't know. Poor Tim." His entire frame, along with his features, drooped with sorrow.

"Indeed." Thetford paused briefly before continuing. "After Eaton was sacked by the assurance company, he found employment with the Amicable Society. What do you know of his work there?"

"Only that he enjoyed it. He liked helping people. No one was friendlier than Tim." Rippon smiled sadly. "I can't think of anyone better to recruit people for a friendly society."

"Do you know if he was pocketing any money meant for the society?" Thetford asked.

"He wouldn't," Rippon said firmly, shaking his head. "You shouldn't speak ill of the dead."

The coroner's brows arched briefly. "I was merely asking a question. It's not my job to form an opinion. Thank you for your testimony, Mr. Rippon."

Unclasping his hands, Thetford moved to stand before the unknown woman with the half-veil. "I appreciate you coming today, Mrs. Atkins." He glanced toward the clerk. "This is Mrs. Charles Atkins." He returned his attention to the lady, who tilted her head back to look up at him. "Will you tell everyone how you knew Mr. Phelps?"

"I met him at church one Sunday." Mrs. Atkins spoke with a breathy rasp. "We became instant friends. He told me of his plan to start a friendly society, which I found to be a wonderful idea. I was eager to provide financial support to ensure its success."

"Did he ask you for that support or did you offer it?"

Mrs. Atkins was silent a moment. "I don't recall." She waved her gloved hand. "It doesn't matter. I invested in the society because I believed it would provide a much-needed service to the ward. My husband, God rest his soul, would have wanted to partner with Mr. Phelps. As a woman, I could not found the society with Mr. Phelps either. I gave him money instead."

"You gave it to him?" Thetford asked with surprise. "Or you loaned it?"

"It was an investment of sorts," Mrs. Atkins explained. "Mr. Phelps explained that I would earn a dividend, but not for a year."

Tilda paid close attention to the reactions of the other witnesses, namely Nevill, Furnier, Giles, and Jarret. The latter seemed genuinely surprised. He turned his body toward Mrs. Atkins and regarded her with open curiosity.

"Were you aware of the accusations regarding members being admitted to the society despite being ill?" the coroner asked.

"I'd heard the rumor, but I can't believe Mr. Phelps would have allowed such a thing to happen," she said with a tsk. "I'm sure it was a clerical error."

Mrs. Cardy, who sat to Mrs. Atkins's right, turned her head and glared at the other widow.

"Did you speak with Mr. Phelps about the matter?" Thetford asked.

"Perhaps. I don't exactly recall—we discussed a great many things." She paused to smile briefly. "We took tea together every Thursday. Last week was the last time I saw him."

"It seems as though you were close friends," the coroner observed. "Do you have any ideas as to who may have killed him?"

"I would never comment on such a ghastly act. Indeed, I don't really wish to be here today, but I'm concerned this entire situation will cast a shadow over the goodness of the Amicable Society. I earnestly believe the society should be preserved." She added the last with a great deal of fervor.

"Thank you, Mrs. Atkins." Thetford pivoted to address the final witness, Mrs. Cardy. "We appreciate your presence here today, Mrs. Cardy, so soon after the loss of your husband. How long had he suffered from consumption?"

"Well over a year," Mrs. Cardy replied. "I can't say for certain. I think one of my daughters is sick now," she added sadly.

Tilda's chest constricted. The poor woman had been through enough.

The coroner's brow creased. "I'm sorry to hear that. Your husband paid an entrance fee to join the Amicable Society. Do you know how much that was?"

"'E said it was six shillings."

"The entrance fee for his age is half that," Furnier said. He glowered toward Mrs. Cardy. "You are mistaken, ma'am."

"I am not mistaken," she snapped back. "I know what my 'usband told me!"

"Do you have a receipt for that fee?" Furnier asked crisply.

Mrs. Cardy crossed her arms and squeezed herself into a smaller shape than she already was. "All my 'usband got was a certificate with 'is name on it."

"Does the certificate include anything about the entrance fee?" Thetford asked.

Mrs. Cardy shook her head, and Thetford's brow creased. "Can you present this membership certificate?"

Her cheeks flushed. "I burned it."

Thetford looked toward Nevill. "I'd like to see what this membership certificate looks like."

Nevill frowned. "I'm afraid I can't help you. That was something Eaton provided to the members he recruited."

"I see." Thetford exhaled, then pressed his lips together. "There is some discrepancy about the entrance fee charged then, and there is no documentation to determine the truth of the matter." He returned his attention to Mrs. Cardy. "What of the weekly dues, Mrs. Cardy? How much did Mr. Cardy pay and to whom?"

"That Eaton fellow came and collected it every Sunday—four pence," Mrs. Cardy replied. "I took on extra sewing and even some washing to pay for it."

"That is also twice the usual amount," Furnier interjected. "Our records show he paid tuppence every week."

Tilda wondered if the records to which Furnier referred could be the ledger Hadrian had seen when he'd touched Phelps's desk.

Mrs. Cardy uncrossed her arms and turned her body toward Furnier, her face flushing. "'E shouldn't 'ave been paying anything since 'e wasn't even supposed to be a member! The society needs to pay us back!"

Furnier clenched his jaw and sat back in his chair, fixing his gaze straight forward.

"Unfortunately, we are not here to discuss what may or may not be owed," Thetford said regretfully. "I am trying to determine who may have killed Mr. Phelps, and I'm sorry to say, Mrs. Cardy, that you have the best motive of anyone. However, I am not sure you had the means or the opportunity to do so. It is my understanding that you were at home with your daughter the last night Mr. Phelps was seen alive. We did not ask her to come and confirm this, but she has done so to multiple people. Do you swear that is the truth?"

"I do," Mrs. Cardy said, her eyes wide. "I 'ave five children, and I would not 'ave left them late at night to do anything."

"Thank you, Mrs. Cardy. I am very sorry for your loss." The coroner turned and faced the jury. "I think you will easily find that Walter Phelps was murdered by a blow to the head with a brass candlestick—one of a pair—that is now missing. He was killed sometime between ten o'clock in the evening and four o'clock in the morning. Several people might have wished him dead, and you've heard from some of them today. Of particular note is the potential fraud of the Amicable Society, in which it solicited members who were ill, perhaps with higher fees for membership. It is up to you to determine if this is a case of murder. You must now deliberate and inform me when you have reached a conclusion. I will dismiss everyone from this chamber so you may discuss the matter."

Thetford turned to the witnesses. "Thank you for your time today. You are dismissed." He looked to the gallery. "Please remove yourselves to the common room."

A constable moved to open the door as people stood. The witnesses began to file out, though a few loitered as the spectators departed.

Tilda noted that Clement was still standing in the corner, furiously scrawling in his notebook.

"I can't see that it will take them long to decide this was a murder," Maxwell said softly as they prepared to leave.

"Particularly since it seems Thetford was able to identify the murder weapon," Tilda said. "And the fact that it's missing."

~

*H*adrian saw the gleam of anticipation in Tilda's eyes. She always looked like that when they uncovered important clues in an investigation.

"The missing murder weapon was perhaps the best piece of evidence to come from the inquest," Maxwell said.

Whilst that may be true with regard to the murder—which was, of course, the point of the inquest—Hadrian found the testimony regarding the society's operations much more helpful. "There was a great deal of good information about the society's membership practices. I wish Thetford had asked Furnier about the records that show what Cardy paid weekly. I think there must be a missing ledger."

"Are you going to ask Nevill and Furnier about that?" Tilda asked.

"I will try," Hadrian replied. "I'm going to attempt to catch them now."

Tilda briefly touched his sleeve. "Be cautious. They are agitated and may not take your inquiry kindly."

Hadrian nodded. "I understand."

They moved into the common room where people milled about. Many went directly to the bar, including Nevill. Hadrian decided to start with him. "I'm going to speak with Nevill first."

"We'll speak with the Furniers," Tilda said, inclining her head toward the center of the common room where Mr. and Mrs. Furnier stood.

Hadrian hastened to Nevill, who held a pint of ale. He'd just taken a sip as Hadrian arrived.

"Afternoon, Nevill," Hadrian said. "I hope the inquest wasn't too much of an ordeal."

Nevill exhaled. "It was unnerving. It seemed as though the coroner thought I could be a suspect in Phelps's murder." Nevill shuddered. "He was a good friend. And he was committed to the success of the Amicable Society. That blasted Eaton took advantage." The color left Nevill's face, perhaps because he just recalled the man had also been murdered. He took a long drink of his ale.

"I do hope the society will continue," Hadrian said. "It provides a good service, and I'm confident you and Mr. Furnier will ensure it operates without further violations of policy."

"We don't really know what happened for sure," Nevill said quickly and with a touch of agitation. "Nor can we ask Phelps or Eaton."

Hadrian wanted to argue that Mrs. Cardy had told them, but he didn't want to anger the man when he was trying to curry his favor. "That is a shame. I hope you won't think me too forward, but I wonder if I might help. It seems the society is in need of a canvasser, and I would offer myself for the position."

Nevill's features twitched with surprise. "You would? But you have a splendid job at a gentlemen's club. Why would you want to leave that?"

"I'd prefer to work closer to the ward or in the ward," Hadrian replied. "I also wouldn't mind sleeping when it's dark," he added with a sheepish smile.

"I suppose that's fair, but a great many men would eagerly trade their job for yours." Nevill frowned briefly. "I can't think we'd pay as well as the club either."

"That may be, but I am ready to try something new. This opportunity might lead to something else."

Nevill studied him a moment. "You may be just what we need.

Are you up to recruiting members and working hard to put all this nastiness behind us?"

"Yes. In fact, that is why I'm so keen to try this." Hadrian met Nevill's gaze with the most earnest expression he could summon. "I believe in the Amicable Society, and I would hate to see it end before it's even really begun."

"Let us speak with Furnier." Nevill drank down the rest of his ale, then looked about, as if to dispose of the empty glass.

Seizing the chance to perhaps see one of Nevill's memories, Hadrian took the glass from him with a smile. "I'll find a place for that for you."

"Thank you," Nevill said with a grateful nod before taking off toward Furnier, who still stood with his wife, as well as Tilda and Maxwell.

Hadrian glimpsed Tilda before the common room faded away. He saw Phelps, and he recognized the setting—Phelps's parlor. Phelps sat in a chair with a glass of something—presumably liquor—in his hand. He shook his head, and Hadrian sensed Nevill was frustrated. Phelps waved his hand and very clearly said, "No." Hadrian could read his lips. After sipping his drink, Phelps adopted a placating expression and said something more. Hadrian tried again to discern his words from watching the man's lips move, but it wasn't as easy as discerning, "No." Whatever he said seemed to soothe Nevill, for the agitation Hadrian felt dissipated. Then the vision faded.

Blinking, Hadrian saw that Nevill now stood with Furnier and the others. Tilda was watching Hadrian with a slightly hooded gaze.

Hadrian deposited the glass on the nearest table and hurried to join them. He'd apparently missed Nevill explaining his idea because Furnier took one look at Hadrian and said, "We don't need a new canvasser. The last one caused enough trouble."

"We need to continue growing our membership," Nevill argued. "A new face out and about in the ward could be just what we need. And Beck is well-spoken and amiable. I think he'll have great success recruiting members."

"We can't commit to anything now," Furnier said firmly. "We must deal with the current problem. A few members have already asked for their entrance fees and weekly dues to be refunded—and they aren't ill."

"Have you considered calling an emergency meeting?" Hadrian asked. "It might be better to address the situation before rumors can take hold. We don't want a misinformed membership."

Furnier's features smoothed slightly. He seemed to consider what Hadrian said.

"Listen to this young man." Mrs. Atkins stood just behind Maxwell. The veil of her hat swept over half her face, leaving one eye and cheek, part of her nose, and her entire mouth visible. She regarded them with an expectant expression. "We must put an end to the gossip about what's happened. The previous canvasser was clearly operating as a rogue agent, but he is, thankfully, gone. We must look to the future, and I think this handsome young man would be an excellent face for the society." She regarded Hadrian with keen approval—and perhaps a bit of prurient interest. "What is your name?"

"Nigel Beck, ma'am. I'm pleased to make your acquaintance."

"You speak with such elegance. You can't be from the ward."

Hadrian didn't want to respond to that directly. "I've worked in a gentlemen's club in St. James for several years. It's not difficult to adapt to their manner of speaking." He was disappointed that she found his speech so distinguished, as he'd really tried to change the way he spoke.

"Well done." Mrs. Atkins looked to Nevill and Furnier. "Hire him. I'll pay his salary if that will persuade you. We need to right this sinking ship!"

"We'll discuss it," Furnier said tightly. He glanced over at Nevill, who nodded, albeit somewhat reluctantly.

"I'll expect your answer—in the affirmative—by Friday." Mrs. Atkins smiled at Hadrian. "Are you a newer member?"

"I just joined this week, in fact." Hadrian gestured toward Maxwell. "Along with my brother-in-law, Albert Harwood. This is my sister, Mrs. Harwood." He motioned to Tilda.

Mrs. Atkins's barely spared a glance for Maxwell or Tilda. She focused even more on Hadrian, her eyes narrowing slightly. "I would like to become more acquainted with you. I've ideas for the society and how you may encourage people to join our movement. Why don't you come for tea tomorrow? Or do you have to work at the club?"

"I can come for tea," Hadrian said, thinking he'd bring Tilda along. But probably not Maxwell as he would almost certainly be at the mercantile house. Hadrian did not feel bad about that. It wasn't that he didn't like Maxwell. He just preferred to conduct the investigation with Tilda and only Tilda. They were a team.

"Wonderful," Mrs. Atkins said before shifting her gaze back to Nevill and Furnier. "Now, when will the emergency meeting be?"

"There won't be an emergency meeting," Furnier said again, sounding as though his teeth were clenched.

Mrs. Atkins waved her hand. "You discuss it, and I'm sure you'll find I'm right."

The coroner stepped out of the inquest room and called for everyone's attention. "The jury has ruled that Mr. Walter Phelps was murdered by a blow to the head. I will assist the police in whatever manner I can as they search for the killer. If anyone has more information to share or learns anything that would be helpful, I advise you to come forward and speak to me or to Inspector Chisholm."

Clement stepped forward, his gaze fixed on the coroner. "When will the inquest for Mr. Eaton be?"

"I'm not certain there will be one," Thetford said.

"He died of natural causes then?" Clement asked.

Thetford exhaled, and his brows drew together. "I am not prepared to say anything further on the matter."

Clement looked about the room, but his gaze didn't settle on anyone. "I can't be the only person wondering if Phelps and Eaton were killed by the same person."

"You may wonder all you like," Thetford said, his voice carrying through the strangely silent common room. "Only the evidence will reveal the truth."

CHAPTER 12

*T*ilda exchanged a brief glance with Clement and managed to silently communicate that she wished to speak with him. A few moments later, he meandered by her, and she whispered, "Call at Number Five White Alley this evening. At the back door."

Clement didn't nod, but their eyes met the barest moment, and she knew he understood.

After milling around the common room a few more minutes, Tilda, Hadrian, and Maxwell took their leave. When they were a distance from the pub, Tilda, who walked between the two men, looked first at Hadrian and then at Maxwell. "Mrs. Atkins called the society a movement. Do you suppose anyone else thinks of it in that way?"

Hadrian chuckled. "Mrs. Atkins seemed quite dedicated to a society in which she cannot even be a member."

"I found that puzzling," Maxwell said. He glanced at Hadrian. "And she was rather taken with you."

Tilda looked toward Hadrian. "I noticed that as well. Perhaps we can use that to our advantage at tea tomorrow."

Hadrian grimaced. "If we must."

Maxwell frowned as they turned into White Alley. "I'm very disappointed I cannot accompany you to Mrs. Atkins's. This job at the mercantile house is becoming a burden, in addition to being horribly tedious. I'm not able to learn anything there. I wish they needed a second canvasser, but it's proving challenging enough to persuade them to hire one—even with Mrs. Atkins offering to pay for the position."

Tilda understood Maxwell's frustration. She disliked not being an investigator out in the open, but at least she was able to make inquiries as Mrs. Harwood. Maxwell was stuck working at a job that only served to support his own disguise. "Perhaps you should try to fill the other open position."

"The third administrator?" Maxwell asked. They'd arrived at Number Five, and Maxwell unlocked the door, opening it for Tilda to walk inside. She removed her hat as Hadrian and Maxwell followed her into the entrance hall.

Maxwell secured the door behind them. "I would have to convince Furnier and Nevill—but mostly Furnier—that I have a higher purpose in wanting to fill this role. I could tell them I have access to a wealthy benefactor who may wish to invest in the society—someone like Mrs. Atkins."

Tilda walked into the parlor and perched on the settle.

Hadrian followed and sat next to her. "But does the society need another Mrs. Atkins? And how would you know a wealthy benefactor?"

"I could say my mother works as a housekeeper in Mayfair," Maxwell suggested as he took one of the chairs. "Perhaps she works for the Earl of Ravenhurst." He smirked at Hadrian.

Hadrian chuckled. "That's not bad."

"It's regrettable we didn't realize there could be a wealthy benefactor in our scheme," Maxwell said to Hadrian. "You could have participated in the investigation as yourself, which would probably have been more pleasing to you."

Hadrian's brows drew together sharply. "Do you think I mind

pretending to work at a gentlemen's club or taking on the role of canvasser? Don't forget that I'm participating in this investigation because I want to, not because I'm being paid."

"I'm aware." Maxwell cocked his head. "And I do find it perplexing."

"You shouldn't," Hadrian said crisply. "I'm doing this because I enjoy it, and because Miss Wren and I work well together."

Tilda sensed an undercurrent of discord between the two men. "I would say it's proven helpful to have the three of us."

She wondered if Maxwell felt threatened because of Hadrian's title. But why would Hadrian be annoyed? He was no longer on the outside. He was very much part of this investigation.

Tilda wanted to return to discussing Maxwell's idea of trying to become one of the administrators. "Since the society already has a benefactress in Mrs. Atkins, it might be more compelling if you had a personal reason for wanting to be involved with the society's growth and management."

"Well, that is rather easy," Maxwell said plainly. "I do have a personal reason. I lost two siblings when they were young, and their funerals were a financial hardship."

Hadrian swung his attention to Maxwell. "I'm very sorry to hear of your losses," he said softly.

Tilda looked at Maxwell with sympathy. "Would you want to share that?"

"It's the truth, so yes, I would. I do happen to genuinely hope the Amicable Society can continue. It will be a great help to many people."

Tilda knew how important that was to him. "You have a true calling to help others. It might also help your cause if you have a plan for how to handle the current situation regarding the members who were admitted fraudulently."

Maxwell blew out a breath. "We've no idea how many there are besides Gilbert Cardy."

"You could offer to audit the membership rolls and finances," Hadrian suggested.

Tilda flashed a smile at Hadrian. "That's a good idea." She returned her focus to Maxwell. "You could tell them it's preferable to have you—a new member, who couldn't possibly have been involved in anything that has gone on before—complete the audit. It may help calm the gossip and allay people's concerns."

Maxwell's eyes gleamed with approbation. "That is brilliant, Miss Wren." He sobered quickly. "Even if they accept me into that position, I can't leave the mercantile house without provoking curiosity as to how I will earn a living, which means I am still not dedicating as much time to the investigation as I would like. The administrators all maintained their jobs, except for Phelps."

"Meaning they weren't paid." Tilda glanced toward Hadrian. "Unlike Ravenhurst will be as the canvasser. Perhaps we can convince Mrs. Atkins that her financial support should include paying a salary to the administrators of the society—or at least one of them."

Hadrian met her gaze then Maxwell's. "We could argue that paying someone to manage things may protect against future attempts at fraud."

"Another excellent idea," Maxwell declared.

"We'll speak with Mrs. Atkins about it tomorrow," Tilda said.

Maxwell's eyes held a sheen of anticipation. Tilda felt a kinship with his eagerness to find new ways to conduct their investigation in order to find the truth.

Mrs. Kilgore entered the parlor. "Pardon me for interrupting. I heard you'd arrived and wanted to ask how the inquest went."

Maxwell nodded at her. "Of course. The jury found that Phelps was murdered, which is no surprise. The coroner interviewed many people, including your cousin."

"I knew she would be there. I hate that she had to endure it. Do you think Chisholm is any closer to arresting the murderer?"

"I don't know," Maxwell replied. "Thetford was able to identify the murder weapon, so that should help."

"We also learned a great deal about how the society operates," Hadrian said. "That will aid our investigation."

Mrs. Kilgore nodded. "Good. I know my husband is eager for you to make progress. As am I. It's not easy being away from home—though I am pleased to help."

"Based on today's testimony from several people, it does seem as though Mr. Eaton was responsible for breaking the society's policy and admitting members who were ill," Tilda said. "Furthermore, it seems he may have been charging them double the entrance fee and doing the same with their weekly dues."

Mrs. Kilgore gasped. "He is truly despicable."

"We should try to confirm that," Tilda noted.

"We learned Eaton was sacked by the Prudential Assurance Company for skimming money," Hadrian said. "Can we assume he was charging a higher amount, depositing the society's stated fees, and then pocketing the difference?"

Tilda had the same thought, but she tried not to draw conclusions before she'd made the proper inquiries. "I don't like to assume anything, especially since Mr. Rippon, who seemed to be a good friend of Eaton, was so adamant that Eaton would never do such a thing." Her gaze met Hadrian's, and she was sure he was recalling the vision he'd seen at the Wolf and Dove, in which the two men appeared to be good friends, especially since the barman said he saw them together regularly.

Maxwell looked to Mrs. Kilgore. "I should mention that Mr. Eaton was found dead."

She gasped once more, her eyes rounding. Her hand fluttered to her chest. "Was he also murdered?"

"That has not yet been determined," Maxwell said.

Mrs. Kilgore turned her head toward the back of the house. "I think I hear someone knocking."

Tilda had thought she'd heard it too. "That will be Mr.

Clement. I asked him to come to the back door. Would you mind letting him in?"

Nodding, Mrs. Kilgore turned and left the parlor.

Maxwell blinked at Tilda. "I didn't know he was coming."

"I invited him after the meeting," she said. "I knew we'd have matters to discuss regarding the investigation."

Ezra Clement entered the parlor a few moments later. His bright yellow plaid pants made the furnishings look even duller. "Good evening, Miss Wren, Lord Ravenhurst." His gaze settled on Maxwell last. "You must be Inspector Maxwell, though I deduced that at the inquest when you sat with Miss Wren and his lordship." He offered his hand to Maxwell, who rose to shake it.

"Welcome, Mr. Clement. Please, sit." He gestured to the remaining open chair and retook his seat.

Clement situated himself. "I'm pleased to make your acquaintance, Inspector, and glad to be a part of the investigative team."

Maxwell scowled faintly. "What have you to share with us this evening?"

"I confirmed that Eaton was indeed skimming money that he collected on behalf of the Prudential Assurance Company. He would tell clients one number that was always higher than what was actually due, and he kept the difference."

"So much for Rippon's insistence that his friend would never do such a thing," Hadrian noted sardonically.

Clement narrowed his eyes slightly as he inclined his head toward Hadrian. "I thought the same thing, so I had a drink with Rippon at the pub. I asked if it was possible that he didn't know his friend very well." Clement's eyes gleamed with anticipation. "Rippon broke down and confessed that he'd lied at the inquest. He hadn't known for certain that Eaton was stealing, but he suspected it. Apparently, Eaton had a younger sister in an orphanage and was trying to save enough money so she could live with him."

"How sad," Hadrian said.

"If it's true," Clement replied. "I've yet to confirm the sister actually exists."

Maxwell frowned. "That's a rather cynical thing to say."

Clement shrugged. "Eaton might have said that to his friend to justify what he was doing. Nobody wants to be seen as a villain —especially villains."

"That's good work," Tilda said, appreciating Clement's commitment to finding the truth. "Thank you, Mr. Clement. What lines of inquiry do you plan to make after today's inquest?"

"Almost too many to count," the reporter replied. "I'm sure you feel the same."

"Quite," Tilda agreed. "Ravenhurst and I are having tea with Mrs. Atkins tomorrow. He's trying to persuade Nevill and Furnier to hire him as their new canvasser, and she is in favor. In fact, she offered to pay his salary. She believes Ravenhurst would be helpful to ensuring the society's good reputation."

Clement's brow creased with confusion. "Does she know he's an earl?"

"No, she just thinks he's handsome," Maxwell replied with a chuckle.

"Well, that could be helpful in many ways." Clement laughed. "I trust you'll let me know how the meeting goes?"

"Certainly." Tilda inclined her head. "Let's plan on exchanging information again, say, Friday evening at the Lion's Heart in Little Moorfields?"

"I'll be there." Clement rose. "I must be on my way. Enjoy the rest of your evening."

After he departed, Maxwell frowned slightly. "I'm not sure I care for Mr. Clement."

"You can trust him," Tilda said.

Maxwell exhaled. "And I trust you. I do not think Sergeant Kilgore or Inspector Chisholm would support his involvement, however."

"Won't they appreciate knowing that Rippon lied today at the inquest?" Hadrian asked.

Tilda met his gaze, surprised that he was, in a way, defending Clement.

"That *was* helpful to learn," Maxwell allowed. "I should share that with Chisholm. I'll don a cloak and go to the police station."

"Could you ask him if we may search Phelps's house?" Hadrian asked. "I think there must be some sort of record of the society's membership and finances."

Tilda knew he was thinking of the diary he'd seen in his vision at Phelps's house when he'd touched the desk. As far as they knew, that diary had not been found, and it would likely be very helpful to their investigation.

"I am sure the constables thoroughly searched the house," Maxwell said. "Chisholm would have told us if they'd found anything like that, for that would certainly be relevant to our investigation. Still, it can't hurt for us to look too. I'll arrange for us to do so tomorrow evening, after I finish at the mercantile house." He stood and turned toward the entrance hall, where Sergeant Kilgore suddenly appeared.

"Good evening, Sergeant," Maxwell said, sounding surprised. "Allow me to introduce Lord Ravenhurst and Miss Wren."

Hadrian stood and greeted the sergeant, but Tilda remained seated.

"I passed a gentleman in extremely bright trousers as I approached the back entrance to the house. I recognized him from the inquest and thought he was a reporter. Mrs. Kilgore tells me that he is. Why did you allow him to come here? And why would you speak with him?" He seemed to direct his questions—and his irritation—at Maxwell.

"He had information to share," Tilda replied, not wanting Maxwell to bear the sergeant's ire. "He spoke with Rippon after the inquest and learned that he lied." She shared the details of what Clement told them.

"I was just about to go to the station to share all that with Chisholm," Maxwell said. "And to arrange for us to search Phelps's house tomorrow evening. Whilst I'm sure he and the constables were thorough, we'd like to look for any society records that may be there."

Sergeant Kilgore nodded. "I'm confident they were thorough, but it can't hurt to search again. You need to work quickly. I know I said you could have a fortnight to complete this investigation, but I do hope you can finish well before then."

Maxwell nodded. "We are endeavoring to do so. In fact, we have a plan to infiltrate the society as employees." He detailed their scheme to have Hadrian hired as a canvasser and for Maxwell to take Phelps's position as administrator.

"Excellent," Sergeant Kilgore said with an approving smile. He looked at Hadrian. "Mrs. Kilgore has told me of your contributions to the investigation and to the household. I was skeptical when I heard you were here, but I can see you are an intrinsic part of this team. I thank you, my lord."

Hadrian inclined his head. "It is my privilege to be of assistance."

Sergeant Kilgore bid them good evening and went back downstairs.

Maxwell eyed Hadrian. "Shouldn't you have left already?"

Tilda realized Hadrian should have departed some time ago to report for his fake job at the gentlemen's club.

"I don't see the point." Hadrian shrugged. "I won't leave the house, and no one will realize I haven't gone to work."

"That makes sense to me," Tilda replied.

Maxwell was pensive a moment. "Yes, our time is better spent investigating than going to fake employment. After speaking with Sergeant Kilgore, I confess I am feeling more pressure to make progress. I think I must resign my position at the mercantile house tomorrow. I'll tell them I've found another position.

Then I'll speak with Furnier and Nevill about becoming their newest administrator."

"That's a great plan," Tilda said in admiration. She glanced at Hadrian, but his features were enigmatic. She wanted to speak with him alone about how to search Phelps's house tomorrow, but that would have to wait. They could not discuss his ability in front of Maxwell. "I'm glad you aren't returning to Mayfair," she said to him.

"As Maxwell said, we should focus more fully on the investigation," Hadrian said. "Though I must wonder how close we are to reaching a conclusion. The objective was to find evidence of fraud. We now know that Eaton was stealing from the society and fraudulently admitting members, not that he can be prosecuted."

"I am not entirely satisfied that Eaton was the sole culprit." Tilda suspected there was more to the relationship between the two dead men—Phelps and Eaton—than they'd yet uncovered. Furthermore, she wasn't sure that Nevill, Furnier, and perhaps Dr. Giles weren't also somehow involved in fraud or corruption. "I think it is our duty to ensure the society will be operating entirely under the law moving forward."

"I completely agree," Maxwell said. "I do think that our current plans—with both Ravenhurst and I infiltrating the management of the society—will bring this investigation to a somewhat rapid end." His gaze focused on Tilda. "I confess I'll be sorry to conclude our partnership."

"Let's not get ahead of ourselves," Tilda said with a smile. "We've plenty of work to do."

CHAPTER 13

The following afternoon, Tilda and Hadrian made their way to Mrs. Atkins's home in Finsbury Circus. The day was cool but so far, dry. Hadrian's back was a bit sore from sleeping on the bed in the garret. The mattress—which was a generous word for what amounted to a thin layer of straw smashed between battered canvas—was not at all comfortable. Indeed, it was likely meant to be the lower portion of a bed with perhaps a horsehair mattress on top of it.

"That's the third or fourth time I've seen you touch your lower back today," Tilda said as they made their way along Coleman Street.

"My bed's a trifle uncomfortable."

Tilda grimaced. "I'm sure it's not at all what you're used to. Is it terrible?"

"It's survivable," Hadrian assured her. "How is yours?"

"I confess the mattress is rather lumpy. But it's tolerable." She glanced at him. "I'm surprised you wouldn't prefer to sleep at home—and you had a perfect reason to do so with your fake job being at night."

"You also had a good reason to return to Marylebone every night, and you chose not to."

"We are equally dedicated then," she said, with a laugh.

Hadrian grinned at her. "I like to think so." They walked another moment or two, and Hadrian turned his mind to the investigation. "I've been thinking about what you said last night regarding Eaton not being the only person behind the fraud with the Amicable Society. I can't help feeling there are things Nevill isn't saying."

"I agree and would say the same of Furnier and Dr. Giles," Tilda said. "I'm curious how much Phelps knew about Eaton's behavior before he died."

"Enough to sack him?" Hadrian mused. "Eaton left the boarding house over a week before he died."

"It's puzzling that Phelps didn't seek to refund the Cardys' money or look into other potentially fraudulent memberships." Pleats formed between Tilda's pale brows, indicating she was deep in thought. "I hope we can find the membership ledger you saw in your vision and that it can answer our questions."

"I'm hopeful we will learn a great many things at Phelps's house with my ability," Hadrian said. "It's unlikely I will see one of Phelps's memories since he is dead, but hopefully we will be able to discern whose memories I do see, which could lead us to the killer."

"I had the same thought about you touching as many things as possible at Phelps's house in order to find some helpful memories." Her brow furrowed again, but this time with worry. "However, I don't want you to suffer from terrible headaches. I think you must choose what to touch strategically, lest you become overwhelmed."

"I appreciate your concern," Hadrian said. "I will be careful."

"You must stop if your head hurts too much," she said.

He flashed her a brief smile. "I promise I will."

"I will hold you to that." Tilda narrowed her gaze at him. "I'll be keeping my eye on you."

Hadrian could find no fault with that. Indeed, he was pleased she cared so much. But he would make sure they did not leave Phelps's house without learning all they could. He was eager to make a discovery that would help them with both the fraud case, as well as with Phelps's murder.

Hadrian knew Tilda wanted to solve his murder, as well as Eaton's, even if they weren't assigned to do so. He would help her in that endeavor.

There was more to Hadrian's need to make himself useful at Phelps's house. He was jealous of Inspector Maxwell and the connection that seemed to be strengthening between him and Tilda.

"How are you finding this investigation?" Hadrian asked. "Is it a chore to seek Maxwell's approval for things?"

"Actually, he indicated that he trusts me and has given me leave to pursue information as I see fit." A smile lifted her mouth. "It's turned out to be a marvelous partnership."

"That's good to hear," Hadrian said, even as his chest felt a bit hollow.

"I'm glad Maxwell is leaving the mercantile house so that he can focus entirely on the investigation," Tilda said. "Then we can make faster progress. Although, as eager as I am to learn the truth, I confess to feeling a little melancholy when a case concludes."

Hadrian felt the same way, but that was largely because he missed working with Tilda when they were between cases. Not just working with her—he missed *her*.

"Will you really miss working with the inspector when we're finished?" Hadrian asked, thinking of what she'd said to Maxwell last night.

Tilda turned her head toward Hadrian. "Are you jealous?"

Hadrian had to check his feet so he didn't stumble. Had she

seen through him and detected how he truly felt? It shouldn't be surprising. She was an excellent investigator after all. But damn, he was still trying to determine his feelings himself.

Tilda cocked her head and blinked at him. He realized from her expression that she'd meant jealousy in a professional sense.

Hadrian exhaled softly. "Yes, I am jealous of the partnership you have with Maxwell."

"I don't know if it's really a partnership," she said.

"You used that word."

"I suppose I did," Tilda said. "Well, he's not a partner in the way that you're a partner. Perhaps that's simply because you and I have worked on several cases together, whilst this is just the first one with Maxwell. If I'm to work on more investigations with him, perhaps we will also become close." She shrugged as if she wasn't discussing a matter that would likely keep him awake tonight.

Hadrian felt as though he'd been stabbed, because whilst he was professionally jealous of Maxwell, it went far deeper than that. It was apparent—only to Hadrian, thankfully—that he had romantic feelings for Tilda. He knew this more and more with each passing day. In fact, as of this moment, he realized it was an incontrovertible truth. He hoped there might be a future in which they were partners in every sense, that she would be his countess.

However, he doubted most sincerely that would ever come to pass. Tilda bore no interest in a romantic attachment with him or anyone else. Though watching her with Maxwell, Hadrian could see where she might change her mind. She and Maxwell had more in common and shared more similar backgrounds. They also worked in the same field, and since it seemed that police wives could be heavily involved in their husbands' work, Tilda and the inspector could truly be professional partners. And romantic ones too.

They turned into Finsbury Circus, and Hadrian strove to put

the melancholy thoughts from his mind. He would enjoy the time he had with Tilda and hoped this would not be their last investigation together.

"I confess it's very strange to be walking as we make our inquiries," Tilda said with a laugh. "I've become used to riding in your coach with Leach ferrying us about."

Hadrian laughed with her. "I know he misses doing so. He does enjoy being a part of our investigations."

"You're going to see him after this?" Tilda asked.

"Yes, I plan to ask for more supplies for the house, since Mrs. Kilgore seems to enjoy them."

Tilda sent him a faint grimace. "Is it too much to ask for more biscuits for the Cardy children?"

"Not at all," Hadrian replied quickly. "I'd already planned to have Leach ask my cook for more."

"Of course you did," Tilda murmured. "You must certainly be the most thoughtful earl in all of London."

Her words helped to banish any lingering disappointment he felt. They shared a strong bond and a mutual respect and concern for one another. If that was all they ever had, he would still find joy in it. And perhaps there was a tiny glimmer of hope that her feelings toward him could change.

Someday.

They approached Mrs. Atkins's house, and Hadrian knocked on the door. A housekeeper answered, a woman in her middle forties with dark brown eyes and a sharply turned-up nose.

"Good afternoon," Hadrian said. "I am Mr. Beck. This is my sister, Mrs. Harwood. We are here to see Mrs. Atkins."

"Come in. She's waiting for you in the parlor, just there." The housekeeper gestured to a doorway off the entrance hall.

Hadrian thanked her, then inclined his head for Tilda to precede him into the parlor.

Mrs. Atkins was seated at a small table, where a tea tray was already arranged. Since she was not wearing her veil today,

Hadrian could see her entire face. She was near in age to his mother, with blonde hair dappled faintly with white. Her eyes were a deep cornflower blue, and her round cheeks were lightly rouged.

She smiled widely at them, her gaze sweeping over Hadrian and barely noticing Tilda. "Welcome. I'm so pleased you could come today. Do sit." She indicated the other chairs at the table. "You look rather dashing, Mr. Beck."

Hadrian had suffered less perusal at the society balls he'd attended—all of them combined. Mrs. Atkins's interest made him slightly uncomfortable, but he knew it was necessary to put up with her for the investigation.

Mrs. Atkins poured the tea and added milk and sugar without asking their preferences.

"I'm most curious about your involvement with the society," Tilda said. "I had the impression that women weren't allowed to do much—though I understand we're supposed to plan a picnic."

"Oh yes, the picnic." Mrs. Atkins waved her hand. "Walter had spoken to me about it and asked if I would coordinate its execution. I'd planned to call a meeting about that to take place during one of the next few weekly meetings. However, this business with that fraudulent member dying and then poor Mr. Phelps being murdered has quite diverted things."

Hadrian prickled at the woman's description of Gilbert Cardy. He hadn't intentionally committed a fraud.

"I would be interested in helping," Tilda said fervently, slipping into her role as Mrs. Harwood, the eager wife of a member. "I greatly admire your involvement with the Amicable Society. My husband and I are also deeply committed to its purpose. In fact, he would be interested in working for the betterment of the society. Do you think Mr. Nevill and Mr. Furnier will be looking for someone to take Mr. Phelps's place?"

Mrs. Atkins's pale blonde brows drew together. "I'm not sure, but that's not a bad idea. Perhaps you should allow me to present the idea to them. They may be more inclined to consider him if I give him my endorsement."

Hadrian wondered if that was true or if Mrs. Atkins simply liked being the center of attention.

"Or perhaps your brother would be interested in being an administrator as well as the canvasser." Mrs. Atkins smiled rather alluringly at Hadrian. "Dare I hope?"

"My talents are better suited to that of canvasser," Hadrian said. "My brother-in-law is more business-minded and would make a better administrator. I am more…social."

"Oh, I can see that," Mrs. Atkins said. "I will speak to Furnier and Nevill about Mr. Harwood, though no one will be able to replace dear Walter—that's Mr. Phelps. He bade me call him Walter some time ago."

"You were close?" Tilda asked.

Mrs. Atkins nodded. "We became very good friends. Having both lost our spouses, we found solace in one another's company. And, of course, he's the reason I became interested in supporting the Amicable Society. I could see his passion for the ward and for helping people here. I knew I needed to be a part of that."

"How exactly have you supported the society?" Hadrian asked. "You mentioned paying my salary, which is most generous of you."

"I did make an investment at the start, but I expect to be repaid in the autumn. At least, that was my arrangement with Walter." Mrs. Atkins lowered her voice to a near whisper. "Nobody knows, but I paid Eaton's salary. That was between Walter and me."

Hadrian wondered how Furnier, as the man in charge of the funds, wouldn't have noticed that. Surely, he would have wanted to know how Eaton was being paid.

"You gave the money directly to Phelps?" Tilda asked, likely thinking along the same lines as Hadrian. Perhaps Phelps had told Furnier that he was funding Eaton's salary.

Mrs. Atkins nodded before taking a sip of her tea. "Oh, that's delicious. What do you think?" She looked expectantly at both Hadrian and Tilda. They exchanged a glance and, obligingly, each took a drink.

"It's lovely," Tilda said with a smile.

"Very good," Hadrian agreed. "Would you mind if I added just a bit more cream?" He reached for the small jug before Mrs. Atkins could.

"Of course," their hostess said.

The minute he touched the china, a vision rose in his mind. He saw Phelps in this very room. He sat on a settee facing Mrs. Atkins. Hadrian was certain he was seeing her memory. Who else's would it be?

Phelps was angled toward her, his arm on the back of the settee. He smiled at Mrs. Atkins, his gaze warm, with perhaps a touch of longing. Looking down, Hadrian saw that Phelps's other hand was touching Mrs. Atkins's thigh. In the memory, Mrs. Atkins was both flattered and pleased.

Hadrian felt a gentle nudge against his arm. That had to be Tilda. He blinked, which ended the vision, then poured cream into his cup and set the jug back down on the tray. Pain sliced through his forehead sharply, and he took a sustaining sip of tea.

"One of the witnesses at the inquest yesterday said that Phelps wasn't from London," Tilda said. "Do you know where he came from?"

"Reading," Mrs. Atkins replied. "He left there after his wife died. Since his grandfather had always spoken warmly of the Coleman Street Ward, Walter came here."

"He must have had considerable means to make such a move," Hadrian said.

Mrs. Atkins wrinkled her nose, but then smiled almost smugly. "We ought not speak of people's money, but sometimes it can't be helped. Walter seemed to do fine for himself, though he was clearly in need of my financial support to fulfill his vision for the society. I was more than happy to contribute. He was very grateful." She looked at Hadrian. "Just as I'm sure you will be glad when I pay your salary to become the new canvasser. When do you think you will start?"

Hadrian wasn't sure he cared for her innuendo. Perhaps she meant nothing by it, but given the memory he'd just seen, he had to wonder if Phelps had been required to demonstrate some kind of gratitude to his benefactress. It could be that Phelps hadn't minded doing that, but Hadrian most certainly did.

"I would like to start immediately," Hadrian said. "I'm keen to identify others who may have been defrauded by Mr. Eaton."

Mrs. Atkins scowled. "Oh, that man! It's a good thing he's dead, for he has maligned this wonderful society."

Hadrian noted that Mrs. Atkins took pleasure in Eaton's demise. He exchanged a look with Tilda, who clearly concluded the same.

"I want to ensure that Mrs. Cardy and the others are paid for the money they put into the society and can never hope to regain," Hadrian added.

"You think there are others—members who were admitted though they were ill?" Mrs. Atkins blinked at him.

They knew there were others because Mrs. Cardy had confirmed it. But Hadrian didn't think they ought to disclose that. He glanced toward Tilda to see what she thought.

She met his gaze with an infinitesimal nod. "It doesn't make sense that Eaton would have only accepted Cardy," Tilda said. "If his goal was to earn money, I should think he would have continued to recruit people."

"That does make sense," Mrs. Atkins said before shaking her head. "It's a terrible shame. Walter was so thrilled to have a canvasser to increase the society's numbers quickly, and it seemed to be working. We had no idea Eaton wasn't following the society's policies. I suppose we ought to refund anybody who paid money, particularly since people like Mr. Cardy shouldn't have been admitted in the first place."

Mrs. Atkins spoke as if she were a co-administrator with Walter Phelps. Hadrian wondered if Furnier and Nevill were aware of that, and if so, what they thought of her involvement.

He also caught her rather cavalier attitude regarding the Cardys' money. "Poor Mrs. Cardy is suffering a great deal," Hadrian said somberly. "She has five children to feed, and one of them is now sick."

"Hmm, yes." Mrs. Atkins sighed softly, then sipped her tea. Setting her cup down, her eyes lit with purpose as she regarded Hadrian once more. "I must send a note to Mr. Furnier about your employment, and I will call on Mr. Nevill tomorrow at his shop. I will ensure you are working as the canvasser by the end of tomorrow."

No, Mrs. Atkins was not at all moved by Mrs. Cardy's plight. Hadrian decided he didn't care for the woman.

Tilda inclined her head toward Mrs. Atkins with deference. "That is most kind of you."

"It is," Mrs. Atkins replied. Her eyes brightened even more, and her lips parted as she sucked in a quick breath before smiling. "Do you know what would be wonderful? We could grow beyond the Coleman Street Ward."

"But it's the Coleman Street Ward Amicable Society," Hadrian said. "I believe the purpose of the society is to serve the residents of the ward."

Mrs. Atkins lifted a shoulder. "We could just as easily call it the Atkins Amicable Society. I must speak to Nevill and Furnier about this idea as well. Don't you worry, this will all come together, and the society will be more successful than ever. Don't you agree?"

"Whatever we can do to help more people would be most agreeable," Hadrian said diplomatically.

Tilda sipped her tea whilst casting Hadrian a dubious glance.

A short while later, they left Mrs. Atkins's house after securing her promise to also speak with Furnier and Nevill about engaging Maxwell as the third administrator. Hadrian did not think the benefactress was as enthused about that prospect as she was of paying Hadrian's salary.

They walked in silence a few minutes before Tilda touched his arm. "Would you mind slowing down?"

Hadrian stopped altogether and faced her momentarily. "Apologies. I fear I am in a hurry to move away from Mrs. Atkins."

"I do understand," Tilda said as they started walking at a more normal pace. "She thinks rather highly of herself."

"Indeed." Hadrian's shoulder twitched as he recalled the many uncomfortable moments of their interview with the woman. "She has quite a vision for the society. And she spoke as if she were jointly managing things with Phelps."

"I noticed that too," Tilda said. "What did you see when you touched the milk jug?"

"How did you know I saw something?" Hadrian was genuinely curious. He knew he hadn't touched his head, despite being in pain for a time.

"Your expression went blank. It's why I elbowed you. I was afraid Mrs. Atkins would notice."

Hadrian nodded. "That is good to know." Often when he had visions, he was not in a situation where others might be observing him. "I saw Phelps in Mrs. Atkins's parlor with her. They were cozied up together on the settee. His hand was on her thigh. She seemed quite pleased about it."

"I see." Tilda's eyes rounded briefly. "That certainly gives new meaning to what she said about Phelps being grateful to her. Goodness, perhaps she will expect something from you for paying your salary." Tilda made a face of distaste.

"I considered the same thing, and that is precisely how I feel about it," Hadrian said. "I did not have the sense she would expect that from your husband," he added wryly.

"She did not seem as excited to hire him as she was you." Tilda smiled sardonically. "Likely because he's married. I do think Maxwell may have to try to obtain the position without a salary, just as Nevill and Furnier do." She glanced over at Hadrian. "How's your head?"

"It hurt at first, but the ache is gone now. I find the pain with visions doesn't last as long as it once did."

"That's wonderful to hear," Tilda said enthusiastically.

"I'll walk you back to White Alley, and then I'll head to the church to speak with Leach." Hadrian had arranged for the coachman to wait for him each afternoon for one hour at the St. Mary Aldermary Church to receive any directions. Along with asking for the supplies, Hadrian also planned to direct Leach to have his secretary deliver money to Mrs. Cardy from an anonymous benefactor. And he would send her the name of a doctor to whom she could take her sick child—as well as inform her that the expense would be paid.

Hadrian knew he couldn't solve every problem, but he tried to help where he could.

Tilda paused as they approached Moorgate. "Nevill's shop is just down Moorgate, isn't it?"

"I believe so." Hadrian pivoted toward her. "Are you suggesting we stop in?"

"I can think of several things I'd like to learn from him, starting with what Mrs. Atkins's role really is with the society." Tilda gave him a sly look. "And I've just the plan for us to find out. I'll tell you about it on the way."

CHAPTER 14

As they walked to Nevill's tailoring shop, Tilda briefed Hadrian on how she wanted to approach their discussion with the society's most amenable administrator. He seemed to possess a gregarious personality, so it hopefully wouldn't take much to persuade him to share information—without him realizing he was revealing important details helpful to an investigation into the Amicable Society.

The shop was relatively small, especially compared to what Hadrian was likely used to on Bond Street, but it was well stocked. There were a few customers inside, one of whom stood at a counter speaking to a young employee behind it. The other patrons browsed the cases and displays.

Tilda glanced about the shop. "I don't see Mr. Nevill."

"Nor do I," said Hadrian.

They walked toward the counter, passing a display with shirts. Hadrian inspected one briefly. "This is very fine work. The stitching rivals anything I've seen at the club."

Tilda silently applauded him for staying in character. Nigel Beck would have seen finer clothing in the course of his employment, whilst Lord Ravenhurst certainly possessed a dressing chamber full of Bond Street finery.

They continued to the counter and stood for a moment. Tilda waited to catch the young employee's attention.

A door to the back of the shop opened, and Mr. Nevill stepped through. His gaze landed on Tilda and Hadrian and lit with recognition. He walked behind the counter to where they stood. "Good afternoon, Mr. Beck, Mrs. Harwood, what a surprise to see you here."

He narrowed his eyes slightly at Hadrian. "Are you not working at the club today?"

"Later tonight. For as long as I'll be employed there," Hadrian added. "I'm hoping to have a change in profession." He gave Mr. Nevill a hopeful look.

"As the Amicable Society canvasser," Mr. Nevill said with a nod. "I must say, I'm in favor of that, but I need to convince Furnier."

"That is actually somewhat why we stopped by." Hadrian glanced at Tilda. "We just came from tea with Mrs. Atkins."

"I'd heard she invited you," Nevill said. "I trust you enjoyed yourselves."

"It was quite pleasant," Hadrian said, and Tilda silently congratulated his prevarication. "She is most keen to have me in the role of canvasser. As you are aware, she's offered to pay my salary and reiterated that today. She plans to speak with you about the matter."

"Mrs. Atkins is always looking for ways to insert herself into the society's business." Nevill sounded beleaguered.

Tilda gave him a brief, understanding smile. "Forgive me, but we wondered if Mrs. Atkins's considerable interest in the society is entirely welcome. She seems very involved for someone who can't be a member."

Nevill blew out an exasperated breath. "Phelps allowed her to participate—to a certain extent. I know he wanted her financial support, but he also desired her goodwill. She is a well-respected member of the ward." He gave them a knowing look. "It's helpful to have someone like her in your corner."

"'Someone like her?'" Hadrian asked, quoting Nevill.

"Someone with money." Nevill regarded Hadrian as if he should have known that.

"Of course," Hadrian said smoothly. "I wondered if there was more to it than that—perhaps her passion for the society. I can see where her avid support would also be helpful."

"I suppose so," Nevill said. "Though she can be rather invasive about it."

"She almost seems like a member of the administration," Tilda noted. "Or perhaps that's just what she would like to be."

"Perhaps," Nevill said thoughtfully. "I can see how you would gain that impression. That's why Furnier doesn't care for her. It's not her place, or anyone who isn't a member, to be so involved. At least, that's his argument."

"So, Furnier won't be in favor of her paying my salary?" Hadrian asked.

"Not necessarily," Mr. Nevill replied, lifting a shoulder. "He knows that if we're to have a canvasser, the funds will need to come from somewhere, since Phelps can no longer pay for it."

Tilda and Hadrian exchanged another look. Their plan did not include telling Nevill that Mrs. Atkins had been funding Eaton's salary.

"Did Phelps not leave his money to the Amicable Society?" Tilda asked.

Nevill leaned his hip against the counter. "I'm not sure he had a will."

"Perhaps the police know," Hadrian suggested.

"That's possible," Nevill said. "I do think they're trying to locate his relatives. Unfortunately, we are of no help. Phelps never spoke of any."

"And he was from Reading?" Hadrian asked.

"That's right." Nevill cocked his head. "How did you know?"

"Mrs. Atkins mentioned it," Hadrian replied. "It seemed they were very close."

"I think she wanted to be." Nevill snorted. "But I don't know that Phelps entirely reciprocated her attentions. She's always struck me as a bit lonely since her husband died a few years ago. And she doesn't have any children. I think that might be why she's so preoccupied with the society. It gives her a purpose. I do agree with her opinion that the Society's reputation needs rehabilitation," he added.

"My husband and I find we are already quite dedicated to the society," Tilda said earnestly. "I look forward to helping plan the picnic, and Albert would like to become more involved. In fact, we discussed with Mrs. Atkins the possibility of him taking Phelps's place."

Nevill's nostrils flared, and his lips parted in surprise. "You discussed that with her?"

Tilda nodded. "Do you think that would be possible?"

Nevill thought a moment, then pushed away from the counter and straightened his shoulders. "Furnier and I haven't discussed it much, though he suggested the two of us could manage things on our own. However, I find him irritating on occasion." He looked at them ruefully. "Phelps was a good mediator between us. I'm not sure it's wise for the society to operate without a third person, but I'll probably have to convince Furnier that someone ought to take Phelps's place."

Nevill fixed Tilda with a curious stare. "Why is your husband's interest so great? He's only just joined."

Tilda looked down for a brief moment before responding. "He has personal experience with losing members of his family. The cost of the funerals was rather devastating. He would like to save other families from such hardship and heartache."

"Too many people have experienced that," Nevill said with a sad shake of his head. His eyes flickered with a bright emotion, and he suddenly slammed his hand on the counter, startling the clients and the other employee with his physical display. "My apologies." He cast a regretful smile toward them before returning his attention to Tilda and Hadrian and speaking in a softer tone. "We need to reaffirm the Amicable Society's purpose and entice people to join."

"We have work to do to reassure people after all that's happened," Hadrian said with a faint grimace.

Nevill pressed his lips together. "There are some people who would like their money returned. They're worried they won't receive their benefits, despite there being no indication that they won't. The situation with Mrs. Cardy is a simple matter of policy being ignored—and apparently fraud was committed." He said the latter as almost an afterthought, which Tilda found perplexing. "Alas, there's nothing we can do about that now."

"There *is* something you can do," Hadrian said insistently but without heat. "You could refund the money to the people who should not have been admitted in the first place."

Raising his hands, Nevill shrugged. "We don't even know who those people are."

"Don't you have a list of the members who were recruited by Eaton?" Hadrian asked, thinking of the ledger he'd seen in his vision when he'd touched Phelps's desk. He didn't know what it recorded specifically, but it was definitely about members. He was certain it was an important clue.

Nevill frowned. "There is a list, but we'll have to visit every single one of them to ascertain their health. I suppose you and Dr. Giles could do that, though he will not appreciate having to take that much time away from his work. He's trying to establish a practice with another physician, and it's challenging, because not many people in this area can afford his service. He's considered moving west, but he tried that when he was first licensed and was not successful."

"That's unfortunate," Tilda murmured.

"He doesn't have the right pedigree," Nevill said with disgust. "Which is apparently important if one wants to be a physician in certain circles. Where the money is, I should say." He looked at Hadrian. "It's like I told you. Wealth matters. So does position. Those of us without those privileges know this in our bones."

Tilda wondered what Hadrian thought of that. To his credit, his features did not reveal whatever his true reaction might be.

"I do think it will be necessary to identify anyone that needs to be refunded," Hadrian said. "I suppose they'll expect the full amount that they paid, which may differ from what the society has a record of. Where is this list you mentioned?"

"I don't know. Phelps had it." Nevill threw up his hands. "How are we supposed to come up with the money that Eaton was stealing? This is why I worry the society won't survive."

Hadrian nodded. "I understand. There has to be a way we can work things out."

"Perhaps Mrs. Atkins would make a benevolent donation to cover the amount of money we would need to refund the people who were defrauded," Tilda suggested. She wasn't sure the woman would, based on her apparent lack of compassion for Mrs. Cardy and her children, but perhaps Hadrian could persuade her. Tilda inwardly cringed at the thought of him having to play on Mrs. Atkins's interest in him.

"I suppose we can consider that," Mr. Nevill said. "I'll speak with Furnier tonight about all this." He fixed his gaze on Hadrian. "You're sure you're up to the task of reassuring the members, ferreting out the sick, and recruiting new ones?"

"I am," Hadrian assured him.

Nevill nodded. "You must excuse me, as I've clients to attend. After I've had a chance to speak with Furnier, I'll send a message to you, probably in the morning. But I do think you can expect to be our new canvasser."

"Thank you, Mr. Nevill. I'm very much looking forward to our association."

Hadrian held out his hand and Nevill shook it. Tilda knew that Hadrian must be seeing a vision and was eager to hear the details.

They left the shop and walked down Moorgate toward White Alley. "Did you see something when you shook his hand?" Tilda asked.

"It was the same vision I saw when I touched the diary on Phelps's desk. I know now that the memory I saw was Nevill's." He glanced toward Tilda. "That is the helpful thing about seeing a vision when touching someone versus an object. I know definitively whose memory I'm seeing."

"Did you learn anything new?"

"It's clear to me that Nevill was angry with Phelps. I felt Nevill's frustration and ire during the memory." He looked over at Tilda as they turned into White Alley. "I think the cause has something to do with that ledger I saw when I touched Phelps's desk. We need to find it. Hopefully, it will help us determine which members require refunds."

Tilda smiled. "I suspect you might want to do this canvassing job, in large part, to ensure everyone who was defrauded is restored."

"I can't say I trust the current society administration to ensure that happens. They seem…less than committed to that than we are."

"I agree." Tilda couldn't help feeling a surge of warmth toward Hadrian. "The irony is that you are precisely the sort of privileged gentleman Nevill seemed to disdain. And yet, here you have a keener sense of doing what's right instead of what is profitable or easy."

"Which is why no one should make assumptions." Hadrian slid her another glance. "Someone very clever told me that."

Tilda laughed. As they reached Number Five, Hadrian stopped and faced her, prompting her to pivot toward him expectantly.

"Do you feel a great difference in our positions?" Hadrian asked. "I realize we come from different social and economic backgrounds, but overall, I feel a connection with you that transcends both those things."

Hesitating, Tilda wasn't quite sure how to respond. She *did* feel the differences between them, just as she accepted them. "We are very different in some ways and similar in others. I think that is what makes us such a good investigative team."

"You have more in common with Maxwell," Hadrian noted. "Does that make you and him a better team?"

Tilda knew Hadrian was jealous of her working with Maxwell. But he'd started this conversation by asking her about their differences. Was there more to Hadrian's feelings than he was saying?

Of course not, she told herself. Hadrian liked working with her as much as she did with him. Today was an excellent example of why their partnership was so beneficial—and satisfying. "It's difficult to think of a better team than you and me," she said with a smile. "Especially after all we accomplished today."

He chuckled. "You're right. I'm off to meet Leach." He continued down White Alley toward Coleman Street, and Tilda watched him walk away. She wondered how she would feel if Hadrian solved crimes with someone else. The image of him working with another woman made her instantly irritated. It also prompted her to ask herself an important question.

Would she feel the same if he were conducting investigations with a man?

～

*A*fter returning from his meeting with Leach, Hadrian learned they were confirmed to visit Phelps's house that evening—under Chisholm's supervision. He would be careful to conduct his scrutiny without drawing the inspector's attention.

After what Tilda had noticed during Hadrian's vision at Mrs. Atkins's house, he would be on his guard.

After a quick dinner, Hadrian, Tilda, and Maxwell made their way to Phelps's house. Maxwell led the way into the narrow alley that led to the back of the dwelling, where there was a small yard with a privy. Tilda and Hadrian followed behind.

They'd already updated Maxwell on everything they'd learned from Mrs. Atkins and from their visit to Nevill at his shop. Maxwell was pleased to hear that Mrs. Atkins was in favor of him becoming a society administrator, and he hoped that Nevill would be able to convince Furnier to accept him, as well as hire Hadrian.

Maxwell had shared that his resignation from the mercantile house had been met with distress. They'd asked him to continue working a few more days whilst they searched for a replacement. He'd consented to working the remainder of the week—Friday and Saturday.

Chisholm was waiting for them at the back door to Phelps's house with a lantern in his hand. "Evening. Where would you like to begin your search?" His tone was derisive.

"Do you find this to be a waste of time?" Maxwell asked, voicing what Hadrian was thinking.

"Yes. But Sergeant Kilgore insisted you be allowed to search the house—*and* that I supervise."

"I suggest we start in the parlor, as that is where Phelps's desk is located. Anything to do with the Amicable Society is likely in there." He gave Maxwell a pointed look. "We searched it *thoroughly*."

"I deeply appreciate you satisfying my curiosity to investigate Phelps's house for myself," Maxwell said. "I'm sure you understand how important it is for me to conduct a thorough inquiry as my position requires."

Chisholm exhaled. "I suppose I do." He went into the house and started through the scullery, moving through the kitchen before continuing upstairs to the ground floor. Maxwell trailed directly behind him, and Tilda and Hadrian brought up the rear.

Tilda stopped short on the landing and glanced back at Hadrian. "Did you hear something upstairs?"

They stood silent for a moment. Hadrian detected a slight scraping sound. "I think so."

"Let's have a look." She moved to the stairs leading up to the first floor. Placing a foot on the first step, she turned her head back toward him. "I see light coming from upstairs," she whispered.

Hadrian nodded in response. It occurred to him that they should alert the inspectors, but he didn't wish to make any noise that would draw attention. So he remained silent and followed Tilda. They crept upward slowly and quietly.

At the top, Tilda paused, going completely still as she appeared to listen. There came another sound, and this time it was most definitely human—a female voice saying something not quite discernible.

The sound came from the right. Tilda pivoted toward the sound and walked through a doorway.

Hadrian was right on her heels and immediately saw the source. A woman knelt on the floor next to a bed that had been pushed out of alignment from the wall. Light glowed from a lantern on the floor on the other side of her.

She pressed on a board and turned her head to look at them, her eyes rounding slightly before she appeared to school her features into a stoic mask.

"Good evening," Tilda said pleasantly, but Hadrian heard the urgency in her tone. "Who might you be?"

The woman's gaze turned wary. "I am Mr. Phelps's new housekeeper. Who are you?"

"I am Mrs. Harwood. My husband is a member of the Amicable Society." Tilda gestured to Hadrian. "This is my brother, Mr. Beck."

Tilda sent him a brief look, and he could tell from her expression that she did not believe the woman was a housekeeper.

Neither did Hadrian.

"Are you cleaning something down there?" Tilda asked.

Hadrian had to stifle a smile at the sardonic lilt of her tone.

The woman sniffed. "Yes, the floor under the bed was quite dusty." She braced her hand on the bed and appeared as if she was going to rise.

Hadrian noted that her hands were empty. "Except you have no cleaning supplies."

Before she could respond, he rushed to assist her, grabbing her hand. He was immediately rewarded with a vision.

He saw Phelps, but he was younger. The woman whose memory he saw held Phelps's hand as they stood beside a bed. In it was a man, perhaps in his early twenties. His eyes were closed, his features ashen. Hadrian had a horrible feeling the man was dead. The woman felt sad, which could support his belief, but she was also oddly hopeful. It was most unsettling.

Hadrian looked down at the woman's hand in the vision and saw that she wore a wedding ring. Before he could detect anything else, the vision faded as the woman released his hand.

Blinking, Hadrian looked at her left hand and saw the same wedding ring. "Where do you and your husband live? Are you residents of the Coleman Street Ward?"

"No." The fake housekeeper glanced toward the door.

Hadrian sensed her desire to flee.

Tilda narrowed her eyes at the woman. "You should know there is a police inspector downstairs. Why don't you tell us what you were looking for under the bed?"

The woman's eyes rounded briefly, and she suddenly dashed around Tilda toward the door. Tilda turned and raced after her.

Hadrian followed. He saw Tilda grab the woman's arm at the top of the stairs. Something fell from the woman and hit the floor. She tried to wrench her arm away from Tilda's grip, then turned and pushed Tilda's chest.

Tilda gasped. Time froze as she flailed.

Hadrian's heart stopped, and his vision tunneled. He lunged forward, praying he could grasp her before it was too late. Except it was.

Tilda tumbled backward down the stairs.

CHAPTER 15

Tilda windmilled her arms as she sought to grab something to save herself from falling. But there was nothing, save the air around her, as she fell backward down the staircase.

She'd seen movement below her on the stairs, just before the woman had pushed her. She could only hope it was one of the inspectors.

Suddenly, a solid form clasped her, stopping her fall, and making her grunt softly at the contact. Her breath came in ragged pants as her heart hammered. The arms around her were strong and safe.

"I've got you," Maxwell said, holding her close. "Are you all right?"

She managed to nod but couldn't quite form words yet. Looking toward the top of the stairs, she saw Hadrian grasping the woman, holding her by both arms. He appeared furious, his face red and his lip curled so that his teeth were partially bared.

"I'm fine," Tilda managed. "She pushed me."

"I saw," Maxwell replied.

Chisholm pushed past them and climbed to the top of the stairs. He set the lantern he carried on the newel.

Tilda turned her head and met Maxwell's concerned gaze. "Truly, I'm fine. We caught her looking for something under Phelps's bed. She said she was his new housekeeper."

Both of those things had to be a lie. Tilda was eager to learn what Hadrian had seen when he'd touched the woman. There was no doubt he'd had a vision, for his gaze had taken on that odd look he had when he was transported into someone's memory.

"You can let me go now," she said to Maxwell.

He loosened his grip, but he made sure she was standing steady on the stair above him before he released her. "You're sure you're all right?"

She nodded. "Thank you. I'm very glad you were there to catch me."

"I am too," he said with warm sincerity, his eyes dark with concern.

Chisholm took custody of the woman, whilst Hadrian bent to retrieve what she'd dropped.

Tilda had heard it hit the floor. "What is it?" she asked as she ascended the stairs. Maxwell followed her.

"A pouch." Hadrian opened it and peered inside. "Full of money." He handed it to Maxwell.

Tilda was certain the woman had found it under the bed. At the top of the stairs, Tilda turned to the right and returned to the bedchamber. Hadrian followed close behind her.

When Tilda had entered before, she'd been focused on the woman. She now noticed the room was disheveled—the dresser drawers were pulled out and clothing was strewn on the floor.

Kneeling where the woman had been next to the bed, Tilda ran her hands over the floor. "This board isn't level with the rest."

Hadrian knelt beside her and managed to pull the board up.

He set it aside and Tilda looked into the space below. "I see something." She reached in and pulled out a stack of letters.

Tilda perused the first letter. "It's to someone named Philip Walters, and it's signed, 'with love, your Ida.' She asks him about London and how things are going with the society. She says she misses him and hopes to see him soon."

"There's something else beneath the floorboards." Hadrian reached into the space and pulled out a metal box. "This is the box I saw in Phelps's memory," he whispered.

"You're certain?" Tilda asked in a barely audible tone.

Hadrian nodded as he opened the box. He removed a photograph of a man and a woman. The. man was Phelps—but a younger version of him—and she was a more youthful likeness of the woman who'd pushed Tilda down the stairs. Hadrian turned it over. "Philip and Ida Walters 1857" was etched on the back.

"Walter Phelps," Tilda said softly, turning her head to meet Hadrian's gaze. "That's an alias. Is there anything else in the box?"

Hadrian looked. "No. And nothing else under the floorboards."

She started to stand, but Hadrian leapt up and helped her.

"Are you all right?" he whispered, holding her hand a trifle longer than was necessary.

"I am." She gave him a brief smile. "Thank you."

He released her, and she turned her attention to Mrs. Walters. She and Chisholm, as well as Maxwell, had followed them into the room whilst Tilda and Hadrian investigated the hiding place under the floor.

Tilda fixed her gaze on Mrs. Walters. "Walter Phelps, or should I say Philip Walters, was your husband?"

The woman pressed her lips together and looked away, focusing her gaze on the hearth. Her features were blank, her jaw clenched.

Tilda stepped toward her. "Did you know that your husband is dead?"

Mrs. Walters darted her gaze back to Tilda, her eyes widening. Then she pressed her hand to her mouth. "I did not."

Tilda didn't believe her. Her reaction seemed artificial.

"Did you find the money in the box under the floorboards?" Maxwell asked.

"It's my money." Mrs. Walters shot a glance toward the pouch in Maxwell's hand.

"Please answer the question," Maxwell said sharply. "Did you take that money from the box?"

"Yes, my husband put it there. For *me*."

"How did you know he'd done that?" Chisholm asked.

Mrs. Walters hesitated. She appeared quite vexed; her sable brows were drawn into a V over her amber eyes. "We have always kept our savings under a floorboard beneath our bed."

Tilda wasn't sure she believed the woman—not when the bedchamber looked as though it had been searched and also since she'd already been dishonest. "Why did you lie about being his housekeeper?" When the woman did not reply, Tilda continued. "Why did your husband tell everyone that his wife was dead?"

Her lack of immediate reaction revealed that she was not surprised to hear this.

"You can answer these questions here or at the police station," Chisholm said darkly. "But you will answer them."

Mrs. Walters's brow creased, but only briefly. She glowered defiantly at Chisholm. The inspector glared back at her.

Though the woman hadn't answered the questions, Tilda offered more—in large part to gauge her reaction. "When did you arrive in London? Did you come from Reading?"

Mrs. Walters's nostrils flared, and Tilda could see the woman's heart was beating furiously and her breath was coming fast. She was trying very hard to remain calm, but she was overexcited, perhaps nervous or even scared.

Maxwell moved closer to Mrs. Walters and gave her a stern stare. "You should know there is a woman who lives across the street who sees everything. She'll know when you've been here, even if you came in the back."

Tilda wasn't sure that was true, but she appreciated Maxwell's bluff.

"Philip stopped writing to me," Mrs. Walters said. "I came to find out why, but now I hear he is dead."

Though Mrs. Walters gave this reasoning, Tilda still didn't believe she wasn't aware that her husband was dead. If she was, she certainly wasn't overly upset about his demise.

"Surely, you must have realized something was amiss when you arrived here this evening?" Tilda noted. "Weren't you expecting your husband to be at home?"

Mrs. Walters pursed her lips. "I assumed he was out."

Tilda gave her a pointed look. "Yet, instead of waiting for him, you searched this room."

"It appears as if she did the same downstairs," Maxwell said. "I don't think she knew where the money was hidden. But why lie about that?"

"It's my money!" Mrs. Walters repeated.

Tilda realized Mrs. Walters had left the letters and the photograph under the floorboards. Apparently, she didn't care as much about those as she did the money. Perhaps she would have taken them, but then heard Tilda and Hadrian approaching and decided to replace the floorboard before she was caught.

"I'm going to take Mrs. Walters to the station," Chisholm announced. "She may be more inclined to tell the truth when she's locked in a cell. Or perhaps charged with murder."

Mrs. Walters gasped and tried to pull her arm from Chisholm's grip. "I did not murder my husband!"

"Whoever said I was speaking of your husband's murder?" Chisholm said shrewdly. He turned to Maxwell. "Will you alert the constable out front that we have Mrs. Walters and need to transport her to Old Jewry?"

Maxwell turned and disappeared downstairs.

Chisholm looked to Tilda and then Hadrian. "I'll need those letters and the photograph."

"Of course," Tilda replied. "I would like to review the letters for any pertinence to the fraud perpetrated by the Amicable Society." Given the money found beneath the floor, Tilda strongly suspected Phelps had been involved in the swindle they now knew Eaton had conducted.

"I'll let you know if we find any," Chisholm said in a tone that brooked no argument. Tilda reluctantly offered the letters to him. "Hold onto them until we are downstairs and I can turn custody of Mrs. Walters over to the constable." He looked sideways at Mrs. Walters. "Let's go." He propelled her toward the doorway and the stairs.

Tilda sifted through the letters she held. "There's only about a half dozen here."

"Are you going to quickly scan them on the way downstairs?" Hadrian asked with a half-smile.

"I will try," she replied.

"We'll descend slowly," he added with a wink before plucking up the lantern that had been next to Mrs. Walters on the floor.

They started toward the stairs, and Tilda did her best to skim the letters with Hadrian holding the lantern for her. She stopped halfway down, her eyes fixing on a line in one of the letters:

I am relieved this will be the last one and look forward to our new life in Cornwall.

"*H*adrian," Tilda whispered urgently. "Listen to this." She read him the line and met his gaze as his eyes rounded.

"What does that mean?"

"I can only guess, but if Mrs. Walters is anticipating a new life and feeling relief over a 'last one,' I'm inclined to believe this entire friendly society is a fraud perpetrated by Phelps." Tilda returned her attention to the letter. "There's more." She read the next few lines.

I need to leave Reading soon. Someone from Maidstone is poking around. Can I come to you, please? Yours, Ida.

"What happened in Maidstone?" Hadrian asked.

"Perhaps Phelps started another friendly society there. I'm reminded of Jarret's skepticism regarding Phelps coming to the Coleman Street Ward to found the Amicable Society. Phelps said his grandfather was born here, but perhaps his true reason for starting the society was to enrich himself."

"He may have even lied about his grandfather," Hadrian said darkly. "It seems Phelps was quite dishonest. Like you said a bit ago, I'm inclined to think he was part of Eaton's fraud."

Tilda's pulse had picked up speed when she'd read the letter, and it continued to thrum as she thought through this discovery. "Or perhaps he was even the instigator. He could have hired and instructed Eaton to recruit ill members and overcharge their fees."

"You should read the rest of the letters before you hand them over to Chisholm." Hadrian flicked a glance toward the entrance hall.

Nodding, Tilda quickly scanned the others, but none contained any damning information such as what she'd just shared with Hadrian. She reread those bits and committed them to memory.

"He's not there?" Chisholm's voice thundered through the house.

Hadrian frowned. "I wonder what that's about."

"We'd best find out." Tilda hurried down the stairs with Hadrian, and they made their way along the short corridor to the entrance hall.

Chisholm still held Mrs. Walters, and Maxwell's brow furrowed.

Hadrian held the lantern up. "What's amiss?"

Chisholm's brows drew sharply together. "The constable is not at his post. Maxwell, you'll need to accompany me. Take the evidence from his lordship and Miss Wren."

Tilda did not take exception to Chisholm addressing her and Hadrian by their real identities. Mrs. Walters would likely be in custody for some time, particularly if they could prove she was part of a conspiracy to defraud the members of several friendly societies.

Maxwell frowned briefly at Chisholm. "I've matters to look into here for my own investigation."

"Actually, you may want to accompany them to the police station," Tilda said. "I've just read something in one of Mrs. Walters's letters to her husband that bears investigation."

Tilda met Mrs. Walters's amber gaze. "You wrote to him that you were looking forward to your new life in Cornwall, as well as expressing relief that 'this will be the last one.' You also mentioned someone in Maidstone 'poking around' and that you would need to leave Reading. What did you mean by 'last one,' and why would you need to leave Reading?"

Mrs. Walters's lips parted, but she clamped her mouth shut. Her jaw quivered, however, revealing her high emotions.

Noting the surprised look on Maxwell's face, Tilda continued speaking to Mrs. Walters. "Am I correct in guessing that 'the last one' refers to the Amicable Society and that its proceeds will fund your new life in Cornwall?"

The woman did not answer. Her gaze was mutinous, which Tilda interpreted as an indication of guilt.

"You must answer," Chisholm said harshly.

Tilda took a step toward Mrs. Walters. "Your husband has defrauded countless innocent people, including a woman whose ill husband paid money into the Coleman Street Ward Amicable Society and is now dead. She is unable to collect his death benefit because he never should have been admitted to the society in the first place. Now, she and her five children are struggling and have had to rely on the kindness of others to pay for her husband's burial."

Mrs. Walters's lips had practically disappeared as she'd listened to Tilda.

"You don't deny that your husband has committed fraud?" Tilda asked gently.

"No," Mrs. Walters croaked.

Tilda let out a quick breath of relief. "How many friendly societies did your husband start?"

"This is the fourth." Mrs. Walters turned her head toward Chisholm. "But I didn't help him! I did what a wife should—I supported my husband and did not interfere with his business."

"And you took the money he stole," Maxwell said with disgust. "You planned a nice life for yourselves in Cornwall, apparently. You are not without guilt, Mrs. Walters, particularly since you pushed Miss Wren down the stairs. Perhaps you can try to redeem yourself somewhat by sharing all that you know."

"I didn't mean to push her—it was an accident. I don't know anything about this society." Mrs. Walters sniffed. "I haven't even been in London."

"You're here now," Hadrian observed drily. "When did you arrive?"

Mrs. Walters narrowed her eyes at him. "Are you really a lord?"

"An earl, yes." He kept his expression pleasant, but Tilda saw the steel in his gaze. He didn't care for Mrs. Walters but wanted her to reveal information, so he would try to put her at ease.

The woman swallowed, and her features darkened with apprehension. "I arrived yesterday."

"But you're not staying here?" Tilda knew she wasn't and wanted Mrs. Walters to confirm it.

"I'm lodging in a boarding house in Cheapside," Mrs. Walters said.

"Why wouldn't you stay here with your husband?" Tilda asked.

Mrs. Walters shrugged. "I was tired and decided to find a boarding house."

"That hardly makes sense," Chisholm said with a faint sneer. "It does not appear you're being honest with us."

"I didn't kill him!" she cried.

Chisholm's eyes glinted with distrust. "I can't say I'm inclined to believe you."

Maxwell regarded Mrs. Walters expectantly. "Was the money you took from beneath the floorboards from the Amicable Society?"

"I don't know where it came from." Mrs. Walters clenched her jaw.

"Who else was involved with your husband's friendly societies?" Tilda asked. "Did he have accomplices?" She was thinking of Eaton and wanted to know if Phelps had hired any canvassers with the other societies he'd formed.

"I don't know. Like I said, I didn't help him with any of that. I was quiet and dutiful, as a wife should be."

Chisholm scoffed. "Dutiful wives don't follow their husbands to London and keep to the shadows upon learning their husband is dead. Nor do they steal into his house and behave like a criminal." He looked to Maxwell. "Let's go. We can finish questioning her at the police station."

Tilda was torn between wanting to accompany them and preferring to stay in the house so Hadrian could use his ability without their supervision. Since she and Hadrian weren't invited, it seemed they would do the latter.

Maxwell took the letters from Tilda and the photograph from Hadrian. "I'll see you later at home."

His use of the word "home" jarred Tilda momentarily. She did not think of Number Five White Alley as home and was surprised he did.

The inspectors left with Mrs. Walters, and Tilda closed the door behind them. She turned to face Hadrian. "At least now we can search the house, and you can touch things without worry of supervision."

"Agreed," Hadrian said. "But I can see you're disappointed you won't be at the station when they continue to interrogate Mrs. Walters."

She smiled. "You know me too well."

He smiled in return, and Tilda's belly did a little flip.

"I wonder what happened to the constable?" Hadrian mused.

"I do too." Tilda glanced toward the closed door. "It's odd that he wasn't at his post whilst Mrs. Walters was here."

"Do you think she had something to do with his absence?"

Tilda narrowed her eyes. "I think anything is possible, especially given what we know about her now."

"Have we solved the fraud scheme?" Hadrian asked.

"Perhaps," Tilda replied. "I'd like to determine the specifics, such as whether Eaton was doing what Phelps instructed or acting on his own."

"It seems likely that Phelps was directing him, since he apparently has a history of committing fraud." Hadrian shook his head. "What do you suppose was his plan with the friendly society? It had to be more than just recruiting men who were ill and overcharging them."

"I think he never intended to pay any of them—ill or not. I wager when we investigate those other friendly societies he started, we'll find that he left with the money before the first year had elapsed."

Hadrian sneered. "Absolutely despicable."

"Yes. Let us find that diary and see if we can learn more about their scheme." She moved into the parlor and went to the desk. Tilda faced him. "Let us discuss how best to use your ability without overtaxing you."

He grimaced faintly. "You should probably know that I already have a headache. Carrying that lantern gave me several of what I think were Mrs. Walters's memories. I saw her lighting the lantern and walking up the stairs and into the bedchamber. She felt anxious and rushed—which makes sense."

"I'm glad you told me," Tilda said, thinking he could just as easily have hidden that fact. "I don't want you suffering. Perhaps we should look around so we can determine what you should touch."

"First, I think we need to search for this diary."

Tilda nodded. "Let's start with the desk. I'll take this side, if you want to take the other." She opened the top drawer on the right side whilst Hadrian moved to the left.

They searched the drawers methodically, moving down each side and opening the corresponding drawers together. Tilda looked over at him to see if he found anything, and he did the same. By the time they reached the bottom drawers, she began to despair of finding the diary.

Hadrian leaned farther over to look into her drawer. "Your drawer is deeper than mine."

Tilda glanced at his, which was open. "It is. Perhaps yours has a false bottom."

Reaching into the drawer, Hadrian removed a few newspapers and set them on the floor. He moved his hands about the interior. "There's a slight gap at the back. Let me see if I can squeeze my fingers into the space." His features creased into a focused expression.

A moment later, he smiled as he lifted the bottom—the false bottom—from the drawer. "There it is."

Tilda looked over his shoulder. "Is that the ledger you saw in your vision?"

He nodded as he set the false bottom atop the newspapers and removed the diary. Grasping the ledger, his eyes glassed over, and Tilda knew he was having a vision. On the one hand, she was sorry they'd hadn't been careful about it—they needed to limit the number of visions he had. But on the other, she was excited about this discovery and was eager to learn what memory he might see.

Several moments passed as Hadrian stood there holding the ledger. Finally, he blinked and set the book onto the desk. He massaged his temple, and Tilda resolved to ensure he would not overtax himself.

"What did you see?" Tilda asked.

"It was murky," Hadrian replied. "I think it was just the same vision I saw when I touched the desk and saw this ledger."

"Nevill's memory?"

"Yes. I saw the same claret sleeve and felt the same agitation. I did see Cardy's name and Nevill pointing at it. He was angry."

Tilda worried about his head. "Is the pain terrible?"

"No. It's already fading. But why don't you open the ledger?"

"Good idea." Tilda opened the book and scanned the first page. There was a single name at the top with two numbers next to it, one of which was clearly a sum. Beneath that were dates and amounts. "This looks to be the record for a member called J. Barnett. The dates listed are a week apart, which could be his weekly dues." Tilda pointed at the number closest to his name. It read twenty-nine. "What do you suppose that is? His age?"

Hadrian looked over her shoulder. Her back grazed his chest, and the contact distracted her momentarily.

"That amount next to his name looks like an entrance fee," Hadrian said. "That's the amount I paid."

"Barnett did not pay an excess amount then."

Hadrian shook his head. "It doesn't appear so."

Tilda turned the page, where there was an identical record for a different man. She turned a few more pages until she reached G. Cardy. The entrance fee was clearly too high. "There he is. And now we can see he was overcharged. I fear we may never learn why Eaton charged people what he did."

"This has to be Eaton's ledger—the one we've been looking for," Tilda said.

Hadrian nodded. "But why would Phelps have it?"

"A very good question." Tilda flipped through the rest of the ledger. The last several pages were empty. "From the dates of the weekly dues, it appears Eaton was recruiting members until a few weeks ago."

"He stopped before Cardy died?"

"Yes, or one could interpret it as he continued to recruit until Cardy died," Tilda said. "Or until his employment with the society was terminated." She pivoted to face Hadrian. He was standing very close, but his proximity was not unsettling. Surprisingly, she found it welcome, perhaps because she'd narrowly avoided injury—or worse—a short while ago. "Do you think Nevill and Phelps were arguing in the memory you saw?"

His long, dark lashes swept over his blue eyes in a quick blink. It was an innocuous movement, but Tilda was bizarrely captivated.

"I do," he replied, jolting her from her senseless reverie. "It's possible they were arguing about Eaton's fraud."

"Perhaps we should speak to Furnier and determine if he knew anything." Tilda turned and surveyed the room. Her gaze went to the doorway into the dining room, and she saw something on the table.

She moved past Hadrian, her heartbeat slowing as she was no longer nearly pressed against him. She hadn't even realized her pulse had sped.

Hadrian accompanied her to the dining room, where an oval table with six chairs occupied the center of the room. A lace-edged tablecloth covered the table, and a half-burned candle lay on its side next to a small dish of salt.

"I wonder if this came from the brass candlestick that was left behind?" Tilda mused. She picked it up and brought it to her nose. "This isn't tallow; it's spermaceti."

"More expensive than tallow," Hadrian noted.

Tilda looked to Hadrian. "Phelps did like to have nice things if he could afford them. And his friendly society schemes ensured he could," she added with disdain.

"May I?" Hadrian held out his hand, and Tilda placed the candle in his palm. Her fingertips grazed his bare flesh, and she tried to pretend the jolt she felt was due to the excitement of the evening thus far.

Hadrian took a deep breath as he wrapped his hand around the candle. His gaze went blank for a moment, then he turned suddenly toward a mirror hanging on the wall opposite where they stood. His chest rose and fell as he breathed deeply. Hadrian set the candlestick down and immediately massaged his temple.

Tilda hated that his ability to see memories caused him pain. "What did you see?"

"Phelps pursing his lips in apparent irritation at the person touching this candle. She's curious and expectant, almost as if he owes her something."

"*She?*" Tilda asked almost breathlessly. "Do you know whose memory you were seeing?"

"I saw her in the mirror," Hadrian said. "It was Mrs. Burley."

CHAPTER 16

Touching the candle, Hadrian had seen Phelps and felt a desire to obtain something, which he attributed to whoever's memory he was seeing. He'd looked down and saw a feminine hand brushing the candle. He recalled there was a mirror and turned his head to see the owner of the memory. Mrs. Burley looked back at him.

"We must call on Mrs. Burley," Tilda said. "Though we need a reason to do so, since we can't say we're investigating a crime."

Hadrian knew how much that bothered Tilda. She wanted nothing more than to be who she was—an investigator. "Perhaps we just say we were walking by and saw Inspector Chisholm escorting a woman out of Phelps's house. We hoped Mrs. Burley might know what's going on."

Tilda's eyes brightened. "Oh, that's brilliant. Mrs. Burley will want to share whatever information she has, *and* she will want to hear that sort of gossip." She wrinkled her nose. "I dislike gossip, but I have no problem playing a role."

"No, you do not," Hadrian noted with admiration.

"We need to take the diary with us," Tilda said.

Hadrian returned to the parlor and fetched it from the desk.

"Should we leave through the front door? What if Mrs. Burley has been watching this whole time?" He frowned. "Our plan won't work."

"Mrs. Burley can't watch everything at every second. As she said herself, she has a household to run. We'll leave through the back."

They departed the house the way they'd come in and made their way to the Burleys' house across the street.

Hadrian tucked the diary into his coat and knocked upon the door. A moment later, Mr. Burley answered, which Hadrian had not expected. He glanced at Tilda and noticed the faintest flare of her nostrils, indicating she was also surprised.

"Good evening, Mr. Burley," Hadrian said.

The man blinked from the other side of the threshold. His small, dark eyes focused on Hadrian. "Good evening. Mr. Beck, is it?"

"Yes," Hadrian replied. "And my sister, Mrs. Harwood."

Mr. Burley inclined his head toward Tilda.

"We were hoping to speak with Mrs. Burley," Tilda said. "We have information she might like to hear."

A faint smile lifted Burley's mouth. "There is no piece of gossip my wife isn't eager to learn, but I'm afraid she's not here. She visits her mother fortnightly, and she won't return until tomorrow afternoon."

Tilda exchanged a look with Hadrian before responding. "I'm sorry to hear that. We were hoping she might know something. We just saw a woman being escorted from Mr. Phelps's house by Inspector Chisholm."

Burley's brows shot up, and he sucked in a quick breath. "Did you recognize the woman?" he asked hesitantly.

"No," Tilda replied.

"You're certain?" Mr. Burley asked, appearing to hold his breath.

Tilda nodded. "Absolutely." She cast her eyes down a moment.

"That's why I was hoping Mrs. Burley was home, so that she could maybe tell us who it was."

"I wish I'd seen her." Burley's mouth was drawn down, and his brow was creased with worry.

"Why is that?" Hadrian asked.

Burley stuck his head over the threshold and looked up and down the street. He lowered his voice, though there was no one around. "I didn't tell the police, but I saw a woman going into Phelps's house late Monday—after midnight."

"Did you?" Tilda asked breathlessly. She was playing the part of a busybody rather well.

"Why didn't you tell the police?" Hadrian asked.

Burley pressed his lips together. "I was worried it might be Mrs. Burley." He grimaced, his features creasing deeply. "She's very curious and sometimes sticks her nose in where she shouldn't. The woman was wearing a cloak, so I couldn't see who she was. My wife wasn't in bed, and I feared she'd gone over to speak with Phelps."

"Why would you think she would do that?" Tilda asked. "Especially after midnight?"

"Sometimes, Florence—Mrs. Burley—has a bee in her bonnet about something. It wouldn't surprise me if she'd gone over to Phelps's house that late. She'd already called on him the day before with Mrs. Cardy—and was upset when he'd told her to mind her own business."

Hadrian wondered if that was the memory he'd seen of Mrs. Cardy in Phelps's house. "Mrs. Burley and Mrs. Cardy called on Phelps together?"

Burley nodded. "Florence was adamant the society should help Mrs. Cardy and did her part by accompanying the poor woman to insist Phelps do something. Phelps's lack of concern made her angry. She complained about him to me several times."

"You thought she went back Monday night to try to convince Phelps to do something?" Tilda asked.

"It wouldn't surprise me," Burley said with a faint shrug. "Some people find my wife annoying, including me sometimes. But she has a good heart and would never hurt anybody. You won't tell the police, will you?"

"Of course not," Tilda assured him. Though Hadrian knew that was a lie. "You don't think she's the woman the inspector escorted away this evening?"

"I don't," Burley said quickly. His neck flushed. "Perhaps I did for a moment, but then I realized it couldn't be. She would not leave her mother, for she requires constant care. Florence's sister lives with their mother, and Florence provides respite for her every fortnight."

"She's a good sister and daughter," Tilda said warmly.

"I'll tell Florence that you saw Inspector Chisholm taking a woman from Phelps's house, if you don't mind," Mr. Burley said.

"Not at all," Tilda replied. "In fact, if Mrs. Burley thinks she might know who the woman is, I'd love to hear. She can call on me at Number Five White Alley if she likes."

Burley nodded. "I'll tell her when she returns tomorrow afternoon."

"Thank you, Mr. Burley. We're sorry to have disturbed you," Hadrian said.

"Not at all. Have a good evening." Burley closed the door.

Tilda and Hadrian turned and made their way toward London Wall.

Hadrian glanced at Tilda. "Well, that was not what I was expecting to hear."

"Nor I," Tilda said. "I think we must consider Mrs. Burley a suspect, regardless of what her husband said. She could very well have been the woman he saw Monday night." She looked over at Hadrian as they turned onto Coleman Street. "You observed her touching the candle in your vision. What if she hit—and killed—Phelps with the candlestick?"

They walked in silence a few minutes. Hadrian thought about

who else the woman could be. "The woman Burley saw could have been Mrs. Walters. I don't think either of us believe she only arrived yesterday."

"No, we don't," Tilda replied. "The woman could also be Mrs. Cardy. You saw her memory in which she was in Phelps's parlor, though that could be from her calling on him with Mrs. Burley on Sunday. Do you recall if she was wearing a cloak?"

Hadrian thought back. "I don't." He frowned, wishing he'd paid closer attention.

"It could also be Mrs. Atkins," Tilda suggested. "It's helpful that we spoke to Mr. Burley, because now we can add Mrs. Burley to the suspect list without having to mention anything about the vision you saw. I was prepared to count her as a suspect based on that, but we wouldn't have been able to share that information, of course."

"I'm curious what Maxwell might be learning from Mrs. Walters at the police station," Hadrian said. "Do you think she's answering their questions now?"

Tilda lifted a shoulder. "It's hard to say. I do wonder whether our investigation will continue, as we are all but certain there was fraud committed by the Amicable Society. We have the ledger showing some were overcharged by Eaton, and Mrs. Walters couldn't deny that her husband had committed fraud."

Hadrian frowned. "Both men responsible for those crimes are dead, so it's not as if they may be prosecuted. I hope we may continue as we are, particularly if Maxwell and I are employed by the society. We seem uniquely placed to find the killer."

"Or killers," Tilda said. "We can't be sure both men were murdered by the same person, though I think it seems likely, since the motive for their deaths could be the same—anger or revenge."

"Are we now officially conducting not one, but two, murder investigations?" Hadrian asked.

A small, sly smile curled her lips. "Perhaps not officially, but no one is going to stop me from investigating."

~

*A*fter arriving at White Alley, Tilda and Hadrian sat in the parlor, sipping port that he'd brought from Ravenhurst House. Bringing the wine was an indulgence, but Hadrian didn't regret it. He was glad that Tilda seemed to enjoy it.

Whilst they were discussing the list of suspects in Phelps's murder, Inspector Maxwell returned. He hung his hat in the entrance hall and joined them. "What are you drinking?"

"Port." Hadrian hoped Maxwell wouldn't have the same reaction the sugar had provoked.

"Did you bring that?" Maxwell asked, appearing curious and perhaps not as judgmental as he'd seemed with the sugar.

"I did. Would you care for a glass?" Hadrian offered.

"I've never had port," Maxwell said. "I suppose I could try a splash."

Hadrian stood and poured a small amount of wine for the inspector. Maxwell accepted it with a nod.

Returning to his chair, Hadrian lifted his glass. "Cheers."

Tilda took a sip and Maxwell followed suit. His face creased, and the muscles around his mouth tightened. Hadrian worried the inspector didn't care for it.

"That's sweeter than I imagined it would be," Maxwell said. "I don't have much experience with wine."

"I didn't either until I met Lord Ravenhurst." Tilda smiled. "I haven't had the opportunity to try much, but I enjoy it, which surprised me."

"Then perhaps I will too." Maxwell took another sip. Whilst his features again registered a reaction, it was less.

"We've news to share," Tilda said. "And we're most anxious to hear what you may have learned from Mrs. Walters."

Maxwell exhaled before dropping onto the settle opposite them. "Unfortunately, Mrs. Walters did not reveal much beyond what you already know. She did tell us that her husband's other friendly societies were in Maidstone, Guildford, and Reading. Chisholm considers her a prime suspect in his murder."

"What is her motive?" Tilda asked.

"That her husband left her and had no intention of living in Cornwall with her." Maxwell gestured with the wineglass. "So, she came to London and killed him."

"Seems a reasonable theory to me," Hadrian said.

Tilda looked to Maxwell. "Was Chisholm able to find out where Mrs. Walters was staying? It would be helpful to search her lodgings."

"In case she hid a brass candlestick there?" Maxwell asked with a faint smirk. "Yes, he'll be going to her lodgings first thing in the morning. Oh, and the constable who was stationed at Phelps's house turned up. He left his post because he'd been lured away by a disturbance. We suspect Mrs. Walters was behind that, but she would not confess to it."

Silence reigned for a moment as they sipped their wine.

"There are other suspects," Tilda said. "Before we list them, let us tell you what we discovered after you went to the police station."

Maxwell regarded her eagerly. "Please."

Tilda exchanged a look with Hadrian. "We decided to call on Mrs. Burley to see if she'd seen Mrs. Walters visit Phelps's house."

Maxwell cocked his head with a faint smile. "I don't doubt that you came up with a reasonable excuse for making this inquiry. What did you say?"

Tilda shrugged. "I played the part of a gossip. What better way to obtain information from Mrs. Burley?"

"Indeed." Maxwell took another sip of port and, this time, did not make a face. "Was Mrs. Burley inclined to exchange gossip?" Maxwell asked.

"I imagine she would have, had she been home," Tilda replied. She went on to explain all they'd learned from Mr. Burley, including what he'd omitted telling the police and why he'd done so.

"So, a female entered Phelps's house after midnight on the night he was killed. That is a fascinating piece of information," Maxwell said. "Well done."

"We'll need to interview Mrs. Burley when she returns tomorrow," Tilda said.

Maxwell pressed his lips together. "We should not. We are not assigned to investigate Phelps's murder."

Hadrian sensed Tilda's frustration as she leaned slightly forward, the muscles of her jaw tight. "Surely we can help Chisholm, since he is busy with Mrs. Walters."

"Eaton's inquest is tomorrow too. Two o'clock at the Swan and Hoop again."

"We should attend." Tilda swirled the small amount of port she had left in her glass. "All of these matters are connected. Whilst I understand we have not been assigned to investigate Phelps's murder, can we agree that we must?" She met Maxwell's gaze with an expectant expression. Hadrian didn't think she would be pleased if Maxwell disagreed.

"Yes, because it pertains to our investigation," Maxwell allowed. "However, we must be discreet."

"Then let us discuss the potential suspects," Tilda said crisply. "Since Phelps's killer may, in fact, be a woman, we can start with them. There are several women who had a motive for murdering him. Most obviously, there is Mrs. Cardy. Her motive is revenge. Then there is Mrs. Walters, whose husband left her and apparently stopped sending her money. He may also have been unfaithful with Mrs. Atkins. As stated earlier, Mrs. Walters's motive is revenge as well."

"And money," Maxwell said.

Tilda looked over at Hadrian. They had already talked through the suspects before Maxwell arrived.

Hadrian continued where Tilda left off. "Mrs. Atkins may also be a suspect. Her motive is not as clear as the others, but we know she possessed some level of interest in Phelps—interest of a personal nature. Perhaps she'd learned he was lying about his wife being dead."

"Now Mrs. Burley is also a suspect?" Maxwell mused.

Tilda nodded. "Her motive is that she was upset about Mr. Cardy being defrauded and Mrs. Cardy and their children suffering as a result."

"There are plenty of male suspects too," Hadrian said. "There's Nevill and Furnier, of course. They would perhaps have wanted to remove Phelps from the society because he'd hired Eaton who was committing fraud."

"There is also Phelps's relationship with Mrs. Atkins. It may be that Nevill or Furnier didn't care for her involvement with the society, particularly since she is not a member."

"I could see that troubling Furnier especially," Hadrian noted.

"Dr. Giles is another suspect," Tilda said. "He was upset to find out that Eaton was admitting men who were ill, and it was Giles's responsibility to ensure that didn't happen. He indicated that he didn't like his reputation being impugned. He had plenty of reason to be angry with Phelps."

"And with Eaton," Maxwell noted with a tip of his head. "Perhaps he killed both men."

"That is a possibility," Tilda allowed.

"Jarret is also a suspect," Hadrian said. "He and Phelps disagreed about the society, and Jarret indicated he was suspicious of why Phelps might want to start the friendly society."

"He also failed to mention that he'd called on Phelps last Sunday," Tilda said. "If not for Mrs. Burley pointing it out at the inquest, we might not know about that. I find him suspicious. I'd like to interview him tomorrow too, if we have time."

Maxwell's gaze turned wary. "We must be careful that we aren't caught investigating Phelps's murder. I am hoping to become a detective inspector."

Hadrian watched as concern filled Tilda's gaze. "We won't do anything to risk your position," Tilda vowed.

"I appreciate that," Maxwell said with a faint smile. "Did you find anything helpful at Phelps's house?"

"Yes," Tilda replied. "We found a ledger under the false bottom of a drawer in Phelps's desk."

Maxwell's eyes widened. "Chisholm and the constables missed something?"

"So it seems."

The inspector chuckled. "Chisholm won't like that. Did you take the ledger?"

"We did." Hadrian stood and fetched it from the dining room table where he'd set it earlier. He handed the diary to Maxwell, who first set his wineglass on the floor.

"It seems to be Eaton's membership record with names of members, the entrance fee they paid, and the dates and payments of their weekly dues," Tilda said as Maxwell thumbed through the book. "Cardy is included." She looked to Hadrian.

"I'm going to use the ledger to hunt down those who were admitted to the society fraudulently," Hadrian said. "I hope Dr. Giles might accompany me."

"You could ask him tomorrow at the inquest, as he should be there." Maxwell cocked his head. "What is your goal in identifying all the fraudulent members?"

"They will give us a full picture of the fraud that was perpetrated by Eaton—and likely directed by Phelps," Hadrian replied. "I also want a complete record of who will need to be reimbursed. Furnier argued that the society's coffers couldn't afford that, which is understandable since the overcharged amount seems to have gone directly to Eaton and, given the money found at Phelps's house, to Phelps. I want to ensure the money these people paid to the society is refunded with due haste."

Maxwell looked at him with something akin to admiration. "That is commendable of you to care about that."

Hadrian lifted a shoulder. "It's the right thing to do."

"You'll find Lord Ravenhurst is incredibly kind and generous," Tilda said to Maxwell, then sent Hadrian a warm glance.

After taking another small sip of port, Maxwell sat forward on the settle. "Tomorrow morning, I must go to the mercantile house, but I will meet you both at the inquest. You'll interview Jarret before that?"

Tilda nodded. "We will call on him at the bank where he works. I've been thinking how to approach him in our disguises, and I think it makes sense for Ravenhurst to want to speak with him about the society before he accepts a position working as the canvasser."

Maxwell grinned. "Excellent idea."

Everyone finished their port, and Tilda stood. "I believe I'll retire."

Maxwell and Hadrian also rose.

"Good night," Maxwell said.

Hadrian met her gaze. "Sleep well."

He watched Tilda depart the parlor and move into the entrance hall. He did not look away until she turned to ascend the stairs and disappeared from sight.

It was strange to be sleeping in this house with her, feeling the way that he did about her, wanting a different relationship than the one they had. Hadrian shifted his gaze to Maxwell and noticed the inspector had been watching her too. Indeed, the expression on his face seemed almost wistful.

Hadrian's chest tightened.

Maxwell turned to face him. "You've known Miss Wren for some time now?"

"Several months," Hadrian replied.

"She's very dedicated to her work."

"She is," Hadrian confirmed. "She's also dedicated to her grandmother and taking care of her household. She's an exceptionally independent woman."

"I can see that," Maxwell said. "I imagine you must find that odd, but I quite like it. Indeed, I find the quality most attractive."

Hadrian bristled at the man's assumption about him and at him calling Tilda attractive. Which was silly. Tilda was incredibly attractive in a myriad of ways. Maxwell would be a fool not to think so.

"Actually, I admire her independence," Hadrian said, hoping he didn't sound defensive whilst also acknowledging that he absolutely was. "It is one of many fine attributes she possesses."

"Indeed, it is." Maxwell glanced toward the base of the stairs where they'd last seen her. "I do wonder why she's not married— precisely because of all those fine attributes. I have to think she's refused many marriage proposals."

"I think you know the answer as to why she remains unwed," Hadrian said flatly. "It lies in her independence. She doesn't see a need to marry."

"That doesn't mean she wouldn't want to," Maxwell argued. "How refreshing it must be for her to not feel as though she must. Well, good night." Maxwell flashed a brief smile before turning and leaving the parlor.

Hadrian frowned at the empty room. It seemed Maxwell was interested in Tilda in a personal manner.

Tilda would not want that. She might accept his friendship, in addition to their current professional association, as she had with Hadrian, but she wouldn't desire more.

Hadrian wondered if he should have informed the inspector of Tilda's preference for maintaining platonic relationships, but he didn't want to speak out of turn. He didn't think Tilda would appreciate him doing so.

There was also the fact that Hadrian was incredibly jealous.

Was his goal to protect Tilda or to dissuade Maxwell in some sort of primal competition for her? The answer was both, and that made Hadrian a trifle uncomfortable.

Did he believe the inspector had a better chance than him? Almost certainly. Maxwell and Tilda had much more in common than she did with Hadrian.

A wave of melancholy swept through him. If he wasn't careful, he was going to turn into a brooding clod.

Hadrian left the parlor and trudged up the stairs, pondering whether he ought to tell Tilda what Maxwell had asked him, or if he should stand by and allow the inspector to make his move.

He didn't like either of those choices. He wanted a third option, one in which he expressed the depth of his feelings to Tilda, and she welcomed them.

Unfortunately, Hadrian believed that was impossible.

CHAPTER 17

*T*he following morning, Tilda and Hadrian left White Alley to call on Jarret at the Imperial Bank on Lothbury. The sky was dark gray, and it looked as though it might rain. Tilda had donned a cloak just in case.

She was eager to speak with Jarret and hoped he would have time to meet with them. "I haven't decided if we should tell Jarret that Walter Phelps's wife is not actually dead, and that Phelps isn't his real name," she said to Hadrian as they made their way along Coleman Street. "I think it may be best for the investigation at this point if we withhold that information."

Hadrian sent her a sideways glance. "Do you think others are already aware she is alive and that Walter Phelps was an alias?"

"I think I want to see people's reactions when they find out both those things."

"Anyone's reaction in particular?" Hadrian asked.

"Nevill and Furnier, as well as Dr. Giles," Tilda replied. "Maxwell is of the same mind. We discussed it briefly this morning before you joined us in the dining room. He looks forward to not having to attend his fake job any longer."

"It's a wonder he's continuing to do so," Hadrian noted.

"Well, whilst his job was 'fake,' it was an actual position he took to ensure he was accepted as a member of the community." She glanced at Hadrian. "Though perhaps he should have invented a truly fake job as you did. You were able to leave immediately," she added wryly. "I commend Maxwell on staying with the mercantile house. I daresay he's as thoughtful as you."

They walked in silence until they reached Lothbury Street.

"I confess, it's been interesting living with you," Hadrian said. "You are most adept at running a household, which I already knew, since you manage your grandmother's. I'm sure they're missing you now."

"Mrs. Acorn can handle things." Tilda referred to her grandmother's housekeeper.

"I wondered if you might have changed your mind about marrying someday. You seem to have taken to the role of pretend wife rather easily."

Tilda laughed. "I've taken on many different roles in our investigations. That doesn't mean I want to actually do any of them." She looked over at Hadrian, curious as to why he'd made the observation. "I have not changed my mind about marriage."

"Not even to someone like Maxwell?" Hadrian asked, his gaze focused straight ahead. "The two of you have so much in common, and you'd be a police wife. You'd be very involved in cases, I should think." Was this coming from Hadrian's jealousy of her partnership with Maxwell? Except Hadrian was asking about marriage and that was an entirely different kind of partnership. Did Hadrian think there was something romantic between her and Maxwell?

"I'm involved in a case right now," Tilda said evenly. "And I didn't have to marry anyone. Nor would I."

He looked her way, and she gave him a smile with a nod, hoping to convey that there was nothing between her and Maxwell. She supposed she could say so, but what if she was wrong about what Hadrian was doing? She didn't want to discuss or draw attention to such matters.

"Shall I take the lead when we speak with Jarret?" Hadrian asked, and Tilda was glad for the change in subject.

"You should," Tilda replied. "You're my brother, and I really have no reason to accompany you on this errand, except that I do. But Jarret doesn't know that, so I will mostly remain quiet— or try to anyway."

They spoke further about the upcoming interview as they approached the bank. Arriving inside, Hadrian asked to speak with Mr. Jarret. They were shown to a small chamber with a seating area.

Tilda again wondered why Hadrian had asked her about marriage and about Maxwell. She decided he'd simply been making conversation.

Hadrian removed his hat as they waited for Jarret. Tilda still didn't care for his fake blond hair. That and his simpler garments made him look very different from the Hadrian she knew. She had to admit he'd surprised her a little with how well he'd transformed into his role as Nigel Beck. It was too bad he was an earl. He was becoming an excellent private investigator.

Isaiah Jarret came into the room. He was around forty years of age with dark, thinning hair and a high forehead. He possessed penetrating blue eyes and a hawk-like nose. He regarded Tilda and Hadrian with guarded curiosity. "Mr. Beck, Mrs. Harwood, I can't imagine why you've come."

"It's a simple matter, really," Hadrian said with a brief smile. "I'm considering working for the Amicable Society as their new canvasser, and since you chose to walk away from the society, I thought I should speak with you before making a decision."

Jarret nodded, his brow creasing briefly. "That's wise of you. Please, sit." He gestured to the chairs and waited for Tilda and Hadrian to take their chairs before he sat. "I think the Amicable Society's cause is noble, and both Furnier and Nevill are committed to its success. I would likely still be involved with it if not for Walter Phelps and our disagreement."

"Because he didn't want to make the society teetotal?" Hadrian asked.

"Yes, but mostly I just didn't care for him." Jarret's tone was laced with disdain. "The longer we were acquainted, the more I didn't think we would work well together."

Tilda clasped her hands tightly to keep herself from interjecting.

Hadrian gestured toward Jarret. "Would you consider working with the society again now that he's...gone? Even though it isn't teetotal?"

"I might consider it," Jarret replied thoughtfully. "Furnier doesn't imbibe alcohol, and I imagine he keeps things as orderly as possible, though it seems there was perhaps some inappropriate activity happening right under his nose."

"You're referring to the members who were admitted despite being ill?" Hadrian asked.

Jarret nodded. "Yes, but it's my opinion that Phelps was likely the poison behind that. The society will be better off without him."

Though Hadrian was doing an excellent job interviewing Jarret, Tilda could not remain silent any longer. "Do you think Mr. Phelps was behind the ill members being admitted?" She asked the question with a measured amount of distress.

Jarret shrugged. "He hired Eaton and should have been managing him, so if he wasn't aware of the canvasser's activities, that doesn't speak well of Phelps's administrative abilities. He was either foolish or in support of the corruption, and I never took him for a fool."

Hadrian cocked his head. "You think he was capable of illegal behavior?"

"I wouldn't be surprised by it. I found him to be insincere, and certain things about him didn't make sense to me after I came to know him better. He was very eager to have Mrs. Atkins as a benefactress, and yet he tried to act as though he had money to support himself whilst managing the society from which he supposedly did not profit. I could never tell if he actually had money. He had a few nice things at his house, but they seemed almost like props."

"What do you mean?" Tilda asked.

"He had those brass candlesticks and a few glass tumblers, but his house was fairly spartan. Those things stood out. There was also a naval dirk that I found intriguing. He said it had belonged to his grandfather who'd served in the Navy. The grandfather that was supposedly from the Coleman Street Ward, and why Phelps came back here to start the society."

"'Supposedly?'" Hadrian said. "You didn't believe him."

"I find myself questioning everything about him after all that's happened. Sometimes I wonder if the entire society was a swindle, but I suppose we can't know."

Hadrian and Tilda exchanged a glance.

"I don't think you need to worry about accepting employment with the Amicable Society now that Phelps is no longer associated with it," Jarret said. "I have to imagine Furnier and even Nevill will be extremely careful going forward."

"What do you mean by 'even Nevill?'"

Jarret chuckled. "I've known Harvey a long time, and he's a bit more interested in appearances than substance. He's a good face for the society, because he knows a great many people and is gregarious. However, his mind for business is not as keen as Furnier's."

Tilda made a show of looking confused. "But he owns his own shop. He must be smart enough when it comes to business matters?"

"Yes, he's smart enough," Jarret said. "Though I have long helped him with his accounting. Don't tell him I told you, as it's our secret."

"We thank you for your time, Mr. Jarret." Hadrian glanced over at Tilda, and she recognized that he was trying to confirm whether they were finished.

Tilda gave him a subtle nod, then rose to indicate that they could leave.

"Happy to be of help," Jarret replied.

Hadrian stuck his hand out and clasped Jarret's palm. Tilda held her breath, hoping that Hadrian would see something useful. The handshake didn't last terribly long, and she worried he hadn't had time to see anything.

They left the bank a moment later, and, unfortunately, it was raining rather steadily. Tilda pulled the hood of her cloak up over her head. "Did you see one of Jarret's memories?"

"I did. He was in Mrs. Atkins's parlor. Phelps was sitting with her on a settee. It reminded me of the vision I saw when we were at her house yesterday, but of course this was from Jarret's perspective, not hers. She and Phelps appeared to be flirting—they were smiling at one another and were positioned quite close together. Jarret was uncomfortable and was eager to leave. That's all I saw, I'm afraid. Handshakes don't typically allow a lengthy vision."

"How's your head?"

"It only aches a little, and I expect the pain won't linger."

Tilda thought for a moment as they approached Coleman Street. "I'm trying to think if the memory you saw reveals anything new."

"I don't know if it did, but it's perhaps further confirmation that Jarret didn't care for Phelps. Not that we needed it since we heard that definitively from Jarret. I'm glad we obtained his perspective about Phelps, as well as Furnier and Nevill."

"Agreed," Tilda said. "However, I don't know if Jarret possesses a strong enough motive to have killed Phelps."

"Jarret certainly made it clear that he thinks the society is better off without Phelps. Isn't that a motive?"

"It is. I'm just not sure it's strong enough compared to other suspects. What does Jarret have to gain? If he was jumping at the chance to involve himself in the society, I might be more convinced."

"I understand what you're saying." Hadrian's brow creased. "Since Jarret was at Mrs. Atkins's house, perhaps she might be able to tell us more about Jarret's relationship with Phelps and what happened when the two men parted ways."

Tilda nodded. "That's a good idea. We can't simply take Jarret's words as truth."

They arrived at Number Five White Alley. As they were quite damp from the rain, they removed their outer garments in the entrance hall.

Mrs. Kilgore appeared. She wore a cloak as if she were going out.

"Are you off somewhere?" Tilda asked.

"I need to run home for a while," Mrs. Kilgore replied with a nod. "Mr. Nevill delivered this." She held out an envelope and Tilda took it.

"It's to Mr. Harwood and Mr. Beck," Mrs. Kilgore said.

Tilda glanced at Hadrian and offered him the note. He shrugged and told her to read it.

Opening the envelope, Tilda removed the short missive and scanned the contents. "He's inviting you to speak with him and Furnier following the inquest today." She looked up at Hadrian. "I hope that means they'll be offering you the job as canvasser."

"I hope so," Mrs. Kilgore put in. "The society needs to reimburse my cousin for the money her husband paid. You still plan to make sure that happens, won't you, my lord?"

Hadrian nodded. "I will do my best."

"You *must* help them," Mrs. Kilgore said imploringly. "It's not fair that my cousin should suffer, and neither should anyone else who was cheated by that horrible Eaton."

Tilda gave her a gentle smile. "We are in agreement about that."

"Thank you. I'll see you later for dinner." Mrs. Kilgore pulled the hood of her cloak up, and Hadrian opened the door for her.

As he closed the door, Tilda narrowed her eyes slightly. "Is there a chance she could be the woman in the cloak Mr. Burley saw? What if Mrs. Kilgore called on Phelps to demand he repay her cousin?"

Hadrian's brows snapped together. "You don't think she might have killed him?"

"I would be shocked if that were the case, but what if she was there and saw something? Though I'm sure she would have come forward and shared all she knew, given her husband's position within the police." Tilda waved her hand. "It was an absurd thought provoked by her donning a cloak."

She handed Hadrian the note Mrs. Kilgore had given her. "Perhaps you'll see one of Nevill's memories."

Hadrian took the parchment, and right away his gaze went vacant. Tilda noted that it was easier to tell when he was having a vision now, perhaps because he'd learned somewhat to seek them out and focus on what he hoped to see. Whilst that was good for obtaining information, it made him appear odd. Someone watching him might wonder what was happening to him, especially if the visions lasted for some time, as this one seemed to. Thankfully, those that accompanied his handshakes were short.

Finally, he blinked and focused on Tilda.

"You look different now when you have visions," she said.

He cocked his head. "Like how you mentioned at Mrs. Atkins's?"

Tilda nodded. "Your eyes appear vacant—like someone who is lost in a reverie. I worry someone will wonder what's happening if they see you in this state."

"I'll simply tell them I am lost in a reverie," he replied with a smirk. His features sobered. "Did I look like that at the bank?"

"No. That was a quick handshake. I only notice it when the visions are longer—usually when you're touching an object like that letter or the milk jug at Mrs. Atkins's house." At Hadrian's nod, she went on. "What did you see?"

"Phelps, Furnier, and Dr. Giles together at Phelps's house. Everyone was agitated and arguing. Giles, in particular, was gesturing wildly. Nevill wanted everyone to calm down. He saw the brass candlesticks on the table, and they held candles like the one we found at Phelps's house last night. Then the memory faded."

"I wonder if there is a significance to him registering the candlesticks," Tilda said.

"I had the same thought, but it could be nothing. We may be attributing relevance to an innocuous glance at the candlesticks because we know the missing candlestick is the murder weapon."

Tilda exhaled. "I would dearly love to find that missing candlestick."

CHAPTER 18

⁂

*H*adrian held the door for Tilda as they arrived at the Swan and Hoop shortly before the inquest for Timothy Eaton was to begin. They made their way to the private dining room where the inquest would be held and found that Maxwell was already there, along with Draper and a few others from the mercantile house.

Tilda pulled her pretend husband aside and told him everything they'd learned from Jarret earlier. Hadrian felt another jealous pang as he watched them together. He mentally chastised himself. Tilda had been hired to investigate this case with Maxwell. That didn't make them permanent partners. It didn't even mean they'd work together a second time.

But Hadrian wasn't concerned about just that. He worried the two of them would enjoy working together so much that they would find a reason to continue doing so. Or that their connection would grow deeper than professional associates, just as his and Tilda's had done.

Only Hadrian wished their relationship would progress even further.

Alas, it would not. Tilda had told him very specifically that her views on marriage hadn't changed. So why was Hadrian worrying about Maxwell at all? Hadrian realized he was being irrational. Of course, generally speaking, matters of the heart weren't logical.

Hadrian refocused his attention on their conversation as Tilda told the inspector about the note that Nevill had delivered, inviting Maxwell and Hadrian to speak with him and Furnier following the inquest.

Maxwell's brows shot up briefly as he looked to Hadrian. "Are we to be offered positions?"

"That is my expectation," Hadrian replied. He scanned the room, looking for Nevill and Furnier, but decided they must already be in the inquest room. However, Hadrian did see Ezra Clement. The reporter stood near the entrance to the inquest room. Clement met Hadrian's and Tilda's gazes but kept his features neutral.

Tilda leaned toward Hadrian. "I look forward to speaking with him at the Lion's Heart later," she whispered.

They moved into the inquest room. The jury of twelve men sat along the far wall, and the coroner, Abraham Thetford, had lined up his witnesses along the wall by the door. They included the society's administrators, Nevill and Furnier, as well as Dr. Giles, and Hadrian also recognized Mrs. Vickers from the lodging house where Eaton lived.

Mrs. Atkins entered a moment later and took one of the witness seats. Hadrian had expected Amos Rippon, Eaton's friend from the Prudential Assurance Company, to also be in attendance, but he was not.

Thetford looked over the room, which was not quite as crowded as it had been for Phelps, and called the inquest to order. "We are here to investigate the death of Timothy Eaton, who was, until recently, the canvasser for the Coleman Street Ward Amicable Society. He was found washed up on the banks of the Thames on Monday and identified on Tuesday, due to the absence of half the little finger on his left hand.

"His death was caused by a knife wound to the chest. I have determined the weapon used was a long, thin blade."

Hadrian immediately thought of the dirk that Jarret had mentioned to Tilda and him earlier that day. He looked over at her, and she met his gaze, giving him a subtle nod. She was thinking the same thing.

Thetford went on to say that the weapon used to stab Eaton had not been found.

He first spoke with Mrs. Vickers from the lodging house, then moved through the rest of the witnesses with alacrity. None of them revealed anything that Tilda and Hadrian didn't already know. The inquest concluded when the jurors rather quickly determined that Eaton had been murdered.

Hadrian immediately turned and, in hushed tones, told Maxwell about the dirk Jarret had mentioned.

Maxwell's brow furrowed. "I reviewed the police report, and it included a description of the items found in Phelps's house. I don't recall anything about a naval dirk."

"We didn't see anything like that when we looked through the house after you left with Mrs. Walters the other night," Tilda whispered.

"I should mention this clue to Chisholm," Maxwell said, glancing toward the front of the room, where the inspector stood with Sergeant Kilgore.

"We need to speak with Furnier and Nevill," Hadrian said. "They're looking in our direction."

"As much as I would like to come along," Tilda said, "I will instead see what I can learn from Mrs. Atkins about Mr. Jarret and his early friendship with Phelps."

Hadrian nodded, and Tilda went into the common room where Mrs. Atkins had gone. Hadrian and Maxwell walked to where Furnier and Nevill stood near the door.

"Let's go into the common room," Nevill said, gesturing for Hadrian and Maxwell to precede him. The four men walked to the corner, away from where people were clustered, to speak.

Nevill directed his attention to Hadrian first. "Mr. Beck, we would like to offer you the position of canvasser."

"I accept," Hadrian said quickly.

"Excellent." Nevill appeared quite pleased whilst Furnier merely nodded. "When can you start?"

"Right away," Hadrian said. "I thank you very much." He looked to Furnier and reached out to shake the man's hand. Bracing himself, he worked to keep his expression normal, though this ought to be a relatively short vision—if he had one.

The common room became Phelps's parlor. Furnier looked toward the fireplace mantel where a knife was displayed. It was long and thin, just like what the coroner had described. It had not been in Phelps's house on either occasion that Hadrian had been in the parlor. The handshake ended, and so did the vision along with it.

Hadrian moved on to shake Nevill's hand. A pain sliced through Hadrian's forehead. Nevill was also in Phelps's house, but Hadrian did not see Furnier. He did see Phelps, who appeared distressed—he was pale, and his features were deeply creased.

Nevill looked down and a man lay prone on the floor of the parlor. Hadrian had never met the man, but he looked as Mrs. Vickers had described Timothy Eaton.

Blood soaked the front of his clothing and his eyes were open, staring into nothing.

The handshake ended and so did the vision. Hadrian managed to keep from gasping, but his heart was thudding madly. He closed his eyes briefly in a long blink to preserve what he'd seen. He could hardly wait to share it with Tilda. He glanced toward where she stood with Mrs. Atkins.

Hadrian couldn't go to her now. They wouldn't have any

privacy to speak. Furthermore, he needed to continue with his inquiries, and that included shaking more hands and potentially seeing more visions. His head already ached terribly.

Focusing on Nevill and Furnier, Hadrian inhaled deeply to calm his still-racing heart. "I would like to speak with Dr. Giles. One of the first things I hope to do is identify those who should not be members because they're ill."

He wanted to say he would use the ledger that Eaton had created, but he couldn't let them know that he had it. They would ask how it had come to be in his possession, and he could not explain that the police had allowed him to search Phelps's house.

"You'll need to identify the people Eaton recruited," Furnier said. His brows gathered in what appeared to be annoyance. "I'm not sure how you will do that." He glanced toward Draper, who stood with the other men from the mercantile house. "I believe some of those people paid Draper at a weekly meeting. You could ask him if he knows the identities of any of those unfortunate people."

"I'll do that," Hadrian said.

Furnier pursed his lips. "I should also add that we're not sure how much longer Dr. Giles will remain with the society. He has indicated he may prefer to leave."

"Why is that?" Maxwell asked.

Nevill glanced toward the doctor, who was speaking to someone Hadrian didn't know. "He doesn't wish to be associated with the society since Phelps was murdered and Eaton was committing fraud. He'd hoped the Amicable Society would boost his fledgling career and perhaps elevate his status, not ruin those things."

Hadrian recalled what Nevill had told him and Tilda about Dr. Giles not having the right "pedigree" to establish himself as a physician. Being the physician for a troubled friendly society would not support his goals.

"But we are going to turn things around," Nevill declared with a smile. "I just feel it, especially if we have a third administrator who might be willing to work hard and instill confidence in the community." He looked at Maxwell as he said this.

"Are you offering me the position?" Maxwell asked. "I would be honored."

"We're willing to give you a chance," Furnier said, almost tersely. "Mrs. Atkins seems to think you would be a fine choice, but I can't tell why she thinks so. Other than you are Mr. Beck's brother-in-law. Apparently, that alone recommends you, at least in her opinion."

Hadrian glanced toward where Tilda was speaking with Mrs. Atkins. The older woman was looking in his direction, and she smiled at him as their eyes met. Hadrian jerked his attention back to Nevill and Furnier.

"I'm glad for the chance to prove myself," Maxwell said. "The Amicable Society performs a necessary and benevolent service that I should like to further. I'm also committed to ensuring that Mrs. Cardy, and others who have paid into the society without any hope of collecting a benefit, are restored."

"We don't disagree," Furnier said crisply. "However, we must find a way to do that, since we do not know where those funds have gone. We can't simply manufacture money to repay these poor people. I find it disturbing that Eaton's body was found without any money. It makes me think whoever killed him stole the funds that Eaton swindled. I fear we may never find out what happened to that money."

Nevill shook his head sadly. "I agree."

Hadrian tried not to look directly at Nevill, lest he somehow convey what he'd just seen when shaking the man's hand. And though Hadrian hadn't seen Furnier in the memory, that didn't mean he hadn't also been there. Hadrian avoided focusing on him too. "Have you any idea who killed Mr. Eaton?"

Nevill coughed and looked away. "No."

"Not specifically, but if someone found out he was cheating

the sick, I can imagine any number of people might have done so," Furnier said.

"Does that number include you?" Hadrian asked. This time, he met the man's gaze.

Furnier's eyes were usually cool, but they appeared particularly frigid now. "No, it does not."

Hadrian had to think Furnier must at least suspect Phelps. He knew about the naval dirk—Hadrian had seen him looking at it on Phelps's mantel. Furnier had to have thought of the blade when Thetford had discussed the murder weapon during the inquest.

"I suspect there is information that hasn't been shared with the police or the coroner," Hadrian said. "Perhaps someone has yet to come forward. Or be completely honest."

"I think most people don't particularly care who killed Eaton," Furnier said with disdain. "I wouldn't hold my breath waiting for someone to be implicated. In any case, I would much rather direct my energy toward the society and recovering from all this turmoil. Nevill and I would like to have an administrative meeting to discuss the future of the society tomorrow evening. We'll meet here at the Swan and Hoop in the back room. Can you both attend?" He looked from Hadrian to Maxwell.

"We'll be there," Maxwell replied. "Thank you again." He shook their hands.

Hadrian looked about to see if Dr. Giles was still present and noted the blond man standing near the doorway. "Please excuse me."

The other men inclined their heads, and Hadrian turned. However, before he could make his way to the doctor, he was intercepted by Draper.

"Did I overhear that you and Albert will be working with the society now?" Draper asked.

"Yes," Hadrian replied. "I'm glad to run into you, because Mr. Furnier suggested I could speak with you about which members may have been recruited by Eaton. I would like to meet with all of them to determine if any are ill, as Mr. Cardy was. We need to refund those men's fees and remove them from the membership rolls."

Draper blinked in surprise. "I'm pleased to hear you want to do this. We need to ensure no one else is paying into the society if they do not meet the requirements of membership. A few of Eaton's recruits came to the meetings on Monday nights, but not consistently."

"You know who they are?" Hadrian asked.

"I do. I'll compile a list. I can deliver it to you, or you are also welcome to stop by my house."

"That would be most helpful, thank you," Hadrian said. "I don't know where you live, however. I live at—"

"Number Five in White Alley." Draper smiled. "I've seen the membership rolls, of course. I'm at Number Twelve in Masons Alley. I'm so pleased to see the society is moving in a better direction with you and Albert. I'd thought to offer myself to the administration, but I'm just glad you're committed to returning the money to those who were cheated."

They parted ways, and Hadrian moved on to find Dr. Giles, managing to catch him just before he left. "A moment, if you don't mind, Dr. Giles." Though Hadrian's head still throbbed, he would try to shake the doctor's hand so that he could see one of his memories.

The younger man turned and faced Hadrian, his brow creased. "Mr. Beck, have you accepted the position as the new canvasser?"

"I have, and I'm hoping I can convince you to stay with the society, at least long enough to identify the members that Eaton recruited and determine if they meet the standards of membership."

"You mean you want to know if they're healthy," the doctor said flatly.

Hadrian nodded. "And if not, we'll need to refund their money."

The physician snorted. "I've no idea how you plan to do that." He exhaled, then inclined his head to move away from the door. Hadrian followed him to a spot near the wall.

"I don't know if I want to stay with the Amicable Society," Dr. Giles said quietly. "I'm trying to establish my practice, and I thought that working for the society would help my endeavors. So far it has not, and now you're asking me to put in more time without being paid. I must make my career my first priority. I'm getting married soon, and I need to establish a consistent income to support my new family. I've had to act as a surgeon on occasion in order to make ends meet." His lips pulled down, and he appeared disgusted at having to perform as a surgeon, as if it were beneath him.

"I do understand," Hadrian said. A surgeon was not as respected or paid as well as a physician but was likely more necessary in this area as they treated injuries.

"It may be that we move away from the ward," Dr. Giles said. "I thought the society would be different, but it has not provided me with the benefits I was hoping for." The doctor's gaze shot to Tilda. No, not Tilda, but Mrs. Atkins.

Hadrian wondered if Giles had been hoping for more of a financial boon, even though he'd known he wasn't going to make any income from this position until after the first year. Perhaps he'd been hoping that Mrs. Atkins, or others like her, would become his clients.

"You were angry during Phelps's inquest and again today," Hadrian said casually. When Thetford had questioned him earlier, Giles had demonstrated the same frustration he had during Phelps's inquest.

Giles's pale brows climbed his forehead as his blue eyes brightened with outrage. "Of course, I was angry. I'm *still* angry—especially at Eaton. He made a mockery of the society, and I'm sure there are many people who don't trust us now. They don't believe the society will support them in their time of need. It's especially frustrating to me that Eaton was taking money when I wasn't being paid at all."

Hadrian could see where the doctor would have a motive to kill Phelps and even Eaton. He realized Dr. Giles would likely have medical instruments that would match a long, slim blade, particularly if he worked as a surgeon. Perhaps Phelps's naval dirk wasn't the murder weapon. He hadn't seen it protruding from Eaton's chest in Nevill's memory. The murder weapon was still unconfirmed.

"I believe very much in the society," Hadrian said. "I'm going to do my best to restore its good reputation, and I hope you'll give me the chance to do what's right by the people who were wronged by Eaton."

Dr. Giles blew out a breath. "I don't know if I can take the time to do that, not unless I could be paid, as I'm sure you will be."

"Think about it," Hadrian said with a smile, and then offered his hand to the doctor. "Whatever you decide, I appreciate all you've done."

The doctor shook his hand, and Hadrian quickly saw different visions of medical situations, including Giles wielding a long blade that absolutely could have been used to kill Eaton. He also saw Furnier and Nevill in the meeting room at the Swan and Hoop, but not Phelps. Giles was gesturing wildly with his hands and felt extremely agitated, whilst Furnier and Nevill were frowning at him. Nevill held up his hands in a placating fashion.

Giles withdrew his grip from Hadrian's, and the vision dissipated. After so many visions, Hadrian's head was throbbing in agony.

"I'll consider helping you with the Eaton members." The doctor's tone held a bitter edge. "I'll let you know at the meeting tomorrow night." He turned and left the pub.

Hadrian pivoted and went to find Tilda. Perhaps he'd have a chance to speak with her privately, though he couldn't see how. Frustration simmered through him, and he massaged his temple to ease the pain in his head.

Unfortunately, Tilda was still with Mrs. Atkins, and now Maxwell was with them as well. Hadrian preferred to avoid Mrs. Atkins, but he saw no other choice but to join them. Indeed, he ought to propose she pay the doctor a salary because his contributions were vital to the society.

Fixing a smile on his face, Hadrian walked over to them.

Mrs. Atkins fluttered her lashes at him as he made eye contact. "Mr. Beck, I understand you've accepted the position of canvasser. I'm so delighted. I'm paying your salary, and I do hope you appreciate that. You do, don't you?"

"I do. Thank you. The society is very lucky to have your benevolent support," Hadrian said diplomatically.

"So long as you're grateful," she said, pointedly touching his sleeve. "I would like you to come for dinner tomorrow evening. We can talk about the future of the society."

Hadrian clenched his jaw, then managed an apologetic smile. "I'm afraid we have an administrative meeting."

Mrs. Atkins pouted. "I should have been invited to that. Where are you meeting? I will come too."

"I don't think it's our place to invite you," Maxwell said a tad awkwardly. "Our apologies, Mrs. Atkins. Perhaps you'd like to speak to Mr. Nevill and Mr. Furnier about that."

"I thought you were a new administrator," she said petulantly.

"I must prove myself first," Maxwell explained.

"I see." Mrs. Atkins pursed her lips. She did not look pleased.

"We'll discuss your involvement with them," Hadrian said. "I'd like to propose another way you can contribute, since you're so keen to see the society succeed. Dr. Giles is an important asset, and we may need to provide him with a salary, lest we lose him to other endeavors."

Mrs. Atkins waved her hand. "Bah. Giles just wants to elevate his position. He's been trying to needle his way ahead for some time. It's the only reason he joined the society and agreed to be the physician." She lowered her voice as if she were imparting a secret. "He isn't even really a physician. He's a *surgeon.*" Her nose wrinkled as if she'd just stated that Giles was lower than the manure found on the street.

"I think he is, in fact, a physician," Hadrian said coolly. Mrs. Atkins was not helping to ease his headache. "As well as a surgeon, which makes him incredibly qualified and useful." He realized he may very well be defending a murderer, but he didn't care for Mrs. Atkins's superiority.

Before the woman could respond, Tilda smiled brightly. "We should be on our way. I need to attend to dinner."

Hadrian wanted to kiss her in gratitude. They bade Mrs. Atkins farewell and left the pub, making their way toward London Wall.

"Thank you for ending that conversation," Hadrian said with great relief.

"You seemed to need rescuing," Tilda said.

"I most definitely did. Were you able to learn anything about her relationship with Phelps?" Hadrian asked.

"A bit," Tilda replied. "I asked if they'd planned to marry."

"You had to gossip again?" Hadrian asked with a smile.

Tilda chuckled. "Somewhat. She said she had no plans to marry him or anyone else, that she doesn't want to do that again. I have the impression she enjoys being an independent widow of means, which I can wholly understand."

Hadrian glanced at Maxwell to see the man's reaction to her statement, but he didn't seem to have one.

Tilda went on. "She said they cared for each other, and she believed their liaison was special—that they were dedicated to one another, I believe she said. However, there was an edge to her tone, and I'm not entirely sure if she was exaggerating, or if she was perhaps lying to herself about what was really happening between them."

"That's an interesting perspective," Maxwell said. He looked to Hadrian. "How was your conversation with Dr. Giles?"

Hadrian was itching to tell Tilda what he'd seen when shaking everyone's hands, but that would have to wait. Instead, he shared what he'd learned from Dr. Giles. "I do think he's still a suspect," Hadrian concluded. "He was angry about Eaton profiting from the society, whilst the doctor's career has not been aided by his involvement. I'm not sure he's going to help me identify which of Eaton's recruits are ill."

"That's unfortunate," Maxwell said. "Whatever happens with the investigation, I hope those people get their money back."

"It depends on if the funds can be recovered," Tilda said. "I wonder how much was under Phelps's floorboards and if it can be proven to belong to the society."

Hadrian glanced over at her. "Giles suggested that whoever killed Eaton stole the money from him."

"That's a fascinating idea," Tilda replied. "And believable. Who do we think killed Eaton? And where? It seems the knife Jarret told us about could be the murder weapon, but does that mean Phelps killed him?"

Anticipation pulsed through Hadrian. He wanted to respond that Eaton had been killed at Phelps's house and that both Phelps and Nevill had been present. He'd never been more frustrated by Maxwell's presence than he was in that moment. The man had completely come between him and Tilda and the way they worked together to solve things.

"It occurred to me whilst I was speaking with Dr. Giles that the blade used to kill Eaton could have been something from a surgeon's kit," Hadrian said. "Dr. Giles has worked as a surgeon on occasion in order to meet his financial needs."

Tilda's eyes gleamed with interest—and admiration. "Excellent deductive reasoning."

Hadrian preened inwardly at her praise, which was a trifle silly. And yet it wasn't—he was beginning to acknowledge just how much her opinion meant to him.

Maxwell came to a stop and turned toward Tilda. "We shouldn't accompany you to Mrs. Burley's house. You'll be better on your own." He glanced at Hadrian. "We'll loiter at the end of the street."

"Brilliant," Tilda replied. "Then afterward, we'll meet with Clement at the Lion's Heart. I do hope we'll be able to narrow the list of suspects soon."

"For which crime?" Maxwell asked with a faint smile.

At least for Eaton's, Hadrian thought to himself. He began to despair that he wouldn't be able to tell Tilda what he knew until after they met with Clement. He disliked that she didn't have all the information he did and would be making further inquiries without it.

This wasn't efficient.

And it was damned frustrating.

CHAPTER 19

*W*hilst Hadrian and Maxwell loitered on London Wall at the end of Second Postern, Tilda made her way to Mrs. Burley's house. She knocked on the door and was pleased when Mrs. Burley answered almost immediately.

The older woman brightened upon seeing Tilda. "I saw you walking up the street, Mrs. Harwood. My husband said you called yesterday, and that I missed something very exciting at Mr. Phelps's house. Do come in!"

Tilda braced herself for the gossip session that was to come. "Thank you." She stepped into the small entrance hall that was really just a landing for the stairs leading up to the first floor.

Mrs. Burley closed the door, then moved past Tilda into the small parlor that looked out to the street. "I planned to call on you tomorrow, but I'm glad you came today, as I was feeling rather impatient to speak with you." She laughed brightly. "Can I offer you tea?"

Tilda gave her a pleasant smile. "No, thank you. I can't stay too long, as I need to meet Mr. Harwood."

Mrs. Burley nodded and gestured toward the seating area. She took a seat in a well-worn chair upholstered with yellow damask. "Mr. Burley says you saw a woman being taken away by Inspector Chisholm from Mr. Phelps's house last night. I'm very disappointed I missed that."

Tilda sat opposite her hostess in a chair with a dull yellow cushion. "Yes, my brother and I just happened to be walking by last night and saw what happened. I almost didn't come here to ask, but I'm afraid my curiosity got the better of me." She cast her gaze down briefly as if she were embarrassed.

"I do understand." Mrs. Burley gave her a knowing look. "I wonder who it was."

Seizing the opportunity to obliquely ask about Mrs. Cardy's visit to Phelps, Tilda grimaced faintly. "Do you think it may have been Mrs. Cardy? I can imagine her confronting Phelps. I might do that if I were in her position. In fact, I thought I'd heard she called on him before he died." It was a risk to mention that last part since there was no such rumor, and if there was, Mrs. Burley would surely have heard it.

Mrs. Burley met Tilda's gaze. "Where did you hear that?"

"I don't recall. Is it not true? I wouldn't blame her for seeking him out."

"It *is* true," Mrs. Burley said softly and exhaled. "However, Mrs. Cardy didn't visit Phelps on Monday night—it was Sunday afternoon, and I was with her. But you mustn't tell anyone because I was not forthcoming about our visit at the inquest. I didn't want the police to have any more reason to suspect Mrs. Cardy of murdering Phelps. She didn't do it."

"You're certain of that?" Tilda asked.

Mrs. Burley's eyes flashed with annoyance. "She was at home with her children. She has a stronger alibi than I do."

"Of course," Tilda said quickly. "But I hope you aren't suggesting you may have killed him." She donned a look of horror that prompted Mrs. Burley to wave her hand.

"It wasn't me either." Mrs. Burley's brow creased as she

appeared to think for a moment. "Could the female visitor on Monday night have been Mrs. Atkins?"

"Why would she have gone to Mr. Phelps's house so late?" Tilda asked.

Mrs. Burley shrugged. "I suspected she and Mr. Phelps were engaged in an affair. They seemed to have a tendre for one another. At least, she seemed to. I'm not so sure about Mr. Phelps."

Tilda widened her eyes and parted her lips to appear rapt. "Why is that?"

"I think Mrs. Atkins may have believed they were closer than they actually were," Mrs. Burley said in a confidential tone. "I happened to see Mr. Phelps with another woman last Sunday. They met at the Black Anchor. Mr. Burley and I were there for supper."

"Indeed?" Tilda asked breathlessly. "What did the woman look like? Perhaps she was the one taken away by Inspector Chisholm last night."

Mrs. Burley's eyes rounded, and she sucked in a breath. "You may be right. She had dark hair and was perhaps in her middle thirties. I made a point of walking past their table to see her better. Her eyes were an unusual amber color."

Tilda suspected the woman was Ida Walters based on that description. "You saw them on Sunday, you say?"

Mrs. Burley nodded. "I don't know if they were romantically inclined, but their heads were bent close together, and they seemed rather intimate. Come to think of it, the woman was flushed."

"Was she agitated?" Tilda asked. If the woman was indeed Ida Walters, which Tilda was inclined to think, she'd arrived in town sooner than she said. This was not surprising as they'd all believed she was lying. Tilda would share this information with Inspector Chisholm. Perhaps he could use it to press more of the truth from Mrs. Walters.

"Do you think she was the same person Inspector Chisholm took away last night?" Mrs. Burley asked.

"She could be," Tilda said slowly, as if she were pondering the idea. "I did not see her very well as it was dark and she was wearing a cloak. I would guess she was probably in her thirties, so perhaps it was the same person."

Mrs. Burley lifted her chin. "I've half a mind to call at the police station and offer my assistance to Inspector Chisholm. I could meet this woman he has in custody—assuming he still does —and see if she is the same person."

"That would probably be helpful," Tilda said. In fact, she would plan on telling the inspector what she'd learned. However, she didn't want Chisholm to come to White Alley. She wanted to visit the police station and interview Mrs. Walters, if he'd allow it.

Tilda put her mind back to the gossip session with Mrs. Burley. "I wonder what Mrs. Atkins would say if she knew Mr. Phelps had another…friend."

"I believe she'd be jealous." Mrs. Burley cocked her head.

"Would she?" Tilda frowned. "She doesn't seem sad about his death."

"She doesn't strike me as the sort of person who allows melancholy to overtake her. When her husband died, she didn't even mourn for a year. But I don't know her well. We aren't friends," she added with a chuckle, as if the notion were amusing.

Tilda believed that. She couldn't imagine Mrs. Atkins would consider someone of Mrs. Burley's station her equal. "Why then do you suspect she'd be jealous?"

"I've observed Mrs. Atkins to enjoy the attentions of various gentlemen, especially Mr. Phelps," Mrs. Burley said thoughtfully. "I don't think she'd care to share him with someone else. She'd take that as a personal slight."

"I see." Tilda agreed with Mrs. Burley's assessment of Mrs. Atkins. "Have you seen her go to Mr. Phelps's house before?"

"Once or twice," Mrs. Burley replied. "But Mr. Phelps has many visitors. Mr. Nevill calls on him, and they often return together to his house after the society meetings on Monday night." She blinked. "I saw them on last Saturday evening together, but it was odd. Mr. Phelps left his house and returned a short while later with Nevill. I didn't see them leave."

"Why was that odd?" Tilda asked. "You said Mr. Nevill visits regularly."

"Yes, but Mr. Nevill doesn't typically visit on Saturday evenings, and it was quite late, nearly midnight, when they arrived together. Sometime later, two night soil men came around, and I noticed neither was the usual night soil man, Mr. Oldham. He either works alone or brings his son, who is around ten years of age."

Tilda resisted the urge to ask Mrs. Burley why she paid such close attention to her neighbors. Whilst Tilda found it annoying, in this case, the woman's behavior was most helpful. "You're sure it wasn't Mr. Oldham and his son?"

"No, it was two grown men in heavy cloaks, which I suppose is what I found strange. They didn't look to be dressed for taxing night soil work. I saw the cart parked in front of Mr. Phelps's house, then they pushed it toward London Wall without going to anyone else's yard."

"That *is* odd." Tilda imagined a night soil cart would be an excellent way to dispose of a dead body, but she didn't have enough information about Eaton's death to make any conclusions. "Did you ever find out what happened?"

"No, but I should inquire. Mrs. Oldham is a friendly sort. They just live over in Evans Court."

Tilda stored that information away for later. She wanted to speak with this night soil man, Mr. Oldham. But she also didn't want Mrs. Burley seeing her doing so. "When do you plan to do that?"

Mrs. Burley waved her hand. "I'll speak with her at church on

Sunday more than likely. I've a busy day tomorrow already with my daughter-in-law."

Moving on to a new subject to see what else she might learn from Mrs. Burley, Tilda adopted an eager expression. "I've just come from Eaton's inquest."

Mrs. Burley clapped her hands together. "I heard that was today. I'm sorry I missed it. Do tell me what happened, if you please."

Tilda provided a description of the events and tried to make it as interesting and gossip-worthy as possible. "One of the most exciting things that happened today is that my brother was hired as the new canvasser for the Amicable Society."

Mrs. Burley's brows rose. "How splendid! That must be quite different from working at a gentlemen's club." Confusion marred her brow. "In truth, I can't imagine why he'd prefer that. I should think working in the West End with the wealthy would be fascinating. Think of the gossip he hears." Her eyes glowed with excitement.

"Nigel isn't one for gossip," Tilda replied. "I think that's frowned upon at the gentlemen's clubs anyway."

"I suppose it would be," Mrs. Burley said with a disappointed frown.

"Well, I'm sure he'll do a better job than Timothy Eaton did," Tilda said firmly. "He certainly has no plans to swindle anyone. In fact, he's very committed to ensuring all those hurt by Mr. Eaton's actions will be reimbursed."

"Do you think there's a great many more people than just Gilbert Cardy?" Mrs. Burley asked.

Tilda lifted her shoulder. "I think there must be. Nigel has vowed to discover the depth of Mr. Eaton's cheating. He'll also ensure that Mrs. Cardy receives the money her husband paid into the Society."

Mrs. Burley put her hand to her chest. "Bless him. I'm so pleased to hear this. It's a relief to know Mrs. Cardy will be taken care of. I do wonder about the future of the Amicable Society."

"My husband and I are quite dedicated to it already," Tilda said softly. "In fact, Mr. Nevill and Mr. Furnier have offered Albert the position of their third administrator, at least temporarily. That was the other exciting thing that happened. We hope they will want him to stay on permanently."

"Really?" Mrs. Burley's eyes flashed with surprise. "That is a shocking development, considering how new you are to the society. I wonder why they didn't ask Mr. Draper, since he's been involved since the beginning. Perhaps he wasn't interested. And he is somewhat soft-spoken. He may not have been the right choice."

"It seems many people are upset about what Mr. Eaton was doing," Tilda said. "I've heard rumors that some have asked to leave the society and have their fees refunded."

Mrs. Burley nodded. "I've heard that too, but I think it's mostly bluster. Still, Nevill and Furnier should not underestimate people's outrage." Her eyes narrowed briefly. "I share their anger. I don't think anybody in the society is sad that Mr. Eaton met his maker."

"You think he deserved to die?" Tilda asked.

"I think what he did was despicable, and I would not fault someone for being angry enough to kill him. He hurt people's livelihoods and their children. Poor Mrs. Cardy has five of them, and one is now sick. The money her husband paid into the society could be used for the child's care. It's terrible."

Tilda glanced out the front window toward Mr. Phelps's house. She thought of Hadrian's visions, of seeing the administrators meeting there.

"You say you saw Mr. Nevill calling at Mr. Phelps's house often," Tilda said. "Did you ever see Mr. Furnier or Dr. Giles there?"

"Sometimes, but not nearly as much as Mr. Nevill. That's

because he and Mr. Phelps are—rather, *were*—friends. I don't think the same could be said for Mr. Furnier and Mr. Phelps."

"What about Dr. Giles?"

"I can't say I've noticed that he's particularly friendly with any of them. But then he's very smitten with his betrothed." Mrs. Burley smiled. "It's always heartwarming to see people in love. I am not above trying to assist with matchmaking," she added in a low tone, followed by a chuckle. "I did that for all four of my sons. I'm surprised your brother is not yet wed. Or is he widowed?"

"He's unmarried," Tilda replied, thinking it was time to make her exit.

Mrs. Burley's eyes lit with excitement. "I was hoping you would say that. I'd love to introduce him to my niece. She's very pretty and will be an excellent helpmate. Perhaps you and Mr. Beck—and Mr. Harwood, of course—could come for dinner next week?"

Tilda felt an odd prick of irritation at the notion of Mrs. Burley trying to match Hadrian with her niece. And it wasn't due to Mrs. Burley being a busybody. Tilda found she just didn't care to think of Hadrian marrying. It would impact their partnership, she reasoned. Whilst that was true, she couldn't help acknowledging she was being rather selfish. If Hadrian wished to wed, she would have no say in the matter. Furthermore, he *would* marry. He was an earl. It was required.

"I'll speak with them about it," Tilda said noncommittally. "I should be going."

Mrs. Burley stood. "Perhaps next time you can stay longer. I've enjoyed sharing gossip." She smiled broadly as she showed Tilda to the door.

Tilda bade Mrs. Burley farewell and hurried along Second Postern toward London Wall. Hadrian and Maxwell were waiting just around the corner.

"How did it go?" Maxwell asked eagerly.

"Very well. I'll tell you about it on the way to the Lion's Heart." They walked east along London Wall, with Tilda between the two men. "It seems we were right about Mrs. Walters's dishonesty. Mrs. Burley reported that she saw her with Phelps at a pub on Sunday. They seemed close—intimate, I mean—with their heads bent together."

"How can you be sure it was Mrs. Walters?" Hadrian asked.

"I can't, of course, but Mrs. Burley's description of the woman matched that of Mrs. Walters. Mrs. Burley asked if she could be the same woman I saw Inspector Chisholm escorting away last night, and I said it could. Now Mrs. Burley may call at the police station to see if she can help."

Hadrian chuckled. "She is very much a busybody, isn't she?"

"Quite," Tilda said. "She mentioned seeing the woman at the pub with Phelps because we were speaking about his potential liaison with Mrs. Atkins. Mrs. Burley indicated that he may not have been as committed to their association as Mrs. Atkins was."

"That is interesting," Maxwell said. "Could jealousy have been a motive for Mrs. Atkins to kill him?"

"Jealousy or a need to keep Phelps's attention completely on her," Tilda replied. "I don't think Mrs. Atkins likes to share." She glanced at Hadrian, whose expression flickered with distaste.

"Mrs. Burley and I also spoke about Eaton's fraud, and whilst she is very upset, I'm not convinced she would have committed murder. She was thrilled to learn that my brother would be working as the new canvasser and will ensure that the people who were swindled would be reimbursed." Tilda wondered what would happen if their investigations concluded before Hadrian could meet that objective. They hadn't discussed that.

"That all sounds most helpful," Maxwell said.

"I haven't told you the most interesting thing I learned." Tilda waggled her brows. "Mrs. Burley saw Phelps leave his house late Saturday."

"The night that Eaton was killed," Hadrian said.

Tilda nodded. "Phelps returned to the house with Nevill after midnight. Mrs. Burley did not see them leave, but she noted that the regular night soil man was not on the route that night. She observed his cart parked in front of Phelps's house, then two men pushed the cart toward London Wall without stopping at anyone else's yards. She knew it wasn't the regular night soil man—a man called Oldham who lives in Evans Court—because it's usually him and his son. However, these were two grown men in cloaks, which she also found strange, because they seemed over-dressed for such strenuous work."

"You think they were Phelps and Nevill?" Hadrian asked. His eyes glowed with excitement and his tone was slightly elevated.

Tilda had the sense this information was of particular interest to him. Did it have anything to do with what he'd seen whilst shaking hands at the inquest? Tilda could hardly wait to find out. "Since the cart was parked in front of Phelps's house, it makes sense. And I can't dismiss the idea that a night soil cart is a perfect vehicle in which to transport a dead body to the Thames."

They all stopped on the pavement. Maxwell pivoted toward Tilda. "You think they killed Eaton together?"

"We must consider the possibility," Hadrian replied, though Maxwell had asked Tilda.

Hadrian *definitely* knew something that supported Phelps and Nevill working together. Tilda wished she could think of a way to be alone with him to hear what he knew!

"Except we don't know that Eaton was at Phelps's house that night," Maxwell pointed out.

"That's true," Tilda said, glancing at Hadrian, whose jaw had tightened. He gave Tilda an almost imperceptible nod, and she knew in that moment that Eaton *had* been there. Hadrian had seen it.

Tilda's pulse picked up speed. "Mrs. Burley didn't report seeing Eaton going to Phelps's house that night, but she could have missed him, since she doesn't spy at *every* moment." She met Hadrian's gaze and silently communicated that she understood.

Maxwell's brow furrowed. "We should speak with the night soil man."

"I agree," Tilda said. "However, we need to meet Clement at the Lion's Heart now. I suggest we call on the night soil man tomorrow morning."

"Unfortunately, I will not be able to join you as I promised the mercantile house one last day of work." Maxwell exhaled. "I'll be anxious to hear what you learn. Well done tonight, Miss Wren. You're an excellent investigator."

"Thank you," Tilda replied, and they started walking again. "I'd also like to pay a visit to the police station in the morning. Mrs. Burley is busy tomorrow, so she won't be going. I want to tell Inspector Chisholm what we've learned. I'm hoping he'll allow me to interview Mrs. Walters regarding the new information I obtained from Mrs. Burley, that Mrs. Walters did, in fact, lie to us about when she arrived in London."

"He won't like you treading on his investigation," Maxwell warned. "Just be sure to have a reason to speak to Mrs. Walters that pertains to the fraud we're investigating."

"Certainly," Tilda said. "I'm anxious to speak with her about the friendly societies her husband started. My hope is that we will be able to persuade her to finally provide all the information she's withholding."

"I'll be sorry to miss it," Maxwell said with a soft grunt.

"One last thing." Tilda looked at Hadrian. "Mrs. Burley has in mind to match you with her niece and has invited us all to dinner next week."

Hadrian's nostrils flared as he regarded her. "How did you respond?"

"I said I'd speak with you about it. With any luck, we'll have solved these investigations and won't be here." She decided now was as good a time as any to ask about helping those cheated by

Eaton and Phelps. "What will happen with the Amicable Society once we leave? I'm not sure anyone besides Ravenhurst—and you too, Maxwell—is committed to reimbursing those who were swindled."

"I share the concern that those people will be forgotten," Maxwell replied with a dark look. "Though I've only been here just over a week, I find I feel rather passionately about the society and what it should do. I might have actually wanted to be an administrator."

Tilda smiled at him, but Maxwell was looking ahead as they walked. "You have a kind heart, Inspector."

"I do not plan to turn my back on those who were wounded by Phelps's and Eaton's malfeasance," Hadrian said firmly. "I've already sent money—anonymously—to Mrs. Cardy, and I'll do whatever it takes to ensure everyone who was admitted to the society improperly is financially restored."

Maxwell paused and turned his head toward Hadrian. "That is most generous of you."

Hadrian shrugged. "I try to help where I can. I would say that the society should take care of reimbursing those people, but we can't be sure all the money stolen from them can be recovered. And even if it is, I'm not sure the Amicable Society will remain. How can it continue if one or more of its leadership are arrested for murder?"

"That is a very good point," Maxwell said as he continued walking. "One we cannot discount either, for the remaining administrators—and the doctor—are prime suspects in both murders."

Tilda knew one thing for certain: Phelps and Nevill were at the top of the list of suspects for Eaton's murder.

And Hadrian knew why.

∾

*H*adrian began to accept that he wouldn't be able to inform Tilda of what he knew until later this evening, probably after Maxwell retired. At least she was aware that he had information to share—that much he'd been able to communicate.

There was no way he was going to participate in a match-making endeavor with Mrs. Burley's niece, unless it would somehow help their inquiries. He doubted it would be necessary because he agreed with Tilda that their investigations would likely be concluded soon. That filled him with anticipation, but also with a sense of disappointment, as it would mean he would no longer see Tilda every day. At least until their next investigation.

Assuming there was one.

Hadrian could not assume, however. Particularly when Tilda believed that assumptions were to be avoided. He'd do his best to manage his expectations accordingly. Which was to say, he oughtn't have any.

They turned into Little Moorfields, where the Lion's Heart Pub was located. It was outside the Coleman Street Ward, which meant they were less likely to encounter someone who knew them as the Harwoods and Nigel Beck.

If, by chance, they did see someone, they would say that the reporter had approached them after recognizing them from the inquests and was interviewing them about the Amicable Society. Furthermore, Hadrian and Maxwell would say they'd welcomed the opportunity to discuss the society's attributes in an effort to rehabilitate its reputation.

Clement was already there when they arrived. He sat at a table in the corner and waved at them as they entered. Once they were seated, they ordered food and drink. Hadrian was looking forward to the ale in the hope that it would ease his lingering headache.

"It's been a busy day with Eaton's inquest," Clement said. He already had a pint of ale and took a sip.

"Quite," Tilda agreed. "We've been conducting many inquiries. Last night, we were at Phelps's house under the supervision of Inspector Chisholm, and we found a ledger with a record of the men Eaton recruited to the society."

"Did that reveal anything new?" Clement asked.

"It confirmed that he charged a higher entrance fee and weekly dues for some people, including Mr. Cardy. Presumably, he was assessing higher amounts to those who were sick."

"He could explain that away as those members being higher risk, hence they would pay more." Clement nodded. "Clever."

"I hadn't considered that, but you're correct," Tilda said. "The ledger was actually the least exciting thing that happened. We encountered Phelps's wife searching the house for money, which she found under the floorboards in his bedchamber."

Clement's jaw dropped. "His wife? She isn't dead?"

"Definitely not," Hadrian replied. "Nor is her name Phelps."

Clement leaned forward over the table, his eyes gleaming. "Tell me everything."

Tilda and Hadrian detailed all they'd learned about Ida Walters, including the fact that she'd lied about a great many things, such as when she'd arrived in London.

"She's a prime suspect in her husband's murder then," Clement said.

"I should think so," Maxwell replied. "But it's not my investigation."

Clement studied him a moment. "And yet you seem to be investigating Phelps's murder."

"As it pertains to my investigation regarding the fraud against the society," Maxwell said a bit stiffly, as if he didn't like Clement questioning him. "Since we now know Phelps started other friendly societies and stole money from them, we can deduce he was behind the swindle at the Coleman Street Ward Amicable Society."

"I wonder if he and Eaton worked together or had their own separate schemes going," Clement mused.

"That is a question we're still investigating," Tilda said. "Though it may be one that we don't find the answer to." She regarded Clement expectantly. "What have you to report?"

Last time they worked with Clement, Tilda and the reporter had traded pieces of information one at a time. Clement would share something, then Tilda would do the same. It was an equitable exchange to prove they were both trustworthy. Hadrian expected she was doing the same now. She was waiting for Clement to share something before she told him about their leads into Eaton's murder.

Clement met her gaze briefly before glancing at Hadrian and Maxwell. "I confirmed that Timothy Eaton does indeed have a sister in an orphanage in Whitechapel. She's eleven years old, and without Eaton contributing money to her upkeep, they are going to turn her over to a workhouse soon." Clement exhaled. "It seems Eaton had a somewhat good reason for his crimes."

Hadrian felt a rush of empathy for the young man. Though Eaton had gone about things the wrong way, he may have felt he hadn't any other choice to help his sister. "It's too bad Eaton didn't have her move into Mrs. Vickers's lodging house with him."

"It may not have been that simple," Maxwell said, sounding a trifle cross. "How is a young working man like Eaton to take care of his younger sister, particularly if he has no experience with that? It isn't our place to judge."

"I wasn't judging," Hadrian retorted. "It's just too bad families can't always stay together."

Maxwell's gaze was cool. "I realize that is foreign to you, my lord, but here, it's all too commonplace."

Hadrian clenched his jaw. He wasn't going to debate Maxwell, particularly when the man certainly knew better than Hadrian on this issue.

"I wish I had more to share about Eaton to help find his murderer," Clement said.

"As it happens, we've made progress on that front." Tilda told him about the naval dirk that Jarret had mentioned, as well as Nevill being a possible suspect. She did not tell him about the night soil men or the suspicion—which was more than that given Hadrian's vision—that Nevill and Phelps may have worked together to kill Eaton. She concluded by simply saying that they were making further inquiries.

Clement inclined his head. "It sounds as though you have good leads. I want to look into these other friendly societies that Phelps—rather, Walters—started. A story about a man who serially swindled people using friendly societies will be of great interest to my readers."

"You'll travel to Reading?" Maxwell asked, appearing surprised.

Clement nodded. "And Maidstone and Guildford, but perhaps I will start by visiting the police station first thing tomorrow to see if I may interview Mrs. Walters."

"She isn't very forthcoming," Maxwell said flatly. "Most of what she says is a half-truth or an outright lie. I think your time is better spent going to Reading."

"Why do you suppose Phelps came to London alone?" Clement asked.

"My best guess is that he perhaps wanted to move on without her," Maxwell replied. "But that's only my intuition."

Clement looked at Tilda. "Do you agree?"

She lifted a shoulder. "I don't know. He was carrying on some sort of affair with Mrs. Atkins, though that could have entirely been for the benefit of the society—or, perhaps more accurately —the benefit of his purse as he sought to gain her financial support. Hopefully, we will soon learn more about Phelps. Nevill and Furnier have just hired Ravenhurst as the Amicable Society's new canvasser, and Maxwell is going to serve as a third administrator, at least temporarily, whilst they decide if they want him to stay permanently."

Clement looked at Hadrian first and then Maxwell. "Are you now? That will give you excellent access to the society's records and doings. You should be able to determine whether Nevill and Furnier were part of the swindle or not."

"I can't imagine they are," Hadrian said. "Both of them are longtime residents of the ward. Nevill has a business there, and Furnier has a job and a wife. That would be rather audacious to cheat their neighbors, and if they had, I don't know how they could expect to continue with the society. Wouldn't they cut their losses? It seems to me Phelps started another friendly society with the intention of stealing its coffers and likely hired Eaton, who'd already cheated at the Prudential Assurance Company, to assist him."

Clement's face creased into a faint grimace. "What you say has merit. I did learn something else that may be important. Furnier and his wife have lost four children, which is why they were keen to be a part of the Amicable Society. I would be surprised if Furnier had planned to commit fraud through the society."

"How sad," Tilda said. "I have found Furnier to be disagreeable, and it seems he has good reason to be."

Hadrian met her gaze and nodded gently, feeling sorry for Furnier. He slid a glance toward Maxwell, who'd also lost family members. But then so had Hadrian and Tilda.

Whilst that was true, losing children was a terrible pain. Hadrian need only look at his mother to see the grief she still carried over losing Hadrian's younger brother, Gabriel. Only recently, in fact, she'd tried to communicate with him in the afterlife.

"I think Dr. Giles is a likelier candidate for participating in the swindle," Maxwell said. "He had motive, due to his desire to establish himself as a physician. Money would allow him to elevate his position and perhaps find his fortune in his chosen career."

"I agree," Hadrian said. "Dr. Giles has been very disappointed and angry about what's happened with the society. He believes it's cost him professional advancement, which is what he was hoping for when he agreed to work with them."

Hadrian recalled the visions he'd had of the administrators arguing and he wished, not for the first time, that he could hear what was being said when he saw a memory. "Perhaps tomorrow night, when we attend our first administrative meeting, Maxwell and I will find out more about the inner workings of the society. Hopefully, we'll have a better sense of whether the three men have a strong enough motive."

Clement tapped his fingers on the table briefly. "It could be Dr. Giles. You did mention that he'd worked as a surgeon and has blades that could match Eaton's wound. Has anyone spoken to Thetford about whether a surgeon's tool might have been used?"

Tilda blinked. "No, but we should." She looked over at Maxwell, and he nodded.

"I'll send Thetford a note," Maxwell said.

Their food and ale were delivered, and they all tucked in for a few minutes.

"You'll be traveling for a few days then?" Tilda asked Clement.

"Likely tomorrow and the next day," he replied. "If I learn anything important, I'll send a telegram. I think I'll delay trying to interview Mrs. Walters until after I return. Then I will be armed with the truth of what happened in those places when I question her."

Maxwell regarded him with surprise. "You speak like an investigator, Mr. Clement. That would all be most helpful, thank you."

Clement inclined his head. "Of course. I suppose I am an investigator of sorts. I ferret out the truth so that I may reveal it to the public." He gave Maxwell a sly smile. "I want to see you catch the murderer as much as you want to catch him—or her."

"Well, I appreciate the help," Maxwell said.

They finished dinner and parted ways with a plan to meet again on Monday. As they made their way back into the Coleman Street Ward, Maxwell glanced over at Tilda and Hadrian. "We shared far more information with him than he did with us."

"We did," Tilda agreed. "But the inquiries he'll conduct outside London could be of great use to us, particularly in determining Mrs. Walters's involvement. I imagine the police will want to prosecute her for her crimes relative to the friendly societies, whether she killed her husband or not."

"Most definitely," Hadrian replied.

"I regret telling the mercantile house I'd work through the end of the week," Maxwell said with a slight frown. "I would much rather call on the night soil man with you tomorrow."

Tilda sent him an encouraging smile. "We'll report every detail. Very soon, you'll be able to focus completely on the investigation."

Which meant he'd be spending more time with Hadrian and Tilda. Whilst Hadrian didn't dislike the man, he found him frustrating at times. He seemed to find ways to emphasize the differences between himself and Hadrian. And Hadrian wasn't entirely sure how to take that.

There was likely nothing to it. Hadrian was merely being defensive because he was jealous of the man. He needed to move past that. He had no claim on Tilda, and the sooner he accepted that and rid his mind of romantic thoughts of her, the better.

CHAPTER 20

Upon returning to White Alley, Tilda, Hadrian, and Maxwell once again settled in the parlor to drink port. Tilda grew more anxious by the minute as she yearned to hear what Hadrian had seen.

Finally, Maxwell stood. "I should turn in. I have to be up early to work at the mercantile house. One last time." He offered a weak smile. "Good night."

He left the parlor, and Tilda waited until she heard his foot-falls on the stairs before turning to Hadrian. Her pulse was already thumping. "Tell me everything you saw at the inquest." She spoke in a low tone.

Hadrian glanced toward the staircase and stood from his chair, moving to the settle where Maxwell had been sitting. He motioned for Tilda to join him. This way, they could sit close together and talk quietly.

Tilda sat beside him and clasped her hands in her lap whilst she waited for him to speak.

"Waiting to tell you what I saw has been interminable," Hadrian said with excitement.

"It seems to have something to do with Nevill." She sucked in a breath as she voiced her suspicion. "Did you see him and Phelps kill Eaton?"

His eyes darkened. "Not quite. When I shook Nevill's hand earlier, I saw him standing over Eaton's body in Phelps's parlor. Phelps was there too. I can't be certain there wasn't anyone else present. The vision was very quick since we were only shaking hands, but I can say that I saw Eaton dead. He was on the floor, and his chest was covered in blood."

"Now we know *where* Eaton was killed," Tilda said. "Do you have any idea when?"

"It was dark, and since Mrs. Burley saw Phelps and Nevill enter Phelps's house Saturday evening and the coroner determined Eaton's death to be late Saturday or early Sunday, I think we can deduce that the memory I saw occurred Saturday night."

Tilda nodded. "What else do you recall about the vision?"

"Eaton's chest was bloody, but there was no weapon in sight," Hadrian replied. "He could have been killed by the naval dirk—I'll share more on that in a moment. Or he could have been killed by one of Dr. Giles's surgical instruments. Just because I didn't see the physician in the vision doesn't mean he wasn't there."

"What do you know about the dirk?" Tilda asked, hanging on his every word.

"When I shook Furnier's hand, I saw a memory in which he stood in Phelps's parlor. His gaze fixed momentarily on a naval dirk, such as Jarret described, displayed on the mantel."

Tilda frowned. "I don't recall seeing that either time we were in the parlor."

"I don't either, which makes me think it's the murder weapon and was disposed of."

"That makes the most sense," Tilda said. "You learned so much today," she said earnestly, but then felt a wave of concern. "Your head must have ached terribly."

"I confess it did." Hadrian's brow creased in a brief grimace, and Tilda hated that he'd been in pain. "I had a third vision when

I shook Dr. Giles's hand. That is when I saw him using medical instruments, including a blade that could have been used to kill Eaton. I also saw a memory in which he stood in the meeting room at the Swan and Hoop with Furnier and Nevill."

"But not Phelps?" Tilda asked.

Hadrian shook his head. "Furnier and Nevill were frowning, and Giles was waving his hands with agitation. I had the sense that Nevill was trying to placate him, but of course, I don't know what they said. It flashed through my mind so quickly. I couldn't make any more sense of it than that."

Tilda was quiet a moment as she thought through everything he'd just revealed. "So we know Eaton was killed at Phelps's house on Saturday night, and the naval dirk was probably the murder weapon. Both Nevill and Phelps were there. But none of that is evidence we can share with Maxwell or Chisholm."

"That's all right, in my opinion, since the best person is already on the case," Hadrian said with confidence. "You."

Tilda felt as though she was actually blushing, which was incredibly odd. "I have excellent help. Your visions have led us here. We just need to find evidence we can present."

Hadrian chuckled. "We've been in this position before."

Indeed they had. "I wanted to tell you that I managed to ask Mrs. Burley about Mrs. Cardy visiting Phelps. She confessed to me that she accompanied Mrs. Cardy to see him on Sunday, just as her husband told us. She also said I mustn't reveal that, since she didn't tell the police, nor did she disclose it during the inquest."

"Did she say why she kept it to herself?" Hadrian asked.

"She didn't want to give the police any more reason to suspect Mrs. Cardy. She is adamant Mrs. Cardy's alibi is true." Tilda smiled faintly. "She went so far as to say she was a likelier suspect in Phelps's murder."

"Whilst that is all good to know, I don't know that we can definitely remove Mrs. Cardy from the list of female suspects who Burley may have seen going to Phelps's house on Monday evening."

Tilda gave him an approving nod. "You're starting to sound like me. I do hope the night soil man will be able to testify that Phelps and Nevill used his cart Saturday night. But we still need to find evidence that Eaton was there—and was killed there."

"Let's see what the night soil man tells us," Hadrian said. "I'm trying to determine Phelps's motive for killing Eaton, if he was indeed responsible, or even partly responsible. It's clear to me why Nevill or the doctor would kill Eaton—they learned of his swindle and became angry."

"You're assuming Nevill and the doctor were not in on the fraud," Tilda noted. "That is why these crimes are intricately tied together. Until we learn exactly who perpetrated the fraud and who was aware of it when, it's hard to know for certain who has the best motive, or any motive, for killing Eaton and Phelps. I do want to start our day tomorrow at the police station, speaking with Mrs. Walters. I hope she can fill in the holes of the fraud scheme, at least somewhat."

"Provided Chisholm allows us to speak with her. And that you can persuade her to talk." He gave Tilda a half-smile. "I have every confidence in the latter and will simply hope for the former."

"We're very close, Hadrian," Tilda said softly. "I know this has not been our typical investigation, but I am very glad you made yourself a part of it. If you had not, I am certain I would have found a way to include you."

Hadrian grinned. "That is most pleasing to hear. I confess I still worry I will be replaced by Maxwell."

She wanted to reassure him. "I know you're jealous of my partnership with him in this, but it's really a three-way partnership with you, if that isn't clear."

Hadrian nodded. They sat for a moment in silence, and Tilda realized they were sitting as close as they had been that day in the coach some weeks ago when they'd kissed. Sitting here in the quiet house, alone together, the excitement of investigative discovery simmering between them, Tilda could imagine kissing him again. With triumph over their shared work and perhaps something more.

Tilda abruptly stood as an irrational fear—of something she couldn't name—tripped through her. "I suppose we should go up to bed." That sounded very wrong. "Not together. You're welcome to stay down here. *I'm* going to go to bed."

She hoped she didn't sound flustered, but she was. She hadn't meant to say anything provocative. And really it hadn't been. It was just that her thoughts had taken a turn where they shouldn't have. Not that Hadrian knew that. Nor would she tell him.

A small smile cracked Hadrian's lips. "I'm tired. It's been a long day. I'll walk you upstairs." He rose.

"You're sure your head is all right?" Tilda asked.

"It still mildly aches—the port helped. I do have lavender upstairs and will sleep with it beneath my pillow."

Tilda smiled. "I'm glad you thought to bring that with you." She made a note to carry some with her, perhaps an oil. She wondered if smoothing it on his temples would help right after he had a vision. Now she was imagining herself massaging it into his skin, and her entire body trembled.

Exhaling, she left the parlor and made her way to the stairs. Hadrian ascended behind her, and on the landing, she turned to face him.

"I think we should call on Chisholm and make our inquiry with the night soil man as our true selves. I don't want anyone to see Mrs. Harwood and Nigel Beck at the police station. We will enter through the back in any case."

"I won't complain about not donning the wig and facial hair," Hadrian said with a grin.

Tilda looked forward to seeing the Hadrian she knew. "I do think we're close to solving things."

He cocked his head. "Do you? Every time I think an investigation feels that way, something happens to send us in a new
direction."

"We can't seem to have a simple case." Tilda gave her head a
shake with a small smile.

Hadrian laughed softly. "No, we cannot."

"Good night then," she said.

"Good night, Tilda. Sleep well."

His gaze lingered on her, and Tilda felt a warmth spread
through her, almost as if he'd embraced her, which was silly.

She went to her room and closed the door. It took her too long to
fall asleep, and she could not blame it entirely on the investigation.

~

*T*ilda had risen early so she could wash the dark powder
from her hair. It felt wonderful to have clean locks and
to reveal her natural color. She entered the kitchen and saw
Hadrian waiting for her near the back door. He looked very
handsome with his dark hair and sparkling blue eyes. His
costume was still simple compared to what he wore as an earl,
but he looked like *him* and not Nigel Beck.

His mouth spread into a wide smile upon seeing her. "I recognize you. It's been some time."

She laughed, and Mrs. Kilgore waved at them as they left.

They kept their heads bent and pulled their hats low as they
hurried along Coleman Street. They did not relax their postures
or speak until they reached Gresham Street and crossed over to
Old Jewry. And even then, it was just to mark their passage and
where they would go to enter the station through the rear.

Upon arriving, they asked to speak to Inspector Chisholm. A
constable showed them to his office, a small space with a window
high on the wall and a narrow fireplace.

Chisholm stood behind his desk and looked toward them with surprise as the constable announced their arrival. "I wasn't expecting you. And certainly not looking like that."

"We thought it best if Mrs. Harwood and her brother weren't seen walking into the police station," Tilda explained.

"It's better if someone recognizes Lord Ravenhurst?" Chisholm asked with a frown. He waved his hand at the constable who took his leave.

"We did come in through the back entrance," Hadrian said. "I believe you'll be glad we've come when Miss Wren explains the purpose of our visit."

Chisholm's brows shot up. "Have you learned something? I just saw you at the inquest yesterday."

Though Tilda had seen him, they hadn't spoken. Their only communication had been to make eye contact and then purposely ignore one another. "I spoke with Mrs. Burley yesterday after the inquest. Since she likes gossip, I pretended to want to share information with her."

Chisholm gestured for them to sit in a pair of mismatched wooden chairs. When they were seated, he sat behind his desk. "I take it she revealed something new?"

"She saw Phelps with a woman at the Black Anchor on Sunday evening when she and Mr. Burley were dining. The description she gave matches that of Mrs. Walters, right down to her amber eyes, which Mrs. Burley saw in close proximity because she made a point of walking by their table to observe the woman more closely."

"Of course she did," Chisholm muttered. His eyes gleamed with satisfaction. "I knew Mrs. Walters was lying."

"I think we all did," Hadrian said.

Tilda sat forward in her chair and pinned the inspector with a firm stare. "We'd like to speak with her, using her dishonesty as leverage to persuade her to finally speak the truth."

"Well, now, this is my investigation," Chisholm said, his brows pitching together.

"You would be present, of course. We want to know the specifics of the other friendly societies her husband started, as well as his plans for the Coleman Street Ward Amicable Society. Of particular interest is whether he tasked Mr. Eaton with defrauding the ill citizens of the ward."

"I think we all assume he did," Chisholm said, echoing Hadrian's comment.

"We don't care to make assumptions, Inspector," Hadrian said smoothly. "May we interrogate Mrs. Walters with you?" He smiled pleasantly, but there was a steel to his gaze, and Tilda thought the inspector wasn't likely to refuse an earl.

After a long moment, Chisholm nodded. "Let's go."

The inspector stood, and Hadrian and Tilda followed him to the door. He led them downstairs to a room and told them to wait.

A few minutes later, Chisholm and a constable entered the room with Mrs. Walters. She looked a bit disheveled compared to when they'd seen her last, and she wore a heavy scowl.

The constable sat her on a bench on the wall opposite the door and stood close beside her. Did they think she was violent?

"Mrs. Walters took a swipe at one of our constables when she was brought in," Chisholm explained. "She's lucky we don't put her in handcuffs."

The woman surveyed Tilda and Hadrian with interest, her gaze sweeping over them. "You look different."

Tilda offered a mild smile. She had no intention of explaining anything to her or identifying who they were. "You look much the same. It is our hope that you will be more forthcoming with your testimony today when we ask you questions. However, we do expect you may lie, as you did about when you arrived in London. We will discover what else you've lied about as we have agents visiting Reading, Maidstone, and Guildford to discover the heart of your and your husband's crimes."

Mrs. Walters's eyes rounded slightly, and she swallowed visibly. Her gaze darted to the inspector.

Chisholm crossed his arms over his chest. "We know you had dinner with your husband on Sunday and lied about when you arrived. It appears you were the woman who visited him late Monday—right around when he was killed. Looks as though you'll be facing a charge of murder and likely hanging."

The color drained from Mrs. Walters's face. "I told you I didn't kill him! I wasn't lying! Not about that," she added in a lower tone.

"Why should we believe you?" Tilda asked. "Perhaps you could demonstrate your newfound honesty by telling us about the friendly societies your husband started. What was his objective?"

Mrs. Walters's jaw clenched, and her knee moved up and down, making her appear incredibly nervous.

"How you behave now could determine your punishment," Chisholm warned.

"We saw there was money to be made from burial societies," Mrs. Walters said. "My sister's son died, and they'd belonged to a burial club. It paid for my nephew's funeral."

Tilda wondered if the vision Hadrian had seen of Mrs. Walters and her husband with a deceased person had to do with her nephew.

Mrs. Walters continued. "We pretended to have children and joined the club—that was in Salisbury, where we lived originally. We said the children died, and we collected the death benefits. We did this a few times in different places. Philip had the idea to start a club, which is what we did. That was in Maidstone."

She went on to explain how Philip Walters had founded that first burial club with another gentleman. Just before they reached the end of the first year when members could begin to collect benefits, he'd left town with all the club's funds. He'd done this two more times—in Guildford and Reading. Then he'd come to London to do the same in the Coleman Street Ward. He'd started the Amicable Society with the intent to fleece its members and flee London.

"It was to be the last time." Mrs. Walters wrung her hands. "We were going to settle in Cornwall. We would have had enough money to live comfortably."

"What happened?" Tilda asked gently, sensing Mrs. Walters's agitation didn't just stem from being caught. "Why didn't you come to London with your husband?"

"He didn't want me to. He thought he could gain more sympathy if he was a widower." She looked down at the floor. "But then he stopped writing to me. That's when I came here to see him."

"When did you actually arrive?" Chisholm asked.

"Last Sunday," she replied. "I did stay at a boarding house because I knew I couldn't go to his house. I had a boy deliver a note, asking Philip to meet me at the Black Anchor."

"And that's where you were seen together," Tilda said with a nod. "What did he tell you?"

Mrs. Walters sniffed. "He said he had to move on sooner than he expected and was angry that I'd come." She lifted her gaze finally and her eyes were wet with tears. "He didn't want to go to Cornwall—he said he wasn't going to fetch enough from this society. He'd decided to go to Bath next to start a new society. I told him I didn't want to continue with these schemes. We had enough money. He disagreed." Her features stiffened, and she looked angry. "I threatened to expose him to the Amicable Society. I was there at the meeting on Monday—in the common room at the Swan and Hoop. He saw me and told me to come to his house later that night."

"So it was you who called on him?" Chisholm asked sharply.

"Yes, but I didn't kill him." Her voice broke, and she brushed her hand against her cheek. "Why would I? I loved him. I wanted him to come with me to Cornwall like we'd planned." Her lip quivered. "He was already dead when I arrived."

Chisholm uncrossed his arms. "What time was that?"

"Just after one o'clock."

"Describe what you saw," Chisholm instructed.

"He was in the parlor on the floor. His head was bashed in, and there was blood and other…" Mrs. Walters squeezed her amber eyes shut and shook her head. "I was very upset. I ran out and didn't return until Thursday."

"That was to find the money?" Tilda asked.

Mrs. Walters nodded. "What will happen now?"

"You'll be prosecuted for fraud and for pushing Miss Wren down the stairs, at least," Chisholm said tersely.

Blanching, Mrs. Walters sent an apologetic look toward Tilda. "I didn't mean to push you. I—I was just trying to get away."

Chisholm grunted. "Regardless, you could have caused her great harm. We'll verify what you've told us." He narrowed his eyes at her. "And we'll know if you've lied."

"I haven't," she swore, her voice climbing with distress. "I hoped to change his mind, to persuade him to take the money from this society and be done with it all. What reason would I have had to kill him?"

"Perhaps you didn't mean to," Hadrian said blandly, though there was a dark glint in his eye.

Everyone knew what Hadrian was saying. Mrs. Walters swallowed.

Tilda could think of at least two reasons Mrs. Walters had for killing her husband—anger at his betrayal of their plan, and jealousy if she somehow learned of his association and potential affair with Mrs. Atkins. But she didn't voice them. Phelps's murder was Chisholm's investigation, and she wasn't sure he'd appreciate her input.

Tilda glanced toward the inspector before fixing her gaze on

Mrs. Walters once more. "I've one last question. Did your husband hire Eaton as a canvasser to recruit people who were sick and overcharge them for fees and dues?"

Mrs. Walters's brow furrowed. "We didn't ever use a canvasser before, and Philip never admitted members who were ill. That would have drawn attention. If he was doing that, it's no surprise the scheme failed. I knew he was too greedy." She closed her eyes briefly.

"Thank you, Mrs. Walters." Tilda nodded at Chisholm to indicate she was finished.

"Wait, I have a question," Hadrian said. Tilda looked over at him, curious what he wanted to ask. "Mrs. Walters, do you know who Mrs. Atkins is?"

She shifted on the bench, and her features hardened. "She's a benefactress who's been supporting the Amicable Society."

"Have you met her?" Hadrian asked.

Mrs. Walters's amber eyes flashed with surprise before darkening. She hesitated before responding. "Yes."

Tilda glanced at Hadrian, so pleased he'd started this line of questioning. "When?"

"I called at her house on Monday." Mrs. Walters cast her eyes toward the floor again and spoke in a quieter tone.

"What happened?" Chisholm demanded. "You should not be keeping important information from us."

"Nothing happened," Mrs. Walters replied defensively. "I said I knew 'Phelps' from before he came to London." She said the name 'Phelps' in a derisive tone. "I told Mrs. Atkins he was a philanderer, and she should not trust him. She laughed and said she liked philanderers because they didn't expect much."

"Take her back to her cell," Chisholm said to the constable.

Hadrian stepped forward quickly and offered his hand to Mrs. Walters to help her up. "Thank you for your honesty today."

Tilda knew he was trying to see a memory, perhaps to determine if the woman was hiding anything else. She took a step toward them as Mrs. Walters stood, hoping to give him a little more time to see something. "It speaks well of you that you're forthcoming now and admitting your crimes. If there is anything else you ought to divulge, you must do so now."

Mrs. Walters shook her head, then withdrew her hand from Hadrian's. "I didn't see anyone else. After I saw my husband had been killed, I rarely left the boarding house until I went back to his house on Thursday. I was too upset. And perhaps a little afraid."

"Why?" Tilda asked gently.

"If someone would kill Philip because of what he'd done, mayhap they'd kill me too. I doubted anyone here knew about me, but I couldn't be sure." She sounded genuinely frightened, which—at least to Tilda—supported her declarations of innocence.

Chisholm inclined his head toward the constable, who then led Mrs. Walters from the room.

Once they were gone, Chisholm exhaled. "That was very helpful. Now we know Phelps was killed between ten, when Mrs. Burley saw him enter the house with Nevill, and one."

Tilda couldn't help thinking Nevill was now the prime suspect in both murders. He had motive and was seen at both murder scenes. Of course, only Tilda and Hadrian even knew where Eaton had been killed. She looked to Chisholm. "Mrs. Walters is almost certainly the woman Mr. Burley saw."

"Agreed," Chisholm said. "Still, I'll confirm the time she says she was there with Burley."

"I imagine this will conclude Maxwell's investigation," Chisholm said. "Mrs. Walters confirmed that her husband started the Amicable Society with the intent to commit fraud."

"We still don't know if he and Eaton were working together," Hadrian said.

Chisholm's brows drew together. "Does that even matter at

this point? I'm sure the victims of this crime only care about recovering their money."

"We are still in the process of identifying those victims," Hadrian noted. "I don't think the investigation can be concluded until that has happened. And how will they recover their funds? What of the money Mrs. Walters found at her husband's house? I should think that would be payable to the victims of his fraud."

"It will be," Chisholm said. "Once Mrs. Walters's trial is complete. If she'll admit her guilt, things should happen fairly quickly."

"What is your next step in determining Phelps's killer?" Tilda asked. "Do you believe Mrs. Walters that she didn't kill him?"

"I'm inclined to, but she's not trustworthy," Chisholm replied. "Nevill remains a suspect. If Mrs. Walters was the woman who called on Phelps that night, that may eliminate Mrs. Cardy and Mrs. Atkins as suspects. Though I'm not sure Mrs. Atkins had a strong motive anyway."

"What of Furnier or Dr. Giles?" Tilda asked. "Surely their motives are the same or similar to that of Mr. Nevill."

"Yes, but they weren't seen at his house Monday night, and Nevill was." Chisholm's gaze glimmered with purpose. "It's time for me to have another conversation with the tailor and to search his residence."

"To hopefully find the missing candlestick?" Hadrian asked.

Tilda doubted the inspector would be so fortunate. Keeping the murder weapon would be an incredibly foolish thing to do.

"That or any other evidence," Chisholm replied.

Tilda and Hadrian took their leave a few minutes later, departing as they'd entered, through the rear of the station.

Waiting until they were nearing Gresham Street, Tilda looked over at Hadrian. "What did you see when you helped Mrs. Walters up?"

"She was at Mrs. Atkins's doorway speaking with Mrs. Atkins. I couldn't hear what she was saying, of course, but I was able to discern Mrs. Atkins's derision. She was looking at Mrs. Walters as if she were a street urchin begging for food."

"I'm not surprised that she found Mrs. Walters wanting," Tilda said with a shake of her head. "Anything else?"

"Mrs. Atkins waved her hand dismissively and laughed, just as Mrs. Walters described. This angered Mrs. Walters. That's all I saw."

"Well, it's good to have confirmation, since Mrs. Walters isn't reliable."

They turned to walk along Basinghall Street. "You didn't offer any information to help Chisholm with the murder investigation," Hadrian said.

"I didn't think he'd want my input."

"Do you think Nevill is the strongest suspect now?"

Tilda didn't immediately respond as she was still considering this latest development about Mrs. Walters and Mrs. Atkins meeting. It didn't appear that Mrs. Atkins was aware of Mrs. Walters's identity, however.

"He does seem the likeliest culprit," Tilda said. "I do wonder why Mrs. Atkins hasn't mentioned the woman who called on her about Phelps on Monday. It seems as though she should have shared that information at Phelps's inquest."

"It does indeed," Hadrian replied. "Does this make her look more guilty?"

"It certainly raises questions. We should perhaps try to learn more from her, but I almost hate to ask you to participate, given the way she behaves with you." She sent him an apologetic glance.

Hadrian chuckled. "I have survived many a managing mother in Society as they sought to match me with their daughters. She is not terribly different. I confess, I find her company distasteful, but my reasons go beyond her fascination with me. I don't care for her disregard of Mrs. Cardy and the others who have suffered from Eaton and Phelps's fraud."

Tilda smiled at him as they continued past Gresham Street on their way to Evans Court. "I am not surprised to hear that. We will discuss Mrs. Atkins and what to do about her later. Let us turn our attention to the night soil man. I hope we'll be able to speak with him."

"You didn't mention him to Chisholm either," Hadrian noted.

"I'm not sure he pertains to Chisholm's investigation. Since the inspector seems inclined to keep the cases separate, who am I to ignore his preferences?" She lifted a shoulder, and Hadrian laughed.

"You are as cunning as you are curious. I shall be forever grateful that we are partners."

His words warmed her in ways she would rather they didn't, reminding her that their association went deeper than the investigations they worked to solve. She met his gaze briefly. "So shall I."

CHAPTER 21

*H*adrian enjoyed these days when they were in the thick of an investigation. He especially loved watching Tilda in her element. She'd managed things very well at the police station. Chisholm had no idea that she'd out-investigated him. At least in Hadrian's opinion.

They arrived at Evans Court, and Tilda paused, touching Hadrian's sleeve so that he stopped with her. He pivoted to face her. "What is it?"

"For the purposes of this inquiry, I will be Miss Wren, but as when we called on Mrs. Vickers, you should not be the Earl of Ravenhurst."

He nodded. "I understand. As it happens, I am also Hadrian Becket." He smiled at her.

Her mouth quirked up. "I've watched how you've become more of him than the earl these past several days. Has it been difficult? You made it look rather easy. I know the lodgings are not what you're accustomed to, and the wardrobe probably isn't either." Her gaze flicked to his simple, dark garments.

"It has been different, and I've learned a great deal." Hadrian imagined he would reflect on the period he'd lived here in the Coleman Street Ward for some time.

"But do you miss your home and its comforts?" she asked.

"No more than you, I imagine. I know you miss your bed," he said with a chuckle.

"True," she said with a rueful smile. "I'm going to tell Mr. Oldham we're looking for a missing man. I'd rather not mention Timothy Eaton unless it becomes necessary. I want to hear what he knows before we give him too much information."

Hadrian nodded and they continued into the alley. They found Mr. Oldham's lodging, a narrow, rather ramshackle house at the end of a terrace. Hadrian knocked on the door.

A woman slightly older than Hadrian answered. Her light brown hair was scraped atop her head beneath a cap, whilst a few strands flowed loose. She eyed Hadrian and Tilda with a bit of suspicion.

Tilda smiled. "Good morning. I'm an investigator looking into the disappearance of a man from the Coleman Street Ward. My name is Miss Wren, and this is my associate, Mr. Becket. Can we trouble your husband for a few minutes of his time? We understand he is the night soil man for this area."

The woman's features relaxed somewhat, though there was still a touch of wariness in her gaze. "I'll ask 'im if 'e wants to speak with ye." She did not invite them in and closed the door in their faces.

"I suppose we wait," Hadrian said wryly. "Should I have offered money?"

"Let's see what happens. But yes, we may need to do that." She looked over at him. "You don't mind?"

"Not at all."

They waited a few minutes, and Hadrian began to worry that their errand would be for naught. But then the door opened, and a man with dark, receding hair and a razor-sharp nose regarded them cautiously. "I'm Oldham. Who're ye looking for?"

"A man called Thomas Edgars," Tilda said with ease. "Specifically, we'd like to speak with you about last Saturday night, when he went missing. We understand you might have loaned your night soil cart to someone."

Oldham's eyes narrowed. "I do that sometimes—when I want a night off. I don't know anybody named Thomas Edgars."

"Who borrowed your cart last Saturday?" Tilda asked.

"Neither of 'em were Thomas. I can't 'elp you." Oldham started to close the door, but Hadrian put his hand on the wood to stop him.

"We understand this is an inconvenience. Perhaps I can make it worth your time." Hadrian reached into his pocket and pulled out a few coins, which he offered to the man.

Oldham hesitated the barest moment before taking the money and tucking it into his pocket. "A couple o' fellows asked to borrow me cart. They came 'ere asking just as I was getting ready to leave. Promised they'd 'ave it back within an 'our—but they were late."

"Do you know their names?" Tilda asked.

"I've seen 'em about, but I don't know 'em personally."

"Could you describe them?" Hadrian prompted.

"One of 'em 'ad long, dark side whiskers. I remember, 'is eyes were small and shifty. 'E was on the 'eavier side. Smelled like booze. Other one 'ad gray hair and a round nose. 'E kept to the background and the drunk did the talking."

"Was he actually drunk?" Tilda asked.

Oldham shrugged. "Could've been."

"So this wasn't really an instance of you wanting to take the night off," Tilda said. "These two approached you to borrow your cart. Do you know why?"

Oldham blew out a breath. "I don't ask. It 'appens from time to time, usually during the day though. People want to use me cart to move something. They paid me a decent sum, so I didn't care."

Tilda gave him a pleasant nod. "May we see your cart?"

The man looked to Hadrian, but didn't say anything. He didn't have to, because Hadrian knew he wanted more money.

Withdrawing another few coins, Hadrian pressed them into the man's hand, which had shot out the moment Hadrian reached into his coat pocket. "Where's your cart?"

Oldham took them around the end of the terrace to a small yard with a privy and the night soil cart. Though the cart was empty, the stench of offal was pungent. Hadrian resisted the urge to reach for his handkerchief to cover his nose. He glanced at Tilda and saw her nose wrinkle.

They moved close to the cart, and Tilda peered inside. It was empty, but there was soil embedded in the corners. She reached inside and plucked a piece of fabric a few inches in size from a splinter of the wood.

She held it between her gloved fingers and lifted it to peruse it more closely. It appeared to be broadcloth and was dark blue with a very subtle and simple plaid pattern. She turned it about. There was a white mark on the other side, like chalk.

"This seems as though it's from a piece of clothing," she observed. She looked to Oldham. "I imagine you pick up any number of things in your nightly collection."

"I do," Oldham said with a nod. He scrutinized the fabric a moment. "That was from the night those blokes borrowed the cart."

"How do you know?" Tilda asked.

Oldham looked at Hadrian again expectantly.

Hadrian handed the man a few more coins.

"When the blokes brought the cart back, there was a large piece of that fabric—enough to spread over the cart a few times over." Oldham made a face. "But it was soaked with pig's blood, and they asked me to burn it. Paid me extra."

Hadrian exchanged an excited look with Tilda.

"Did they dispose of a pig?" Tilda asked.

"Assume so." Oldham shrugged. "I didn't ask."

Tilda handed the scrap of fabric to Hadrian, who'd removed his glove. Right away, he was inside Nevill's shop. He saw the fabric spread out over a table with a pattern marked out in chalk. Nevill—Hadrian assumed it was his memory he was seeing—swept it up and walked to the front part of the shop. Phelps stood there, waiting with a small lantern in his hand. It was night.

Blinking, Hadrian met Tilda's gaze and nodded. He didn't want to give the scrap back to her yet in case he might see something else.

Tilda looked to the night soil man. "Thank you for your time, Mr. Oldham." She turned and started toward the street.

Hadrian joined her and focused on the fabric in his hand as they walked. He tried to think of what the fabric had been used for.

There! He was back in Phelps's house. Nevill and Phelps lifted Eaton onto the fabric, which had been laid out over the floor of the parlor. Then they rolled him inside it.

"Hadrian!" Tilda gripped his arm, startling him from the vision.

He realized he was falling. She tried to keep him upright, but gravity would not be denied. He managed to put his arms in front of himself to break his fall and landed on his knees.

"Are you all right?" Tilda's tone was fraught with concern as she crouched beside him.

"I'm fine. I don't know what happened. One moment, I was in Phelps's parlor, and the next I was pitching forward." He took a breath to try to slow his pulse and pushed himself up.

Tilda clasped his arm and helped him as best she could. "I know what happened. You were seeing a vision and trying to walk at the same time. I'm not sure you've ever done that before. I would advise you not to try it again."

He saw that she was frowning at him. No, not frowning, just regarding him with grave concern. "I'm fine, but your counsel is well received. You're right—I haven't ever done that before. I'm not sure why I did. Honestly, I didn't think about it. I had the fabric, and I focused on trying to see what Nevill did with it."

Realizing he no longer had the fabric piece in his hand, he glanced at the cobblestones and saw that he'd dropped it. Tilda bent and retrieved the swatch. "I'll keep this for now." She tucked it into her pocket.

"You sure you want to put something that has spent a week in a night soil cart in your pocket?" Hadrian asked wryly.

She lifted a shoulder. "What choice is there? Are you ready to continue walking?"

"Yes, though my head is throbbing." He winced as he touched his temple.

The furrows in Tilda's forehead deepened. "No more visions today."

"We'll see what happens." Hadrian wasn't going to promise anything, especially not when they were so close to solving at least Eaton's murder. They continued on their way from the alley. "I saw Nevill in Phelps's parlor. They lifted Eaton onto the fabric and rolled him up."

"Did you see them put the body into the cart?" Tilda asked.

Hadrian shook his head and immediately regretted it as the pain sharpened. "No, I lost the vision along with my balance. I could try again."

"We don't need you to," Tilda said firmly. "We'll learn the rest from Nevill. Could you tell how he was feeling?"

"In the first vision at the shop, he was extremely agitated and upset and angry at Phelps. At Phelps's house, he was disgusted, almost sick."

"Nevill certainly seems guilty, along with Phelps. Too bad he's dead or we could use them against one another to learn the truth." Tilda slid him a sideways glance. "We'll need to come up with a way to provoke him to confess what happened when we call at his shop. First, we'll need to return to White Alley and disguise ourselves as Mrs. Harwood and Mr. Beck."

Hadrian noted her slightly pursed lips. "You don't look happy about that."

"I didn't think we were finished disguising ourselves, but I'm not looking forward to powdering my hair again."

"I will miss the way you look," he said. "But it's only temporary. And perhaps not for much longer at all."

"Let us hurry." Tilda quickened her pace. "I'm quite anxious to speak with Nevill, knowing what we know now."

"What if Inspector Chisholm has taken him to the police station?" Hadrian mused.

Tilda exhaled. "I suppose that's possible. We must be careful not to encounter Chisholm, lest he wonder why we're making these inquiries."

"We may very well uncover Eaton's murderer today," Hadrian said. "I wonder how Chisholm will take that."

"I'd like to think he'd be grateful, but he may not appreciate our involvement in his investigation." She straightened her shoulders. "In the end, if the killer is caught, it shouldn't matter." She turned her head and met Hadrian's gaze. "Hopefully he soon will be."

~

*T*ilda lamented her transformation back into Mrs. Harwood. She truly hated powdering her hair. Thankfully, she'd had Mrs. Kilgore's assistance, as it was difficult to accomplish a thorough job of it on her own. It was much easier for Hadrian to don his hairpieces. Tilda wished she'd thought to obtain a wig from Mrs. Longbotham.

Disguised once more as Mrs. Harwood and Nigel Beck, Tilda and Hadrian made their way to Nevill's shop in Moorgate. There were a pair of employees inside, each working with a customer, whilst a few other patrons poked around the shop.

Nevill was not present, but then he'd come from the back last time they visited. Tilda hoped that would also be the case this time. She and Hadrian looked about for several minutes before one of the employees was finally free. When none of the other clients approached him, Tilda did so.

"Good afternoon," she said to the young man, recognizing him from the last time they'd been to the shop. "We're looking for Mr. Nevill."

"Mr. Nevill's not typically here on Saturday afternoons. Can I help you with something?"

Tilda exchanged a disappointed look with Hadrian. "We'd like to have a coat made for my brother here."

The young man nodded. "Shall I show you some plates and fabric swatches?"

"I know what fabric I'd like," Hadrian said. "Dark blue broadcloth with a simple plaid. It almost doesn't look like plaid at first glance. A friend has a coat made from it, and I'm sure he said it came from this shop."

"That is very specific." The young man's face creased. "I'm not sure we have something exactly like that at the moment."

Tilda pulled the swatch from her pocket and held it out in her palm. She displayed the side without the chalk mark. "This is the fabric. My brother's friend gave it to us."

The clerk nodded. "We did have that, but I'm afraid we don't right now." He gave them an apologetic grimace. "It actually went missing last week. I'd just marked out a pattern for a coat on it."

That explained the chalk, Tilda thought.

"You've no idea what happened to it?" Hadrian asked.

Tilda wondered how they could lose an entire bolt of fabric. But, of course, they hadn't. Nevill had taken it and not told anyone. Which he wouldn't have, given what he'd used it for.

The young man shook his head. "I was hoping I just put it

somewhere and didn't remember and that it would turn up. Do you want to see other swatches?" he asked Hadrian. "We have some other very nice blue plaids."

"I'll think about it," Hadrian said with a vague smile. "We appreciate your time." He and Tilda turned and left the shop.

"When Nevill wasn't there, I was prepared to be disappointed," Tilda said.

"You seemed to be for a moment," Hadrian noted.

"I was, but we were able to obtain confirmation that this fabric came from his shop. And now we have proof to present to others—since we cannot share your vision—that Nevill was involved with at least the disposal of Eaton's corpse." She paused and turned to face Hadrian. "Except we can't prove that Eaton's body was wrapped in the fabric, just that the broadcloth came from Nevill's shop and a piece of it was found in a night soil cart that he and Phelps paid Oldham to borrow."

"We also have Oldham's testimony that he burned a large piece of that fabric soaked in supposed pig's blood." He gave her a sardonic look. "We don't really think the night soil cart was used to dispose of a pig, do we?"

Tilda shook her head. "Absolutely not. That ties Nevill to the disposal of *something* bloody. But we don't yet have evidence that Eaton was at Phelps's house on Saturday night. We're going to have to coax a confession out of Nevill."

"We've done that before," Hadrian said. "Using the information we have from my visions."

Tilda nodded. "The meeting at the Swan and Hoop is tonight. Let's see if we can provoke a confession from Nevill."

"What are we going to tell Maxwell?" Hadrian asked.

They began walking once more. "We'll tell him about our meeting with the night soil man and finding the fabric," Tilda replied. "Since Oldham described Nevill as one of the men who borrowed the cart, we wondered if the chalk mark might indicate the fabric came from his tailoring shop."

Hadrian grinned. "Genius. That leads us directly to Nevill's shop, and we can inform Maxwell of what we learned from the employee."

"Precisely." Tilda exhaled. "It's too bad we can't tell Maxwell about Nevill and Phelps standing over Eaton's dead body in Phelps's parlor. But hopefully the 'pig's blood' that the night soil man reported seeing on the fabric, and the fact that they paid him to dispose of it, will convince Maxwell that they were transporting a dead body."

Silence reigned for several minutes as they walked. Tilda thought through ways they could provoke Nevill to confess.

"If we can provoke him to confess about Eaton, perhaps he'll do so about Phelps too," Hadrian said as they turned into White Alley. "Whether Nevill killed either man, or both of them, he's been hiding things."

"That is certainly true. Once he knows we're aware of that, he should begin to unravel." She shot him a look full of anticipation as the scheme crystallized in her mind. "And I know exactly how to pull the thread."

CHAPTER 22

As soon as Maxwell arrived at White Alley from the mercantile house, Hadrian and Tilda updated him on everything they'd learned that day—minus the memories Hadrian had seen and from which he was still suffering a slight headache.

Then they reviewed the scheme Tilda had concocted for provoking Nevill's confession at the meeting. Hadrian had helped, but Tilda had laid out the plan. He was looking forward to executing it, but was disappointed that Tilda would not be a participant, since she would not be allowed into the meeting.

Instead, Tilda would remain in the common room in the company of Mrs. Furnier and Mrs. Draper, if they came. She'd even brought some items to mend, though neither required mending, nor was she actually going to conduct a repair. By her own admission, her lack of skill at needlework was only surpassed by her complete disinterest.

Just as they were preparing to leave, Mrs. Kilgore came upstairs carrying a small basket. "These just arrived for you. They're biscuits."

"Who are they for?" Maxwell asked.

"All of you. There's a note," Mrs. Kilgore said.

Maxwell pulled a small piece of parchment from the basket and read it aloud, "Congratulations, Mr. Harwood and Mr. Beck."

"Not for all of us then," Tilda noted with a smirk.

Mrs. Kilgore grimaced. "Sorry, Miss Wren."

Tilda waved her hand. "It's fine. It appears someone is congratulating them on their new positions with the society, and that does not include me. Who delivered them?"

"A young boy," Mrs. Kilgore said. "He came to the back door. I didn't recognize him."

Maxwell returned the note to the basket and withdrew a round biscuit stamped with a pineapple design. "As it happens, I'm feeling a bit peckish. Thank you, Mrs. Kilgore. We'll be back later."

He popped the biscuit into his mouth, and the three of them departed on their way to the Swan and Hoop.

"I wonder who sent the biscuits," Tilda mused.

"Mrs. Atkins?" Hadrian suggested.

"Seems like she might have just sent them to you," Maxwell cracked.

Tilda laughed as Hadrian rolled his eyes.

"Well, they are delicious, whoever sent them," Maxwell said. "That was very thoughtful. I must say, I've enjoyed many things about this investigation, including the sense of belonging that many people here seem to feel. We have something like that at the police station, but it's not quite the same. I'll probably be back there soon enough, as this investigation is winding down."

Hadrian wouldn't walk away without ensuring things were made right. That was not an investigator's job, but Hadrian hated thinking of people like Mrs. Cardy and her children suffering as a result of the money swindled from them. He also thought of Eaton's sister in the orphanage and didn't want her going to a workhouse. "I will not consider our work done until we have restored the funds that were stolen from everyone who was cheated by Eaton and Phelps."

"You still plan to meet with Draper to determine who those people are?" Maxwell asked.

"I do," Hadrian said. "I will set that up with him after the meeting, I hope. We'll see how things progress."

Tilda gave them a rueful smile. "I hope the plan goes well. I'll be sorry to miss its execution."

"We will share every last detail," Hadrian promised.

"All that matters is that you obtain Nevill's confession," she said.

They went into the pub. Mrs. Furnier and Mrs. Draper were sitting together at a table near the door to the meeting room. "I'll join the ladies," Tilda said. "At least I brought mending to pretend to work on today."

"We'll see you after," Maxwell said.

He and Hadrian made their way to the open door into the meeting room.

Nevill, Furnier, and Draper were already there. Nevill looked a bit pale, and he was not his usual smiling self. Hadrian assumed he'd spent some time today being interviewed by Inspector Chisholm and wondered how that had gone. Hadrian knew without a doubt that Nevill had not been forthcoming about his role in Eaton's death and would have had to maintain his deceit when speaking with Chisholm. He was likely spent.

"We can sit, if you'd like." Furnier gestured to a table arranged with six chairs. "We're just waiting for Dr. Giles."

Draper looked toward the doorway. "Here he is."

Dr. Giles strode inside, assessed the room, and closed the door. He removed his hat and set it on a hook near the door where others had put theirs. Hadrian added his hat to the wall, and Maxwell did the same.

Furnier positioned himself at the head of the table, and Nevill sat to his left. Draper sat beside Nevill, whilst Hadrian and

Maxwell took the chairs opposite them. This left the seat at the other end of the table open for Dr. Giles. However, he didn't sit. He moved to stand behind the chair and braced his hands on top of the back.

"Would you like to sit so we may begin?" Furnier asked with an arched brow.

"I don't need to sit." The doctor's mouth was set in a firm line. The muscles of his neck were tense, and his brows pulled together. His blue eyes sparked with high emotion. "I would like to resign from the Amicable Society. When I accepted Phelps's offer to work with the society, I never envisioned the disaster it would become. Desperate people cheated of their money. Two people dead." Dr. Giles shook his head. "I can't imagine why you all want to continue, but I do not. I don't think the Amicable Society is salvageable."

"I can't disagree," Furnier said, which seemed to surprise both Nevill and Draper, who swung their heads toward him.

Draper even gasped. "We can't abandon the society," he argued. "It provides a much-needed service for the ward."

Dr. Giles cut his hand through the air. "There are other burial societies."

"But our Amicable Society is more than that," Draper said. "We help people in time of illness, and we, as members, look out for one another. We are a friendly society, and that is much more than a simple burial club."

"We are a friendly society founded on decidedly unfriendly intentions," Dr. Giles said darkly.

It sounded to Hadrian that Giles knew Phelps had started the society with ill intent. Did all of them know?

"What are you saying?" Draper asked. "That the Amicable Society was never meant to be a friendly society?"

Furnier shot Dr. Giles a frigid stare. "Let us not revisit what's happened. Dr. Giles, if you would like to disassociate yourself from the Amicable Society, we cannot force you to stay, nor will we try. Perhaps we should all take your lead and step away from this failed endeavor."

Draper looked earnestly about the table. "I believe we can start fresh with new leadership." He pinned his gaze on Furnier. "We have Mr. Beck and Mr. Harwood to help. We can move forward with the picnic and plan other events that will instill confidence and a sense of brotherhood within the ward."

Brow furrowing, Furnier contemplated Draper's heartfelt plea. "I did envision Mr. Beck working as an officer of goodwill, perhaps even more than recruiting new members."

Dr. Giles threw his hands up. "This is a waste of time. The police haven't even caught who killed Phelps or Eaton. Their behavior and murders are a stain on the society, even if no one else will be defrauded because they're both dead."

Maxwell and Hadrian exchanged a look. It was time.

Hadrian looked at the doctor. "It's interesting you commented that the Amicable Society was founded fraudulently. I find myself wondering what you know about what has transpired—and possibly haven't revealed." This wasn't part of the plan, but they hadn't anticipated Giles saying something like that, and Hadrian wanted to know what he'd meant.

The doctor's lips parted, but he clamped his jaw shut very quickly and exchanged a look with Furnier and Nevill. Draper appeared confused. It certainly appeared to Hadrian that they knew something they hadn't revealed. Perhaps Tilda's scheme would provoke confessions from everyone.

"Harwood and I have something to share." Hadrian looked toward Maxwell.

"I have an old friend who is a constable with the police," Maxwell said. "He told me that Phelps's wife turned up here in London. She isn't really dead."

All the men at the table, save Hadrian and Maxwell, appeared surprised, but Hadrian couldn't know if that was because they'd believed her to be dead or they'd known she was alive and were shocked that she was here.

Maxwell continued. "Mrs. Walters—Phelps isn't their real name—has had much to say." He paused and looked at each of the four men who'd been with the society. "The man you knew as Walter Phelps was actually called Philip Walters, and he started several friendly societies or burial clubs in other cities, solely with the intent to steal the money that people paid in before there was even an opportunity for it to be paid out."

"Bloody bastard," Dr. Giles swore.

Hadrian looked at the doctor. "You didn't know? You said the society was started with 'unfriendly intentions.' I took that to indicate that you might have been aware of Philip Walters's plan."

Dr. Giles's face lost a shade of color. "I didn't know he'd started the society with an explicit plan to steal everything. We all thought he'd hired Eaton to conduct the fraud of admitting members who were ill and overcharging them." He glowered at Nevill. "At least, that's what Nevill told us after Phelps died. Personally, I assumed Phelps was betting on them dying before they'd have to collect. He purposely kept me from being a part of admitting those members because he knew I wouldn't allow it based on their health."

Furnier's mouth was tight, his expression one of cold anger. Nevill was still pale, and his body was moving as if he were tapping his foot or making some other nervous motion. Draper's eyes were wide, and he kept looking from Furnier to Giles, and then to Nevill, and then repeated the circuit. Giles clenched the back of the chair, his knuckles turning white.

"You all knew about the fraud," Hadrian said.

"And lied about it since learning the truth, particularly at the inquest." Maxwell narrowed his eyes. "You all appear complicit." He fixed his gaze on Nevill and told the lie Tilda had concocted to provoke Nevill. "Mrs. Walters arrived in London on Saturday and went to her husband's house. She saw Phelps and another man pushing a night soil cart." He paused before continuing, his gaze sweeping around the table.

Hadrian tensed, knowing what was coming next.

"She said whatever was in the cart appeared bloody," Maxwell finished.

This revelation was met with more shock and gasps from everyone, even Furnier.

"Who was with Phelps?" Giles asked, his eyes bulging.

"There was a piece of fabric attached to the inside of the cart," Hadrian said. He looked at Nevill and watched the remaining color in his face drain away. Moisture dappled his forehead.

Maxwell withdrew the scrap of fabric that had come from the night soil cart and placed it on the table in front of him. "This is the broadcloth that was found in the cart. It came from Nevill's shop."

The other men at the table swung their heads toward Nevill.

"What have you done?" Furnier demanded.

Nevill's shoulders shook. "God forgive me." He began to sob.

Suddenly, the door burst open, and Mrs. Atkins swept in. Tilda was on her heels, her green eyes wide.

"I should be a part of this meeting," Mrs. Atkins declared with great hauteur. "I have important things to say."

Furnier stood and glowered at her. "Right now, there is nothing more important than Nevill explaining why he has committed murder."

CHAPTER 23

*T*ilda had tried to stop Mrs. Atkins from storming into the meeting, but the woman was adamant that she be allowed to participate. Now, it seemed she'd entered at the precise moment when Hadrian and Maxwell had orchestrated Nevill's confession.

Tilda quickly met Hadrian's gaze. He gave her an infinitesimal nod that told her they'd executed the plan.

Nevill was seated at the table, his head bent and his shoulders shaking as he sobbed.

"Pull yourself together, man," Furnier snapped. He looked down his nose at the distraught Nevill. "Did you and Phelps kill Eaton together? And then you killed Phelps? I wouldn't have imagined you could be capable of murder, but it seems I was wrong."

Nevill lifted his head and wiped his hands over his face. He drew a deep, shuddering breath. "I swear I didn't kill anyone."

Maxwell fixed his gaze on Nevill. "What—rather, who—was in the night soil cart? We know you borrowed it along with Phelps."

"And don't say it was a pig," Hadrian warned.

Tilda wanted to join in the interrogation, but her participation would draw questions. Whilst she and her partners acknowledged it was possible their true identities may come to light before the end of the evening, they hoped to remain in disguise for a little while longer. Hadrian still hoped to ensure the people who were cheated by Eaton and Phelps were financially restored.

"It was Eaton in the cart," Nevill said, looking and sounding defeated. "But I didn't kill him. Phelps did. He came to my house and told me I had to help him with a problem, but that first we had to stop at my shop to fetch some fabric. He didn't explain anything. He was a friend in distress, so I complied."

"What on earth are you saying?" Mrs. Atkins shrieked. "What night soil cart? What happened to the pig?"

"There was no pig," Tilda said softly. "Mr. Nevill is confessing that he helped Mr. Phelps with a problem, and it appears that may have been disposing of Mr. Eaton's body."

Mrs. Atkins sucked in a breath as her hand fluttered before her chest. "I feel faint."

Hadrian bolted from his chair and pulled it toward Mrs. Atkins. She sat down soundly, and Hadrian had to keep it steady.

"My fan…" Mrs. Atkins managed as she held up her reticule with a shaking hand.

Tilda opened the reticule and retrieved a fan, which she opened and handed to Mrs. Atkins. But the woman didn't take it. She glowered at Tilda in silent remonstration. Clearly, Tilda needed to fan her. Clenching her jaw, she did as the woman wanted.

Hadrian exchanged a suffering glance with Tilda before returning to stand near the table.

"Please continue," Maxwell prompted Nevill. "You owe everyone here the complete truth."

Nevill gave a faint nod. "We arrived at Phelps's house, and

Eaton was dead on the floor of the parlor. There was a great deal of blood." Nevill's face turned green.

"Why didn't you fetch a constable?" Furnier demanded.

"I wanted to, but Phelps swore it was an accident." Nevill wrung his hands, and the pitch of his voice rose. "He was afraid he'd hang. He said he'd caught Eaton in his corruption and confronted him. Eaton came at him, and Phelps grabbed his knife from the mantel to defend himself. I-I believed him."

"But you don't believe that's true now?" Maxwell asked.

Nevill shook his head. "The night Phelps died—when I went back to his house after the meeting—I learned he'd been part of the original swindle."

Tilda stopped fanning Mrs. Atkins and stepped toward the table between Hadrian and Maxwell. "How did you discover his role?"

Nevill blinked at her, as if he was surprised to hear her ask the question. Tilda simply hadn't been able to remain quiet another moment. "When he went to pour the wine, I noticed a diary on his desk. It was open, and I saw a name at the top of the page that I didn't recognize. But there were amounts listed, and I could see they were entrance fees and weekly dues, only for more money than we typically charge."

Tilda and Hadrian looked at one another. That had to be the ledger they'd reviewed.

"At first, I thought it must have belonged to Eaton, and he'd catalogued the members he'd recruited, as well as the amount of money he'd charged," Nevill continued. "However, it was written in Phelps's handwriting. It was *his* recordkeeping. He knew about the corruption."

"And you discovered his deceit," Maxwell said with a frown. "That would have been an excellent motive to kill him. You were, apparently, the last to see him alive."

Nevill did, in fact, appear quite guilty.

"I didn't kill him," Nevill cried, his eyes wide. "And I didn't kill

Eaton. I did help take his body to the Thames, and I lied about that. I'm so ashamed." Tears streamed down his cheeks once more.

"You'll go to prison for that," Furnier said.

"You definitely won't be part of the Amicable Society anymore," Draper declared.

Giles stared at Nevill in cold fury. "When you told us Phelps and Eaton had worked together to swindle the society, you could have told us the entire story but didn't. How can we trust anything you say?"

Nevill put his hand on his heart. "I swear I'm telling the truth now. I will go to the police, and I will tell them everything."

Maxwell stood. "Nobody here is without blame. You all agreed to keep the corruption quiet."

"We saw no point in having it made public," Furnier said tightly. "It wouldn't solve anything and would only drag the society further into the mud. The best we could do was try to make things right and move forward."

"I had nothing to do with any of this, but I don't disagree with them trying to protect the society," Draper said. "It shouldn't fall apart because of the corruption of two terrible men." He turned his head toward Nevill. "I even understand what you did in helping Phelps. You were trying to protect the society. That's probably why you killed him too. He ruined everything and dragged you into it."

Nevill shook his head wildly. "But I didn't kill anyone!"

"I agree with Draper," Furnier said quietly. "It only makes sense that you killed Phelps. If you truly cared for the society and those of us associated with it, you would confess your guilt and end this nightmare."

"But I didn't kill anyone," Nevill repeated, his voice pitching down as he lowered his gaze to the table. He sniffed and rubbed his hand across his nose.

"I am sorry it's come to this," Furnier went on. "But I just don't see how the society can recover." He looked to Maxwell and Hadrian. "I'm afraid your services will not be needed."

Hadrian locked his gaze with Furnier's. "I'm committed to ensuring that the people who were cheated receive their money. Don't you have a lockbox with the society's funds?"

"I do," Furnier replied. "With the society ceasing to operate, we'll have to refund everyone's money, not just those who were cheated, and there isn't enough since Eaton and Phelps stole some of it."

"We'll have to find an equitable way to refund the fees," Hadrian said. "Unless a benefactor or benefactress wants to step in to help." He glanced toward Mrs. Atkins where she sat in the chair.

"This is a travesty," she cried. "I'm not giving money to a failing, corrupt society."

Tilda thought it seemed as if the Amicable Society was well and truly dead.

"We can rebuild the society," Draper insisted. He looked to Furnier. "I will help you."

"I appreciate your zeal, Mr. Draper, but I'm afraid it's too late," Furnier said sadly. "Please help Mr. Beck in his endeavors to return the money, and I will also do my part."

Mrs. Atkins stood and moved toward the table, her gaze fixing on Draper. "We will find a way to start a new society." She shifted her attention to Hadrian and smiled, in spite of the tense mood in the room. Tilda resisted the urge to roll her eyes.

"Can I count on you to join us, Mr. Beck?" Mrs. Atkins asked.

"Certainly," Hadrian replied after a moment's hesitation. "You should accept Draper's help too."

Tilda could see that Hadrian had debated whether he should commit, knowing their time in the Coleman Street Ward was coming to an end. Though, if Nevill was telling the truth, Phelps's murderer was still at large.

She looked about the room and reckoned the culprit had to be there, whether it was Nevill and he was lying, or perhaps it was Furnier, or Dr. Giles, or even Mrs. Atkins. What of Mr. Draper? They hadn't considered him before, but he seemed very invested in maintaining the society. She also couldn't completely discount Mrs. Walters, though the woman claimed to have told the complete truth. Still, people like her and Nevill could not be entirely trusted after they were found to have lied about so much.

"Someone must alert the police about Nevill," Giles said. "I'll fetch a constable."

"You don't need to," Nevill said, rising in a wobbly fashion. "I will turn myself in."

Dr. Giles sent him a dubious glower. "Forgive me if I don't trust you. I'm fetching a constable." He stalked from the room.

Mrs. Furnier and Mrs. Draper had come into the room but stayed near the doorway. Now, they each went to their husbands. Mr. Draper embraced his wife, whilst Mr. and Mrs. Furnier clasped hands briefly. The Furniers whispered to one another, and Tilda wondered what they were saying.

Hadrian leaned toward Tilda. "Do you believe Nevill's claims of innocence?" he whispered.

"He's made himself very unreliable. The evidence leads to him. Nevill looks unsteady on his feet. Perhaps you should help him sit down." She didn't want to outright ask Hadrian to touch Nevill in the hope of seeing the murder, not with Maxwell standing so close.

Hadrian's eyes lit with understanding. "I'll do that." He moved around the table to where Nevill stood with his head down.

Tilda watched as Hadrian murmured to Nevill, then took the man's hand to guide him to a chair near the wall away from the table. It took them a few moments, and Tilda anticipated Hadrian would have plenty of time to see a vision.

But after Nevill was seated, Hadrian met her gaze and gave his head a small shake. Either he hadn't seen anything, or he hadn't seen anything helpful. That was a shame.

"That was not quite the confession we expected," Maxwell said, drawing Tilda to pivot toward him. "But if I were facing hanging, I would probably say whatever I could to avoid it."

"Nevill's declarations of innocence won't save him if he's proven to be guilty, and there is plenty of evidence."

Maxwell nodded. "I hope Chisholm isn't too upset that we discovered the killer, particularly since he probably spent time interrogating Nevill today. I imagine he won't be happy that he didn't catch Nevill in his lies."

"Nevill has fooled everyone," Tilda said. "I think Chisholm will just be grateful the case is solved."

Hadrian returned to the table and asked Draper and Furnier if they could meet the following day to come up with a plan to repay the members.

"I still say we try to maintain the society," Draper said. "Especially if there isn't enough money to refund everyone. We can do it. I'd be happy to step in as the third administrator since Nevill can't continue." He stared at Furnier expectantly, as if he were the sole arbiter of whether the society lived or died. Tilda supposed that was true, since he was the only remaining person who'd started it.

Furnier looked at his wife, who gave him a slight nod. "I'll consider it."

"You should appoint him," Hadrian said. "If the society is to continue, you need another administrator."

"I said I'd consider it." Furnier inclined his head toward Hadrian. "I'll meet you at Draper's house tomorrow."

"Thank you."

A few minutes later, Chisholm arrived with a pair of constables. He was furious that Nevill had lied to him repeatedly and did not believe Nevill's insistence that he hadn't killed anyone. In fact, he was going to recommend Nevill be charged with murdering both Eaton and Phelps.

Whilst Maxwell spoke with Chisholm for a few minutes, Tilda and Hadrian stepped away.

"You didn't see anything when you touched Nevill?" Tilda asked.

"I saw a longer version of when he came upon Eaton's body. In the memory, he entered the house and walked into the parlor. I felt his shock and anguish at seeing the dead man. I'm confident he didn't kill Eaton. What's more, I'm not entirely convinced he possesses the amount of immorality or desperation necessary to have killed Phelps."

"That's an interesting way of putting it," Tilda said. She glanced toward Chisholm. "For now, we must allow the police to do what they will."

The constables placed handcuffs on Nevill, who had started sobbing again, and led him from the room. Chisholm and Maxwell approached Tilda and Hadrian.

Chisholm's brows were drawn tightly together, and his lips were pursed. He did not look pleased. "Apparently, you withheld information from me this morning regarding a night soil man." He glanced at Maxwell, who must have just informed him of the evidence they'd accumulated against Nevill.

"We didn't have solid information when we saw you," Tilda said smoothly. "And once we had a strong suspicion as to Nevill's involvement, we came up with this plan to hopefully provoke him to confess. I'm glad it worked."

"You should have told me everything this morning so that I could have interviewed the night soil man," Chisholm said tersely. "Instead, I wasted my time with Nevill, who continued to lie."

"I daresay he won't be lying anymore," Hadrian said. He met Chisholm's gaze with what Tilda would describe as his best earl expression—it exuded authority and did not encourage debate. "All's well that ends well, isn't it, Inspector?"

"This is not how I care to conduct my investigations."

Chisholm slid an angry glower toward Maxwell. "Your investigation is also complete."

Maxwell didn't appear at all bothered by Chisholm's ire. "We've a few loose ends to tie up with the society. I imagine we will conclude our investigation at the Amicable Society meeting on Monday evening."

"Well, I need all three of you to come to Old Jewry tonight to explain everything you know." Chisholm turned and went to speak with the Furniers, who'd lingered near the far end of the table, before leaving.

Mr. and Mrs. Draper had already departed the meeting room, as had Mrs. Atkins. Now, Mr. Furnier was watching Tilda, Hadrian, and Maxwell warily.

"It's suspicious that we've spent so much time speaking with the inspector," Tilda murmured.

Maxwell moved closer to the Furniers. "What did the inspector say to you? He asked us to come to the police station to give testimony."

"He asked us to do the same," Furnier replied. "That's all he asked of you?"

Hadrian nodded. "He also expressed his appreciation for our help in catching Phelps's murderer."

"And Eaton's." Furnier blinked. "I'm in shock that Nevill would do any of this. I believed he had a kind heart. He's certainly…friendlier than I am."

Mrs. Furnier patted her husband's arm. "Friendliness is not goodness. Mr. Phelps was friendly enough too."

Furnier vaguely nodded. "The inspector said Dr. Giles is at the police station giving his testimony now. I'd like to speak with him about the society." He looked to Maxwell and Hadrian. "We really were trying to protect this fledgling society. It seems Phelps never meant for it be successful, but we did."

"I hope you will decide to sustain it," Maxwell said. "I agree with Draper that it's a benefit to the ward."

"I agree with that too. But I don't know that I'm the right person to continue with it." Furnier gave them a sad smile—the only smile Tilda had ever seen him crack.

"I know you've suffered losses, Mr. Furnier," Tilda said softly. She also glanced at Mrs. Furnier. "You are perhaps the *best* person to ensure the society's success."

Mrs. Furnier nodded at Tilda and curled her arm through her husband's. "I'll make sure he considers it."

Furnier looked to his wife and a more genuine smile—one filled with love—lifted his features. "Let us go to the police station now." He glanced back at Maxwell and Hadrian. "I'll see you tomorrow."

After the Furniers left, Tilda turned toward Maxwell. "You seem genuinely interested in the society's future."

Maxwell lifted a shoulder. "I do live in the ward—at the police station. I think I'd like to retain my membership. Provided they don't kick me out once they learn I've lied about who I am." A faint smile crossed his mouth.

"I felt guilty committing to the society, knowing I won't be there," Hadrian said quietly. "I was encouraging Furnier to appoint Draper. The society needs people to continue. I feel badly that they are relying on us as part of the society's rebirth."

"I understand." Tilda met Hadrian's gaze. "I'm sure you won't abandon them entirely."

"No, I won't do that," Hadrian assured her.

"Neither will I," Maxwell said. "Shall we go to Old Jewry?"

Tilda nodded, and the three of them made their way to the common room. Mrs. Atkins was seated at a table and immediately stood upon seeing them. Tilda heard Hadrian exhale.

"I'm quite serious about the society continuing," Mrs. Atkins said without preamble. "I'm trusting you both to be my advocates, since Furnier and Nevill won't allow me to participate officially. Not that Nevill will have any say going forward. Perhaps Dr. Giles will be stepping in."

"Actually, Draper has put himself forward to be an administrator," Maxwell replied. "Dr. Giles said he wants to remove himself from the society completely."

Mrs. Atkins frowned. "That's a shame. He was a good representative for the society with that engaging smile of his."

Tilda stifled a smirk. Mrs. Atkins was easily won by an attractive face.

"I'm not surprised Draper would offer himself," Mrs. Atkins continued. "He has been a staunch advocate for the society, and his wife too. In fact, if the society falls apart, I may work with them to found a new one."

"How wonderful to create a society that would also accept women," Tilda said.

Mrs. Atkins's gaze snapped to her and widened briefly. "I didn't say we'd be doing *that*."

Tilda considered asking why. Since they were women starting a society, it seemed only natural that women would be allowed membership. But she glimpsed futility in the endeavor and decided to remain silent.

Turning toward Hadrian, Mrs. Atkins fluttered her lashes. "I don't suppose you'd care to see me home, Mr. Beck?"

"I'm afraid we're expected at the police station," he said apologetically, but Tilda knew he was relieved to have an excuse to refuse the woman. "Have a good evening."

Tilda and Maxwell bid Mrs. Atkins good evening as well, then followed Hadrian from the pub. Something wasn't sitting quite right with Tilda. She wasn't sure if it was Chisholm's anger at how the case was resolved, or if the case wasn't *actually* resolved. She still wasn't completely convinced that Nevill had killed Phelps, and, thanks to Hadrian, she was certain Nevill hadn't helped Phelps kill Eaton.

But if not Nevill, who was Phelps's murderer?

CHAPTER 24

After spending a few hours at the police station, Tilda had arrived back at White Alley late and in the company of Hadrian and Maxwell. She found herself wanting to discuss the case, primarily with Hadrian, so they could talk about his visions and how they might use them to find Phelps's killer.

It seemed Maxwell was as convinced as Chisholm that Nevill was guilty of both murders. But Tilda didn't hold that against him. Maxwell didn't have the benefit of everything Tilda and Hadrian knew, nor could he.

The evidence had been enough to convince Sergeant Kilgore that Nevill should be charged with the murders of Eaton and Phelps. Indeed, he hadn't required much persuasion.

Since they'd returned to White Alley so late, Tilda had retired immediately. She'd been hungry but was too tired to eat. Hadrian and Maxwell had gone downstairs to the kitchen to forage for whatever they could find. Tilda was sure Mrs. Kilgore would have assisted them.

Still, when Tilda woke the next morning, she found Mrs. Kilgore was up early too. Tilda made her way to the kitchen and encountered the woman brewing tea with an odd odor.

"Good morning, Mrs. Kilgore," Tilda said. "What do I smell?"

"I'm making special tea for Inspector Maxwell. He is rather unwell." Mrs. Kilgore's face was creased with concern.

Tilda tensed with alarm. "What's wrong?"

"Some sort of stomach gripe," Mrs. Kilgore replied as she poured the tea into a cup. "He's down here on the cot in the storage cupboard." She inclined her head toward the front of the house, where a narrow corridor led to that cupboard. "He was just coming in from the privy after being sick when I came downstairs. I made him lie down in the cupboard rather than go all the way back up to the garret."

"Let me take him the tea," Tilda said. She picked up the cup and made her way to the cupboard. It was windowless and only large enough for the narrow cot and a crate that sat on its end next to it. There was also a bucket beside the bed, and from the smell, it seemed Maxwell's illness persisted.

"I've brought tea," she said softly, placing the cup on the table. She plucked up the bucket and took it to the corridor.

Mrs. Kilgore hurried toward her to take it up. "I'll wash it out and bring it back."

"Miss Wren?" Maxwell croaked.

"I'm here." Tilda moved toward the bed. Since there was nowhere to sit, she knelt on the stone floor.

Maxwell's lips parted, and he appeared to be breathing heavier than he ought. His skin looked clammy. "Did Mrs. Kilgore tell you I'm ill?"

"Yes, but I can see that for myself," she said drily, thinking the situation could use some lightness. She was quite worried at how poorly he looked. "I think we should send for Dr. Giles."

"That would be good, actually. I fear I am most unwell."

"When did you began feeling ill?" Tilda asked, thinking it had come on rather quickly. He'd been fine last night.

"In the middle of the night. I thought I was just feeling poorly because I didn't eat much. Ravenhurst and I didn't want to trouble Mrs. Kilgore last night, so we had cheese and bread. And I'm afraid I overindulged on those biscuits someone sent."

Tilda frowned. "You wouldn't be this ill from not eating enough or from having too many biscuits."

"I am not used to eating such things." Maxwell moaned.

"If I had to guess, I would say it looks as though you've eaten poison," Tilda said. "But that can't be." Or could it? They'd no idea who the biscuits had come from. If they had indeed been poisoned, it would mean someone had intended to harm Maxwell.

And Hadrian.

Tilda's pulse quickened. "Did Ravenhurst eat any of the biscuits?"

Maxwell's eyes closed. "I dunno."

"You should drink this tea. Mrs. Kilgore brewed it to help you feel better."

"Not just yet," Maxwell murmured. "I want to rest."

Tilda frowned as she stood. She didn't like this one bit. Turning, she hurried from the cupboard and went back to the kitchen. "Have you seen Lord Ravenhurst?"

Mrs. Kilgore shook her head. "Not this morning."

Perhaps he wasn't ill. Or perhaps he was and hadn't been able to leave the garret. Tilda hastened to the stairs and quickly ascended to the ground floor. Then she raced to the front of the house. But as she reached the stairs, she stopped short at seeing Hadrian coming down. He was dressed as usual and wore his blond wig and facial hair.

"You're all right?" she asked, sounding breathless, but then her heart was pounding with fright.

"Yes." He reached her at the bottom of the stairs, his forehead pleating. "Why wouldn't I be?"

Tilda touched Hadrian's sleeve. "Maxwell is violently ill. Will you fetch Dr. Giles? I'm worried Maxwell's been poisoned."

Hadrian's eyes rounded. "How would that have happened?"

"I can only think the biscuits that were delivered may have contained poison. Maxwell said he ate too many. Did you have any?"

"I did not, but I did see Maxwell eat several. He couldn't seem to help himself, which he found ironic since he doesn't typically eat such things. He said they reminded him of something his mother used to bake at Christmas."

Tilda's heart squeezed. She hated that something which had given Maxwell joy may now be causing him distress. "He began feeling unwell in the middle of the night, and it's not a mild illness. I wish we knew where those biscuits had come from."

"Didn't Mrs. Kilgore say they were delivered by a boy?"

Tilda nodded. "I'll speak with her whilst you fetch Dr. Giles."

First, Tilda checked on Maxwell and found him peacefully asleep. When she returned to the kitchen, she was surprised to find Mrs. Kilgore had prepared a plate of eggs and toast for her.

"You must be hungry," Mrs. Kilgore said. "You didn't eat at all last night."

Tilda's stomach growled in response. "I am, thank you."

Mrs. Kilgore poured tea. "Don't worry, this isn't the medicinal brew I made for the inspector. This is his lordship's blend."

After taking a few bites, Tilda sipped her tea and looked at Mrs. Kilgore. "Do you recall anything about the boy who delivered the biscuits?"

"He was around ten or eleven, I'd say. He had freckles. Why?"

"Because I fear Inspector Maxwell has been poisoned and that the biscuits are the source."

Mrs. Kilgore gasped. "I had no idea!"

"You wouldn't have," Tilda said gently. "I'm sure Maxwell didn't taste anything wrong with the biscuits. If it's arsenic, as I suspect, there wouldn't be any strange flavor. Ravenhurst has gone to fetch Dr. Giles."

"Thank goodness." Mrs. Kilgore looked a bit pale. "Why would someone want to poison the inspector?" Her eyes rounded. "And his lordship! Do you think it's to do with your investigation?"

"We are investigating the fraud, and it's evident that Phelps and Eaton were responsible. Since they are both dead, they can't poison anyone. Furthermore, no one is aware that we're investigators, as far as I know."

What if someone had discovered their true identities? Tilda wondered if Phelps's or Eaton's murderer could have sent the poisoned biscuits. Except that Nevill was in custody. But what if Tilda's suspicion was correct and Nevill hadn't killed Phelps? What if Phelps's killer feared they were close to discovering their identity and tried to poison them? Tilda's name hadn't been on the card, but that didn't mean she wouldn't eat the biscuits.

Mrs. Kilgore gave her a frank stare. "I'm no inspector, but it seems to me that you've been investigating the murders in addition to the fraud." She lowered her voice, though there was no one to hear them talking. "I'll tell you a secret. You're a better investigator than some of the police inspectors."

Tilda couldn't help smiling. "Well, I'll tell *you* a secret. I can't seem to help myself when it comes to solving murders. If someone is killed in my vicinity, I am bound to investigate."

"I read about the Levitation Killer murders—you solved that case. You ought to work for the police. Except I know they wouldn't hire you." Mrs. Kilgore appeared disappointed by that.

"No, they won't. I do sometimes work with an inspector at Scotland Yard. Unofficially," Tilda added. "It's been nice to have an official assignment with Inspector Maxwell."

Mrs. Kilgore glanced toward the cupboard where he was resting. "He's a good man and a fine inspector. The two of you seem to be well matched. As partners, I mean."

"I'm distressed that he was poisoned," Tilda said.

"The biscuits were for both of them," Mrs. Kilgore said pensively, her brow creasing as she leaned on the worktable.

"And they were sent in congratulations, presumably because

of their new appointments with the society." Tilda tried to think of who all knew about the appointments—the Furniers, Nevill, Dr. Giles, and the Drapers. But why would any of them want to poison Maxwell and Hadrian?

"Perhaps it was an accident," Mrs. Kilgore suggested. "I've heard of that happening when someone grabs the wrong ingredient." She grimaced. "That would be awful. I'm not sure I could live with myself."

A banging on the front door drew Tilda and Mrs. Kilgore to turn their heads toward the stairs. Tilda jumped up and ran to answer the summons.

Tilda opened the door to see Dr. Giles standing on the doorstep. She looked past him, but Hadrian was not present. "Where is Ha— Nigel?" In her agitation, she'd nearly used his real name.

"He went to meet with Draper and Furnier. I'm supposed to attend as well, but it sounds as though Mr. Harwood is quite ill."

"Yes, please come in." Tilda welcomed him inside and took his hat, which she placed on a hook. "He's downstairs so he could be closer to the privy."

Tilda led him to the kitchen and introduced her "sister." Mrs. Kilgore explained Maxwell's symptoms.

Dr. Giles frowned. "Mr. Beck said you suspected poison and that it may have been from some biscuits that were delivered from an anonymous source."

"That's right," Tilda said. "Let me show you to Albert."

"I'd like to look at the biscuits when I'm finished examining him. Do you still have them?"

Tilda looked to her "sister."

Mrs. Kilgore nodded. "I'll fetch them whilst you're in with Mr. Harwood."

Leading Dr. Giles to the cupboard, Tilda motioned for him to enter.

The doctor leaned over Maxwell. "Has he been sleeping for a while?"

"Not terribly long. We spoke briefly, but he was tired. His color actually looks a little better."

The doctor poked and prodded at Maxwell, who finally opened his eyes. He blinked several times. "Giles?"

"Yes. How are you feeling, Mr. Harwood?"

Maxwell's brow furrowed. "Who's Harwood?"

Tilda tensed. Had Maxwell forgotten their disguises due to being ill?

The doctor glanced at Tilda. "It's not unusual to suffer from delusions." He'd set his bag on the floor and opened it to retrieve a stethoscope. He pulled down the bedclothes and listened to Maxwell's chest.

"What are you doing?" Maxwell asked. His words were slurred, making him sound as if he were inebriated or half asleep.

"Just making sure you're all right," Dr. Giles said cheerfully. He continued listening to Maxwell a moment longer, then returned the stethoscope to his bag. "How are you feeling now?"

"Tired."

The doctor asked Maxwell about his symptoms, and it seemed he was doing better. He didn't need to run to the privy, nor was he feeling nauseated. Tilda relaxed slightly. Perhaps he hadn't been poisoned after all.

As Maxwell's eyes began to close again, the doctor leaned down and sniffed Maxwell's neck. He straightened and turned to face Tilda. "It's arsenic poisoning. But not a lethal amount. In fact, I'd wager he vomited a good amount from his system, according to what your sister said. He should be well enough in a day or two."

"Really?" Tilda sagged with relief. Only for a moment, however, as she realized someone had set out to hurt him—and Hadrian.

Giles inclined his head toward the kitchen. "I'd like to look at the biscuits now to see if I can determine if they are the source of the arsenic."

"They have to be." Tilda led the doctor back to the kitchen, where Mrs. Kilgore had set the basket of remaining biscuits on the worktable.

"How many did he eat?" Dr. Giles asked.

"Probably a half dozen," Mrs. Kilgore replied, her eyes darkening with concern. "Is it poison?"

"Arsenic," the doctor replied. "Though there can't have been too much. Six biscuits could have been lethal. I wonder if the intent wasn't to kill Mr. Harwood but just to make him ill. Thankfully, he'll recover."

Mrs. Kilgore exhaled. "I'm so glad. My husband would be—" She snapped her mouth closed and her eyes rounded briefly. She'd clearly forgotten herself. "My husband would have been upset. I'm a widow," she added.

But the doctor wasn't paying much attention to her, fortunately. He was studying the biscuits. "I can't really tell if these contain arsenic. We'd have to feed them to someone or an animal, such as a rat, to see the effects and know for sure. You're certain these are the source?"

"They have to be," Mrs. Kilgore said. "There's no arsenic in the house."

"Did Harwood eat at the pub last night, perhaps?" the doctor asked.

Tilda shook her head. "I know he did not."

Dr. Giles frowned at the biscuits. "I've seen that pineapple stamp before."

"Do you know who made them?" Tilda asked, her pulse quickening.

"It may be a common stamp, but I've seen biscuits like these at an Amicable Society meeting," Dr. Giles said. "Mrs. Draper has brought them on a few occasions."

Draper. Tilda had thought of Mr. Draper as one of the few

people who was aware of Hadrian's and Maxwell's appointments. But why would he want to poison them?

"Why would Mrs. Draper send arsenic biscuits to your husband?" the doctor asked, echoing Tilda's thoughts.

"They arrived yesterday with a note congratulating my husband and my brother," Tilda replied. "It wasn't signed, so we've no idea who sent them."

Dr. Giles shook his head. "I can't think why Mrs. Draper would want to poison your husband or your brother."

Tilda recalled Mrs. Burley wondering why Mr. Draper hadn't been asked to fill in as the third administrator instead of Maxwell. Her reasoning was that Draper had been involved with the society since the beginning, but then she'd gone on to say he was soft-spoken and perhaps not the best person for the position.

But Draper was clearly very invested in the society. Indeed, he'd been quite zealous about it at the meeting last night. He and Mrs. Atkins were a pair given their obsession with the society.

Tilda's blood chilled. What if Draper had wanted a position and was upset when Maxwell and Hadrian, who were newcomers, were appointed? She looked at the doctor. "Do you think Draper could be capable of such a thing?"

"Draper? Or Mrs. Draper?" Dr. Giles blinked. "I'm struggling to imagine it. But this stamp is the same as what Mrs. Draper has used before." A deep frown creased his features. "Draper was very outspoken when Gilbert Cardy died and we found out he'd been admitted as a member despite being ill. Draper insisted the society pay out a benefit. We explained that it wasn't possible, that even if Cardy had been admitted appropriately, benefits are only payable after one year. *No one* is eligible yet."

"Did that satisfy Draper?" Tilda asked.

"It seemed to, but he was still upset on the Cardys' behalf. Several people were."

"I need to know if he was upset enough to act," Tilda said, thinking that Hadrian was with Draper now. And if Draper or his wife had sent arsenic-laden biscuits, what else were they capable of?

Dr. Giles lifted his hands. "I don't know." His features arrested, then he drew in a deep breath. His eyes widened before he settled his focus on Tilda. "I just remembered that Draper had been friendly with Eaton. I'd seen them together a few times."

Tilda's heart was now pounding. "I'm going to Draper's house."

"I'll go," Dr. Giles said. "You should stay here, just in case."

Tilda ignored the doctor's words and started toward the stairs. She wasn't going to stay here and not ensure Hadrian was safe.

CHAPTER 25

*A*fter calling on Dr. Giles and ensuring he would pay a
visit to Maxwell, Hadrian made his way to Draper's
house. Whilst Hadrian was concerned about Maxwell, he wanted
to keep the appointment with Draper and Furnier. Hopefully,
Maxwell would feel better later, and Hadrian would update him
on what happened.

Draper's lodgings were a set of rooms over a millinery shop
on the second floor. Mrs. Draper welcomed Hadrian inside and
showed him to a small parlor where Draper was waiting.

"Good afternoon, Mr. Beck," he said with a nod.

Mrs. Draper looked to her husband. "I'm going to take the
children over to visit my mother whilst you meet." She departed
the parlor.

"I didn't realize you had children," Hadrian said.

"Two," Draper replied. "A boy and a girl, aged two and four."

"How delightful," Hadrian said with a smile. "I'm sorry to
arrive early," Hadrian said. "Dr. Giles will be late, if he comes at
all. I had to fetch him to call on my brother-in-law, as he is taken
ill."

Draper's brow creased with concern. "I'm sorry to hear that. Mr. Harwood won't be here today either then?"

"Definitely not," Hadrian said.

"That sounds worrying."

"Hopefully it's nothing serious." Hadrian didn't want to mention the potential of poison when they weren't certain.

"So it's to be just you, Furnier, and me," Draper said.

"We'll see if Giles shows up." Hadrian held up the ledger he and Tilda had found at Phelps's house. "Hopefully this will provide us with a list of the members Eaton recruited, and we can determine how much money we need to repay them."

Draper extended his hand. "May I?"

"Of course." Hadrian gave the diary to him and idly realized he hadn't ever shaken the man's hand.

Draper sat and opened the ledger to peruse it. Hadrian glanced about the room whilst Draper reviewed Eaton's accounting. There was a photograph on the mantel of Mrs. and Mr. Draper on their wedding day. A pair of painted candlesticks framed the photograph, one on either side. Hadrian noticed the half-burned candles didn't match. One was tallow and the other spermaceti—it looked like the one he'd had seen at Phelps's house in the remaining brass candlestick.

Hadrian moved closer. It didn't just look *similar*... Curious, Hadrian removed the candle from the holder. He was suddenly in Phelps's parlor, where he seemed to spend so many of his visions of late.

He was holding the candle in his left hand, and he was bent over. As he straightened, he pivoted. He saw Phelps's body in exactly the same position he'd viewed it the morning he and Tilda had happened by his house.

Phelps's head was bashed in, but the blood had not settled. It was still oozing from the wound, spreading on the floor beneath Phelps's head. Hadrian realized that in his right hand, he held the missing brass candlestick. His heart began to pound. He couldn't see whose memory this was, but he could certainly guess.

Perhaps the man would move in such a way that his reflection would be visible in the mirror that hung in Phelps's dining room. Unfortunately, he did not. The man stood over Phelps's body, breathing heavily and then swearing under his breath.

"What have I done?"

The man didn't speak the words aloud, but Hadrian heard them in his mind as if he'd thought them. He also felt an overwhelming sense of shock and horror mingled with fury.

"Mr. Beck?"

Hadrian blinked and the vision faded. A terrible pain blistered through his head. He took a deep breath before turning to face Draper. He still held the candle in his hand.

"What are you doing?" Draper asked.

"I just noticed your candles didn't match." Hadrian shrugged, then returned the candle to its holder. Ice coated his skin as he realized he was in the presence of Phelps's murderer.

"When did you start taking money at the society meetings?" Hadrian asked, his heart continuing to race. He worked to keep his tone even.

"I don't recall exactly, but sometime after the new year," Draper replied as he continued to flip through the diary.

"And how did that come about?" Hadrian moved toward the doorway to the small entry hall, which took him past where Draper was sitting. "Were you recruited for the position?"

Draper looked up from the ledger. "They asked at a meeting if anyone would volunteer to help collect money. I raised my hand. I've always been keen to help the society."

"I see. All this turmoil must be very upsetting for you." But was it disturbing enough for him to kill?

It seemed to have been—Hadrian was convinced the man was a murderer. But what could Hadrian do about it right now? He had no proof beyond what he'd seen when he touched the candle.

He'd have to coax a confession out of Draper, as they'd done with Nevill. Hadrian tried to think of how to do that, but he wanted someone else present to hear the confession. Hopefully, Furnier would arrive soon.

"What do you think of the ledger?" Hadrian asked.

Draper frowned. "There are a great many members listed here who should not have been admitted due to illness. They appear to have paid inflated entrance fees, as well as weekly dues." He closed the book with a snap. "I don't know how we can repay all that. But where has the money gone? Shouldn't the police have recovered it from Eaton or Phelps?"

Hadrian thought of the notion that Eaton's killer had stolen whatever money Eaton may have had. Since they knew Phelps had killed him, it seemed plausible that Phelps would have had all the ill-gotten money. Perhaps the entire sum had been beneath the floorboards and was indeed in police custody. Hadrian would confer with Inspector Chisholm and hopefully match up the amount of those funds with Phelps's ledger.

It occurred to Hadrian that money was not Draper's motive. What was it then? The only thing that made sense was Draper's passion for and dedication to the society. If he'd learned of Phelps's corruption, he could have been angry enough to kill him. Hadrian had felt the man's rage in the vision along with his surprise. Perhaps he'd confronted Phelps and killing him had been triggered by emotion.

"We should speak with the police about the money," Hadrian said. "And we should prepare ourselves for the possibility that we won't recover all that was stolen."

Draper's eyes flashed with anger. "It's not fair. People work hard, and every shilling counts."

Hadrian wondered if he could provoke Draper into confessing something. "It's good that Phelps and Eaton are dead."

"I confess I'm shocked by Eaton's behavior," Draper said. "I've known him for some time and never would have believed he was corrupt—at least not on purpose. It seems likely to me that Phelps told him to admit members who were ill and to over-charge them."

"Eaton's colleague from the Prudential Assurance Company confirmed that he had a history of stealing." Hadrian realized he shouldn't have shared that. Why would he know such information?

Draper blinked in surprise. "How do you know that?"

Hadrian shrugged. "I don't recall where I heard it. Perhaps I'm wrong." He wanted to deflect Draper's attention. "You knew Eaton to be a good man?"

"I did. You must be mistaken. I'm sure Phelps corrupted him."

"You sound rather certain," Hadrian said. "Do you have any proof that Phelps did that?"

A look of unease passed over Draper's features as he glanced away. "I just know that he did."

Hadrian sensed the opportunity to provoke a confession, but wished Furnier was there. Where the devil was he? "It sounds as though Phelps ruined a good man *and* robbed the society. That's bloody enraging."

Draper's eyes gleamed with righteous fury. "You're damned right it is."

"I can see where someone might have killed him. Even by accident," Hadrian added softly.

Two things happened at once: Draper rose and dropped the diary on the chair, and Hadrian heard a shuffle outside, perhaps signaling Furnier's arrival.

Hadrian pivoted to make his way to the door just as it opened. But it wasn't Furnier on the other side of the threshold. It was Tilda.

Her eyes rounded, and he heard her shout his name just as he felt something crash onto his head. The blow sent him to his knees, and in a horrid flash, it was a cold night in January when he'd been stabbed and fell to the cobblestones.

But Hadrian refused to lose consciousness this time.

~

*E*verything froze as Tilda watched Draper strike Hadrian over the head with a small table he'd swept up. Hadrian fell forward to his knees, where he swayed. Then he collapsed onto the floor.

Tilda rushed forward, desperate to reach Hadrian.

"Bloody hell!" Dr. Giles shouted from behind her.

She dropped down next to Hadrian as Dr. Giles moved beside her. "Put the table down, Draper! What are you doing?"

"He killed Phelps," Hadrian muttered. He moaned softly and touched his head. "Is it bleeding?"

Tilda looked at his scalp. "No, but your wig is askew," she whispered.

"Did you say Draper killed Phelps?" the doctor asked, his voice rising.

"Yes," Hadrian groaned. "He has the candle from the missing brass candlestick on his mantel."

Tilda's gaze shot to the mantel. Right away, she saw how the candles were different. "Brilliant investigative work," she murmured to Hadrian.

"I saw him do it," Hadrian whispered.

Tilda nodded, eager to hear the details when he could share them.

Draper's eyes were wide. He still held the table aloft.

"What are you going to do?" Tilda asked him. "You've already killed one man, poisoned another, and now you've struck my brother. Do you hope to kill the three of us and flee?"

"I didn't mean to do any of it," Draper croaked. He lowered the table slowly.

"What on earth is going on?"

Tilda recognized Furnier's voice but didn't dare turn her head away from Draper.

"Draper killed Phelps, poisoned Mr. Harwood, and just hit Mr. Beck," Tilda replied.

"He poisoned Maxwell?" Hadrian said, his voice low and unsteady, so that it was possible no one noticed he'd called Maxwell by the wrong name.

"Yes. We puzzled that out, and I rushed over here. But you were busy unmasking him as the murderer." She felt an enormous sense of pride, along with something else she couldn't quite identify. She just knew she felt more drawn to Hadrian than ever before, and she didn't know if it was because of her worry for his safety or her admiration for him solving the case.

Or if it was both of those things as well as some deeper sentiment.

Furnier came to stand near Dr. Giles so that Tilda could see him from the corner of her eye. She still wouldn't take her gaze off Hadrian and Draper.

"Someone must fetch a constable and Inspector Chisholm," Tilda said.

"Perhaps you should do that whilst we guard Draper," Dr. Giles suggested.

Tilda wasn't leaving Hadrian. "I'm staying with my brother since he's wounded." How she wished she had her pistol to train it on Draper until the police arrived.

"I'll go," Furnier said. "Giles, you should look at Beck's head." He departed swiftly.

"Now would be a good time for you to have your pistol," Hadrian said quietly.

"I was just thinking the same thing," Tilda replied softly. "Can you stand?"

"Yes." He rolled to his side.

Tilda helped him rise, then guided him to a chair. "Sit, please."

"You don't have to tell me." Hadrian dropped into the chair with a grimace.

Furnier returned, but before Tilda could ask why—in extreme irritation—Chisholm appeared behind him with a constable.

"The inspector was already on his way here," Furnier explained. "I encountered him just outside."

"Mrs. Kilgore sent me," Chisholm said.

"Who is Mrs. Kilgore?" Dr. Giles asked.

"My sister," Tilda replied.

"Isn't the sergeant also called Kilgore?" Dr. Giles asked. "And who is Maxwell?"

Tilda and Hadrian exchanged a long look, but before they could respond, Inspector Chisholm spoke.

"Mr. and Mrs. Harwood have been investigating the fraud of the Amicable Society on behalf of the police. Mr. Harwood is Inspector Maxwell and Mrs. Harwood is a private investigator." Chisholm paused as the three men gaped at him. "Mr. Beck has been assisting with the investigation."

Hadrian pulled the wig from his head and gently touched where he'd been struck. Wincing, he lowered his hand, and the wig, to his lap.

Tilda faced Draper. "Why did you send biscuits poisoned with arsenic?"

Draper grimaced. "I only wanted Harwood to be ill for a while so I could become an administrator. I hate working at the mercantile house—we all do. Harwood hardly worked there and then resigned his position. He didn't say where he would be working instead, but next thing I hear, he's an administrator for the society. I've been a member longer *and* I've been taking money." He sent a disgruntled look at Furnier. "Why wouldn't they ask me? It should have been me."

"But you were *going* to become an administrator," Furnier cried.

"That was after Nevill was arrested." Draper's face had turned bright red. "I sent the biscuits before that happened."

"And we weren't paying Harwood," Furnier said. "None of us are paid, only the canvasser receives a salary."

"I'm not even paid." Dr. Giles glowered at Draper. "Not yet anyway."

Tilda cocked her head at Draper. "Did you think any of this through?"

"No," Hadrian replied, though she hadn't asked him. "He killed Phelps in a rage after going to confront him about his swindle with Eaton." He winced as he turned his head to look at Draper. "Do I have that right?"

Draper nodded. "I didn't mean to kill him." He frowned, and an angry light glinted in his eyes. "He was arrogant and unapologetic. He offered to pay me to keep quiet, said he would leave London."

"That was Phelps's plan all along—to leave London with the society's money," Tilda said.

"It wasn't just that he'd cheated everyone. He corrupted Eaton." Draper sneered. "Tim was a good man and my friend. He came to see me and told me everything that Phelps had hired him to do. Tim didn't realize how bad it would be at first, but he needed the money for his sister. After Cardy died, Tim told me that Phelps was going to blame the fraud on him and that he'd given Tim some money to leave town. Only it wasn't enough. I told Tim to go back and demand that Phelps turn himself in. Tim planned to do that and must have, but Phelps killed him."

"How do you know Phelps killed him?" Chisholm asked sharply.

"Because when I went to see Phelps, I asked if he knew where Tim had gone. Phelps acted strangely, and he said Tim had got what he deserved. He tried to blame everything on him." Draper's voice was climbing. "I was tired of his lies. The society deserved better than him!"

"That's when you struck him with the candlestick?" Tilda kept her voice even.

Draper nodded.

Chisholm fixed his dark gaze on Draper. "Sounds as though I'll be charging you with the murder of Walter Phelps and the attempted murders of Inspector Maxwell and Lord Ravenhurst." He closed his eyes briefly, then sent Hadrian an apologetic glance.

"*Lord Ravenhurst?*" Furnier gasped as Draper paled.

"I struck a peer?" Draper asked faintly.

"An earl." Tilda narrowed her gaze at Draper. "Why would you take the candle from Phelps's house and use it here in plain sight?"

Draper stared at her a moment. "It was a good candle. I didn't think anyone would notice."

"Where is the brass candlestick you used to kill Phelps?" Chisholm asked.

Casting his focus to the floor, Draper mumbled his response. "Hidden under my bed. I was going to sell it in a month or so."

Tilda concluded that Draper wasn't terribly bright. He seemed ruled by emotion and perhaps economy, as evidenced by his reusing of Phelps's candle, regardless of the risk that possessing it would implicate him in a murder, and his intent to sell the weapon he'd used to kill Phelps. He'd made a series of poor choices and hadn't seemed to fully consider the consequences.

Chisholm looked to the constable. "Handcuffs, if you please, Selby."

The young constable made his way to Draper and placed the cuffs on his wrists.

"What of my wife?" Draper asked, his voice breaking. "My children?"

"I will explain to them what has happened," Tilda said. "It may be best if you go now before your family returns. Mrs. Draper can visit you later." If she wanted to. Though Tilda had questions for her about the biscuits. "Wait," she said to Inspector Chisholm. "I want to ask Draper about the biscuits he sent to Inspector Maxwell."

"Yes, I would like to know how much arsenic was used," Dr. Giles said. "It will help determine the inspector's recovery."

"I added arsenic when my wife was distracted with the children," Draper replied. "I didn't add much. I really was only trying to make him sick. I made sure all the biscuits went to Harwood and Beck."

Dr. Giles glared at Draper. "You fool. You endangered your wife by allowing her to cook with the poison."

Draper blanched. "I thought it would be fine if she didn't eat any."

"Let's go," Chisholm said, inclining his head toward the door.

The constable took Draper by the arm and guided him out.

Chisholm looked to Tilda and Hadrian. "I'll expect you to call at the station later to provide testimony. My apologies for revealing your identity, my lord. That was not my intent."

"I do hope you won't be charging Nevill with murder now that Draper has been arrested," Tilda said.

"He was still involved with Eaton's death," the inspector replied.

"Yes, but only to dispose of the body," Tilda argued. "He didn't kill the man—there's no proof that he did and every indication that it was Phelps. We know he left his house to fetch Nevill, who he had stop at his shop for the fabric with which to wrap the body. I believe that indicates Eaton was already dead at Phelps's house."

Chisholm's brows pitched down over his eyes. "Nevill is still guilty of aiding a murderer."

"Yes, but he's not a killer." Tilda knew Nevill wasn't blameless, but he shouldn't hang for a crime he didn't commit.

"I suppose not." Chisholm did not sound pleased. He departed, leaving Tilda and Hadrian with Furnier and Dr. Giles.

"Let me tend to your head," Dr. Giles said. He'd brought his bag with him and set it on the table that Draper had used to hit Hadrian.

Dr. Giles parted Hadrian's hair and gently prodded at the spot where Draper had hit him. "You've a contusion, and a bump has formed. I'd say it's good you were wearing that hair piece or you might have sustained a cut or abrasion."

Hadrian smiled at Tilda. "I'm glad it was good for something."

"Are you really an earl?" Dr. Giles asked.

"Yes. Am I all right then? No concussion? I had one in January, and this doesn't feel as bad as that, thankfully."

Dr. Giles asked several questions and concluded that Hadrian was not concussed. He instructed him to be cautious for the rest of the day.

"What of Maxwell?" Hadrian asked. "Will he be all right?"

"Was he really poisoned?" Furnier asked, his face pale.

The doctor nodded. "But he'll be fine."

Tilda was eager to see Hadrian back to White Alley so he could rest. However, she also felt the need to stay and speak to Mrs. Draper about what had happened. She looked to Hadrian. "You should return to White Alley. I want to stay so I may tell Mrs. Draper about her husband. Perhaps Dr. Giles can walk with you."

"I'll just wait for you." Hadrian gave her a weak smile, and she could see he was in pain. She wondered how much was from the blow to his head and what was due to the vision he'd had. Tilda had no doubt he'd seen something and looked forward to hearing the details.

"Mrs. Harwood, perhaps I should stay with you," Dr. Giles said. "Mrs. Draper may be overcome when she hears the news of her husband's arrest. She may require a physician."

Tilda appreciated the doctor's concern. "Thank you, Dr. Giles."

"I don't mind walking you, my lord," Furnier said to Hadrian. "It's the least I can do. I feel horrible about all that's happened. I just wanted to help others during difficult times. Mrs. Furnier and I have lost four children, and it's devastating, especially if you can't care for them in death the way they deserve to be. I don't want anyone to have to feel they are failing their family—in life or death."

"That is precisely why you should consider maintaining the society," Hadrian said. "I do appreciate your offer to accompany me, but I'll wait for Mrs. Harwood. You're still planning to have the weekly meeting tomorrow night?"

Furnier nodded. "We must. Many members are demanding at least an explanation of what's happened and what the future of the society will be. Others want their money refunded."

"Perhaps we can find a way forward," Dr. Giles said, surprising Tilda.

"I thought you planned to resign." She met the doctor's gaze.

"I did, but Furnier has reminded me of why I agreed to help in the first place." The doctor sent Furnier a brief smile.

"It wasn't to improve your position?" Hadrian asked.

A bit of pink stained Dr. Giles's cheeks. "I genuinely wanted to help, just as I hoped my association with the society would boost my prospects. Is that so terrible? When I learned of Phelps's corruption, I became concerned about my future. I will shortly have a wife to care for." He took a deep breath. "I am still committed to the society and what we originally set out to do. If we can persuade Mrs. Atkins to be a true benefactress, we may be able to find a way forward."

"If she won't support you, I will," Hadrian said, looking from the doctor to Furnier.

Tilda's heart swelled. She knew he would help, but hearing his pledge made her happy, nonetheless.

Furnier gaped at him. "You'd just give us money?"

"The police recovered money from Phelps's house—his wife found it under the floorboards in his bedchamber," Hadrian explained. "We'll find out how much and whether it can cover what the society owes to those who were swindled. I'll make up any difference, and I'll set up a small fund to help you restart the society as you intend it to be." He gave them a brief smile. "I have faith the two of you can do right by the denizens of the Coleman Street Ward."

Furnier put his hand to his chest. "I don't know what to say, my lord. Your generosity overwhelms me."

"I would appreciate it if you said nothing. No one else needs to know who your benefactor is. And it is still my hope that Mrs. Atkins will also provide her financial support."

"We may have to invite her into the administration," Furnier said with a touch of disdain.

Dr. Giles sighed. "I suppose there are worse things."

"With a woman in the leadership, you might consider allowing women to join the society." Tilda couldn't stop herself from making the suggestion.

Furnier appeared skeptical whilst Giles nodded. "We can certainly discuss that," the doctor said.

A while later, after speaking with a very distraught Mrs. Draper, Tilda and Hadrian made their way toward Old Jewry. Hadrian explained the vision he'd seen when he'd picked up the candle and how he'd managed to provoke a near-confession from Draper.

"Rather than completely confess, he tried to kill you instead," Tilda said, looking over at Hadrian.

"I suppose he did." Hadrian wobbled, and Tilda threaded her arm through his and pressed herself to his side.

"Careful," she murmured.

Hadrian stopped and pivoted toward her slightly so they were almost facing one another. "Thank you."

Tilda met his gaze and allowed herself to just stand here with him in this moment. "I was very worried. You're sure you're all right?"

"I am. It's nice to know you care so much."

"I do." It sounded like a confession, and she supposed it was. She'd been trying so hard to maintain a strictly professional friendship, but their connection was much deeper than that. It was time she embraced it.

Tilda slipped her other arm around him and pressed herself against him. Hadrian's arms encircled her, and they stood together like that for several moments.

Heat rose up from Tilda's chest into her face. She pulled back and looked up at him. Then she laughed.

Hadrian arched a brow. "What do you find amusing?"

"Your dark hair and your blond side whiskers—one of which is starting to peel away." Tilda giggled.

He touched the side of his face and felt the hair piece where it was coming off. "I'm glad to not have to wear these again."

"And I will be most relieved not to have to powder my hair anymore."

"Will you go home tonight?" he asked as they continued walking.

"I suppose I could, but I'm concerned about Maxwell. I think I'd like to stay and make sure he recovers. And I do wonder if we ought to attend the Amicable Society meeting tomorrow night." She glanced over at Hadrian and felt another rush of admiration for him. "Your offer to support the society was incredibly generous. Why do you want to do it anonymously?"

Hadrian shrugged. "This is not my home. Once they learn who I am, they'll see me as an outsider." He met her gaze briefly. "Which I am. I wasn't even supposed to help with this investigation," he added with a smile.

"I'm very glad you did. This was particularly complicated, and I'm not sure we could have solved these murders without your help—and not just because of your visions. You were able to provoke Draper into admitting his guilt."

"I just found myself wondering what Tilda would do," Hadrian said, his eyes glowing with respect.

Tilda laughed. Then she felt humbled. She'd never intended to train Hadrian to become an investigator, but that had just… happened. "I imagine you're anxious to return to your responsibilities. I feel bad that you've lost a week. Won't they have missed you in the Lords?"

Hadrian waved his hand. "Not for a week. But I do have matters I must attend. I may go to Westminster tomorrow and return for the Amicable Society meeting."

They were nearing the police station. "I hope this won't take too long. I'm concerned about Maxwell and want to make sure he's improving."

"I hope so," Hadrian said. "If not, Draper's situation will become much worse."

CHAPTER 26

*D*r. Giles called on Maxwell again Sunday evening and declared him to be on the mend. Maxwell had even managed to ingest some broth, and Tilda was most relieved.

By Monday morning, Maxwell had left his cot in the storage cupboard and even bathed. He'd indicated his intention to attend the Amicable Society meeting, and Tilda could see there was no stopping him.

Hadrian had gone to Westminster but was now back at White Alley. However, instead of walking to the meeting at the Swan and Hoop, Hadrian had insisted they take his coach, since Maxwell was still a bit weak. Tilda sat with him on the forward-facing seat, which Hadrian understood, given Maxwell's condition. Leach had been delighted to be driving them once more.

As they entered the common room, Tilda immediately noticed Ezra Clement sitting at a table sipping ale. He lifted his glass toward her.

"Clement is here," she said to Hadrian and Maxwell. "I'm eager to learn what he discovered on his travels."

"As am I," Maxwell said. "Do you think we have time to speak with him before the meeting starts?"

"We may as well try." Tilda led them to Clement's table.

The reporter picked up his ale once more and rose. "It seems you've solved the case whilst I was away. I only returned this afternoon."

"We have," Tilda replied. "But your efforts will be of great use in the prosecution of Mrs. Walters. At least, I assume they will be."

"Most definitely," Clement said as he proceeded to tell them about how Mr. and Mrs. Walters had cheated many people in several places with fake burial clubs. Phelps had gone by many aliases, including Wallace Philips and Philip Wallace. The Coleman Street Ward Amicable Society was actually his first friendly society—and would be the last.

"With the number of people he's cheated, I'm surprised Phelps lasted as long as he did," Clement noted. "I'll publish a series of articles starting tomorrow. I don't suppose you have any information about the future of the Amicable Society? I'd like to include that in my story."

"We don't know yet," Maxwell replied. "If you'd care to wait around until the meeting concludes, we may have a better answer for you."

"I'll do that, thank you." Clement inclined his head, then sat back down.

As Tilda turned from Clement's table, Isaiah Jarret was just walking into the pub. He removed his hat and looked about somewhat cautiously before his gaze settled on Furnier.

"I wonder what Jarret is doing here," Hadrian said softly.

"Perhaps he's decided to give the society another try," Tilda mused. "I hope that bodes well for the future of the society. Perhaps others will also give it a second chance."

Tilda noted that several other wives were in the common room, including Mrs. Furnier and Mrs. Burley. Dr. Giles's fiancée, Miss Trimble, was also present.

Mrs. Burley gaped upon seeing Hadrian. "What has happened to Mr. Beck's hair?"

"That will be revealed shortly," Tilda said. She hadn't washed the powder from her hair since her identity would not be revealed. For propriety's sake, she would remain Mrs. Harwood. No one needed to know that Miss Matilda Wren had resided with an earl and an inspector, even though she'd had a chaperone. In fact, they'd decided that Hadrian wouldn't be revealed as Lord Ravenhurst either. Maxwell had asked Furnier and Giles to keep Hadrian's identity quiet, at least until they were gone.

Everyone seemed rather subdued after hearing of Draper's arrest, which had spread since yesterday. However, Mrs. Atkins arrived with her usual boisterous, self-important demeanor. Tilda wasn't sure the woman was capable of restraining herself.

Furnier then shocked the ladies by inviting them to come into the meeting room. Even Mrs. Atkins seemed surprised.

"I wonder why we're being included," Mrs. Burley commented as she walked into the room with Tilda.

"There are to be some announcements," Tilda said. "Perhaps Mr. Furnier understands the importance of ensuring everyone hears the news."

"That's precisely it," Mrs. Furnier said pertly. She smiled at Tilda.

Tilda sat between Hadrian and Maxwell in the front row.

Mr. Furnier cleared his throat and welcomed everyone. "I know it has been a very long week and much has happened. Some may think the Coleman Street Ward Amicable Society is finished, but I am here to tell you we will forge on." He glanced at Dr. Giles, who sat behind the purple covered table. "Dr. Giles and I are committed to ensuring that those who were cheated will have their fees refunded."

"How will you do that?" someone asked.

"We are working with the police to recover at least some of the money that Eaton and Phelps stole," Furnier replied.

"Though, that may not be enough. We do have one anonymous benefactor who has donated to our cause, and we hope to solicit another." He looked pointedly at Mrs. Atkins, whose hand fluttered to her chest.

"You want me to pay for those men's crimes?" she asked, her voice tinged with disdain.

"We'd be grateful if you were able to donate money to help the society survive and move forward. Dr. Giles and I would be pleased to recognize you as the society's benefactress or even have you as a member of our leadership, if you are so inclined."

"Will women be admitted?" Mrs. Burley asked.

Mrs. Atkins turned her head to look at Mrs. Burley. "I don't know that we should—"

"We will discuss that," Dr. Giles said, cutting Mrs. Atkins off. Tilda buried a smile.

"What about Mr. Beck?" Mrs. Atkins asked. "Will he still be employed as our canvasser? I'd already agreed to pay his salary."

Furnier inclined his head toward Hadrian.

With a nod, Hadrian stood and turned to face the members. He smiled faintly. "I will not be staying with the society. I have been investigating the society along with Inspector Maxwell and Mrs. Harwood." He gestured to Maxwell and Tilda.

This revelation was met with surprised murmurs and a few gasps.

Maxwell rose. "I am Inspector Maxwell with the City of London Police. I was charged with infiltrating the Amicable Society and investigating it from within. I was aided by Mrs. Harwood and Mr. Beck, who are private investigators. We hope you will forgive us for the deceit, but it was necessary to discover what happened. Perhaps surprisingly, I have found that I am quite invested in the Amicable Society now. I've discussed matters with Mr. Furnier and Dr. Giles, and I will be staying on as an administrator. The Coleman Street Ward is my home, and

I'm eager to support this fine endeavor—and ensure there is no further corruption."

"Can't do better than an inspector in charge," someone called out.

This was met with murmurs of agreement.

"I agree," Furnier said. He gestured to an empty chair behind the table. "Please come and join us, Inspector Maxwell." Furnier went on to apologize for his part in not coming forward immediately when he'd learned of Phelps's corruption. "My aim has been, and will remain, the success of the Amicable Society and the prosperity of its members."

Cries of "huzzah" rang through the room, and the business meeting soon commenced, complete with the odd rituals Hadrian and Maxwell had described to Tilda last week. She could hardly believe that was only a week ago.

However, there was one thing missing. She turned to Hadrian. "I thought there was a hat of cock feathers?" she whispered.

He chuckled softly. "Perhaps Phelps was the only one who would wear it."

Following the meeting, Mrs. Atkins cornered Hadrian. Tilda was going to rescue him, but Maxwell asked if he could speak with her. "Would you join me in the common room for a few minutes?"

Nodding, Tilda left the meeting room with him. He guided her to an alcove in the farthest corner where there was a private table.

"Do you mind if we sit?" he asked. "I'm a bit fatigued."

"You should have rested another day," Tilda said, sliding into a chair.

He smiled as he sat. "It warms me that you care so much."

"I'm very glad the poison will not have lasting effects. And I'm pleased that you'll be staying on with the society."

Maxwell lifted a shoulder. "I can't really explain it, but through this assignment, I've developed a connection to the ward that I didn't have before. I've decided to live at Number Five permanently."

Tilda blinked at him in surprise. "That is a large house for just you."

"Actually, I was hoping it wouldn't be just me." He leaned slightly forward over the table, his eyes glowing with anticipation. "I know this is sudden, but I've come to admire you greatly, Miss Wren. And I believe we work well together as an investigative team. So well that I also believe we would make an excellent team in matrimony. It is my greatest hope that you will consent to be my wife." He smiled.

Her surprise was now shock. Tilda had not expected this at all.

Maxwell continued. "Before you answer, let me present my argument. I am not asking you to become a housewife. I recognize and, indeed, admire your passion for investigation. I support your continued work as a private investigator, and perhaps we will continue to partner together on cases for the police. We should generate enough income to hire someone to cook and clean, so you won't have to do those things." He looked at her expectantly, but Tilda was too flabbergasted to respond.

"I realize it's a change for you to move here from Marylebone and your grandmother. However, perhaps she could live with us too."

Tilda immediately thought of her grandmother's household. Number Five White Alley would not support a housekeeper, maid, and a butler—her grandmother's house barely did that. Furthermore, Tilda could not uproot her grandmother from her home.

But could Tilda make that change? There was an unexpected appeal in his proposal. He saw her as an equal and valued her as a person with her own plans. He was also a very good man. Maxwell was kind, handsome, caring, and they shared many of the same principles. If she wanted to marry, Maxwell would be an excellent match. Her grandmother would be ecstatic. So much so that she may even consider leaving Marylebone.

But marriage meant surrendering her independence, and Tilda had no desire to do that, no matter how much sense a match with Maxwell might make.

Maxwell put his hand to his head briefly. "I forgot the most important part. I've grown to care for you, Miss Wren. I greatly respect your intellect and am drawn to your kindness and warmth. It would make me beyond happy—and proud—to call you my wife."

His words were incredibly flattering, and they brought her reluctance into sharp relief. Her independence notwithstanding, she did not feel "drawn" to Maxwell in any similar fashion. If anything, his words provoked a startling realization: she *was* drawn to someone else.

And she'd nearly lost that person, which had jolted her. Tilda had been scared she would lose Hadrian, not just as a partner, but as a vital part of her life. Which he had very much become.

The acknowledgment shook her.

Tilda blinked. She focused on Maxwell across the table. He was attractive and clever, and she liked him immensely. But she didn't want to marry him.

"You are a wonderful man, Inspector Maxwell. And you will make some lucky woman very happy someday."

His features fell, and his lips lifted into a sad smile. "However, you are not that woman."

Tilda shook her head gently. "I'm afraid not. I value my independence far too much, and I'm rather set in my ways and committed to managing my grandmother's household." She had a terrible thought. "Does this mean you can't live at White Alley?" Perhaps he was counting on her to make that work.

"I will still live there," he said. "I'm sure Mrs. Burley would appreciate the chance to play matchmaker for me." He smirked, and Tilda was grateful for his humor.

"I know she would. Be careful." Tilda chuckled.

They rose from the table, and Maxwell looked at her sideways. "Is it truly your independence that is stopping you from accepting my proposal?"

"Yes." She wouldn't reveal the rest. She was barely comfortable with acknowledging it herself.

Maxwell nodded. "I just... That is, I wondered if there was perhaps another reason. Or another...person."

She followed his gaze to Hadrian, who was still in Mrs. Atkins's clutches—literally, as she was touching his arm.

"No," Tilda replied, perhaps a tad too quickly.

"We should probably rescue Ravenhurst," Maxwell said with a laugh. "And then I suppose we'll say goodbye." He met her gaze.

"For now," Tilda said firmly. "I'm confident we'll meet again. Perhaps we'll even investigate another case together."

Maxwell nodded. "I hope so."

❧

*H*adrian was relieved when Tilda and Maxwell came to rescue him. Not just because he was eager to be away from Mrs. Atkins's fawning. He'd seen Tilda and Maxwell sitting together with their heads bent toward one another in what appeared to be an intimate conversation. An irrational fear had lodged in Hadrian's chest. He worried that things were about to change.

A short while later, they left the pub and dropped Maxwell back at White Alley. Tilda packed her things whilst Hadrian fetched his. Then they said goodbye to Mrs. Kilgore, who would be returning home the following day after ensuring the inspector was well enough to care for himself.

Hadrian had shaken Maxwell's hand, and Mrs. Kilgore had

given Hadrian a surprising hug. She thanked him profusely for helping her cousin, Mrs. Cardy.

As Hadrian escorted Tilda to the end of White Alley, where Leach stood with the coach, he began to relax. Had he thought she may not be coming with him?

Perhaps not that, but he realized he'd been anticipating… something.

They climbed into the coach and sat together on the forward-facing seat. It felt good and familiar to have Tilda beside him. Hadrian stretched his legs out. "I hope our next investigation is a little closer to home."

"I won't argue with that," Tilda said. "I'm sure you were eagerly welcomed back at Westminster today."

"Yes, though I confess I wasn't there very long. I visited the orphanage where Timothy Eaton's sister lives and arranged for her to move to a school in Kent."

Tilda gaped at him. "You did?"

Hadrian nodded. "I couldn't rest knowing she was going to a workhouse."

"You are the kindest man," Tilda whispered, her gaze warm and her lips curving into a beautiful smile. Their gazes held a moment before Tilda looked away, and her features straightened. "I've a case I need to work on that I set aside whilst we were assisting Inspector Maxwell. I'm relieved it only took a week instead of a fortnight."

"Honestly, it felt like a month."

Tilda nodded. "It really did." She looked over at him. "You're sure your head is all right?"

"It only hurts if I touch it, so I don't."

"And no other headaches? You shook a few hands at the pub and then you shook Maxwell's hand before we left. No visions or pain?"

"Neither. I don't always see a vision when I touch someone."

He hadn't seen one with Mrs. Kilgore either, and her head had nudged his jaw.

"I know, but isn't that typically with people you know, such as me and your mother?"

"Typically." Now that Hadrian thought about it, the lack of any vision from the several hands he'd shaken today was a trifle odd. "Perhaps I'm learning to control it more. I didn't *need* to see any visions today."

She sent him a smile. "That would be wonderful, wouldn't it?"

Her concern for him never failed to infuse him with a sense of joy. It seemed they'd shared a strong moment of connection yesterday after leaving Draper's lodgings. She'd been frightened for his safety, and he'd sensed a deeper sentiment within her.

Or had he?

He wasn't sure he wanted to know. Perhaps that was the source of his unease. His feelings for her had only grown stronger this past week as they'd lived and worked together. He was going to miss her horribly—more than he had before when they'd finished an investigation.

But he couldn't assume she felt the same. Particularly after he'd seen her talking privately with Maxwell at the Swan and Hoop. Hadrian was overcome with curiosity and—he realized— an unshakeable dread.

Hadrian decided it was best to know the truth rather than imagine what they'd discussed. "I saw you and Maxwell speaking at the pub."

"Did you?" Tilda brushed an invisible speck from her skirt. "I was going to tell you about it. Maxwell, ah, proposed marriage."

Whatever Hadrian had expected, it wasn't that. They hadn't even been acquainted a fortnight! His gut clenched, and his breath halted in his lungs as he realized she hadn't revealed her response.

"What did you say?" He worked to draw a deep breath.

"I politely declined, of course." She arched a brow at him. "Did you think I would accept? You know I value my independence and that I've no desire to wed."

He lifted his hand. "I make no assumptions. I could see where you might consider marriage to an inspector."

"Yes, you've pointed out the things Maxwell and I share in common," she said wryly. "He did present a compelling argument, and I confess I thought about it for the barest moment. But I can't surrender my independence."

That she'd thought about it made Hadrian both uneasy and surprisingly encouraged. If she could consider marriage, even briefly, perhaps she might someday consider it with him.

Was that what he wanted?

He could envision it quite easily. And it was most appealing. It would also be challenging, given their differences. Still, it would be manageable. If they both wanted the same thing.

"I don't think you'd have to completely surrender your independence to marry," Hadrian said evenly. "Your husband should know that you need to manage your own life and will see you as a true partner."

"That was part of Maxwell's proposal," Tilda said.

"Then I give him great credit." Hadrian angled himself toward her. "You still declined?"

She did not look at him, but she clasped her hands briefly before pressing them flat on her lap. "I realized I would never be drawn to the inspector in the way he said he was drawn to me. I don't develop close relationships very often or very easily." She sent him a nervous look, and Hadrian's pulse picked up.

He waited to see if she would say more.

Her gaze fixed on the opposite side of the coach. "We have that sort of...closeness. I was very afraid I would lose you, and not just as an investigative partner. I did not want to lose that... closeness."

Hadrian's chest filled with hope. "We do have that," he said softly. "And I don't want to lose it—or you—either. You've become very important to me, Tilda."

She met his gaze. "And you have to me." She cleared her throat and looked away more quickly than he would have liked, but he could see that she was struggling with whatever newfound emotions she was feeling.

That made Hadrian a little giddy.

"I'm just glad we can continue as we have been." She looked over at him. "You still wish to do that?"

"Most definitely." Hadrian decided he would reveal some of what he was feeling. "I should confess that my jealousy of Maxwell went beyond professional sensibility. And hearing that he wanted to marry you made me…upset. I'm glad you said no."

She looked at him in surprise. "You felt that strongly?"

He nodded. "I feel quite strongly about you. If I'm honest, I think of the kiss we shared, and I don't regret it. In fact, I would kiss you again if I knew you were amenable."

Her lips parted, and she swallowed. "I think of it sometimes too." Her voice was soft, and Hadrian could see her pulse in her neck.

He sensed her apprehension. "I'm a patient man."

She exhaled. "Thank you. I need to make sense of things. This past week has been intense, particularly spending so much time with you and Maxwell. There has been little escape." She sent him an apologetic smile. "Perhaps you could come for tea later this week."

Hadrian's stomach flipped, and he had to keep himself from grinning like a fool. "I would be delighted."

A short while later, they arrived at her grandmother's house in Marylebone. He walked her to the door and bid her goodnight.

He whistled on his way back to the coach.

CHAPTER 27

ilda's grandmother was thrilled to have her back at home, as was the rest of the household. She'd taken the last two days to rest and reacclimate herself and was now ready to return to work. In fact, she'd just sent a note to the person who'd hired her to find some stolen items and would hopefully meet with her in the next few days.

And today Hadrian was coming for tea—he was due any moment. Tilda's grandmother already had plans to take tea at a neighbor's house, though she'd considered canceling in favor of seeing Hadrian. She enjoyed his visits, which often occurred after they finished a case.

The tea and scones were already on the table in the parlor thanks to Mrs. Acorn. She was just finishing her arrangement, when Tilda heard Vaughn open the door and welcome Hadrian inside.

"It's good to see you, my lord," Vaughn said. "We heard all about your exciting case in the City. Are you glad to be back at home?"

"I am, thank you, Vaughn. The investigation was most invigorating."

"I'm sure there will be another shortly," the butler noted.

"Has Miss Wren received more inquiries?" Hadrian asked.

"Just one, but I'm not interested in it," Tilda replied from just inside the parlor.

Hadrian stepped over the threshold. His head and hands were bare as he'd given his hat and gloves to Vaughn. The towering butler shuffled to a table where he set the accessories.

"You look lovely," Hadrian said with a warm smile. "I've missed your blonde hair."

Tilda touched the back of her head. Clara had done another of her intricate styles, which Tilda had surprisingly missed—not necessarily how it looked, but having the help. Tilda hadn't ever wanted a maid, and now she found she liked having one, particularly after living in the City the past week, where she'd cared entirely for herself. That realization made her slightly uncomfortable. She told herself that enjoying the help of a maid did not diminish her independence. "I've missed my hair too."

"That powder was in your clothing," Mrs. Acorn noted. "But Clara is a wonder with laundering."

Hadrian smiled at the housekeeper. "Good afternoon, Mrs. Acorn. It's a pleasure to see you."

Mrs. Acorn blushed faintly. "It's always nice to welcome you, my lord. Mrs. Wren is sorry she isn't here but hopes to return before you leave." She gestured to the table. "Enjoy your tea."

When she was gone, Tilda moved to the table and poured out. She made Hadrian's cup the way he liked it.

"I'm afraid I can't use sugar now without thinking of Inspector Maxwell," Hadrian said.

Tilda sat. "I had the same thought. Speaking of him, he sent a note this morning. He's been promoted to Detective Inspector. I'm so pleased for him."

Hadrian smiled as he took the opposite chair. "That is excellent news." He sipped his tea. "I take it I shouldn't leave until after your grandmother returns?"

"She would appreciate that," Tilda replied. "Thank you." She helped herself to a scone.

"Have you settled back in?" Hadrian asked.

She nodded. "And you?"

He put a scone on his plate. "I've noticed something odd," he spoke softly, though he didn't really need to. Vaughn was in the entrance hall, but his hearing was not the best. "You recall how I didn't see any visions on Monday at the society meeting?" At Tilda's nod, he continued. "I haven't had any—not even a glimpse —since. I've been to Westminster and to my club. I typically see a flash of *something* when I am in such places."

Tilda paused in spreading jam on her scone. "When was the last time you had a vision? You were at Westminster on Monday before the meeting, weren't you?"

"The last vision I had was the candle at Draper's house."

"That is perplexing," Tilda said. "Have you ever had such a period where you haven't seen visions?"

Before he could answer, there was a commotion in the entrance hall. Tilda heard the door open. An unmistakable voice made her freeze.

"Are you a butler? How on earth can Barbara afford a butler?"

Hadrian leaned slightly forward. "Who's that?" he whispered.

Tilda clenched her jaw. "My mother." She set her scone down and prepared herself for the coming storm.

Tilda's mother swept into the parlor, her orange-red silk skirts swirling. Her pale blonde hair was piled high atop her head and her hazel eyes surveyed the room briefly before settling first on Hadrian and then Tilda.

"Welcome, Mother. We were not expecting you," Tilda said evenly. "Unless we somehow missed your letter."

She waved her hand. "I did not send one. I only made the decision to come yesterday after a friend told me she read about you working as an *investigator*." She flicked a glance toward Hadrian, who stood. He wore an amiable expression.

Tilda looked up at Hadrian. "Allow me to present my mother, Lady Edith Pierce. Mother, this is Lord Ravenhurst."

Hadrian bowed. "Lady Pierce. Your husband is a baronet?"

Tilda's mother's brows arched in surprise. "Lord Ravenhurst? How do you know one another?" She appeared utterly aghast, but then she would never have expected her daughter to be acquainted with an earl.

Glancing at Hadrian, Tilda murmured, "Yes, her husband is Sir Bardolph Pierce." She returned her gaze to her mother. "Ravenhurst assists me with my investigations."

Gasping, Tilda's mother's hand fluttered to her chest. "My goodness, but that is shocking."

Tilda rose from her chair reluctantly. "Why are you here?" She hadn't visited London since last autumn, and Tilda did not expect to see her for at least another few months.

"As I said, I heard you were working as an *investigator*," Tilda's mother said dramatically. "Why on earth would you do that when you should be looking for a husband? I was concerned it may be too late for that, but my hope is rekindled now." Her gaze settled on Hadrian once more, and she smiled.

"Lord Ravenhurst is my investigative partner," Tilda reminded her, though she'd little hope her mother would accept that truth.

"He's here for tea," her mother said with a faint shrug. "That is nearly courting."

Tilda exhaled with exasperation. "It is not."

Tilda's mother pursed her lips. "Hmm. I would join you, but I'm exhausted after my trip. Where is Mrs. Acorn? I'm afraid I didn't bring my maid. She was feeling a touch under the weather."

"I'm here," Mrs. Acorn called just before she stepped into the parlor. Her eyes were slightly wider than usual, and Tilda could see she was as surprised by their sudden guest as Tilda.

"My mother is here for a visit," Tilda said tightly. "She did not

bring her maid. I am happy to assign Clara to her for the duration of her stay."

Her mother's gaze snapped back to Tilda. "Who is Clara?"

"Our maid," Tilda replied.

"You've a butler *and* a maid? Is this because you're an investigator? Don't tell me you earn enough money to afford such luxu-
ries. I can't believe it."

"Your daughter is quite accomplished," Hadrian said
smoothly. "My own mother hired her to conduct an investigation."

Tilda's mother narrowed her eyes briefly as she regarded
Hadrian dubiously. "Indeed? Well, I shall have to hear more about
this, I suppose." She sent Tilda a look of deep concern. "I came
here to demand you cease that work at once. It's unseemly."

Tilda opened her mouth to defend her work, but there was a
second commotion in the entrance hall. She heard another
familiar voice—that of Inspector Teague from Scotland Yard.

Turning to Mrs. Acorn, Tilda gave her a pleading look. "Please
show Lady Pierce upstairs so she can rest." She tried to summon
a smile for her mother and failed. "I'll see you later, Mother."

Mrs. Acorn followed Tilda's mother from the parlor, and
Tilda sent a brief look at Hadrian, who was regarding her with
curiosity.

"I want to know more about that situation," he said softly.
"But it sounds as though you have another caller. What a busy
afternoon. Here, I'd hoped to have you to myself."

His words sent a ripple of heat through Tilda. She didn't have
time to consider her reaction, which was probably for the best.
She still hadn't worked through the unfamiliar new feelings she
had for Hadrian.

Vaughn trudged into the parlor. "Inspector Teague is here. Is
now a good time?"

Tilda exhaled and smoothed her hand down her hip. "Yes.
Show him in."

The butler departed and a moment later, Teague strode in. In his middle thirties, he had dark red hair and sharply assessing brown eyes. He looked toward Hadrian. "I thought I recognized your coach outside."

"Afternoon, Teague," Hadrian said. "I trust you are well."

"Well enough." The inspector moved his attention to Tilda. "I hear you conducted a successful investigation in the City. And you." He glanced at Hadrian.

"We did indeed." Tilda clasped her hands in front of her waist. "Have you come to hire me for an investigation?"

Teague's features darkened. "I have not. But I wanted to alert you about something that will be of interest. I probably shouldn't, but I can't keep it from you. Not after all we've been through together."

"That sounds almost ominous," Tilda said with curiosity.

"It's not good," Teague replied with a frown. "Inspector Padgett was found dead last night."

Tilda sucked in a breath. Padgett worked for the Metropolitan Police and had been the inspector assigned to Hadrian's attack several months earlier. Padgett had buried evidence in Hadrian's case, as well as in another regarding the man who was murdered by the brigand who'd attacked Hadrian. Padgett had left the police, but his behavior hadn't been investigated.

"Dead or murdered?" Hadrian asked, his tone carrying a rough edge.

"The inquest is tomorrow, but the coroner will no doubt say it's murder," Teague said. "I came here because Padgett was found with a piece of paper in his pocket that is most confounding."

The hair on Tilda's neck stood up. "Why?"

"Because it bears your father's name."

AUTHOR'S NOTE

Funerals and burials were very important to people in the Victorian era in the United Kingdom, regardless of class. The death of Queen Victoria's husband, Prince Albert, in 1861 changed the way in which people mourned. Queen Victoria herself wore black "widow's weeds" for the rest of her life. Mourners, particularly widows, adhered to very specific behaviors in how they interacted outside their home. There was no social contact for at least a year.

It was shameful to have to bury a loved one in a pauper's grave. Burial clubs and friendly societies offered an opportunity for working class people to pay into a fund that would provide a benefit upon a family member's death. This benefit would pay for the necessary funeral and burial. There were about 100 burial clubs and friendly societies in London during this era, and smaller towns had multiple such organizations.

Death was expensive. Women, particularly widows, wore black, including a veil, for at least one year. It was not uncommon to dye clothing black and then bleach it again after the mourning period, rather than suffer the expense of purchasing black clothing. Mrs. Cardy borrows black clothes rather than dye any of her own, and she certainly can't afford to buy new garments. Professional mourners were often hired to accompany the procession to the graveyard, not as a luxury, but as a necessity to following the appropriate custom of the time. If possible, mourners would also have the coffin drawn in a hearse by black horses. People would go into debt to pay for such extravagance, which was how burial clubs and friendly societies helped.

Burials clubs were rife for corruption, however. Proof of death was not required until 1875. Meetings were always held in pubs where members would drink and even use club funds to pay for the drink. In 1846, these clubs were no longer allowed to enroll children under the age of six due to infanticide. Many people murdered family members, usually children, to collect the death benefit. One of the most famous of these murderers was Mary Ann Cotton. Though she was only prosecuted for killing her stepson (and subsequently hanged), she likely killed eleven of her thirteen children and three of her four husbands.

Friendly societies were regulated, while burial clubs were not. The societies required medical certificates to prove death. However, it wasn't difficult to obtain a medical certificate before 1874, as one didn't need to produce a body. Someone could just report the death, which could lead to corruption if someone "died" several times. Dying repeatedly meant being able to collect from multiple clubs and societies, for people could belong to as many as they liked or could afford.

ALSO BY DARCY BURKE

Historical Mystery

Raven & Wren

A Whisper of Death

A Whisper at Midnight

A Whisper and a Curse

A Whisper in the Shadows

A Whisper of Secrecy

A Whisper in Darkness

Historical Romance

If the Duke Dares

Because the Baron Broods

When the Viscount Seduces

As the Earl Likes

Until the Rake Surrenders

Since the Marquess Demands

What the Scoundrel Desires

How the Devil Sins

The Phoenix Club

Improper

Impassioned

Intolerable

Indecent

Impossible

Irresistible

Impeccable

Insatiable

The Matchmaking Chronicles

Yule Be My Duke

The Rigid Duke

The Bachelor Earl (also prequel to *The Untouchables*)

The Runaway Viscount

The Make-Believe Widow

Marrywell Brides

Beguiling the Duke

Romancing the Heiress

Matching the Marquess

The Untouchables

The Bachelor Earl (prequel)

The Forbidden Duke

The Duke of Daring

The Duke of Deception

The Duke of Desire

The Duke of Defiance

The Duke of Danger

The Duke of Ice

The Duke of Ruin

The Duke of Lies

The Duke of Seduction

The Duke of Kisses

The Duke of Distraction

The Untouchables: The Spitfire Society

Never Have I Ever with a Duke

A Duke is Never Enough

A Duke Will Never Do

The Untouchables: The Pretenders

A Secret Surrender

A Scandalous Bargain

A Rogue to Ruin

Love is All Around

(A Regency Holiday Trilogy)

The Red Hot Earl

The Gift of the Marquess

Joy to the Duke

Wicked Dukes Club

One Night for Seduction by Erica Ridley

One Night of Surrender by Darcy Burke

One Night of Passion by Erica Ridley

One Night of Scandal by Darcy Burke

One Night to Remember by Erica Ridley

One Night of Temptation by Darcy Burke

Secrets and Scandals

Her Wicked Ways

His Wicked Heart

To Seduce a Scoundrel

To Love a Thief (a novella)

Never Love a Scoundrel

Scoundrel Ever After

Legendary Rogues

Lady of Desire

Romancing the Earl

Lord of Fortune

Captivating the Scoundrel

Contemporary Romance

Ribbon Ridge

Let Go (a prequel novella)

Get Lucky

Sparks Fly

Fall Hard

Can't Stop

Break Free

Hold Me

Turn On

So Right

This Love

Prefer to read in German, French, or Italian? Check out my website for foreign language editions!

ABOUT THE AUTHOR

Darcy Burke is the USA Today Bestselling Author of historical romance and mystery and contemporary romance. Darcy wrote her first book at age 11, a happily ever after about a swan addicted to magic and the female swan who loved him, with exceedingly poor illustrations. Join her Reader Club newsletter for the latest updates from Darcy.

A native Oregonian, Darcy lives on the edge of wine country with her guitar-strumming husband, incredibly talented artist daughter, and imaginative, Japanese-speaking son who will almost certainly out-write her one day (that may be tomorrow). They're a crazy cat family with two Bengal cats, a small, fame-seeking torbie named after a fruit, an older rescue Maine Coon with attitude to spare, an adorable former stray who wandered onto their deck and into their hearts, and two bonded boys (a Russian Blue and a Turkish Van) who used to belong to (separate) neighbors but chose them instead. You can find Darcy in her comfy writing chair balancing her laptop and a cat or three, attempting yoga, folding laundry (which she loves), or wildlife spotting and playing games with her family. She loves traveling to the UK and visiting her cousins in Denmark. Visit Darcy online at www.darcyburke.com and follow her on social media.

facebook.com/DarcyBurkeFans

instagram.com/darcyburkeauthor

pinterest.com/darcyburkewrites

goodreads.com/darcyburke

bookbub.com/authors/darcy-burke

amazon.com/author/darcyburke

threads.com/@darcyburkeauthor

tiktok.com/@darcyburkeauthor

www.ingramcontent.com/pod-product-compliance
Ingram Content Group UK Ltd.
Pitfield, Milton Keynes, MK11 3LW, UK
UKHW010637141025
8379UKWH00011B/65